Above Suspicion

THE HAGGERTY MYSTERY NOVELS
BY BETSY BRANNON GREEN:

Hearts in Hiding

Until Proven Guilty

Above Suspicion

Silenced

Copycat

Poison

Double Cross

OTHER NOVELS
BY BETSY BRANNON GREEN:

Never Look Back

Don't Close Your Eyes

Foul Play

Above Suspicion

A NOVEL

BETSY BRANNON GREEN

Covenant Communications, Inc.

Cover image by © Marty Honig, Photodisc Green Collection

Cover design copyrighted 2006 by Covenant Communications, Inc.

Published by Covenant Communications, Inc.
American Fork, Utah

Printed in Canada
First Printing: October 2003

10 09 08 07 06   10 9 8 7 6 5 4

ISBN 1-59156-310-0

For the Graces who have blessed my life:
Grace Vann Brannon, my grandmother
Grace Elizabeth Green, my daughter
Abbie Grace Acker, my granddaughter

ACKNOWLEDGMENTS

As always, I owe the biggest debt of gratitude to my husband, Butch, for his patience, support, and free editorial advice. Thanks also to my kids, who make many sacrifices so that I can have the time I need at the computer. I'm so grateful to Katie Child and the other wonderful people at Covenant who work diligently to make my books as good as they can be. And finally, a special thanks to the teachers of Hueytown Kindergarten. They've nurtured and encouraged and prodded and advised me from the beginning of this writing adventure, and I'm really going to miss them.

CHAPTER 1

As the sun rose over the white sand beaches behind the Bethany Arms Hotel, Mary Grace O'Malley dropped a pile of sheets onto the floor of the laundry room. She loaded both washers and added the recommended amount of industrial-strength detergent. The wash cycles started, and she leaned against the window to watch the waves, painted pink by the sun, pound against the shore.

Her appointment with Justin's lawyer was only minutes away, and she didn't have a second to spare, but the incoming tide was irresistible. So she stood and stared for a moment, wondering how it would feel to be that powerful. Finally, with a sigh, Mary Grace pulled her thoughts back to practical issues.

Leaving the laundry room, she walked toward her office. She needed to go over her figures again before Heath arrived. After their meeting, she would help Lucy clean up the mess created by the continental breakfast they provided for their guests, then prepare the additional rooms reserved for the weekend.

When she reached the small office, Mary Grace sat behind Justin's big, imposing desk. Opening her file of financial statements, she tried to concentrate, but her eyes strayed back to the window and the beach. Heath was going to say the same thing this morning that he had every time they'd met since Justin died. A part of her wanted to follow his advice, but the other part . . .

She transferred her attention from the window to the framed snapshot of Justin taken several years earlier. He was standing in front of his sailboat, smiling at the camera.

"He loved that old boat," Heath Pointer said from the doorway, and Mary Grace looked up, startled. Heath was an attractive man in his early forties who always dressed like a model from *Gentlemen's Quarterly.*

"Good morning, Heath."

He pointed out the window. "If you'd listen to me, you could be lying out on that beach instead of cooped up here with a stuffy old lawyer." He gave her a charming smile, then waited for her to assure him that his self-description was erroneous.

Instead, Mary Grace responded, "I never was all that crazy about lying on the beach."

Heath cleared his throat. "Aztec made another offer yesterday." He moved into the office and dragged the chair from in front of the desk around to the side before sitting down. "If you sell the Arms, you'll have almost a million dollars after taxes and legal fees."

"I'm happy running the Arms, and money doesn't interest me," she said.

"Money interests everyone," Heath assured her. "And you're just breaking even with the Arms. There are several repairs that need to be made, and advertising, while essential to success, is something you can't really afford."

She was pleased that he had introduced this subject for her. "You're exactly right," she agreed wholeheartedly. "I do need to make repairs and advertise. That's why I asked you to come over today. I want you to help me get a business loan."

Heath frowned. "How much?"

Mary Grace pushed her proposal across the desk, and he picked it up.

Heath read for a few seconds, then his eyes widened. "Pretty comprehensive."

"There's no point in doing it at all if I'm not going to do it right."

"If you borrow this kind of money and sink it into the Arms, you'll be committed. Are you sure you want to run a small-time hotel for the next thirty years?"

"I love the Arms," she said softly.

"That doesn't mean you have to sacrifice your life for it." Heath's tone was gentle. "The Arms was Justin's dream, not yours. And he never meant for you to work so hard. You have to get up before dawn to wash sheets and towels for the guests. Then you have to spend time in the kitchen to compensate for the fact that your cook is blind . . ."

Mary Grace couldn't control a laugh. "Lucy is not *completely* blind."

"Close enough," Heath muttered.

"She's worked at the Arms for years, and I can't fire her just because she's getting old." Mary Grace tucked a wisp of dark hair behind her ear. "Besides, she's talking about retiring."

Heath leaned back and crossed his legs so that one tasseled, Italian leather shoe swung very close to her. "I hope she retires soon, for your sake. And in the meantime, why don't you consider dropping dinner from your list of services? That would save you time and money."

"Dinner at the Arms is legendary," she reminded him.

"It's expensive," he reiterated. "But delicious," he relented with a smile. "What's on the menu for tonight?"

Mary Grace recognized the hint. "Lasagna, and you're welcome to join us."

"I might just take you up on that. And don't dismiss Aztec's offer without giving it some thought. I've studied it carefully, and it's a good one."

"I appreciate your concern and your advice, but I'm not ready to sell the Arms. So you can tell the people from Aztec to stop making offers."

Heath smiled. "For such a pretty girl, you sure are a tough negotiator."

"I'm not trying to get a better offer out of Aztec," Mary Grace insisted. "I really don't plan to sell."

Heath glanced at his watch. "Okay, then. I'll call around and see if I can find any takers on a small business loan." He stood and moved toward the door. Mary Grace accompanied him, and just before he stepped into the hallway, he turned to face her. "Hey, I've got an idea. As good as dinners at the Arms are, you must get sick of them. Why don't you let me take you out to a restaurant for dinner?"

For a second Mary Grace was too surprised to respond. She had always thought of Heath as Justin's friend, Justin's lawyer. The idea of a personal relationship with him was unnerving. Pasting a polite smile on her face, she shook her head. "Thank you for the invitation, but there can't be dinner at the Arms without a hostess. My presence is required."

Heath frowned. "Don't you ever take a night off?"

She walked into the hall, hoping to rush his departure. "No. Never."

"Well, maybe we could go to lunch sometime," he suggested as she led the way through the lobby.

"You know I'm chained to this place, Heath," she discouraged him gently. "Breakfast, lunch, and dinner." She opened the front door. "But thanks anyway."

Accepting defeat, Heath continued outside. Mary Grace followed him as far as the cobblestone drive that encircled the courtyard in front of the Arms. She watched Heath climb into his gold-tone Volvo, then waved as he drove away. Surveying the courtyard, she realized that the grass was going to have to be cut before her teenage yardman returned from vacation the following Saturday. It had been awhile since she'd pushed a lawn mower, but maybe it was like riding a bike—something you never forgot.

Mary Grace returned to the lobby of the Arms and straightened magazines on an antique occasional table. She pulled dead leaves off a plant and stirred the sea breeze potpourri on the registration desk. Then, accepting that she could delay it no longer, she went to the kitchen and called for Lucy.

"I'm here, Mary Grace," a voice responded from the storage room.

Mary Grace stuck her head in to see the elderly black woman with cotton-white hair stretched out on a cot, watching *The Today Show* on a small television. "Is something wrong?" she asked.

Lucy nodded. "I got to feeling a little dizzy and knew you'd want me to lie down before I fell."

Mary Grace controlled a sigh. "I certainly wouldn't want you to fall. I'll clean up the dining room."

"Don't worry about dinner. I'm sure I'll be better by then."

Mary Grace didn't comment but instead pulled a metal cart from the kitchen into the dining room and started collecting dishes and silverware. The buffet table only took a minute, but the long banquet table where her guests had eaten was a mess. The snowy white linen tablecloth was littered with crumbs, and two crystal jelly jars were turned on their sides, the contents seeping into the expensive fabric.

As Mary Grace pried a spoon covered with cheese grits from a butter plate, she rejoiced that the Lovejoys and their demon children would be leaving the next morning. Glancing down, Mary Grace saw a strawberry and two squashed grapes under the table. She crouched to retrieve them and was in this undignified position when she heard footsteps echoing on the hardwood floor of the lobby. Before she had time to stand, the form of a tall man filled the doorway.

The chandelier in the lobby was at his back, causing a shadow to hide his features. But there was something familiar about the way he stood with his feet wide apart and his head thrust forward. Mary Grace felt her scalp start to tingle . . .

The man was holding several bulky pieces of luggage, which he dropped abruptly, then stepped into the dining room, and her eyes focused on his face. The dark, wavy hair was cut a little shorter than it used to be. The brown eyes were older, wiser. Only his lazy grin was just as she remembered. "Hey, Gracie," he said.

Mary Grace had thought about John Wright many times during the past five years, but never had she imagined that when and if she ever saw him again she'd be crawling on the floor holding squashed fruit. She stood and clasped her sticky hands behind her. "Nobody has called me that for a long time," she told him.

He took a step closer and looked around the dining room. "So you *own* this place?" he asked.

"I do," she confirmed. "What brings you to Bethany Beach?"

"Business." He smiled. "I called last week to make a reservation, but the girl who answered the phone said it wasn't necessary since you always have plenty of vacancies."

Mary Grace wished fervently that her desk clerk had prepared her for John's impending arrival. "We have rooms available, but I'll warn you in advance that the Arms is not luxurious."

"I've been on the road for three weeks, so luxury is a distant memory. I just need a quiet place to work for a few days. And this looks perfect."

She wiped her hands on the already-soiled tablecloth, then walked past John Wright and into the lobby. "Would you like a room that faces the beach or the courtyard?"

"It doesn't matter," he said as he followed behind her. "I'll be too busy working on my article to look out the window."

"Article?" she asked as she opened the hotel register.

"I'm an investigative reporter for the *Savannah Sun Times,* and I'm here to write a story."

She paused in her efforts to find the correct page in the register. "You always said you were going to be a journalist. Did you get to play for the NBA too?" she asked, then regretted the question, realizing she had shown him that her memories of him were quite detailed.

He shook his head with a smile. "No, I lost my edge during my mission and had to give up on a pro basketball career." He ran his hand along the polished mahogany surface of the registration desk. "This place is pretty nice."

Mary Grace was instantly conscious of all the needed repairs and wished that he had waited to come until after the improvements had been made. "It's a wonderful old house," she told him with pride. "But we're a little off the beaten path, and I don't advertise much anymore, so I'm surprised you found us."

John gave her another smile. "I met Stan Guthrie at the Atlanta airport last summer, and I asked him about you. I'll admit it was a shock to learn you were here. I figured you'd be in a desert with dirt under your fingernails instead of running a classy little hotel. What happened to your dreams of being an archaeologist?"

"Circumstances changed my dreams," she responded vaguely.

"That happens sometimes." He studied her for a few seconds, then continued. "Anyway, when I got the assignment to come to Bethany Beach, I decided to stay here so I could see how your life has turned out."

She laughed. "I don't think my life has 'turned out' yet. I'm just kind of in a holding pattern."

His eyes surveyed her quickly. "You cut your hair."

Mary Grace absently put a hand to her head. For years she'd worn her hair long, but recently Jennifer had convinced her to try a more sophisticated look, and now the bottom layer barely brushed her collar. "Yes."

"I like it. Even though it makes you look so . . . mature and serious."

"I am very serious," she assured him. "And mature."

"But you're not computerized?" he asked as she wrote his name in the register.

"We don't have many guests at a time, so this system still works for us," she told him as she mentally added a computer to her list of things she would buy with her renovation money. Then, reaching behind her, she took a set of keys off a hook. "You'll be in the Robert E. Lee Room, court-side. It's the most convenient to the parking lot and should be quiet."

"Thanks." He took the key, and she couldn't help but notice that he wasn't wearing a wedding ring.

After pausing to let him retrieve his luggage, she led the way outside. "Follow me, please."

"Don't you want my credit card number?" he asked.

"My desk clerk will be in soon, and she'll handle the payment arrange-ments with you." Mary Grace glanced at him. "I'll trust you until then."

"I guess I have an honest face," he said, and she smiled.

She opened the door with her passkey, then stood back and admired the room with pride. The furniture was mostly antique, and a large, limited-edition print of General Lee himself hung above the huge, four-poster bed.

"Wow," John said as he stepped inside. He put his suitcases down and walked around, looking at the Civil War memorabilia. "Is this stuff authentic?"

"Mostly. Some are reproductions."

"Are all your rooms named after Civil War generals?"

"Confederate generals," she corrected.

He returned from his tour of the room to stand beside her. "That was clever."

"I can't take credit for the idea," she told him.

"And you said your rooms weren't luxurious," John said with satisfaction. "You should have seen the Annie Oakley Motor Inn that I just checked out of."

Mary Grace smiled at this. "Well, I've got to get back to work. Call the desk if you need anything, and stop by after ten o'clock to give the clerk your credit card number."

Before John could reply, Mary Grace left the Robert E. Lee Room and took two calming breaths as she returned to the lobby. John Wright was staying in her hotel. She couldn't wait to call Jennifer and give her the news. When she walked through the front door, she saw that her teenage desk clerk had arrived.

"Oh, my gosh!" the girl cried with her hand to her heart. "I saw our new guest!"

"Mr. Wright?" Mary Grace clarified.

"Didn't you recognize him? He's John F. Kennedy, Jr.!" Windy exclaimed.

Mary Grace exhaled slowly. Windy worked for almost nothing and was eager to please, but she was not the brightest person. "John F. Kennedy, Jr. is dead. He and his wife and sister-in-law were killed in a plane crash several years ago."

Windy grasped Mary Grace by the arm. "Don't you see? He must have faked his death, and now he's hiding out! He probably stays in small towns like Bethany Beach to keep from being discovered by the press." Windy held to her original theory.

Mary Grace couldn't control a laugh. "Windy, John Wright *is* the press. He works for the *Savannah Sun Times.*"

"John Wright must be a fake identity," Windy insisted. "And he probably uses his *real* first name to keep from getting confused!" She lifted her eyebrows meaningfully.

"I can promise you that John Wright is not a famous dead person," Mary Grace reiterated. "We knew each other when we were in college."

"Oh, I get it," Windy replied with a conspiratorial nod. "He asked you to cover for him. I can understand that you want to help him, but it seems like you could tell me, since I work here and everything . . ."

Mary Grace shook her head and moved away from the desk. "He'll be back in a little while to pay for his room." She stopped and glanced at the teenager. "And he said he called last week and you told him he didn't need to make a reservation."

Windy looked down at her faded blue jeans. "If I'd have known I was going to meet someone important today, I'd have dressed better."

"Dressing professionally is something you should do every day, regardless of who you expect to meet, and record keeping is very important. I've asked you to make reservations when people call."

The girl was instantly contrite. "I'm sorry! But when he called, those Lovejoy people were checking in. Their kids were jumping on the couch, and it made me so nervous I forgot."

Mary Grace sighed. "It's okay. Just try to remember next time," she said, then walked back to her office. The answering machine was blinking, and she checked her messages. There were two calls—one from her mother and one from Bobby Chandler. She didn't have time for a lengthy conversation with her mother, but it seemed wrong to return one call and not the other. She had just about decided not to call either of them when the phone rang. It was Bobby.

"I called a few minutes ago, but no one answered," he said.

"Sorry. I was taking an unexpected guest to his room."

"Oh, an unexpected guest," Bobby sounded impressed. "That's a good thing."

An image of John Wright's face floated before her, and Mary Grace suppressed a sigh. "Maybe."

"How did your meeting with Heath Pointer go this morning?" Bobby asked.

"About like you'd expect. He tried to talk me into selling the Arms."

"But you resisted?"

"Firmly," she assured him.

"I hate to agree with your snooty lawyer on anything, but you ought to unload that place," Bobby advised. "Justin will forgive you."

"I've already discussed this enough for one day."

"Am I invited for dinner?" Bobby changed the subject.

"Of course. You have a standing invitation. But I have to warn you that Heath may also be there."

Bobby groaned, and Mary Grace had to laugh.

"Lucy and I made lasagna," she told him. "Maybe that will compensate for the company."

"I'll be there," Bobby promised, concluding the conversation.

After they hung up, Mary Grace reviewed her list of reservations for the weekend. The Lovejoys were leaving the next day at noon, but the ladies from Haggerty were due in just a few hours. That would fill four of her remaining rooms. A couple from Texas who had spent their honeymoon at the Arms in 1978 would arrive by six o'clock and had requested the Robert Hatton Room. Her perusal was interrupted by a sharp knock. Mary Grace looked up to see John Wright standing in the doorway. He held an American Express card in his hand.

"The girl at the front desk says she doesn't remember how to do credit cards," he explained.

Figuring it would be useless to get mad at Windy, Mary Grace stood. "I'll take care of it for you."

He stepped aside to allow her through the doorway, then followed her into the lobby. When they arrived at the registration desk, Windy gave Mary Grace a sheepish look. "Sorry."

"It's okay," Mary Grace said. "Just watch me so you can do it next time." She pulled out the old manual imprint machine while John leaned on the aged wood. He extended the card toward her.

"I didn't know anyone used those things anymore," he commented as she made an impression of his card onto the carbon paper.

"We like to keep things simple." Mary Grace tried not to sound like she was making excuses for the Arms. "How many days are you planning to stay?"

"At least through Friday. I have to be at my next assignment on Monday, so I'll finish up before then."

Mary Grace made a notation on the slip, then handed it, along with the credit card, to Windy. "Can you handle it from here?" she asked the girl.

Windy nodded. "I'll call this in and be right back," she told John with a giggle.

Hoping to distract John from Windy's peculiar behavior, Mary Grace asked, "What are you working on? Or are you allowed to say?"

He leaned closer and whispered, "I think I can trust you. I'm investigating an unsolved mystery that began twenty-five years ago. A girl named Victoria Harte was killed in a motel here. Have you ever heard of her?"

Mary Grace frowned. "No, but our mayor is Richard Harte."

John nodded. "Victoria was his sister."

Windy returned at this moment. "His credit card is good," she announced. John raised an eyebrow, and Mary Grace regretted the girl's lack of tact.

"That's a relief, I can tell you," John teased.

"I had no doubt that it would be," Mary Grace said with as much dignity as she could muster. "It's just standard procedure," she added with an embarrassed look in John's direction.

"No problem," he assured her.

Windy gave the card and the charge slip back to their new guest. "Thank you, Mr. *Wright*." She emphasized his last name, then winked at Mary Grace.

Mary Grace was glad that John didn't even seem to notice the girl. "I hope you enjoy your stay," she told him, then turned and walked to her office. She didn't realize that John had followed her until he spoke from the doorway.

"You look natural in here," he said.

"I should, I certainly spend enough time at this desk."

"I guess running a place like this takes a lot of dedication." He looked around. "It must be about a hundred years old."

"Almost," she affirmed. "It was built in 1910 by a railroad baron named Peter Bethany. It was *one* of his family's summer homes."

John whistled in appreciation. "The architecture is kind of unusual. It's shaped almost like a V."

"Peter Bethany could afford the best, so he brought in craftsmen from the northeast who were skilled in building homes that could withstand high winds. The shape of the house protects the courtyard from gusts blowing up from the ocean. They built it up here near the bluff to avoid flooding, even during hurricanes. Because of that, it's one of the few surviving structures from its era."

John seemed impressed by this information. "So when was it turned into a hotel?"

"In the 1940s. But then it changed ownership several times, and by the time Justin bought it, the Arms had fallen into disrepair. He restored it and made a good living."

"No easy task, I'm sure. This Justin—is he your husband?"

She shook her head. "Just a friend."

Now it was John's turn to look embarrassed. "I'm sorry."

She smiled. "That's okay. Lots of people make that assumption."

"Did you buy this place from him?"

"No," she told him. "Justin left it to me when he died."

John looked even more uncomfortable. "I'm sorry again. Did he die recently?"

"He's been gone for almost four years." She forced a smile.

There was an awkward silence, then John said, "Can I ask a favor?"

She nodded. "Of course."

"I need to fax some information to my office in Savannah." He held up a handful of papers, and his eyes strayed to the economy fax machine on the credenza behind her desk. "If it wouldn't be too much trouble," he added.

"It's no trouble." She extended her hand, and he relinquished the pages.

"I hate to bother you, but I'm already in the doghouse with my editor, and if this arrives after my deadline, I'm toast." He gave her the fax number, and she put the papers into the tray. There was a few seconds of awkward silence. Neither of them spoke while they watched the first page slip slowly into the machine.

Finally Mary Grace felt obligated to make conversation, "What could possibly be interesting enough about a twenty-five-year-old murder for the *Savannah Sun Times* to send a reporter all the way to Bethany Beach?"

John leaned his hands against the edge of her desk. His shirt-sleeves were rolled up, and as Mary Grace saw the muscles in his fore-arms flex, she wondered if he still played basketball to keep in shape. "Summers are always a little slow news-wise," he told her. "So somebody came up with the idea of doing a series of articles on old unsolved murders. They've given me a less-than-generous expense account and sent me to little towns across the southeast."

Mary Grace raised an eyebrow. "Maybe your limited expense account was the *real* reason you wanted to stay here—since my rates are cheap."

He looked over her shoulder out the window at the beach. "I'll admit I was pleased to get a bargain."

She removed the papers from the fax machine and handed them back to him. "All done."

He took the pages. "Thanks. Now I'll get to work." With a wave, he turned and left the room.

Mary Grace stared at the empty doorway for several minutes after John left. Then the phone rang and she picked it up absently. "Bethany Arms."

"Gracie?" It was John's voice. "The phone in my room doesn't work."

She cleared her throat. "It sounds like it's working fine to me."

"I'm calling on my cell phone. The one in the Ulysses S. Grant Room is dead as a doornail."

"Robert E. Lee," Mary Grace corrected. "The jack is probably loose. I'll be right there."

She hung up the phone and walked out of her office. When she passed the front desk, she saw Windy painting her fingernails. "Windy," she whispered, "please don't paint your nails at the front desk."

Windy looked up with a blank expression. "Why not?"

Rather than try to explain professionalism to Windy, she said, "It's a waste of money for me to buy that expensive potpourri when the only thing our guests can smell is nail polish."

Windy considered this for a few seconds, then nodded as she put the little bottle of polish away.

"We've got several guests arriving today," Mary Grace told the girl. "Please check the register, then turn on the air conditioners in the appropriate rooms."

"Who'll answer the phone while I'm gone?" Windy asked as she blew on her damp nails.

"I will," Mary Grace replied.

With a shrug, Windy sauntered slowly toward the back door. Once the girl had disappeared, Mary Grace took a deep breath, then walked outside and down the sidewalk to the Robert E. Lee Room. John was unpacking his clothes when she knocked on the open door.

John smiled. "Well, that was quick service." He pulled dress shirts from a suitcase and hung them on the wooden rack provided for that purpose.

"Service is something we're very serious about here at the Arms," Mary Grace assured him as she walked across the room. She leaned over the desk and pushed the loose phone cord firmly into the jack, then stood and picked up the receiver. The dial tone hummed steadily in her ear. "All fixed." She turned back toward the door, but his voice stopped her.

"I might be getting a fax back from my office."

She nodded. "If you get anything, I'll have Windy call you."

"Your desk clerk?"

"Yes."

He walked over and stood a little closer than absolutely necessary. "Her name is Wendy?"

"No, W*i*ndy," Mary Grace emphasized the vowel sound.

John frowned. "Windy isn't a name, it's an atmospheric condition."

She smiled. "I can't be held responsible. I didn't name her."

John acknowledged this with a little nod. "It says on my welcome note that you provide a continental breakfast for all your guests."

His close proximity was unnerving, so she took a step back. "Yes, from seven to nine during the week, eight to ten on weekends."

"It also says that a buffet dinner is served every night at seven o'clock."

"That is correct. It's included in the price of your room."

He gave her a speculative look. "So, do you join your guests for meals?"

Mary Grace nodded, then turned her stare to the picture of General Lee. "Yes, it's a long-standing tradition."

"Well then, I'll look forward to seeing you tonight."

Mary Grace nodded, then walked back to the lobby. She sat down at the desk and dialed a number from memory. Jennifer Sanders Guthrie answered on the third ring. "Hello!"

Mary Grace could hear the twins in the background. "Jen, it's me, Mary Grace."

"Calling me in the middle of the day? Did someone die?" Jennifer demanded.

Mary Grace laughed. "Not that I know of. What are you doing?"

"Wiping noses, cleaning toilets, thawing hamburger . . ."

"You're watching Judge Judy, aren't you?"

"It's very educational," Jennifer admitted without a trace of guilt. "It really should be on PBS. So what's up?"

"Do you think Stan would keep the boys for you tonight so you could come for a visit? I'll make you a root beer float."

"I'm due for a night out, but what's the occasion?"

"I just have some interesting news and wanted to share it with you. Be here at nine o'clock. I'll be finished with dinner by then."

There was a brief pause, then Jennifer said, "I know you don't expect me to wait until tonight to find out your news. The suspense will kill me."

"Not if the twins haven't," Mary Grace responded with confidence. "See you at nine."

CHAPTER 2

After a thirty-minute conversation with her mother, Mary Grace went to the kitchen to be sure that Lucy was working on dinner. The cook was nowhere to be seen, but the pans of lasagna they had made the night before were stacked in the refrigerator. She found Windy in the Elisha F. Paxton Room, looking through a fashion magazine.

"Did you turn on the air conditioners in the rooms with reservations?" Mary Grace asked as they returned to the lobby together.

Windy nodded, then extended the magazine. "Do you think this would look good on me?"

Mary Grace glanced at the model wearing shiny red boots and a neon-green miniskirt. "I think the boots would clash with your hair," she responded. "Now I need to you to man the front desk." Mary Grace checked her watch. "It's almost three o'clock, and the ladies from Haggerty will be here soon."

As if on cue, the front door opened, but it was John Wright instead of the harmless little old ladies from Georgia. Mary Grace felt a blush rise in her cheeks. Then she glanced at Windy, who looked like she was about to ask for his autograph. Mary Grace stepped forward before they could embarrass themselves further.

"Can I help you?" she asked in her most professional tone.

John gave her that lazy smile, and her cheeks grew hotter. "I'll just bet you can. I need directions to the public library."

"Two blocks down Beachside Road, then turn left on Sand Castle Drive," Mary Grace provided.

"I also need a map of the area so I can begin my investigation."

Mary Grace opened her mouth, but before she could respond there was a disturbance at the door. Everyone turned as four elderly women in different shapes and sizes walked through. Miss Eugenia Atkins led the way, carrying a duffel bag with *Free to the first 1,000 ticket holders* emblazoned on the side and four Wal-Mart sacks. She was a tall, heavyset woman with white-gray hair and skin turned brown by the sun.

Her sister, Annabelle, was younger and smaller. She had a sprinkling of freckles across her nose, and while her hair was also gray, it was cut in a modern bob. She trailed a few feet behind Miss Eugenia, pulling a suitcase with a built-in dolly.

Miss George Ann Simmons, who was tall and thin, came next and had no luggage. Her jet-black hair contrasted sharply with her pale skin, and the way she wore it in a bun at the back of her head emphasized her long neck.

Miss Polly Kirby brought up the rear, clutching a tapestry-print overnight bag and looking nervous. She had always reminded Mary Grace of a cupcake—sweet with fluffy, white hair and a pink complexion.

Mary Grace turned to the ladies with genuine pleasure. "Welcome to the Arms!" she greeted. "You make the first week of June something to look forward to each year."

"Humph," Miss Eugenia said with a look at her companions, and Mary Grace raised an eyebrow.

"Did I miss something?"

Miss Eugenia shook her head. "No," she replied. "It's just that *someone* in our group suggested going to the Georgia coast this year instead of coming to the Arms."

"Just to keep our tax dollars in our home state," Miss George Ann explained quickly.

"But I talked them out of it," Miss Eugenia claimed.

"Since we didn't want to desert you," Miss Polly added as she dabbed perspiration from her face with a lace handkerchief.

Mary Grace knew the ladies meant no harm, but was galled to have this announcement made in John Wright's presence. "I appreciate that very much, but I don't want you to feel obligated to come here each summer. Next year if you want to stay in Georgia and bolster your own state's economy, I will understand completely."

Annabelle leaned onto the wooden counter. "This is the last year I'll be going anywhere with them. I've made that clear."

Mary Grace waited for Annabelle to explain this comment, but Miss Eugenia spoke instead. "Annabelle got married in December, and she doesn't like to leave her new husband."

"We are still practically on our honeymoon," Annabelle elaborated. "And the only reason they wanted me to come along was so we could split the cost of gas the usual four ways."

"That's not the only reason," Miss Eugenia corrected. "Coming to the Arms has been our tradition for over thirty years, and it would be bad luck to break it. And besides, we needed you to drive us in your nice new car."

Miss George Ann lifted her nose into the air, making her neck appear even longer. "And it's unbecoming for a woman your age to even say the word *honeymoon*, Annabelle, much less claim to still be *on* one."

Annabelle looked offended by this remark, so Mary Grace introduced John before things could get worse. "These ladies live in the small town of Haggerty, Georgia, and come here for a week every summer," she told him, and he nodded to each of the new guests.

Then Miss Eugenia studied him thoroughly. "You look so familiar to me."

Mary Grace saw that Windy was about to divulge her JFK, Jr. theory, so she spoke quickly. "He is a reporter for the *Savannah Sun Times*. Perhaps you've read one of his articles?"

"I guess that's possible," Miss Eugenia murmured.

"But not likely," Annabelle added. "Eugenia spends her spare time watching soaps, not reading the paper."

"I read an occasional paper," Miss Eugenia corrected. "The obituaries are the only way I can keep up with all my friends."

"Okay, let's get you ladies settled," Mary Grace said briskly. "I know you requested the Edward Kirby Smith Room, Miss Polly, but the hot water isn't working there, so I've put you in the Henry Lewis Benning Room instead."

The older lady nodded, then turned to John. "I like to stay in the Edward Kirby Smith Room since my own last name is Kirby," she enlightened him. "I've always thought the general and I might be related."

John's eyebrows rose as Mary Grace turned to Miss George Ann. "Of course, you're in the Stonewall Jackson Room."

Miss George Ann sniffed. "Since I really *am* related to him," she said with a look at Miss Polly. "I have a certificate from the Daughters of the Confederacy that proves it," she added as if someone had disputed this fact. Then Miss George Ann returned her attention to Mary Grace. "My luggage is in the car if you'll have the bellboy bring it in."

There was no bellboy, so this task would fall to Mary Grace, but she nodded. "Yes, ma'am."

"You look so pretty, Mary Grace," Miss Polly said quietly. "Did you dye your hair?"

"No, but I did get it cut."

Miss Polly nodded. "Very attractive."

Mary Grace smiled. "Thanks." Then she turned to the sisters. "Miss Eugenia, I thought I'd put you in the Nathan Bedford Forrest Room."

Miss Eugenia seemed pleased with this arrangement. "That has always been one of my favorites."

"And Annabelle," Mary Grace continued, "you are next door as usual."

Annabelle accepted this announcement without comment.

"Windy, will you escort Miss George Ann and Miss Polly to their rooms?" Mary Grace requested. "And I'll take Miss Eugenia and Miss Annabelle to theirs."

The girl obeyed, but her eyes remained focused squarely on John Wright until she walked out the door. Miss George Ann and Miss Polly followed right behind her. After a quick wave to John, Mary Grace led the sisters through the rear exit and onto the sidewalk that ran along the beach side of the Arms.

"Is dinner still at seven?" Miss Eugenia asked.

"Yes, ma'am," Mary Grace replied.

"Well, we'll all be looking forward to visiting with you then." Miss Eugenia glanced at her sister. "As soon as I get unpacked, we can go for a walk on the beach."

"As soon as I get unpacked, I'm going to call Derrick." There was a little edge to Annabelle's voice.

"A few days away from your husband won't kill you," Miss Eugenia said sagely, and Annabelle rounded on her sister.

"You're just jealous that you don't have a husband!"

"Jealous!" Miss Eugenia repeated. "Of that little pip-squeak?"

Mary Grace unlocked the doors and put their luggage inside while the sisters quarreled. Then she waved good-bye and returned to the lobby. She was surprised to see John Wright still standing by the desk. "Your new guests arrived like a tornado," he commented.

"That's a pretty accurate description, but they are regulars and I appreciate their business," Mary Grace said in defense of the ladies from Haggerty. "I thought you were going to get a map."

"I wanted to ask you to recommend a good place to buy one."

Mary Grace glanced up from the guest register. "Any of the stores that line Beachside Road will have one."

John leaned on the desk, his face close to hers. "Your desk clerk seems a little . . . slow."

Mary Grace sighed. "She's just starstruck."

John glanced around the room. "Who's the star?"

"You," she replied with reluctance.

John's eyebrows shot up. "Me?"

"She thinks you're John F. Kennedy, Jr."

John frowned as he considered this. "He's dead."

"I know that," she agreed, "and you know that, but Windy thinks you faked your death and have spent the last few years hiding from the press in small towns like Bethany Beach."

John rubbed his chin thoughtfully. "So who was in the plane that crashed and what have I done with my wife and sister-in-law?"

Mary Grace couldn't resist a quick look at his unadorned left hand. "Windy's theory still has some holes in it."

John flashed her one of his smiles, then headed for the door. "I'll try to figure that out while I find a map."

As Mary Grace watched him disappear, the phone rang and she picked it up absently. It was Mr. Lovejoy telling her that they were driving to Daytona for the evening and wouldn't be eating dinner at the Arms. Mary Grace rejoiced silently, then wished them a safe and pleasant trip and hung up with a sigh of relief.

Windy returned, and Mary Grace asked her to stay at the front desk while she delivered Miss George Ann's luggage. Then Mary Grace changed into jeans and a T-shirt and went out into the hot sun.

It took forever just to get the lawn mower out of the equipment shed. Refusing to be discouraged, Mary Grace dragged the machine to the courtyard and tried to start it. Fifteen minutes later, she was sweating and her arms were aching. She was glaring at the lawn mower, when the second-honeymooners arrived.

"Leo Rayburn." The husband approached her and held out his hand. He was in his early fifties, tall and fit, with sandy red hair and lots of freckles. Mary Grace wiped her palm on her jeans before extending it. "And this is my wife, Farrah."

Farrah lived up to her name with long legs, a mane of curly blonde hair, and enough eye makeup to make Tammy Faye Baker seem demure. Even though she was also past her prime, Farrah looked good in her short shorts, indicating that she made a point to stay in shape. Mary Grace nodded at Farrah. "It's nice to meet you." She turned back to Mr. Rayburn. "I'm Mary Grace O'Malley. I spoke to you on the phone."

"You're the owner?" Mr. Rayburn asked with a surprised glance at the lawn mower.

Mary Grace sighed. "I don't normally cut the grass, but my yardman is out of town," she explained briefly.

"Don't you have a pool?" Farrah wanted to know as her vacuous eyes explored the landscape.

"No. Just the beach," Mary Grace replied with determined cheerfulness.

"Leo," Farrah whined, pulling on her husband's shirtsleeve. "You said they would have a pool."

"The Arms has never had a pool," Mary Grace pointed out, wondering if Farrah's memory was as bad as her manners.

Leo looked a little embarrassed as he addressed his wife. "I said after all these years they might have had one put in. But we don't need a pool, honey-pie," he placated. "Look how clear the ocean is."

"But there's so much *sand*," Farrah replied, her lips pouting.

"It will be fine," he promised, then turned to Mary Grace. "Do you need a hand with that?" Before Mary Grace could decline, Mr. Rayburn leaned forward and pulled the chain one quick time. The lawn mower sprang to life, and Mary Grace gave it a resentful look. Then she smiled at her guests.

"Thanks!" she hollered over the roar of the lawn mower. "My desk clerk is in the lobby, and she can get you settled."

"We want the Robert Hatton Room, since we stayed there before," Leo yelled with a smile at his wife.

"It's all been arranged," Mary Grace assured loudly. "Windy will give you the key." Then she put her hands on the handle of the mower and started pushing.

It didn't take long to cut the grass in the small courtyard. Once she was through, Mary Grace stood back and surveyed her handiwork. There were a few strips of long grass marring the green surface, but considering her lack of landscaping experience, she couldn't be disappointed. Mary Grace towed the lawn mower back to the shed and was attempting to get it inside when a familiar voice spoke from behind her.

"Let me get that," John said pleasantly. Then, without waiting for her permission, he reached over and lifted the mower with negligible effort into the shed.

Mary Grace saw several pieces of grass stuck to her ankles and felt a trickle of sweat run down her spine. She hated for John to see her in this condition, but there was no means of escape, so she turned around. "Thanks."

His eyes scanned her appearance as she closed the shed. "So is working in the yard at your hotel a hobby or something?"

She shook her head. "No, it was an isolated emergency. Did you get a map?" she changed the subject quickly as they walked toward the lobby.

John nodded. "A nice one, color coded so I can easily find government buildings, historical sites, and tourist attractions." They reached the front door of the Arms, and he opened it for her. "I also made an appointment to talk to the victim's brother, Mayor Harte, tomorrow morning."

Mary Grace considered this. "That sounds like a good place to start. Did you find the library?"

He nodded. "I'm headed there now."

Anxious to get cleaned up, Mary Grace took a step down the hall. "Well, good luck. And I guess I'll see you at dinner."

John smiled. "For sure."

After a shower, Mary Grace went to the kitchen. Once they had the lasagna baking, she helped Lucy chop heads of lettuce for a huge salad. Then they arranged frozen breadsticks on pans so they would be ready to go into the industrial-sized oven once the main course was done.

"What's for dessert?" she asked as she checked the clock at six-thirty.

"Oh dear me," Lucy replied, putting a hand to her head. "I forgot all about dessert."

"Don't you have some frozen pies or something?" Mary Grace asked with a hopeful glance at the freezer.

Lucy shook her head. "No, we used the last of them last night. I'm so sorry." The old woman squinted at the cupboards. "Maybe I could make a cake or something."

"There's not enough time," Mary Grace said, still thinking. "I guess I could ask Bobby to pick up some ice cream and let the guests make their own sundaes. If we're lucky, they'll think we planned it."

The old woman giggled. "Maybe it can become a Friday night tradition."

"Hmmm," Mary Grace murmured as she walked toward the door that led into the hallway. "I'm going to call Bobby, then change for dinner. I'll be in my apartment if you need me." She walked quickly back to her apartment and reached Bobby at his office. He agreed to stop by the grocery store to get ice cream for dessert. She hung up the phone and it rang again immediately. This time it was Heath Pointer.

"Mary Grace?" he asked, and she could barely hear him over the static on his cell phone. "Is that you?"

"It's me. Where are you calling from? Australia?"

Heath laughed. "Close enough. I'm in Andalusia, and it doesn't look like I'm going to make it back in time for dinner."

Mary Grace sighed with relief, then said, "Well, the invitation is an open one. You can come another night."

"I'll be looking forward to it," he replied. "I'll probably talk to you tomorrow."

Mary Grace said good-bye, then hung up the phone. Determined not to be at a disadvantage when she saw John Wright again, she went to work on herself. She took special care with her hair and applied makeup liberally. Finally she put on her favorite dress and hurried from her room to face her guests.

She stopped by the kitchen, where Bobby was unloading bags onto the counter. "I don't know how I can ever thank you," Mary Grace told him as she transferred the ice cream into the freezer.

Bobby smiled. "How about a lifetime of free meals at the Arms?"

Mary Grace looked over her shoulder at him. "I've already given you that." Then they heard voices from the dining room. "I guess I'd better get to work."

He followed her through the door, and they found the ladies from Haggerty arguing about where they should sit.

"I prefer to be near the window so I can see the tide," Miss George Anne Simmons stated firmly. "We're at the *beach*. If we can't see the *water,* it's pointless."

"Well *I* like to be near the door," Miss Eugenia Atkins disagreed.

"Why don't both of you sit on opposite ends of the table," Mary Grace suggested diplomatically. "Then both of you will be comfortable."

The ladies exchanged a glare, then followed this recommendation. Just as they took their seats, John Wright walked in.

"Good evening, ladies." He stepped up to scoot Miss Polly's chair under the table. "I must say you all look wonderful tonight." He spoke to the room in general, but his eyes were on Mary Grace.

The Rayburns arrived, and Mary Grace made brief introductions. "I wonder how she keeps her eyes open with all that goop on them," Miss Eugenia whispered as the honeymoon couple took seats at the other end of the table beside Miss George Ann.

Mary Grace checked to be sure that Leo and Farrah hadn't heard this remark, then asked Bobby to say the blessing on the food. Immediately following Bobby's "amen," there was a crash in the kitchen. Mary Grace ran toward the door with Bobby at her heels. They found Lucy sitting on the floor, surrounded by lasagna.

"I didn't see the stool." Her lip trembled as she pointed to the offending object. "Two whole pans of lasagna ruined."

Mary Grace surveyed the disaster area and tried to think of a comforting response. "There's one pan left," was all she could come up with.

"That's not enough to feed everyone!" Lucy wailed.

"Bobby and I won't eat any lasagna," Mary Grace proposed, and Bobby nodded in agreement.

"Me either," John Wright contributed gallantly from behind them.

Mary Grace glanced back at him, torn between gratitude and embarrassment. John leaned down and helped Lucy to her feet.

"I'll clean up this mess if I can just find the broom," Lucy peered around the room.

"Nonsense," Mary Grace said briskly as she picked up the broom that was right in front of Lucy. "I'll clean up the mess. You need to call your son and have him come pick you up."

"You can't clean the kitchen," John objected. "You've got guests waiting. I'll clean it up."

Mary Grace shook her head vigorously. "You will not. You're a guest here, and in spite of what you've seen since you arrived, we have very high standards at the Arms."

John gave her a compassionate smile, which only made her feel worse. "Of course you do."

"I'm not a guest, just a freeloader," Bobby said. "So I'll sweep up the lasagna."

Mary Grace opened her mouth to object, but John took her by the elbow and guided her away from the mess. "It's really your only option," he whispered. The warmth of his fingers against the soft skin of her arm was distracting, and Mary Grace couldn't think of a response. "You've got to get back in there before all your guests come to check on *us*."

Reluctantly she allowed him to propel her. "I can't leave Bobby here cleaning my kitchen," she said with an anxious look over her shoulder.

"It's almost done already," Bobby said as he swept the soggy mess onto the dustpan. "Just take the surviving lasagna and put it on the buffet table. And if it wouldn't break the house rules, maybe he could carry the salad." Bobby waved the dirty broom at John.

John picked up the salad bowl and waited while Mary Grace put on oven mitts before lifting the last pan of lasagna. Then they walked into the dining room together.

"Nothing to worry about, folks," Mary Grace said with a reassuring smile. "My cook had a little accident, but she's fine, and dinner will continue as scheduled." Mary Grace placed the lasagna in the center of the buffet table, then took the salad from John's hands and put it to the left. "I'll be right back with the bread," she told the ladies. "Help yourselves."

She walked into the kitchen, where Bobby was arranging bread-sticks on a platter. He had one of Lucy's aprons tied around his waist. "What are you doing?" Mary Grace asked, gesturing at the apron.

"Somebody has to pour tea and keep the bread plate refilled."

"Oh, Bobby." Mary Grace felt tears spring into her eyes.

"I feel terrible about all this," Lucy said from her perch on a stool. "I'd help, but I think I might have twisted my ankle."

This remark alarmed Mary Grace. "Do you want me to take you to the emergency room?"

Lucy shook her head. "No, Jerome will be here in a minute, and if he thinks it's bad, he'll take me."

Mary Grace looked from Lucy to Bobby, unsure which situation was causing her the most anxiety.

"Don't worry about me, Mary Grace," Bobby insisted. "I used to wait tables in college, so I have experience. And who knows, maybe I'll get a tip."

"Don't worry about me either, honey," Lucy said bravely. "I'm sure my old leg will be fine."

Bobby picked up the platter filled with breadsticks and pushed open the door, then waited for Mary Grace to precede him into the dining room. With a sigh, Mary Grace took her seat at the table.

"So you spent your honeymoon here in the seventies?" Miss George Ann was asking the Rayburns.

"Yes," Leo said, then sent a warm look in his wife's direction. "We recently renewed our vows and wanted to come back for a second honeymoon."

Farrah batted her bright blue eyelids.

Miss Polly put a hand to her ample chest. "That is so sweet."

"Why anyone would want to have a second honeymoon is beyond me," Miss Eugenia said as she settled down at the table with her plate full of food. "Seems to me folks should get all that taken care of the first time."

"Try to keep from being an embarrassment," Miss George Ann replied.

Mary Grace was looking for a way to intervene when Farrah surprised her by commenting, "I wanted to go to Cancun, but Leo made me come back here instead."

There was a brief silence, then Mary Grace responded, "At least here you can drink the water."

Farrah blinked stupidly as an embarrassed look spread across Leo's face.

"And there's no language barrier or currency exchange issues," John added.

Mary Grace gave him a grateful smile as Miss George Ann asked, "What did you say happened to your cook?"

"She tripped and dropped two pans of the lasagna," Mary Grace admitted. "So everyone may not get their fill of the main course, but we have plenty of bread and salad."

"It's just as well," Miss Eugenia told them from her seat near the door. "A serving of lasagna has an atrocious number of fat grams, and I don't even want to think about the calories."

"You never used to think about calories," Annabelle said with a trace of sarcasm.

Miss Eugenia picked up her plate and moved two seats down so she was closer to the other guests. "That was before the doctor discovered my condition."

"You have a condition?" John asked politely as Bobby started pouring tea.

Miss Eugenia nodded and covered the top of her glass. "I'll just have water, thank you."

"Me too," John said with a smile up at Bobby.

"I was recently diagnosed with high cholesterol," Miss Eugenia continued the discussion of her health problems, "and as a result my doctor put me on a low-fat diet."

"Dr. Fisk thinks I might be borderline hypoglycemic," Miss Polly contributed.

Miss Eugenia dismissed this with a wave of her hand. "If Dr. Fisk says he *thinks* you *might* be *borderline* hypoglycemic, that means there's nothing wrong with you. He just didn't want to tell you that because you might stop coming in for checkups, and he'd lose money."

Miss Polly's lips opened in a perfect O. "Why, that would be dishonest."

"Dr. Fisk *is* dishonest," Miss Eugenia said as she helped herself to another breadstick. "Don't you remember last year when the newspaper said he'd been involved in Medicare fraud?"

"I certainly remember," Annabelle contributed from across the table. "I took Agnes Halstead for a checkup during the scandal, and when Dr. Fisk walked into the examination room she said, 'Oh, Dr. Fisk, I'm so sorry you got caught stealing money from the government.'"

Miss Eugenia shouted with laughter. "That Agnes! She never was one to beat around the bush."

"What did Dr. Fisk say?" Miss George Ann wanted to know.

Annabelle shrugged. "He handled it like a gentleman. He said, 'I'm sorry, too, Miss Agnes.'"

Miss Polly took the lace handkerchief from the neckline of her dress and dabbed at her forehead. "Well, even if Dr. Fisk had some bookkeeping problems in the past, I don't think he would give me a false diagnosis."

Miss Eugenia opened her mouth to respond, but Farrah Rayburn spoke first. "Do you have to give yourself shots?" she asked Miss Polly with a little shudder.

Miss George Ann narrowed her eyes at the other woman. "Of course not. That's just for diabetics—not people who might be borderline hypoglycemic."

Farrah's cheeks turned pink, and Mary Grace decided to step in before someone got seriously offended. "There are so many diseases, it's hard to keep them all straight," she said with a sympathetic look at Farrah. Then she turned to Miss Eugenia. "If you'll provide me with a list of your dietary restrictions, I'll make sure that we have something you can eat at each meal. You too, Miss Polly."

Miss Eugenia seemed pleased by this offer, but Miss Polly shook her head. "Oh, I don't have any restrictions."

Miss Eugenia gave her a disparaging look. "If he didn't restrict your diet, you don't have hypoglycemia."

"Would anyone care for more salad?" Mary Grace asked to forestall Miss Polly's response. She stood and carried the salad bowl around the table, serving guests personally. The conversation tapered off for a few minutes while everyone ate. As he had promised, John got a healthy portion of salad and several breadsticks, but no lasagna. Mary Grace returned to her seat and nibbled on a piece of cucumber, trying not to watch Bobby as he performed his duties as impromptu waiter.

"The hot water in the Edmund Kirby Smith Room wasn't working last year when we came either," Miss Polly said after a few minutes. "When do you think it will be fixed? Not that I don't love the Henry Lewis Benning Room," she was quick to add.

"I'm terribly sorry for the inconvenience," Mary Grace said. "And I'm just about to take out a construction loan so I can make some major renovations. I hope that by next year the Edmund Kirby Smith Room will be available."

"Who's going to do your financing?" Annabelle asked.

"I'm not sure," Mary Grace replied as she pushed salad around on her plate. "My lawyer is handling it."

"Well, be sure you get a competitive rate," Annabelle advised. "And stick with banks. Private investors are easier to find, but they usually have nasty little clauses that give them the right to call your loan for unconventional reasons."

Mary Grace smiled. "It sounds like you know your business."

"I should," Annabelle said with a sigh. "I spent thirty years working for a bank."

"And what brings you to Bethany Beach, Mr. Wright?" Miss George Ann asked.

John looked surprised by his sudden inclusion in the conversation. "I'm investigating a murder," John told them with a wink at Mary Grace. All the old women leaned forward in unison.

"A murder?" Miss Polly breathed.

"Who died?" Miss Eugenia wanted to know.

"Not here I hope!" Miss George Ann sounded genuinely afraid.

"The victim was a seventeen-year-old high school student," John elaborated. "She didn't die here at the Arms, but she was stabbed at a local hotel."

Fear registered on the faces of her guests, and Mary Grace rushed to clarify. "The girl died over twenty-five years ago."

"Oh, thank goodness," Miss Polly said with relief.

Miss Eugenia narrowed her eyes at John. "Were you playing a trick on us?"

John shook his head, looking innocent. "Oh no, I would never do that. But Mary Grace is right. The victim died twenty-five years ago."

"And why are you interested in it?" Annabelle asked.

"My newspaper has me doing a series of reports on unsolved murders in the southeast," John told them. "This is my fourth. I've already been to towns in North Carolina, Mississippi, and Georgia."

"We're from Georgia!" Miss Polly cried. "I hope you didn't find any murderers in Haggerty!"

"Not so far," John replied with a smile.

"Did you solve any of the old murders?" Annabelle inquired. "Or in your articles do you just rehash the event itself?"

John leaned forward with a satisfied smile. "As a matter of fact, I solved one of them outright and gave the police significant leads on another."

Everyone seemed impressed, and Mary Grace couldn't help but say, "You must either be very lucky or very good."

John turned to her and smiled. "Maybe a little of both."

"Do you think you can solve the murder here in Bethany Beach?" Miss Polly asked.

John nodded. "I'm going to try. And in the meantime, I'll be able to enjoy these luxurious surroundings and the company of lovely ladies." He glanced at Mary Grace, and her cheeks started to burn.

"Oh, Mr. Wright, you are such a charmer," Miss Polly said with a little giggle.

Miss Eugenia frowned. "And I still haven't figured out why you look familiar to me."

"My desk clerk thinks he bears a remarkable resemblance to John F. Kennedy, Jr.," Mary Grace admitted.

Miss Eugenia clapped her hands. "That's it. He's the spitting image of John-John."

All eyes turned to John. "Well, what do you know," Annabelle said in amazement.

"You're John F. Kennedy, Jr.?" Farrah asked.

"No, honey," Leo was quick to say. "Mr. Wright just *favors* him."

Miss George Ann gave Farrah an impatient look, then turned to John. "It must be so annoying to be constantly mistaken for a famous person."

John shrugged. "Actually, this is the first time it's ever happened."

"I'm surprised by that," Miss Eugenia told him. "The likeness is quite pronounced."

"Maybe I *am* JFK, Jr.," John said with another wink at Mary Grace.

Miss Polly put her hand to her mouth in a girlish gesture. "Mr. Wright is teasing us again."

Before Mary Grace could think of a way to regain control of the conversation, Miss George Ann claimed John's attention. "How many more murder cases do you have to write about?"

"Just two more, then I'll be through."

"What will you do after that?" Miss Eugenia asked.

"I'll go back to Savannah and get my next assignment. Something dull and boring, I'm sure. But maybe next summer they'll run a series on," he paused for a second to think, then continued, "the greatest love stories in the southeast. Then I can come back to Bethany Beach and interview all of you." He looked around the table. "I'd start with Miss Polly."

The plump woman blushed crimson. "Oh, Mr. Wright, I don't have a love story to tell."

"Now you're being modest," John said with a smile. Then he looked at the other guests. "I'll bet I could get lots of interesting love stories here."

"I had the most wonderful husband in the world," Miss Eugenia provided helpfully.

"May he rest in peace," Miss Polly added as she dabbed her eyes with her ever-present handkerchief.

"And now Eugenia has a boyfriend who is half her size," Annabelle contributed with relish.

Miss George Ann lifted her chin a notch higher than usual. "Annabelle just got married again at sixty-five. *That's* a story in and of itself."

John turned to Mary Grace. "And what about our lovely hostess? Do you have a love story you could share?"

"No," she answered.

John looked surprised. "Come on, Gracie, you must have dated a bunch of guys."

"Gracie?" Miss Polly repeated in confusion, and John smiled.

"Mary Grace O'Malley is a such a mouthful. I've always preferred to call her Gracie."

Annabelle's eyes widened. "You and Mary Grace *know* each other?"

"We met one summer during college," John told them.

"Well, I declare," Miss Eugenia said.

"In fact, Gracie here broke my heart," John continued, obviously enjoying himself.

"I did not," Mary Grace denied quickly as her guests turned curious eyes toward her. "John is teasing us once again."

Miss Eugenia ignored this and addressed John. "How did she break your heart?"

"I followed her around Panama City like a puppy that summer, but she wouldn't go on a date with me. She wouldn't even dance with me!"

All the old ladies turned with scandalized expressions toward Mary Grace. "And he seems like such a nice young man!" Miss George Ann voiced the universal disapproval.

"I just felt that we didn't have anything in common," Mary Grace defended herself with a stern look in John's direction. "And he didn't follow me around."

"Gracie worked in a little souvenir shop, airbrushing T-shirts," John told the old ladies with a mischievous glance at Mary Grace. "I bought a dozen of them. Now do you think I needed that many shirts saying *Welcome to Panama City?*"

"Of course not." Miss George Ann had chosen sides. "You just wanted to be near her."

"And I did agree to dance with you that last night," Mary Grace added. "But you had to leave."

"Was it just coincidence that you came to the Arms?" Miss George Ann pressed for more details. "Or did you come here to pursue a romance with Mary Grace?"

John laughed. "I'm here to work, but a little romance sounds nice."

Mary Grace tried to hide her embarrassment. "Oh for goodness' sake."

"You can at least revive your friendship!" Miss Polly exclaimed with delight.

"I certainly hope so." John leaned back and crossed his arms over his chest. "But I still find it hard to believe that Gracie hasn't had any romances in five years."

"I didn't say I haven't had any romances," Mary Grace amended as she stood. "I just said I haven't had any I care to share." She gave him a smile over her shoulder as she walked to the kitchen to get dessert.

CHAPTER 3

When Mary Grace pushed her way into the kitchen, she saw Bobby standing at the big stainless steel sink, scrubbing lasagna pans. She immediately started shaking her head. "Oh no. I draw the line at letting you wash our dishes."

He smiled. "That's probably a good thing, since I don't have much experience in the kitchen. Annie and I ate out most of the time." She watched his eyes cloud with misery. "I'd probably break something."

"Help me get the ice cream out," she said briskly, hoping to distract him from his unhappy memories. "Once my guests have finished dessert, I'll come back and load the dishwasher." She pushed a metal cart toward the freezer. "And please take off that apron. There is a limit to the amount of humiliation I can stand."

Bobby laughed. "I'd say your limit is pretty high. I remember a certain hot pink bathing suit with green polka dots that your mother bought you when we were about twelve . . ."

"Keep the apron on, just don't mention that bathing suit again," Mary Grace begged. "Did Lucy go home?"

Bobby nodded. "Yeah, her son came to get her, although she seemed to be walking on that ankle just fine."

"There's probably nothing wrong with her, but I can't take any chances." Mary Grace stacked the gallons of ice cream and toppings as Bobby reached up to take bowls off a high shelf.

"So," Bobby said. "What's with you and John Wright?"

"What do you mean?" Mary Grace asked casually.

"Did you really break his heart?"

She rolled her eyes. "Of course not."

Bobby raised his eyebrows. "He was pretty convincing in there. And I've noticed that when you're around him you blush—a lot."

She felt her cheeks get hot. "I'll explain as soon as we get finished with dinner," Mary Grace promised as she prepared a tray full of toppings, including fruit for those watching fat grams, then turned toward the door. "I might as well get this over with."

When Mary Grace returned to the dining room, John and the Rayburns were gone.

"Mr. Wright said to tell you that he had work to do, and the honeymoon folks said they were going to walk on the beach," Miss Eugenia informed her.

Mary Grace forced a cheerful smile. "That's fine. But for those of you who have stayed for dessert, there is plenty of ice cream. We have vanilla, chocolate, and even some frozen yogurt for those of you who have dietary restrictions," she announced. "Just come on up and fix whatever you'd like."

Mary Grace helped her guests make their dessert choices. Once everyone was served, she sat beside Miss Polly and listened to the ladies discuss their plans for the next day.

"We've got reservations for the tour of the Pirate Ship at nine o'clock, then we'll have lunch at the Sand Dollar," Miss George Ann told the group.

"I thought we were going to the Oyster Bar," Annabelle said with a frown.

"I made a little adjustment to our usual schedule," Miss Eugenia explained. "The Sand Dollar is near the outlet mall, and I want to shop after lunch. I've lost so much weight since I've started my low-fat diet that my clothes are just hanging off of me."

Annabelle gave her sister a disparaging look. "You've only lost six pounds."

Miss Eugenia sniffed. "Six pounds can make a huge difference on someone with my frame."

"I don't see why we can't sleep in," Annabelle complained. "After all, this is supposed to be a *vacation*."

"You can sleep at home," Miss George Ann pointed out. "While we're here we need to see all the sights."

"We've seen them all, year after year," Annabelle said wearily.

Miss George Ann nodded. "That's what makes it a tradition."

"Well, ladies," Mary Grace said briskly as she stood and stacked the empty ice cream dishes on the metal cart, "it sounds like you have a busy day planned for tomorrow, so I know you'll want to get a good night's sleep. I hope to see you all at breakfast," she added, then pushed into the kitchen.

"Did they leave?" Bobby wanted to know from his position at the sink.

"No, but I don't think they'll stay long now that the food is gone." Mary Grace put the leftover ice cream into the freezer and the dessert dishes into the warm water. After rinsing them quickly, she started loading the dishwasher while Bobby wiped down the counters. "We don't have to do a perfect job," she told him. "We'll just hit the high spots, and Lucy can finish up tomorrow."

Bobby nodded as he took out the broom and started sweeping. Jennifer arrived while they were putting the tablecloths into the washers. Mary Grace gave her friend a quick hug, then made introductions.

"Jennifer, this is Bobby Chandler—childhood friend and former resident of Augusta. Bobby and his wife have separated, so he's temporarily living with his grandfather, but I have complete confidence that he will gain her forgiveness and be back with her soon."

She waved toward Jennifer. "Bobby, meet Jennifer Guthrie—wife of Stan, mother of Will and Wes, former college roommate of yours truly. She lives in Destin, which isn't that far away, but I still have to bribe her to come visit me every now and then."

"Nice to meet you," Jennifer said, reaching a hand out to Bobby.

He shook her hand gently. "Likewise."

Jennifer turned to Mary Grace. "So, where's my root beer float?"

Mary Grace laughed. "I haven't made it yet. Come on." She led the way back to the kitchen. Bobby and Jennifer sat at the counter and watched as she made floats with an experienced hand. After distributing the drinks, she took a seat across from them.

"Okay," Jennifer said between slurps. "What's your exciting news?"

"Well, for starters, I think Heath Pointer was flirting with me today."

Jennifer choked on her float. "Justin's old lawyer?"

"What do you mean by 'flirt'?" Bobby wanted to know.

Mary Grace smiled. "Heath's far from ancient—only about fifteen years older than we are—and by 'flirt' I mean that he sat a little closer than absolutely necessary and asked me out to dinner."

Jennifer pushed her float away. "Well, that killed my appetite."

"What did you say?" Bobby asked.

"I told him I was too busy. Which is true," Mary Grace added when Bobby raised an eyebrow.

"So, what's the other news?" Jennifer asked. "And I hope it's better than your lawyer asking you out to dinner."

"John Wright is here."

Jennifer's mouth fell open. "*The* John Wright?"

Bobby looked between them. "What does that mean? Is he famous or something?"

"John Wright was madly in love with Mary Grace a few years ago," Jennifer responded, watching her friend closely. "Is it the same guy?"

"One and the same," Mary Grace agreed. "But he was *not* madly in love with me. He just couldn't believe that any girl could resist him and considered my refusal to date him a challenge. And I have Stan to thank for his presence here."

"My Stan?" Jennifer confirmed, and Mary Grace nodded.

"They met in the Atlanta airport awhile back, and Stan told him I ran the Arms."

"Why didn't you like him?" Bobby asked.

"I liked him fine," Mary Grace began, but Jennifer interrupted.

"John is a staunch Mormon, and since Mary Grace hadn't joined the Church yet, she thought he was a little—extreme." She turned to Mary Grace. "You might as well start at the beginning of that summer."

"This could take awhile," Mary Grace warned Bobby.

He stared at his empty root beer glass. "Time is something I've got plenty of."

Mary Grace took a deep breath. "My parents bought a vacation house in Bethany Beach before I was born. Every summer, as soon as school let out, we'd leave Atlanta and drive down here. Mother and I would stay all summer while my dad commuted on the weekends. I laid out on the beach, read books, and worked for Justin at the Arms," she began with a glance at Bobby. "But the summer after my freshman year at Emory, I got a better offer."

Bobby frowned. "I thought you liked it here."

"I love it here. But Jennifer's uncle owns a souvenir shop in Panama City. He offered us a rent-free garage apartment and the chance to airbrush T-shirts all summer." Mary Grace shrugged. "I couldn't resist. Besides, I'd be in a different town from my parents."

Bobby nodded. "I understand. So you deserted your folks?"

Mary Grace nodded. "And Justin." She turned to Jennifer. "Even though I had worked for him every year since I was six."

Jennifer frowned. "Why would he hire a six year old?"

"He saw me on the beach and said he needed someone to pick up trash around the Arms, water plants, sweep the courtyard—that sort of thing. It was mostly a way to keep me busy and give me some spending money. My parents had known him for years, so they agreed."

Jennifer shrugged, then picked up the story. "Anyway, my uncle was a slave driver! We worked twelve hours a day and barely had any time to look for cute boys."

Bobby raised an eyebrow. "Sounds like you were making good money."

Jennifer waved this aside. "The money was incidental to me. My purpose in going to Panama City was to find Mr. Right."

"That was Jennifer's purpose—not mine," Mary Grace clarified.

Jennifer continued without a pause, "But my uncle kept us so busy, the only guys we met were single adults in his ward."

"Single adults?" Bobby repeated. "Ward?"

"In the Mormon Church we call our congregations 'wards,' and unmarried, college-age people 'single adults,'" Jennifer explained.

"They were nice kids," Mary Grace informed him.

"I guess I shouldn't complain," Jennifer said with a sigh. "My husband, Stan, was one of them. I met him the first week, and it only took me a month to convince him that he was *my* Mr. Right."

"So you weren't looking for Mr. Right?" Bobby asked Mary Grace.

She shook her head. "No. My future was planned, and it didn't include marriage."

Jennifer smirked. "She met Mr. *Wright* instead. John and some of his teammates showed up at the church one Saturday morning to play basketball."

"Teammates?" Bobby questioned.

"They played basketball for Duke University," Mary Grace told him.

"Stan invited them to a weenie roast on the beach that night." Jennifer glanced over at her friend. "Mary Grace caught John's eye right away. He made a point to sit by her, then asked if she'd be at church the next day."

"But I wasn't a Mormon back then," Mary Grace picked up the story. "It was a miracle Jennifer had convinced me to attend the single-adult cookout."

"Since Mary Grace wouldn't come to church, John started hanging out at my uncle's store, which could have gotten us fired since having boys visit us on the premises violated one of the many terms of our employment."

Bobby raised an eyebrow. "He fell in love at first sight?"

Mary Grace laughed. "In the beginning he was trying to convert me to Mormonism, but it didn't take him long to start asking me out. But he bought a T-shirt every time he came in, so Jennifer's uncle didn't complain."

"All summer long Mary Grace steadfastly refused to date him," Jennifer told Bobby.

"Why?" he asked. "Was something wrong with the guy?"

Mary Grace shook her head. "No, he was nice enough and certainly handsome. But he was just so . . . Mormon. I had been raised to believe that Sundays were meant for sleeping in, reading the paper, and maybe a matinee. John thought that Sundays were to be spent attending one church meeting after another. I planned to be an archaeologist—traveling wherever that might take me. John was going on a two-year mission, and when he came back he'd be looking for a little Mormon wife who would have lots of babies and keep his shirts ironed." Mary Grace shrugged. "It was an impossible combination, so I resisted. For his own good."

"John was persistent," Jennifer mused.

"And I have to admit that he was starting to wear me down toward the end," Mary Grace remembered.

Jennifer smiled. "I invited her to a tri-stake Farewell to Summer dance. I didn't expect her to come, but she did. Then she wore this gorgeous white dress that set off her tan. She looked so incredibly beautiful I actually felt sorry for John."

"So, did you get the reaction you were hoping for?" Bobby wanted to know.

Mary Grace shrugged. "He seemed to appreciate my efforts."

"He was spellbound," Jennifer amended. "He asked her to dance and, to my utter amazement, Mary Grace accepted. I'll never forget, the song was an oldie—'You're Just Too Good to Be True.' But before they made it all the way onto the dance floor, Courtney arrived."

"Courtney?" Bobby prompted.

"John's sister," Mary Grace provided. "She said his mission call had come in the mail from Salt Lake, and she had been sent to bring him home. His parents were waiting up to watch him open the letter."

"He gave Mary Grace the sweetest smile of deep longing, then waved good-bye to all of us and left with his sister," Jennifer said dramatically.

"She's exaggerating," Mary Grace assured Bobby.

"And you never heard from him again?" he asked.

"Not until he walked into the Arms this morning."

"Sometimes life throws us curves," Bobby philosophized. "We both had our lives planned out. I married my high school sweetheart intending to live the rest of my life with her, but now I'm on the verge of a divorce. You wanted to be an archaeologist, but ended up saddled with the Arms."

"My life is just the way I planned it," Jennifer pointed out.

"So far," Bobby muttered, then turned to Mary Grace. "Why did you quit school and start working at the Arms?"

Mary Grace sighed. "I came to Bethany Beach at the end of that summer to spend a few days with my parents before returning to Emory. I stopped by the Arms to apologize to Justin for deserting him, and I was shocked by his appearance. He had lost so much weight, and his skin was kind of gray and all his hair was gone."

Bobby nodded. "Cancer."

Sadness clouded her face. "By then, the disease was in an advanced stage. He'd had chemotherapy and radiation." She looked up at them. "There was nothing else the doctors could do, and he only had a few months to live. He needed help running the Arms, and I couldn't refuse. Not after all he'd done for me."

"So you stayed here to help him out?" Bobby guessed.

Mary Grace nodded. "It was supposed to be just for a little while. At first I worked at the front desk, but as Justin's health got worse, I had to do more. Soon I was paying the bills and cohosting dinner."

"You and Justin were always very close. I know it must have been painful to watch him deteriorate," Bobby said softly.

"It was, but I'm thankful we had that time together. He wanted to die at home and couldn't do that without someone here to keep track of the medication and schedule the nurses. So finally I moved into the Nathan Bedford Forrest Room."

Bobby sat up straighter. "That was asking a lot of you."

She shrugged. "He didn't ask. I offered."

"Did you miss college and your friends?" Bobby asked.

"It wasn't so bad," Mary Grace told him. "Justin loved to hear every detail of my life, so I entertained him with stories about school and Panama City. When I ran out of those we talked about the hotel business in general and specifically how to run this place. And he could go on for hours about Peter Bethany and the history of the Arms."

"And I called regularly to cheer her up," Jennifer interjected.

"And you forgot John Wright?" Bobby asked Mary Grace.

She smiled. "Actually, I thought of him often. All summer he'd been little more than a nuisance, but once we were apart . . ." She looked at Bobby. "It was like I never appreciated him until he was gone."

Bobby's expression became more serious. "I know exactly what you mean."

Mary Grace gave him a sympathetic smile. "Annie still won't return your phone calls?"

He shook his head, then glanced at Jennifer. "A few months ago, I developed a friendship with a coworker. It wasn't an actual affair, but when my wife found out, she was, well, devastated. I know I deserve everything she's dishing out and more, but . . ."

"She will eventually find it in her heart to forgive you, and then your marriage will be stronger than before," Mary Grace said gently. Bobby didn't look convinced, so she continued. "There's even a silver lining to my story of unrequited love."

Bobby laughed. "Which is?"

"The first night we met, John told me that by the end of the summer I'd want to be a Mormon."

"So you investigated?" he asked.

"Not right away. I didn't even own a Bible, let alone a Book of Mormon, so research would have been difficult. But one day after I moved into the Arms, I saw two young men riding past on bicycles. It was cold and had started raining. They pedaled by slowly, their heads down against the wind. The skies were so dark that the streetlamps had come on, and I guess it was a combination of the moisture in the air and the artificial light, but as they passed under the streetlamp, it looked like they had halos."

She glanced up at her friends and shrugged. "Without really thinking, I opened the door and called for them to stop. When they got closer, I could tell from their white shirts and short haircuts that they were Mormon missionaries. Two months later I was baptized." She turned to Jennifer. "My interest in learning about the gospel was mostly a result of your wonderful example, but I have to admit that John was part of it too."

She turned back to Bobby. "You know my parents weren't religious, so I was unfamiliar with the Bible and didn't really even know how to pray. Those two young missionaries opened up a whole new world for me."

"How did your parents feel about you joining the Mormons?" Bobby asked.

"They said it was my decision," Mary Grace replied. "Their ambivalence toward religion worked out well when I wanted to join the Church but has been a roadblock in trying to share the gospel with them since." She sighed, then continued. "Anyway, the support of ward members and the bishop was invaluable to me during those last awful days before Justin died. He wanted to be cremated, and I honored his wishes. Afterwards I met with Heath Pointer and found out that I had inherited the Arms. Heath advised me to sell immediately, but that seemed so ungrateful. Instead, I've done my best to run the Arms like Justin taught me."

"You didn't want to go back and finish college?" Bobby asked.

Mary Grace shook her head. "It wasn't that I didn't want to finish, but I couldn't work twenty-four hours a day at the Arms and go to school too."

For a few minutes they were quiet. Then Jennifer studied Mary Grace with narrowed eyes. "You have a funny look."

"What do you mean by funny?" Mary Grace asked.

"Kind of flushed and, oh I don't know. Just funny," Jennifer replied, still frowning. "Honestly, Mary Grace. You're a beautiful woman. You don't have to dodge unwanted advances from your lawyer *or* John Wright. If you'd give the single adults a try . . ."

Mary Grace laughed. "The only single adults in my ward are minors."

"You could attend regional conferences and meet eligible men from all over the southeast." Jennifer's eyes lit up as she considered the possibilities. "Stan and I could go with you to the first few so you wouldn't be alone . . ."

Mary Grace raised her hand to interrupt. "What would you do with Will and Wes while you and Stan chaperon me?"

Jennifer bit her lip, then smiled. "We'll leave the boys with Stan's mother. She's always complaining that she doesn't get enough time with them."

Mary Grace stood and rinsed their glasses in the sink. "It's not that I don't appreciate your offer, but I don't have time for single-adult conferences or even a social life. I can fend off Heath Pointer, and John Wright will only be here for a few days. Once he writes his article, he'll go back to Savannah and that will be the end of the story."

Jennifer studied her closely. "So, *now* do you find John attractive?"

Mary Grace searched for an honest answer. "Anyone with eyesight would find John attractive, and we have a lot more in common now that I've joined the Church."

"What are you saying?" Jennifer whispered.

Mary Grace laughed. "I'm not saying anything. John isn't interested in me anymore, so his attractiveness is not an issue."

Jennifer's eyes narrowed. "How do you know he isn't interested anymore?"

Mary Grace shrugged. "A man like John is bound to have a girl-friend. He might even be married and just not wear a ring."

"He's not wearing a ring?" Jennifer asked shrewdly. "And you noticed?"

"John's marital status is not important," Mary Grace said with a trace of impatience.

"I don't know." Jennifer chewed her lip. "What if the tables are turned and you fall in love with him this time?"

Mary Grace sighed. "I'd have to be out of my mind to fall in love with John Wright."

Bobby stood and squeezed Mary Grace on the shoulder. "And since you're the most sensible person I know, I'm not worried in the least."

Mary Grace smiled. "I appreciate the vote of confidence. I'll be right back," she told Jennifer, then she walked with Bobby to the door. She tried to reimburse him for the ice cream, but he refused payment.

"I ate for free and I'm not a guest, so it's only fair that I should contribute."

"Thanks, Bobby," Mary Grace said as they passed through the lobby. "Come back for dinner again tomorrow night."

He nodded, then stepped outside. "I will."

"Have you tried sending Annie flowers?" she asked as an after-thought.

"I've tried everything," he replied with a sad smile, then he disappeared into the night.

After Bobby had gone, Mary Grace walked back into the kitchen where Jennifer was trying unsuccessfully to stifle a yawn. "Well, I guess I'd better get home too. There's a fine line between bonding and bondage, so I can't leave Stan alone with the boys too long."

"I'm really glad you came over. It's been fun."

Jennifer smiled. "Just like old times." Her smile dimmed. "You're sure you'll be all right?"

"I'll be fine."

Jennifer looked skeptical as Mary Grace opened the front door again.

"Give the boys a hug for me. Stan too." Mary Grace waved to her friend, then walked down the hall to the laundry room and moved the tablecloths from the washers to the dryers.

Afterwards she was headed to her apartment when she glanced out the back door. The beach beckoned, so she went out into the clear night. A full moon was shining on the incoming tide, and she marveled at the beauty of this little piece of earth. Kicking off her shoes, she started walking barefoot down to the damp sand. As the water bubbled around her toes, she closed her eyes and let herself remember . . .

* * *

She was in Panama City that summer five years before. They arrived at the cookout and got their food, then Jennifer started flirting shamelessly with Stan Guthrie. Feeling like an extra wheel, Mary Grace walked to a rock on the periphery and sat down. While trying to balance the paper plate on her lap, she mentally chastised herself for allowing Jennifer to drag her along to the church social. She could be home eating something she liked and watching television in air-conditioned comfort. Then John Wright and his friends arrived.

They caused a little stir in the group of single adults, which drew Mary Grace's attention originally. But unlike Jennifer, she wasn't looking for romance, so after watching briefly, she returned her gaze to the ocean. A few minutes later she was surprised to see John taking a seat beside her on the rock. After introductions, he took a big bite of hot dog, then smiled.

"Mary Grace O'Malley," her name rolled off his tongue, and the memory was so vivid she could see the sprinkle of freckles across his nose, the wisp of curls that rested on the collar of his shirt, and the little cleft in his chin. "Melodious but unwieldy. I think I'll call you Gracie."

She didn't really care what he called her, so she shrugged, then angled her head more toward the waves. Undeterred, he asked if she came to Panama City often. "I've never been to Panama City before," good manners forced her to tell him. "I usually spend the summers in a little town called Bethany Beach near Destin."

"This is my first time too," he told her. "My coach at Duke roped me into helping him do kiddie basketball clinics at a junior college here—not that I'm complaining. We get to stay in the dorms for free, and the money's not bad. What about you? Where do you go to school?"

"Emory."

John raised his eyebrows, apparently impressed. "I'll bet you are an education major. All the good little Mormon girls are."

"My major isn't education, and I'm not even a member of your church," she told him. "I was forced to come by my roommate, who *is* a good little Mormon girl."

He laughed at this remark, then swallowed another big bite of his dinner before asking, "What is your major, then?"

"Archaeology."

He put down his hot dog and stared. "You want to dig up bones and study mummies?" he asked in a half-amused tone. "And get *dirt* under your fingernails?"

She ignored the last part and nodded. "I'll start applying for an archaeological internship next year. If I'm accepted, I'll basically work for free for a while after I graduate. Then, hopefully, I'll be invited to join a team as a paid member."

"What about a husband and family?" he asked.

"That's too far into the future for me to even consider right now."

He studied her for a few seconds, then shook his head.

"What?" She was a little defensive about her choice of career fields.

"You're a puzzle."

She gave him a look that would have withered a lesser man. "Because I've chosen a field of study that is predominantly male and will require me to delay marriage?"

He wadded up his napkin, indicating that he was through eating. "I thought most women your age dreamed of finding the perfect man, then buying a wedding dress, picking out china patterns, and knitting baby booties."

She stared at him in horror. "When and if I ever do marry, I won't wear a silly white gown, the only china I'm interested in picking out is from ancient civilizations buried deep in the ground, and I don't think *anyone* knits booties anymore."

John leaned a little closer and laughed. "You may set archaeological science back a thousand years, Gracie."

"Why would you say that?" she asked with a frown.

"Because you're so beautiful that all the 'predominantly male' archaeologists will turn clumsy in your presence and destroy countless invaluable artifacts."

She gave him a small smile, then, in an effort to redirect the conversation, asked, "What's your major? Besides basketball."

"Journalism," he said without hesitation. "After my dazzling pro career, I plan to be a famous international newspaper reporter."

"Do you have a particular NBA team in mind?"

He considered this. "Not really. I'll take whoever is lucky enough to draft me."

"A particular newspaper you want to write for?"

He grinned. "The *New York Times.*"

She shook her head. "You dream big."

He lifted a strand of dark hair that hung all the way down her back. "Did I mention that you are incredibly beautiful?"

"I believe you did."

He stood and offered to take her plate to the garbage. As he moved away, he told her, "You may not be a Mormon yet, but I'm preparing for my mission, and I practice on everyone. By the end of the summer, you'll be begging me to baptize you . . ."

* * *

The past faded from her memory as a light breeze lifted the hair off her neck and brought Mary Grace back to the present. Rubbing her hands up and down her forearms, she watched the waves. Then a voice spoke from behind her. "I think these might belong to you."

She turned and saw John Wright holding her sandals. "Thanks." She took them from him.

He was wearing cutoff sweatpants and an old Duke University T-shirt. The change from a business suit made him seem younger and more familiar. "It's a beautiful night." He pointed to the lights in the distance. "I guess that's Destin."

"Yes."

"This reminds me of that summer in Panama City before my mission."

"Hmmm," she murmured.

John was quiet for a few seconds, then said, "I'm about to take a walk down the beach. Would you care to go with me?"

Mary Grace knew that she should refuse, but her feet seemed to have a mind of their own, and she fell into step beside him.

"I'm surprised you're not married," he told her as they walked along the water's edge.

She looked out at the waves. "Not yet."

John leaned down to pick up a seashell and threw it into the waves. "Stan told me you joined the Church."

She nodded. "The missionaries found me here at the Arms, which is another reason I'm glad I wasn't in a desert somewhere, digging up artifacts."

"I'd like to hear your conversion story," he said.

"Sometime I'll share it with you," Mary Grace promised, then she took a deep breath and asked, "What about you? Are you married?"

John shook his head. "It's a nice concept, and I really do think that the greatest potential for happiness is within a family setting. But personally, I just haven't found anyone that I want to spend this life with, let alone the eternities."

They reached the edge of the private beach and turned around, then headed back toward the Arms. "I'm sorry you didn't get to play basketball professionally," she told him. "It seemed like something that was very important to you."

"It was before my mission. Afterwards it didn't seem nearly as vital." He looked over at her. "And how about you? You longed for adventure and travel. Are you really content managing a hotel?"

She considered this for a few seconds. "I'll admit that sometimes I get a little restless, but overall the rewards have been worth the sacrifices."

His expression became pensive. "I thought it would be impossible for you to get more beautiful," he said softly, "but I guess some people just get better with age."

Mary Grace was glad that the darkness covered her discomfort. "I guess we'll have to test that theory when I get to be about ninety," she said lightly, and he smiled as they reached the back entrance of the Arms.

"Well, thanks for the sweet dreams," he said.

She gave him a startled look. "I've given you sweet dreams?"

He winked. "Not yet, but you will." With that, he walked inside. Mary Grace gave him plenty of time to clear the lobby before she entered. Then as she locked up, she admitted to herself that it was very likely that John Wright would make an appearance in *her* dreams that night as well.

* * *

As darkness settled over the Arms, a figure stepped out of the shadows near the bluff. He adjusted the brim of his hat so that it concealed his face. Still staring at the Arms, he dropped a cigarette and ground it into the damp sand with the heel of his shoe. Then he turned to his companion. "Let's get busy."

CHAPTER 4

On Saturday morning Jennifer called before daybreak. "Both the twins are running fevers," she told Mary Grace. "I guess that's my punishment for taking a break from motherhood."

Mary Grace laughed. "It's germs that make people sick, not mothers who take breaks. But I hope the boys will be okay."

She heard Jennifer sigh. "It's probably just ear infections. They get them all the time. We're on the way to the after-hours clinic right now, but I wanted to check on you."

"I'm fine," Mary Grace assured her. "You just take care of those boys and leave John Wright to me."

"I guess that's my only choice," Jennifer muttered. "But if John Wright breaks your heart, I'll kill him."

Mary Grace laughed. "You can't kill anyone because I don't have time to visit you in prison. Now let me get to work."

"Call me often so I'll know you're okay."

"That's a promise," Mary Grace told her as she hung up.

After a quick shower, Mary Grace went to the kitchen to help Lucy with breakfast, and by the time the guests started wandering in, everything was ready. When the ladies from Haggerty arrived in the dining room, they filled their plates and Miss Eugenia came over to stand beside Mary Grace while she ate.

"It seems awfully quiet here, and the parking lot isn't even half full."

Mary Grace nodded. "Yes, ma'am. I'm hoping things will pick up soon."

Miss Eugenia frowned. "I only asked because I have some young friends who really need a vacation. They have a daughter who won't be two until October and a son who is only six weeks old. The mother had a hard time with the delivery and had to have an emergency hysterectomy afterwards. Physically she seems fine now, but they had hoped to have a large family, and emotionally, she's still struggling. I thought a few days on the beach might be just the thing to cheer her up."

"Well, I have plenty of vacancies if they'd like to come."

Miss Eugenia chewed her bran muffin thoughtfully. "Money's not an issue, but Mark is very busy with his career, and he's recently been called to be a bishop in the Mormon Church."

Mary Grace's eyes widened, and she smiled. "You're in luck. It just so happens that I joined the Mormon Church myself a few years ago, so I'm obligated to help a bishop in need."

Miss Eugenia seemed pleased at this fortuitous turn of events. "But I'm not sure he would agree to come unless we could present it in such a way that he didn't have much choice."

"What do you mean?"

"Well, you know how sometimes companies will have a contest to generate interest? They give away a TV or a car or a free vacation."

"You want me to give your friends a free stay at the world-renowned Bethany Arms Hotel?" Mary Grace asked with a raised eyebrow.

Miss Eugenia had the good manners to look ashamed. "I don't expect you to give it to them. I'll pay for their room. I just want you to make up a contest and let them win so they'll feel obligated to come."

Mary Grace frowned. "Don't you think if I call your friends and tell them they've won a free vacation here where you are, they'll get suspicious?"

"We'll admit up front that I entered them in the contest," Miss Eugenia said. "That will make their good fortune seem logical instead of coincidental."

"I can't lie," Mary Grace told her.

"No," Miss Eugenia agreed. "You really will have to have a contest. It just won't last very long nor be widely publicized."

"How long do you think this contest should last?"

Miss Eugenia had an answer ready. "Just about enough time for me to write their names on a piece of paper."

Mary Grace smiled. "As soon as you finish your breakfast, come to my office and we'll take care of it."

"Take care of what?" Annabelle wanted to know as she came to the food table for more orange juice.

"Mark and Kate have won a free vacation here at the Arms," Miss Eugenia announced.

Annabelle's eyes narrowed. "I didn't know there was a contest." She studied Mary Grace for a few seconds, then addressed her sister. "And it seems mighty coincidental that Kate and Mark just happened to win."

"You didn't know about the contest because all you think about is Derrick," Miss Eugenia said primly. "Besides, Kate and Mark are due for some good luck."

Annabelle sighed. "I'm glad that you mentioned Derrick. I need to go to my room and call him before we head out."

"Nonsense," Miss Eugenia dismissed this idea. "You can call him when we get back. That way you'll actually have something to *tell* him."

Mary Grace took a step toward the door. "Just come see me after breakfast," she reminded Miss Eugenia. Then she saw the Lovejoys and their children entering the dining room, so she made a quick escape. She barely had time to get settled in Justin's chair before John knocked on the open office door. Her heart pounded as he gave her a breathtaking smile.

"Good morning," she greeted. "If you're looking for breakfast, it's in the dining room."

"Thanks, but I'm not much of a breakfast eater." He moved a step farther into the small room. "I've come to apologize."

"For what?" she asked cautiously.

"I'm sorry that I teased you about being in my dreams. Some people might consider that comment inappropriate."

She smiled. "Well, was I?"

He shook his head. "I slept so soundly in your incredibly comfortable room that I didn't have any dreams."

"If I ever advertise again, I may quote you."

"Just make sure you spell my name right," he requested with a smile. "Well, I'd better get to my appointment with Mayor Harte. He's working me in between breakfast with the Civitans and a tennis match at the country club."

"Good luck."

He sighed. "I'm going to need it." With a shake of his head, he left the office.

He had only been gone for a few seconds before Miss Eugenia appeared. She placed a piece of paper on Justin's desk, and Mary Grace picked it up. In a bold script, Miss Eugenia had written *Mark and Kate Iverson* and a phone number with a Georgia area code. "So, these are our lucky winners?"

Miss Eugenia settled herself in a chair across from Mary Grace. "Yes."

"You want me to call them now?"

Miss Eugenia checked her watch, which looked like a men's Timex from the '50s. "Yes, this is good."

Mary Grace picked up the phone and dialed the number, composing a spiel in her mind. A woman answered breathlessly after three rings. "May I speak to Mr. or Mrs. Iverson?" Mary Grace asked in her most professional tone.

"This is Mrs. Iverson," Kate responded.

"My name is Mary Grace O'Malley, and I am calling to inform you that you have won a free vacation."

"Well, thank you very much for calling, but we're not interested," Kate replied.

"Please don't hang up!" Mary Grace urged. "I own the Arms, and the drawing is part of a," she glanced at Miss Eugenia, "brief advertising promotion."

The old lady nodded her approval to Mary Grace as Kate spoke again.

"Wait, did you say the Arms?" she asked. "You mean the Bethany Arms Hotel where Eugenia Atkins and her friends are staying as guests this week?"

"Exactly the same one. And as a matter of fact, it was Mrs. Atkins who entered you into our vacation contest." Mary Grace looked down at the piece of paper in her hand. "The drawing was held this morning and you won a," she glanced back at Miss Eugenia, who held up four fingers, "four-night stay, subject to availability, of course. We have vacancies now and would be pleased to have you come right away."

"Well," Kate said slowly, "it does sound nice, but I don't see how we could possibly come now."

Mary Grace covered the mouthpiece and whispered, "She doesn't think they can come now."

"Give me that," Miss Eugenia instructed as she reached for the phone. Mary Grace handed it to her without argument. "Kate? How is Emily?" There was a pause while Kate Iverson apparently gave a report. "And what about little Charles?" Another short pause. "Now, about this mini-vacation you've won. You have to come now while I'm here to help with the babies. Otherwise you won't get any rest."

Miss Eugenia was quiet for a few seconds while Kate replied. Finally Miss Eugenia rolled her eyes in exasperation. "Put him on the phone." She poked a loose hairpin into the messy bun at the back of her head while she waited for Mr. Iverson to be located. "Mark, I entered you and Kate in a contest for a free four-night vacation here at the Arms and you won. Kate is worn to a frazzle and needs a vacation worse than anything. If you come now, I can watch the babies while you and Kate relax." There was another brief pause, then Miss Eugenia continued. "The FBI will give you a few days off, and an opportunity like this doesn't come along every day."

After some additional negotiation, Miss Eugenia hung up with a satisfied smile on her wrinkled face. "They'll leave first thing Monday morning."

Mary Grace nodded. "I'll add them to the hotel register." She followed Miss Eugenia out into the lobby, where the other ladies from Haggerty were waiting. "All ready to go sightseeing?" she asked.

"Some of us more than others," Annabelle replied with a yawn.

"Oh, come on," Miss Eugenia encouraged. "You can write Derrick love notes in the car between stops."

Miss George Ann walked up to Mary Grace with a frown on her face. "There was an unpleasant odor in my room last night. Could you see about it today?"

"I certainly will," Mary Grace promised.

"Probably because there was a *rat* staying in there," Miss Eugenia suggested with a challenging look at her traveling companion.

"My goodness, Eugenia, you are so childish," Miss George Ann responded as Mary Grace ushered them toward the door.

"I'll see you ladies at dinner." Mary Grace waved good-bye, then went into the dining room and cleared the tables. After helping

Lucy clean the kitchen, they discussed plans for dinner. Lucy offered to fix fried chicken, which at one time had been her specialty, but Mary Grace was concerned about Lucy handling a pot of boiling oil with her failing eyesight. So she suggested a spiral-sliced ham and potato salad instead. Lucy agreed and made a list for the grocery store.

When Windy arrived to cover the front desk, Mary Grace went to all the rooms, making beds and replacing towels. She didn't smell anything in the Stonewall Jackson Room, but sprayed it liberally with air freshener, hoping that would satisfy Miss George Ann. There was a Do Not Disturb sign on John's door, and Mary Grace was thankful to have one less room to clean.

Once she was finished, she returned to the front desk where Windy was talking on the telephone. Mary Grace leaned over the girl and opened the reservation book, then wrote Kate and Mark Iverson in for the James J. Pettigrew Room for Monday through Thursday. She was counting up her rather impressive number of guests when John returned from his interview with the mayor.

"Well, I'm back," he announced the obvious.

Windy ended her phone conversation abruptly and stared at him, her mouth hanging open slightly.

"Is the case solved?" Mary Grace asked optimistically.

He leaned onto the polished wood of the reservation desk. "Hardly. I got about as much out of Mayor Harte as I would have from one of the faces on Mount Rushmore."

Mary Grace felt sorry for him. Southerners were polite to a fault but tight-lipped when it came to discussing family skeletons with strangers. Mary Grace noticed that Windy had worked her way over to stand near John so she could study his profile. John gave the girl a quick glance, then continued.

"I stopped by the library, and they have high school yearbooks dating back to the '50s, but you can't check them out. So I thought I'd go back there and take a look at the ones that involved Victoria. Then I have a lunch appointment with one of her old friends, Susie Ireland. Have you ever heard of her?"

Mary Grace nodded. "She was a friend of Justin's and used to visit him occasionally. She owns a jewelry store in town."

Windy edged closer to John, but before Mary Grace could tell the girl to move back, the door opened and a stranger walked in. The man was a little below average height, solidly built with dark hair and eyes. He approached the desk and asked if there was a room available. Mary Grace made a token search of the register before nodding.

"You can have your choice of courtyard or beach," she offered.

"I'll take a room facing the beach, please." He signed his name as Joseph Tamburelli and paid for the James Henry Lane Room in cash. After the financial transactions were out of the way, Mary Grace asked Windy to take their new guest to his room. The girl tore her eyes from John and led the way out the back door.

"Well, two nonreservations in two days. That's probably a record, at least since I've been running the Arms," she said with a smile.

John cleared his throat. "Gracie, I know you're really busy, and I hate to ask, but I need a favor."

"I'll be glad to help in any way I can," Mary Grace offered, then waited for him to elaborate.

"Given enough time, I'm sure I could charm the folks in this town into telling me what they know about the murder of Victoria Harte," John said with a grin. "But I've only been allotted a few days for this story. So I was wondering if you'd come with me to my interview with Susie Ireland. Since you're a hometown girl, I'm hoping your presence will make her more trusting. And unlike Mayor Harte, she might even answer my questions."

Leaving the Arms in Windy's less-than-capable hands for any length of time was terrifying, but the idea of helping John solve his case was too tempting. So after a few seconds of hesitation, Mary Grace nodded. "Okay."

John looked genuinely pleased. "Now that I've got you feeling sorry for me, I have another request."

Mary Grace arched an eyebrow. "Which is?"

"I think the nightly dinners at the Arms would be a perfect forum for me to question locals without putting the guilty party on guard."

"You want to invite the murderer to dinner?" she asked in alarm, and he smiled.

"I'd *love* to invite the murderer, but at the moment I don't know who he is. However, I think that there might be people here in

Bethany Beach who know exactly what happened to Victoria Harte. The trick will be getting them to tell me."

"I guess my answer will depend on *who* you want to invite," she said slowly. "I mean, I can't very well ask the dead girl's brother to come to dinner so you can interrogate him again."

John shook his head. "I did not interrogate Mayor Harte, but I wouldn't ask you to invite him. I was thinking of Dr. Rimson Chandler. He is, I presume, related to your boyfriend."

"Dr. Chandler is Bobby's grandfather, but Bobby is not my boyfriend."

John paused just long enough for Mary Grace to know he doubted this, then he continued. "Dr. Chandler signed the death certificate and listed the cause of death as 'puncture wound to the chest.' The newspaper article said Victoria Harte was stabbed to death. The two descriptions give different impressions."

"What do you mean?"

"Well, *stabbed to death* sounds like multiple wounds administered by a crazed killer. *Puncture wound to the chest* sounds like one well-placed thrust. The killer would have had to be close to the victim and have encountered almost no resistance."

Mary Grace considered this. "I don't know about any of that, but I will ask Bobby to bring his grandfather to dinner tonight. Dr. Chandler is a widower and retired, so he gets lonely. He'll probably appreciate the invitation. But I'll have to warn him that you will be present and asking questions about an old murder."

"Fair enough," John agreed to her condition. "Could you invite Sheriff Thompson, too?"

Mary Grace sighed. "Are you ever satisfied?"

"Is that a yes?" he pressed.

"I'm sure Sheriff Thompson will come if I ask him to," Mary Grace said with a nod.

John smiled. "Good. This might turn out to be a productive day after all. And if I solve the case, I'll put a plug for the Arms in my article. Give you a little free advertising."

"That's very nice of you."

John looked around. "So, where's Stormy?"

"Her name is Windy." Mary Grace needed something to do

besides stare at the cute little cleft in his chin, so she started straightening the desk.

"Whatever her name is, she always smells like Jell-O."

"It's not Jell-O," Mary Grace informed him. "It's fruit-scented body lotion that all the teenage girls love."

"I think she might be on drugs," John said, lowering his voice.

Mary Grace looked up sharply. "What would make you say such a thing?"

"She acts very peculiar, always staring at me and following me around."

Mary Grace winced at this announcement. "She follows you around?"

"Frequently," John affirmed. "And this morning she asked if she could take my picture with her new digital camera."

Mary Grace was horrified. "On behalf of the Bethany Arms Hotel, I apologize. I'll speak to her immediately."

John waved a hand. "That's not necessary. I didn't mind her taking my picture. She brought me a print later, and I signed it simply *John*." He flashed her a smile. "And I was thinking about trying a Boston accent on her."

"Please don't encourage the girl," Mary Grace begged. "Her family is very poor, and Windy depends on what I pay her to make her car payment." She looked up at John. "But I can't have her harassing guests."

"I'm sure you rarely have guests as handsome and interesting as me, so once I leave, she'll probably never be tempted again," John predicted.

Mary Grace rolled her eyes. "What time is lunch?"

"Twelve. We should probably leave about a quarter to," John suggested. "But it might be a good idea for us to go over what I've got before then so you can make educated comments during my interview."

Mary Grace checked her watch. "Why don't you come to my apartment at eleven-thirty. It's down this hall, last door on the left, next to the kitchen."

"It's a date," John confirmed with a smile as he walked out. After the front door closed behind him, she took a few steadying breaths, then went to check on the laundry.

Once she had all the sheets washed and dried, Mary Grace walked to the lobby to talk to her clerk. Reprimanding employees was one of many unpleasant things about running a business, but Mary Grace knew she couldn't ignore the fact that the girl had been stalking a hotel guest. When Mary Grace reached the front desk, Windy was nowhere in sight. However, the Arms' newest guest, Mr. Tamburelli, was talking on the lobby phone, and the ladies from Haggerty were gathered by the door.

"How was the Pirate Ship tour?" Mary Grace asked.

"Fine," Miss Eugenia answered for the group. "We've got lunch reservations at the Sand Dollar, but Polly forgot her sunglasses and we had to come by and let her get them." Miss Eugenia glanced at the plump woman, who apologized, then hurried off to her room. Miss Eugenia took a step closer and lowered her voice. "Who is that man on the phone?"

Mary Grace glanced over her shoulder, then turned back. "He's a new guest named Joseph Tamburelli."

"Where's he from?" Miss Eugenia demanded.

Mr. Tamburelli had listed Chicago as his home address, but Mary Grace had no intention of sharing this information. "Why do you ask?" she countered as the subject of their conversation walked by them and out the door.

"I've had some experience with organized crime," Miss Eugenia said. "And I declare, that man has Mafia written all over him."

"Organized crime?" Mary Grace asked in surprise.

"I helped the FBI crack a big money laundering case a couple of years ago," Miss Eugenia claimed. "You probably remember it."

Mary Grace glanced at Annabelle for confirmation, and the sister nodded. "I don't know how much help Eugenia was, but she was definitely involved with the FBI for a while."

Mary Grace turned back to Miss Eugenia with more respect. "Why do you think Mr. Tamburelli is involved with the Mafia?"

"He's obviously Italian," Miss Eugenia pointed out.

"That is an unfair stereotype," Mary Grace dismissed this immediately.

"He showed up without a reservation," Miss Eugenia added.

"So did John Wright," Mary Grace told them. "It happens occasionally, even at the Arms."

"You'd better keep an eye on him," Miss Eugenia advised. "He looks shady to me."

Mary Grace cleared her throat. "We have no proof that Mr. Tamburelli is a criminal. It's my responsibility to treat him just like all the other guests at the Arms."

"He's sure not a tourist. Did you see those clothes he was wearing? Shiny shoes and dark socks," Miss Eugenia informed them with an air of satisfaction.

Miss George Ann actually smiled. "And I'll bet those tight polyester pants will chafe in this heat."

Mary Grace was so astounded that Miss George Ann and Miss Eugenia were agreeing on any subject that her mouth fell open.

"When he was on the phone a few minutes ago, I heard him set up a meeting with his contact," Miss Eugenia continued her surveillance report.

"How do you know it was his contact?" Annabelle asked. "It might have been his mother."

"Would he call his mother Silverstein?" Miss Eugenia demanded. "And tell her to meet him at the NASCAR Museum at one o'clock and bring binoculars?"

"He said that?" Mary Grace asked, looking at the front door.

"He certainly did," Miss Eugenia confirmed. "Whoever he is, I'm convinced that he's up to no good. So after lunch, we're heading out to the NASCAR Museum to keep an eye on him."

"We're doing no such thing!" Annabelle objected. "You said you needed new clothes from the outlet mall."

"We'll go shopping later, and if you're scared of Mr. Tamburelli, we'll drop you off here before we go to the museum," Miss Eugenia offered.

"I am not scared," Annabelle dismissed this notion. "But what will we do while you're spying on this poor man?"

"Look at the exhibits in the museum," Miss Eugenia informed her sister. "Racing is very interesting."

Annabelle's eyes narrowed. "How would you know?"

"I've always liked it," Miss Eugenia claimed.

"You have not!" Annabelle was indignant.

"Of course I have," Miss Eugenia insisted. "Ever since we saw that ESPN special on Dale Earnhart, Jr., the number eight has been my favorite."

"Let's go to lunch before I kill her," Annabelle muttered to the other ladies, then said good-bye to Mary Grace and led the way outside.

Mary Grace expelled a sigh of relief, then went back to the desk and called Sheriff Thompson. "Hey, Mary Grace," he said when he came to the phone. "How's business?"

"Slow, but steady," she replied. "And speaking of my business, I wondered if you might be interested in joining us tonight. You could help me liven up my dinner conversation."

Sheriff Thompson chuckled. "You must be desperate if you're asking me to provide entertainment."

Mary Grace laughed. "You're very pleasant company, but I have to warn you that a friend of mine is a guest, and he'll be asking questions about an old murder for a newspaper article he's writing. But the food will be good and *free*."

"I'd have to be a fool to pass up an offer like that," the sheriff replied. "What time?"

"At seven o'clock, and please bring your wife." Pete Thompson had been a minor figure in Mary Grace's life for as long as she could remember, but she couldn't recall meeting his wife, Sadie, more than a couple of times. Mrs. Thompson was quiet, almost a recluse, and Mary Grace didn't expect her to come but felt that she should be included in the invitation.

"I doubt Sadie will make it. She doesn't get out much."

"Well, if she doesn't feel like coming, we'll fix her a plate," Mary Grace offered. "Don't be late."

After her conversation with the sheriff, Mary Grace had to wait at the desk for thirty minutes before Windy finally returned. "I'm sorry," the girl said breathlessly as she rushed in. "I had to run an errand."

"You can't just leave the desk unattended," Mary Grace said in exasperation. "I depend on you to be here in case a guest needs something. If you want to run an errand, please ask me first."

Windy twisted a strand of bright red hair around her finger. "I was just gone for a few minutes."

Mary Grace frowned. "And Mr. Wright told me you've been following him around and even asked to take his picture."

Windy didn't need to reply. The guilt was obvious on her face.

Mary Grace took a deep breath and prayed for patience. "You must stay away from Mr. Wright. He's a guest in this hotel, and we have to respect his privacy."

"Yes, ma'am," Windy mumbled.

"I've got a lunch appointment, and you'll be responsible until I get back." Just saying the words made Mary Grace shudder. "You have my cell number?"

The girl nodded.

"I'm going to my apartment now. Call if you need me."

Mary Grace walked down the hall and into the cool confines of Justin's apartment. She changed into a linen dress and respritzed her hair. She was trying to decide whether to freshen her makeup when a knock at her door settled the issue. Turning off the bathroom light, she walked into her living room and admitted John Wright.

"Nice place," he said, taking a quick look around. Mary Grace looked too. She hadn't changed a thing since Justin died, so the room reflected his tastes, not hers. Then he pointed at a painting on the wall of the foyer. "Forrest Merek," he read the name scrawled in a corner. "Is this an original?"

Mary Grace nodded as she studied the geographic symbols in neon colors. "Justin loved it. Before he died, he told me that someday it might prove extremely valuable."

John was squinting at the artwork. "It must be one of his early efforts. My brother is a big fan of Merek's, and the prints he has are all southwest landscapes."

Mary Grace led the way into the living room. "I don't really care for it, but I leave it there out of respect for Justin." She pointed to the couch. "Why don't you have a seat?"

John settled onto the couch, then placed his briefcase on the coffee table. "I'll show you what I've collected so far." He opened his briefcase and removed several sheets of paper, then extended them toward Mary Grace. "This is the original article that appeared in the Destin newspaper the day after the body was found."

Mary Grace accepted the photocopy and read the article. It was only a few inches long. In small but bold print, the headline announced *Mayor's Daughter Found Stabbed to Death in Motel near Bethany Beach.* In regular text below, the murder was described briefly. *Victoria Harte, daughter of Bethany Beach Mayor Anson Harte, was discovered dead in a room of the Seafoam Motel on Highway 25. According to Marshall County Sheriff's Deputy Peter Thompson, the seventeen-year-old victim died from stab wounds shortly before midnight on New Year's Eve. Miss Harte was a student at the Hartford Preparatory Academy for Young Women in Connecticut and was home for the holidays. Deputy Thompson said that a thorough investigation is underway. Information regarding funeral services was unavailable.*

Mary Grace looked up. "I'm surprised that the article is so small. The mayor's daughter getting stabbed sounds pretty newsworthy."

"You would think, but that was the only mention ever made in the paper except for the obituary, which didn't discuss the details of Victoria's death. There was nothing at all in the local weekly paper."

Mary Grace returned the photocopy to him. "That's not as surprising. The *Bethany Beach Beacon* is more of a gossip sheet than a newspaper."

"It seems like this murder would generate plenty of gossip," John said. "And a stabbing death should have been interesting enough for some of the bigger cities around here to pick up the story, but none of them did."

"You think the Hartes kept it quiet?"

"I know they did. There's no other logical explanation." John shuffled through the papers and extracted another one. "There are several other funny things, like the fact that according to the Hartford Preparatory Academy for Young Women, Victoria Harte was *not* a student there at the time of her death. She was enrolled but never attended classes."

Mary Grace raised her eyebrow in surprise. "If the Hartes were controlling the information given to the press, why would they give incorrect information when it would be so easy for someone to check?"

"Why indeed?" John gave her an approving smile. "The woman who used to cook for the Hartes is an alcoholic and spends her evenings at a bar on the outskirts of town. Last night I got there about midnight. By then she'd had several drinks and was more than happy to talk about her former employers. She said that contrary to what this article says, Victoria was *not* at home for the Christmas holidays. She said Victoria hadn't been *home* since September."

"Another lie?"

"The old cook was drunk, but I think she was telling the truth. She gave me details—like the fact that the Hartes canceled their annual Christmas party that year—which would have made sense *after* Victoria's death, but why *before?*"

Mary Grace shrugged. "I do know that the Hartes always have a big Christmas party, even now that it's a new generation in the mayor's office. But what difference does it make if they had the party that year or not?"

"Maybe something was wrong before Victoria was killed. The cook said the family told everyone she was off at school, but the fancy Hartford Preparatory Academy says no. I think she was in Bethany Beach, but not at home."

Mary Grace shrugged. "Quite a few contradictions. So, do you have a theory?"

"My guess is they sent her to school and maybe even thought she was there, but she ran away instead. After they found out she wasn't at the academy, they pretended that she was for some reason."

"To avoid embarrassment?" Mary Grace asked incredulously. "It seems like they'd be telling everyone, trying to find someone who had heard from Victoria or had an idea where she might go."

John nodded. "It's kind of like the way they kept the murder quiet, as if saving face was more important than finding Victoria's killer."

"And they couldn't host their regular Christmas party without having to answer uncomfortable questions about their daughter," Mary Grace guessed.

"Exactly. They canceled the party and laid low. Then, a few days later, the daughter who is a potential embarrassment turns up dead."

"You don't think the Hartes killed their own daughter!" Mary Grace cried.

"No, but there's a good chance that they know who did and covered it up."

Mary Grace shuddered, then studied him through narrowed eyes. "The cover-up is what really bothers you, isn't it?"

"The murder bothers me plenty," John disagreed. "A beautiful teenage girl lost her life. But the fact that her family didn't even seem to care about bringing the guilty party to justice bothers me more."

"She was beautiful?" Mary Grace asked, and John extended a black-and-white photograph.

"See for yourself."

The girl in the picture had long brown hair parted in the middle. She was smiling up into the camera, her teeth perfectly white, her skin flawless, her eyes sparkling. "She *was* beautiful," Mary Grace murmured. "But there's something more." She searched for the right word.

"I see it too—an exotic quality."

"I'll bet she stuck out in Bethany Beach like a tropical fish out of water," Mary Grace said as she continued to stare at the picture. "So, who do you think killed her?"

"If she was stabbed to death, meaning multiple wounds, I would say a stranger who has no connection to her life."

"And therefore will never be found." Mary Grace frowned. "But what if Victoria died of a single stab wound to the chest?"

"Then I think it was a friend or a lover."

"Why would someone who loved her kill her?"

John smiled. "That I don't know." He started collecting his papers and put them back into his briefcase. Once everything was in place, he snapped the case shut and stood up. "Are you ready to go?"

Mary Grace nodded and picked up her purse.

"Ms. Ireland suggested a place called Barnacle Bills," he told her as they walked to the door. "You ever been there before?"

Mary Grace wrinkled her nose. "A couple of times. It's really more of a bar than a restaurant—dark, dirty, and loud."

John flashed her another grin. "Sounds like a perfect place to discuss murder." Mary Grace removed her keys from her purse, and John said, "I'll drive."

She shook her head. "I've got to stop by the grocery store afterwards and get some things for dinner. So I'll follow you."

"I don't mind going to the store with you," John offered.

Knowing that if he came with her to the store she'd be so nervous she'd probably buy all the wrong things, Mary Grace told him firmly, "You've got a murder to solve. You can't waste your time grocery shopping."

With a shrug of acceptance, he held the door open for her and followed her into the lobby of the Arms.

CHAPTER 5

John and Mary Grace arrived at the busy seafood restaurant a few minutes early and were escorted to a booth in the back. John told the waitress that Ms. Ireland would be joining them, then asked Mary Grace to sit beside him. "It will make it easier for me to interview Ms. Ireland if we're across the table from each other."

Mary Grace slid in, and John scooted next to her. Then the waitress handed them a menu to share.

"What's good here?" John asked, his arm brushing against Mary Grace's, which interfered with her ability to think coherently. She moved a little closer to the wall.

"They're famous for their gumbo," she told him.

"Is that what you're going to have?"

She shook her head. "No. I'll get half a turkey sandwich on wheat bread."

John raised an eyebrow. "Are you a health nut?"

Mary Grace gave him a little smile. "No, I just watch what I eat."

John's eyes did a quick appraisal. "I'd say you're doing a pretty good job," he said softly. Before she could respond, Susie Ireland arrived. Mary Grace exchanged greetings with the other woman, then introduced John. After a few minutes of pleasantries, they ordered lunch, then John leaned forward.

"I really appreciate you agreeing to meet with me today."

"I'm not sure why I did," Susie told him honestly, then folded her fingers together. "What I'd give for a cigarette right now." She included them both in a nervous smile. "I gave up smoking years ago, but at times like this I still miss it." She turned toward Mary Grace. "How are things at the Arms?"

Mary Grace gave her standard answer. "A little slow, but picking up."

Susie nodded, then turned to John. "Now, why are you interested in Victoria Harte after all these years?"

"Like I told you on the phone, it's an assignment from my editor," John replied with exaggerated casualness. "Just something to fill up empty pages during the lazy days of summer. So, Victoria was a friend of yours in high school?"

"I suppose we were friends," Susie answered with a restless look around the room.

"You were both cheerleaders," John continued. "You must have spent a lot of time with her, practicing and everything."

Susie nodded. "We saw each other daily until the end of our junior year, when Victoria got kicked off the squad for an honors violation."

"What did she do?" John asked, and Mary Grace could feel the subtle undercurrent of tension.

"What *didn't* she do?" Susie responded with a sigh. "She slept with most of the boys in the junior class, she drank, she smoked pot. I'm not sure what she got *caught* doing."

"You don't sound like you liked her much," John said, and Mary Grace could tell he was making mental notes.

"Oh, don't get me wrong! Vicki was a sweet kid, but she was . . . difficult."

"Difficult?" Mary Grace prompted.

Susie shrugged. "I think she had emotional problems, but back then nobody went to shrinks. So she coped the best she could."

Mary Grace frowned. "By living a wild, destructive life?"

Susie nodded. "I wasn't the least bit surprised when I heard she was dead. I knew she'd come to a bad end." She looked up. "It was almost like she *wanted* to die."

The waitress arrived with lunch, and it took them a few minutes to get situated before John resumed his questions. "Any idea why Victoria was so unbalanced?"

"It was a lot of things," Susie responded. "The boys flocked around her for all the wrong reasons, and most of the girls hated her for the same reasons. It made her popular and lonely at the same time, you know what I mean?"

John nodded. "I think I do."

Susie stirred her gumbo with a spoon. "She acted like she didn't care, but I think she did. She was real smart but had trouble conforming to the structure of a classroom, so her grades weren't very good. And her family redefined *dysfunctional.*"

John raised his eyebrows. "The mayor's family?"

Susie took a small bite of gumbo, then nodded. "The mother was an alcoholic—rarely seen in public. Richard was okay, kind of an overachiever, but he was a lot older than Victoria and joined the army when she was in junior high. And the father." Susie shuddered. "He was the devil."

"The devil?" John repeated.

"He was so mean that Mrs. Harte tried to kill herself more than once, and when Richard left for college, he didn't come back until the old man was dead."

"And when the son returned, he was elected mayor of Bethany Beach?" John asked.

"Richard Harte was appointed to finish the term of the previous mayor, who died in office," Mary Grace provided.

Susie nodded. "But I think everyone is satisfied with the job he's done, so when it's time for reelection, he'll probably stay in office."

John considered this for a few seconds, then turned back to Susie. "So Victoria transferred to a prep school up north for her senior year?" Susie acknowledged this with a tip of her head. "Do you know why?"

"She said it was to get her SAT scores up, but we all figured that the school board had told her parents to make other arrangements."

"You mean they kicked her out of the county high school?" Mary Grace confirmed.

"Basically."

John took a sip of water. "Did you ever talk to Victoria after she went off to prep school?"

Susie had to think for a minute. "No, I don't think I did."

"I heard a rumor that she wasn't at school at all, but really ran away from home."

Susie's expression became guarded. "Where did you hear that?"

"I never reveal my sources," John told her with a charming smile.

"People started talking when she didn't come home for the holidays. Her father said that since her school was up in New England, it would be too expensive to fly her home. But the Hartes had lots of money, so we knew that wasn't the reason."

"Why do you think she didn't come home?" Mary Grace asked.

Susie shrugged. "I figured she stayed at school so she wouldn't have to spend Christmas with her satanic father."

"I guess everybody was pretty scared after Victoria was killed," John commented.

Susie looked surprised. "Scared?"

"That the killer might strike again," John clarified.

"Oh, no, I don't remember ever worrying about that," Susie said. "School started back and we were all busy, and . . ."

"Everybody just forgot about Victoria," John finished for her.

"We didn't exactly forget," Susie said slowly. "But there was nothing we could do for her."

"Did you go to the funeral?" John asked.

"There wasn't one."

John glanced at Mary Grace. "No service at all?"

"Not that I know of. We kept watching the paper because my mother said we should go, but there wasn't ever an announcement."

"Does she have a grave in a local cemetery?" John wanted to know.

Susie put her napkin beside her almost-untouched bowl of gumbo. "I never thought to look, but I suppose so." She reached down and collected her purse. "Thanks for lunch, but I really have to get back to work."

John reached out and grasped her arm. "Who do *you* think killed Victoria Harte?"

Susie pulled her arm free. "Could have been anybody. She picked up men all the time."

"Did she ever date one boy steadily?"

Susie looped her purse over her shoulder. "Like I said, Victoria's name was associated with about every boy in our class at one time or another. The only one I ever remember her dating for more than a week was Randy Kirkland."

"The preacher?" Mary Grace was surprised into asking.

"Well, he wasn't a preacher then, but he was the junior class president and eventually our valedictorian. They dated pretty steady that spring, and I remember being mildly amazed. Of course, it didn't last. By prom time, Victoria was dating a baseball player from Florida State."

Susie took a step away from the table, indicating that their interview had come to an end. John stood and thanked her again, then settled back beside Mary Grace, and they watched the jewelry store owner weave her way through the crowded room toward the front door.

John raised his eyebrows. "Well, that was interesting."

"She didn't really *answer* any of your probing questions, and I thought the remark about Victoria's father was a little strong. It makes me wonder how stable Susie is herself."

"Just because she called the old mayor the devil?" John asked.

"You've got to admit that was a bit much," Mary Grace replied carefully.

"A bit," John agreed. "And I'm sure she's not telling us everything she knows about Victoria or the evil mayor."

"How do you know?"

John smiled. "Women are like that—sneaky and secretive."

Mary Grace opened her mouth to protest, but he laughed before she could.

"Just kidding. I'm a complete stranger, and the questions I was asking are sensitive. It's reasonable to assume that Susie kept a few things to herself—like the fact that Victoria's father was abusive."

"You're sure?"

John's expression turned hard as he nodded. "According to the old cook, he was hardest on the son, but Victoria and the mother got their share of licks." He waved the waitress over and asked for their check. While they waited for her to return, John said, "The fact that the family didn't have a public funeral for Victoria supports my theory that they wanted the whole thing to go away. No investigation, no press coverage, nothing."

"The most interesting thing Susie told us was that Victoria dated Randy Kirkland," Mary Grace said as the waitress put their ticket facedown on the table. "Victoria sounds like the worst kind of bad girl, and Reverend Kirkland is the picture of propriety."

"Maybe he was different in high school?" John proposed, then pulled two twenties from his wallet to cover the bill.

"The junior class president and valedictorian? Sounds pretty circumspect to me."

John frowned as he slid out of the booth. "Yes, Mr. Kirkland definitely warrants more scrutiny. Any chance you could invite him to dinner tonight?"

Mary Grace shook her head. "Not on such short notice. Maybe tomorrow."

"You think he'll come?" John asked as he held the door open for her.

Mary Grace stepped through the door into the hot sunshine, then nodded. "Oh yes, he'll come. Reverend Kirkland visited Justin regularly until he found out I'd joined the Mormons. Then we couldn't get rid of him. Trying to save my soul, I guess."

John raised an eyebrow as they reached their cars. "Reverend Kirkland gets more interesting all the time."

Mary Grace slid into the front seat of her car and tried to close the door, but John put out a hand to block it.

"Don't you want to come to the library with me?" he asked.

She shook her head. So much time spent in his presence had her nerves on edge. She needed to put some space between them so she could think clearly. "I'd like to, but I have groceries to buy."

"What if they refuse to let me look at the yearbooks since I don't have a library card?"

She smiled. "Tell them I gave you permission to use mine. Now I have to get back to the Arms and prepare for all these guests you've had me invite to dinner."

He moved his hand and let her close the door. Mary Grace started her car and pulled out of the parking lot. When she checked her rearview mirror, she saw that he was still standing by his car watching her drive away.

Mary Grace sighed as she parked in front of the Piggly Wiggly. She needed some time to recuperate from close exposure to John Wright, but had none to spare. So she took Lucy's list from her purse and hurried inside. It took her thirty minutes to collect all the necessary items, then fifteen minutes to get away from Miss Iantha Mullins, who'd recently had hip replacement surgery and wanted to give Mary Grace all the details of her ordeal.

John's car wasn't parked in front of the Arms when Mary Grace returned. Relieved, she carried the groceries to the kitchen, then stopped to check on Windy.

"Did you have any problems while I was gone?" she asked the girl.

"Just those Lovejoy people checking out *late*," Windy said. "Then they complained about their room and the quality of our food and even the seaweed in the water." Windy looked up in amazement. "Like we could do something about that."

"Some people just enjoy complaining," Mary Grace told her. "Did you offer them a free night the next time they come?"

Windy gave her a sullen frown. "Why would I do that? They were making all that stuff up."

Mary Grace took a deep breath before she responded. "I know it's annoying to deal with people like the Lovejoys, but the customer is always right. I'll mail them a certificate for a free night's stay."

"It doesn't seem right that they get a free night while the nice guests have to pay," Windy grumbled.

Mary Grace shrugged. "It's not fair, but it's the way the hotel business works. Now, we're having more people than usual for dinner tonight, so I've got to go and talk to Lucy. You won't leave the desk, will you?"

Windy shook her head, and with that small comfort, Mary Grace moved down the hall. "I'll be in the kitchen if you need me."

Mary Grace found Lucy humming cheerfully as she rolled out piecrusts. "Thought I'd make some of my lemon meringue pies for tonight since Dr. Chandler's coming. You know how he loves my pies."

Mary Grace smiled. "Everybody loves your pies. And I was thinking you might want to call your cousin Ernestine to come help you tonight."

Lucy's head bobbed. "Already called her. She'll be here at five o'clock."

"Is there anything I can do?" Mary Grace asked.

"Got the rolls rising, the beans cooking, and the ham warming. About the only thing left to do is peel the potatoes."

Mary Grace tied on an apron and sat down in front of the huge bowl full of boiled potatoes. Then she picked up a paring knife and began to peel. While she worked, Lucy entertained her by describing recent events on a soap opera. A few minutes later, they were interrupted by a voice from the dining room.

"Who in the world could that be?" Lucy demanded with a frown on her face.

Before Mary Grace could reply, John Wright appeared in the open doorway. "I've been looking everywhere for you," he told her.

"Lucy, meet John Wright. John, this is Lucy Dubose."

"Happy to meet you," Lucy said, and John nodded, then took a seat across from Mary Grace.

"So, did you get any new information at the library?" she asked as he leaned forward on his elbows and stared at the bowl of potatoes.

"I got lots of information, no answers," he replied. "If you'll give me a knife, I'll help you with those."

Mary Grace shook her head. "You're a guest here," she reminded him.

"Never turn away helping hands," Lucy overruled her and handed John a knife.

With a shrug, Mary Grace picked up another potato and began to peel.

For the next little while, they worked in silence with Lucy humming in the background. Finally John spoke. "After my research at the library, I drove out to the old Seafoam Motel where Victoria died," John said. "How long has it been deserted?"

Mary Grace paused in her peeling to consider. "Ever since I can remember."

"About twenty years or so," Lucy provided.

John smiled at Lucy, then turned back to Mary Grace. "I got some more pictures of Victoria. You want to see them?"

She nodded as he dried his hands on a dish towel, then reached into his shirt pocket and unfolded several sheets of paper.

"This one is the whole cheerleading squad in their junior year. Here's Victoria." He pointed to the now-familiar face. "And this is Susie." This time he indicated toward a young-looking version of the jewelry store owner.

Mary Grace reached for the papers in his hand. She shuffled through until she found one of the whole junior class. "There's Reverend Kirkland," she identified the minister. Then her fingers outlined the image of Justin, youthful but still serious. "And here's Justin," Mary Grace said a little wistfully, then refolded the pages and extended them back toward him. "When you're finished with those, I'd like to have them."

"These pictures?" John waved the copies.

"Yes."

"You can have them now." He pushed them across the counter, then resumed his potato peeling. "I have an appointment with one of Victoria's old teachers tomorrow afternoon—a retired English teacher named Clarabelle Lowery."

Mary Grace nodded. "I'll have to go with you on that one too."

John looked up. "Why, is she mean to strangers?"

"No, she's an angel to everyone. I'll need to be there to protect her from you."

John laughed. "Well, I'll be happy for the company, whatever the reason."

When the potatoes were finished, Lucy took over. "I can handle the rest of this potato salad. You go ahead and be getting the dishes on the table."

Mary Grace walked to the cabinet, expecting John to head back to his room. But when she pulled out a rolling cart full of dinnerware, John was waiting for her. "My mother taught me how to peel potatoes, but she wasn't a real stickler for manners. I don't know if I'll be able to set a proper table," he said as he surveyed the array of dishes.

"We'll set things up buffet style and let the guests pick their own utensils," Mary Grace explained.

While they were distributing the dishes, a bouquet of roses was delivered. "Who are they from?" John asked, squinting at the card.

"My lawyer," Mary Grace told him as she read the card. *Since I can't be there personally I thought I'd send a little something to brighten your table.* Mary Grace looked up and saw John frowning at the bouquet.

"Your lawyer sends you flowers?" he asked.

Mary Grace put the arrangement in middle of the buffet table. "Actually, this is a first."

Before John could respond, Windy came rushing in. He took one look at the teenager and excused himself.

"Can I leave early tonight?" Windy asked after John was gone. "Some friends of mine are riding into Destin, and they invited me to go along."

Mary Grace nodded. "After you take fresh towels around to all the occupied rooms, you're free to go."

"Thanks!" Windy replied cheerfully. "I'll come in early tomorrow to make up the difference."

Windy rushed toward the linen closet, and Mary Grace went to her apartment. She took a quick shower, then fixed her hair and used perfume for the first time in almost a year. After putting on her second-favorite dress, she stared at her reflection. Looking into her dark eyes, she promised herself that these concessions were not for John's benefit. She was merely trying to help the Arms maintain high standards.

When she reached the dining room, Dr. Chandler and Bobby were just arriving. She greeted the old doctor warmly with a hug. "Thank you for coming tonight."

"It's my pleasure," the elderly gentleman replied.

"Let's go into the dining room, and I'll get you settled." Mary Grace put Bobby and his grandfather near the head of the table as the honeymooners came in. She seated them at the other end to give them a degree of privacy. Mary Grace gave Mr. Tamburelli the seat beside them, since he wasn't much on making conversation. The Haggerty ladies walked in as a group, and Miss Eugenia made a point of taking the empty seat beside Mr. Tamburelli. The other ladies sat across the table from Dr. Chandler and his grandson. When the sheriff arrived, he sat next to Bobby. John chose the chair beside Miss Eugenia as Mary Grace moved to the head of the table and welcomed everyone. She invited Dr. Chandler to say a blessing on the food, then encouraged everyone to fix plates.

"I had Lucy bake a chicken breast for you if you'd rather not eat ham," Mary Grace whispered to Miss Eugenia as the others moved toward the buffet table.

Miss Eugenia eyed the spiral-sliced ham. "Well, just this once it will probably be okay for me to eat pork."

After everyone was seated, Mary Grace made introductions, and John immediately started fielding questions about his career. He told them about his opportunity to serve a mission in South Africa. "When I got home, I finished my last two years at Duke, then took a job as a sportswriter for the *Savannah Sun Times*. When race riots broke out in Cape Town, I told my editor that I had contacts in the area. So they promoted me to investigative reporter and sent me to Africa."

"That's a big assignment for a young man," Sheriff Thompson remarked.

"It was a very lucky break," John agreed.

"So, let me guess. On your first assignment you became the *Sun Times*'s star reporter?" Mary Grace predicted.

"I'm not sure about that," John demurred. "But my success in South Africa did help me get more good assignments."

Then Annabelle pointed her fork at him. "My husband works for the Albany Library, and they subscribe to newspapers from across the country. I told him about you, and he looked up your articles. According to him, you are a very good writer."

John smiled. "Well, tell him thank you very much."

"He also said you made the headlines yourself recently," Annabelle continued.

John's smile remained in place, but his eyes lost all traces of humor. "Just trying to sell a few newspapers."

Miss Eugenia was regarding him shrewdly. "I thought it was strange that a world-traveling reporter would end up in Bethany Beach, Florida. What did you do?"

"I almost got fired," John told them. "Sending me on this little trip into the rural South is my editor's idea of the next best thing."

"You almost got fired?" Mary Grace repeated, and John sighed.

"A few weeks ago, a woman on the mayor's staff contacted me and told me that her boss was a cocaine addict, and his dependency on the drugs had forced him into a relationship with organized crime."

"Just like Deep Throat in *All the President's Men!*" Miss Eugenia whispered.

"The Watergate scandal," Annabelle provided for the benefit of the young people at the table. "Happened before most of you were born. You probably learned about it in history class."

"I'm familiar with Watergate," John told them. "And this scandal was on a much smaller scale. I did some research, came up with corroborating evidence, and convinced my editor to go with the story."

"Derrick said it was front-page news for a week," Annabelle informed the assembly.

"How did that get you in trouble?" Miss Eugenia demanded. "Sounds like exposing a criminal would make you a hero."

"It did until the evidence disappeared and my informant was compromised."

The Rayburns were talking quietly between themselves, and the men seemed focused on eating. But all the old ladies were engrossed in the story. "How?" Miss George Ann asked.

John grimaced. "The mayor admitted to having an extramarital affair with my informant and publicly begged his wife for forgiveness. He claimed that his mistake had put him in a position where a vindictive woman could ruin his family and his career."

"That sounds like a more *recent* presidential scandal," Miss George Ann remarked. "One that may be too risqué to include in the history books."

Murmurs of agreement were heard around the table, then Annabelle asked, "And the voters bought his story?"

John nodded. "And they probably would have even if the incriminating drug test results hadn't disappeared."

"You think the mayor arranged for them to be stolen?" Mary Grace asked.

John ran his hands through his hair. "I know he did, but my editor wouldn't give me time to prove it. We were making some important enemies, and he buckled under pressure."

"And sent you off to write filler for the summer," Annabelle concluded.

John's eyes were angry. "That pretty much sums it up."

"Well, if you do a really good job on these summer murder articles, maybe your editor will let you have your old job back," Miss Polly proposed with optimism.

"That's what I'm hoping," John affirmed.

"Have you solved the murder here in Bethany Beach yet?" Miss George Ann asked, and Sheriff Thompson's eyebrows shot up.

"Not quite yet," John told Miss George Ann.

"He's trying to solve the murder of a teenage girl stabbed to death here twenty-five years ago," Miss Eugenia told Dr. Chandler and the sheriff.

Both men gave John their full attention as he addressed the table as a whole. "I'm sure you remember the incident. Her name was Victoria Harte."

"Why would you be interested in something that happened so long ago?" Sheriff Thompson asked.

"I'm not interested exactly," John replied. "It's just an unsolved murder that my editor assigned to me. I asked Mary Grace to invite both of you to dinner tonight so I could pick your brains," John admitted, then spoke directly to Dr. Chandler. "Since you signed the death certificate." He then turned to the sheriff. "And since you were the deputy who answered the emergency call, I thought I could give my investigation a jump-start by asking you a few questions over a pleasant meal."

"The incident report will be a matter of public record, but I'm not at liberty to say anything else about the case," Sheriff Thompson said firmly.

Dr. Chandler nodded in agreement. "Anything I might remember would be protected under the doctor and client privilege."

John took a sip of water, then spoke to the sheriff. "You know, I was in your office today and asked for a copy of that incident report, and they said it wasn't in the file."

Sheriff Thompson shrugged. "There could be any number of explanations for that. It could have been misfiled, lost, thrown away by mistake . . ."

"Thrown away on purpose," John added.

"That's unlikely," Sheriff Thompson said. "But even if it's true, I can't possibly be held accountable for mistakes made by previous sheriffs or their employees."

John put his fork down, abandoning all pretense of eating. "Actually, there never really was a 'case' to speak of, was there?" The sheriff didn't respond, so John continued. "A young woman dies by violent means in a small southern town, but nobody called in the FBI, appealed to the public through television ads, or even questioned the victim's friends."

The sheriff met John's gaze directly. "I was only a deputy at the time. The family requested that the investigation be discreet, and the sheriff honored their wishes."

John spread his hands in confusion. "Why would the family be interested in discretion rather than catching the killer?"

Sheriff Thompson shrugged. "How can people be expected to think clearly after such a tragedy?"

"Especially a grisly death like Victoria's?" John clarified, and the sheriff nodded.

"The murder scene was gruesome, obviously the work of a deranged person. Since no other crime even remotely similar had taken place in the surrounding areas, we determined that the killer was just passing through. The Hartes were a prominent family—"

"A political family, you mean," John interrupted.

"Okay, a political family," Sheriff Thompson admitted. "If dragging Victoria's name through more mud could have brought her back, I'm sure they would have encouraged us to do so. But Victoria was dead, and nothing could change that. They wanted to protect her as much as they could."

"From what?" John asked.

The sheriff paused, searching for the right words. "She was found in a seedy hotel room, killed by a man she had picked up heaven knows where."

"From what I've been able to determine, Victoria Harte's whole life was fairly scandalous," John pointed out. "I don't see why the circumstances of her death would have surprised anyone."

"There was nothing to be gained by a noisy, embarrassing investigation," Sheriff Thompson maintained.

John turned to Dr. Chandler. "I was able to get a copy of the death certificate, but there was no time of death listed."

Dr. Chandler thought about this for a second. "An oversight. The weather was terrible that night, which confused everything. I must have forgotten."

"Do you remember the time of death?" John pressed.

The doctor shook his head. "No."

"Why wasn't an autopsy performed?"

"She had a knife in her chest. We certainly didn't need an autopsy to determine the cause of death." Dr. Chandler turned to Mary Grace. "When you said your friend wanted to ask a few questions, I didn't anticipate an inquisition."

"I'm sorry, Dr. Chandler," Mary Grace said with a look at John. "I think that's enough questions for tonight."

John accepted responsibility. "I'm the one who should apologize," he said. "But I just have a few more questions, if you'll bear with me." He looked at the sheriff. "I'd like to see the room at the Seafoam Motel where Victoria died. Could you tell me how to arrange that?"

"The property reverted to the county years ago for nonpayment of taxes," the sheriff told him. "I'm sure there's a key around the courthouse somewhere. I'll take you out there and let you look at the room. When do you want to go?"

"Would tomorrow afternoon about three o'clock be okay with you?"

The sheriff nodded. "I'll meet you there."

"And do you know what happened to the old motel registers?" John asked once his tour was arranged.

"They were sold at an auction with everything else when the owner died," Sheriff Thompson replied.

John looked disappointed by this news. "Any idea who bought them?"

The sheriff gave him a hard look. "They were purchased by Justin Hughes."

Mary Grace blinked in surprise. "Why would Justin buy them?"

"Because Justin was the night clerk at the Seafoam for a couple of years," the sheriff replied. "That's where he got his start in the hotel business, and I guess they held sentimental value for him."

"Was Justin working there the night Victoria was killed?" Mary Grace asked.

After a brief pause, the sheriff said, "I believe he was."

The room fell silent as Mary Grace digested this information. Lucy came in with the lemon meringue pies, and as dessert was distributed, the guests engaged in individual conversations. The honeymooners had their heads close together as they shared a piece of pie. Miss Eugenia grilled Mr. Tamburelli about his life in Chicago while Miss George Ann described a pain she'd been having in her lower back for Dr. Chandler.

John scooted his chair close beside Mary Grace and whispered into her ear, "I thought that went quite well."

She turned to him incredulously. "You must be kidding! Dr. Chandler and Sheriff Thompson might not even speak to me again!"

John glanced up to make sure no one was listening, then continued. "Do you know where Justin Hughes might have put the old registers from the Seafoam?"

"Probably in the basement," Mary Grace said. "That's where he stored the ones from here."

"Maybe we could take a look tomorrow, between our appointment with Mrs. Lowery and our trip out to the Seafoam."

Apparently John intended for her to spend all of the next day with him, and even though it was a little presumptuous, she was curious to see the room where Victoria Harte died, so she nodded. "What do you expect to find in the register?"

"Maybe nothing," John admitted quietly. "But let's suppose that Victoria had a new boyfriend—one whom her parents disapproved of. They sent her away to school, trying to discourage the relationship, but she ran away instead. Nobody heard anything from her until she came back to Bethany Beach during the holidays."

"Since she died at the Seafoam, you're assuming that she was staying there?"

"It makes sense to me. And if I'm really lucky, she signed the register."

"If she was hiding from her parents, she wouldn't have used her real name."

"No, but if I can get a sample of her handwriting and compare it to the names on the register . . ."

"A sample of what?" Annabelle asked as she walked up beside them.

Mary Grace smiled as she cut a bite from the pie on her plate. "This pie. Isn't it wonderful? Lucy is the best cook in Florida."

The cook returned as if on cue and offered more pie. "The entire meal was delicious," Leo Rayburn praised.

Lucy beamed at him. "Glad you enjoyed it. More?" she asked Farrah.

Farrah declined with a sweep of her fake eyelashes. "I've eaten too much already."

Leo stood and pulled out his wife's chair. "We're going to excuse ourselves and go for a quick swim."

"Be careful of the undertow," Sheriff Thompson advised.

"And the jellyfish," Miss Eugenia added as she watched the couple leave.

Mr. Tamburelli pushed back from the table. "Thanks for dinner," he said briefly, his eyes on the door.

"Are you going for a swim too?" Miss Eugenia asked, and the man from Chicago gave her a startled look.

"What? Oh, no. Just headed to my room."

As soon as Mr. Tamburelli was gone, Miss Eugenia turned to the sheriff. "That man is extremely suspicious. We followed him to the NASCAR Museum this afternoon, and he spent the entire time on the telephone talking to someone named Silverstein. He never looked at one single display."

"But if there's anything you want to know about racing, I had plenty of time to study each and every exhibit," Annabelle told the remaining guests.

"Why were you ladies following this Tamburelli fellow around?" the sheriff asked with a frown.

"I worked with the FBI to crack a big money laundering case a couple of years ago," Miss Eugenia began.

"Heaven help us," Annabelle interjected wearily.

"So I've learned to spot criminals," Miss Eugenia proceeded as if her sister hadn't spoken. "And Mr. Tamburelli is a criminal type if I ever saw one." She turned to John. "In fact, he might have been sent here by whoever sells drugs to the mayor of Savannah. They may plan to kill you for exposing him!"

The guests at the table reacted in varying degrees of horror to humor.

"If there's the slightest chance that this Mr. Tamburelli is dangerous, you need to stay away from him," the sheriff warned.

"Well, somebody needs to get some information about him," Miss Eugenia insisted. "And since you local authorities don't seemed concerned about him, I'll probably have to call the FBI myself."

The sheriff's eyebrows shot up. "The FBI?"

Miss Eugenia nodded smugly. "I have contacts."

The sheriff scooted his chair back. "I'll take care of it, ma'am." He stood and thanked Mary Grace for the meal. His tone was polite but formal, and Mary Grace knew he was unhappy about John's intense questioning.

Bobby and Dr. Chandler said they would leave as well. Mary Grace walked them to the door and apologized again. "John is a friend from college, and I was just trying to help him," she explained.

The old doctor patted her hand. "It's okay, dear, but you need to encourage Mr. Wright to finish his article quickly and go home. Nothing good can come from digging up old heartache."

By the time Mary Grace returned to the dining room, John was gone and the ladies from Haggerty were embroiled in an argument. "Going to outlet stores and touring pirate ships is one thing, but following around a stranger is where I draw the line," Annabelle declared in a loud voice.

"Is something the matter?" Mary Grace asked the obvious.

"Something is definitely the matter with Eugenia's head," Annabelle said, jabbing her finger toward her sister. "Tomorrow she wants to go to Underwater World just because that Mr. Tamburelli told her he was going there."

"Someone has to keep an eye on him," Miss Eugenia said in her own defense.

"I think you're flirting with him," Annabelle proposed.

"That is absurd!" Miss Eugenia objected vehemently. "You *know* my heart belongs to Elmer! I'm just trying to do my civic duty!"

"Let the sheriff handle it. He said he would," Annabelle reminded her sister.

Mary Grace stepped forward and spoke to Miss Eugenia. "As much as I admire your sense of duty, it probably would be better to let the sheriff worry about Mr. Tamburelli."

"Humph!" Miss Eugenia sniffed. "All my instincts tell me he's not who he claims to be, and someday you're all going to be sorry you didn't listen to me!" With that declaration, Miss Eugenia stalked out of the room.

"Dear me," Miss Polly said in obvious distress.

"Don't mind her," Annabelle told everyone. "She'll be over it by breakfast."

"I think all this arguing has given me a headache," Miss George Ann said as she put a hand to her pale forehead.

Mary Grace included all the ladies in a smile. "Well, it's been a long day, and I'm sure tomorrow will be eventful as well, whether you spend it sightseeing or following Mr. Tamburelli." She led the way toward the lobby. "Remember, we don't provide cleaning services on Sunday. A fresh supply of towels was delivered earlier this evening, but if you need anything else, just let me know."

Once Mary Grace had the ladies in their rooms, she went back to the kitchen. Lucy and her cousin had things under control, so she walked through the back door onto the beach. She knew that the chances of running into John were good. Meeting him on the beach with a million stars overhead was asking for trouble, but she kept walking.

CHAPTER 6

Mary Grace moved slowly up the beach, breathing the salt air and letting the warm breeze pull at her hair. After about a half mile, she turned around and headed back. When she reached the Arms, John was sitting on a porch swing, staring at the surf. He put out a foot to stop the swing's gentle sway and patted the empty space next to him. Slightly apprehensive, she settled beside him, and he resumed pushing his feet against the sand to set the swing back in motion.

"This is a very beautiful place," he said.

"Yes, it is," she agreed.

They were quiet for a few minutes, then Mary Grace asked, "Do you think you'll be able to solve this case by the end of the week?"

"One way or another," he replied obtusely.

"You won't get much more out of Dr. Chandler and Sheriff Thompson. They were both irritated by your questions tonight."

"I expected the doctor to be resentful, but I was surprised by the sheriff's reaction." John stopped pushing the swing and sat forward, resting his elbows on his knees. "It seems like he'd be glad that someone was trying to solve that old case."

"Maybe he thinks if you solve the case it will make him look incompetent."

"I could understand that if it were a current case, but it's an old one. Like he said, he wasn't the sheriff back then. But he saw Victoria dead in that motel room, and that image should haunt him."

"Maybe it's just like they said—impossible to solve, and investigating it will only hurt the people who have already suffered because of the loss."

"Maybe." John smiled again. "But I'm a suspicious kind of person. And I don't see how you could be *sure* a case was impossible to solve unless you knew who the killer was."

Mary Grace considered this ominous possibility. "You think they're protecting someone?" she asked, looking at his profile.

"I think it's possible."

"So Victoria ran away from school and lived—where until Christmas?"

John shrugged. "I don't know."

"Then during the Christmas holidays, she came back to Bethany Beach and stayed at the Seafoam but didn't let her family know she was here?"

"It sounded a little better in my mind, but I guess that's my basic working theory."

"But if she didn't want to see her family, why did she come back at all?"

"I'm still counting on the mysterious boyfriend."

Mary Grace frowned at the retreating tide. "But from what Susie Ireland said, Victoria was very promiscuous, and her parents didn't interfere. How bad could this boyfriend have been that she had to hide him from her parents?"

"Maybe he was married, a respected man in the community, and an association with Victoria would be bad for *him*."

She nodded. "That makes sense." They were quiet for a few minutes, then a couple walked by, hand in hand. "Is that the Rayburns?" Mary Grace asked, peering into the moonlight.

John followed the direction of her gaze with his eyes. "I think so."

"It must be nice to still be in love after so many years."

"They honeymooned here in the 1970s?" he asked.

"Yes."

John looked over his shoulder at the Arms. "This place has a lot of history behind it."

Mary Grace was still watching the Rayburns walk briskly down the beach. "They aren't wet, so they must have decided not to swim." Mary Grace leaned forward to get a better look. "But they *are* covered with sand."

John didn't seem interested in the Rayburns. "Who's that?" He pointed to a figure up on the bluff, silhouetted in the darkness.

Mary Grace squinted. "Based on the moonlight reflecting off his bald head, I'd say it's Mr. Tamburelli." Mary Grace turned back to John. "But why would he be standing up there watching us?" Then a terrible thought occurred to her. "Unless the Mafia *did* send him to spy on you. Or worse!"

John scowled at the figure above them. "Whoever he is, he'd better keep his distance." He laced his fingers together and popped them.

"That will give you arthritis," Mary Grace warned.

"I'll worry about that in thirty years," he said with another glance at their onlooker.

"Annabelle said Miss Eugenia really did help the FBI catch some money launderers," Mary Grace told him.

"So . . ."

"So, maybe she *can* recognize Mafia people."

"I doubt Mr. Tamburelli is a Mafia man." John stood and reached out a hand to help her up. "But I appreciate you being so concerned about me."

She stared at his hand. His CTR ring glittered in the moonlight, and for a second she was transported back five years. They were at the Farewell to Summer dance, the music was playing, and she had just decided to take a chance on John Wright.

"You're not one of those germ fanatics who won't touch other people's hands, are you?" John asked, bringing her back to the present.

She smiled. "No." Then, against her better judgment, she put her palm in his. Heat moved up her arm. She saw the startled look on his face and took a measure of comfort from the fact that he'd been affected by the contact as well. She clasped his hand, pulled herself up, then let go and moved toward the back door to her apartment.

He didn't say anything, but she could feel his eyes follow her until she was safely inside.

After closing her apartment door, Mary Grace took off her shoes and tossed them in the closet, then hung her dress on a hanger before putting on her bathrobe. She checked to make sure her doors were locked and saw the light on her answering machine was blinking. Pushing the button, she sat down to listen.

The first was from Bobby, saying he'd enjoyed dinner. The second was from Reverend Kirkland, accepting the dinner invitation for himself and his wife for Sunday night. The third was from Jennifer. Mary Grace dialed the number quickly.

"I hope I didn't wake you up," she said when Jennifer answered.

"No, we're pretty much staying awake 'round the clock."

"How are the boys?"

"They both have strep throat and infected ears," Jennifer reported. "And as an added little bonus, Will has an unexplained rash. After the doctor gave me the multiple diagnosis, I half expected him to tell me to put a black wreath on our door."

Mary Grace laughed. "I'm sorry. I know it's not funny. Do you want me to bring you some chicken soup or something?"

"No, but thanks anyway. So what's been going on with John Wright?"

"He took me out to lunch today," Mary Grace announced.

"You're lying!" Jennifer exclaimed.

"I *am* exaggerating. He asked me to come to an interview with him, and it just happened to be a lunch meeting."

"Wow." Jennifer still sounded impressed.

"And Heath Pointer sent me flowers."

"In two days you've become a *femme fatale.*"

Mary Grace laughed again. "Hardly. But Miss Eugenia thinks that one of my guests is a criminal."

"Is Miss Eugenia one of those old ladies from Georgia?"

"Yes. They come the first week in June every year."

"And why does she think one of your guests is a criminal?" Jennifer asked.

"It's a long story, and you've got sick children who need you."

Mary Grace heard Jennifer yawn. "That's true. It's about time to give out doses of antibiotics."

"I'll call back tomorrow."

"Okay. And Mary Grace?"

"Yes?"

"Watch out," Jennifer warned.

"For what?"

"Your heart."

The second Mary Grace hung up, the phone rang again. She glanced at the clock as she clasped the receiver. It was ten-thirty.

"Miss O'Malley?" a haughty voice demanded.

"Yes."

"This is Richard Harte. Let me begin by apologizing for calling so late."

Mary Grace had met the mayor a few times, but was not in the habit of receiving phone calls from him any time of day. "No need to apologize," she answered, curious.

The mayor cleared his throat, and when he spoke again, his tone was less friendly. "It has come to my attention that you are assisting a reporter from Savannah in his efforts to humiliate my family."

Mary Grace was surprised by his strong choice of words. "John is not trying to humiliate anyone. He's just writing an article for his newspaper."

"He's a rude, self-serving individual, and I refuse to allow him to further his career at my expense. I insist that you stop supporting him in his efforts."

"He's a guest in my hotel and an old friend," she told the mayor. "I have an obligation to help him."

"I was hoping you'd be reasonable," Richard Harte replied. "But if not, I will be forced to use my considerable influence against you. In a matter of days, the Arms could be nothing but a memory."

"Are you threatening me?" she asked incredulously.

"I prefer to consider it good advice." At this point, Mayor Harte disconnected.

Mary Grace stared at the cordless phone for a few seconds, then returned it to the charger. She looked out the window at the darkness and repressed a little shudder. She wasn't exactly afraid. Mayor Harte had limited influence in Bethany Beach, and his threat to ruin her was probably an empty one. But the fact that he took the time to call—not to mention the tone of his voice—was unnerving. As Mary Grace climbed into bed, she wondered if maybe John might be on to something after all.

* * *

The man stepped away from the sand dune that had concealed him from view while he watched Mary Grace through the picture window in her living room. Once her lights were out, he dropped the last of several cigarettes and made a quick call on his cell phone. Then he walked through the sand down to the water's edge.

* * *

On Sunday morning Mary Grace slept in until six o'clock, then dressed quickly in a pair of jeans and a Bethany Arms T-shirt. When she arrived in the kitchen, Lucy was there rubbing Ben-Gay into her calves.

"Is your rheumatism bothering you?" she asked the older woman politely.

"Mercy, yes. We must be in for some stormy weather. I can always feel rain in my bones long before the weatherman predicts it."

Anxious to keep the smell of Ben-Gay out of the dining room, Mary Grace encouraged Lucy to stay in the kitchen while she arranged the continental breakfast on the buffet table. The Haggerty ladies arrived at five after seven so they could eat before they went to the sunrise service on a retired battleship. Miss Eugenia and Annabelle seemed to be over their argument from the night before, although Mary Grace noticed that they were careful to avoid the subject of Mr. Tamburelli and his possible ties to organized crime.

The Rayburns came in and fixed plates with healthy portions of Lucy's food. "Do you folks have a big day planned?" Mary Grace inquired.

"We've rented a sailboat," Farrah said with a spacey smile.

"Thought we'd get a view of the ocean from a different perspective," Leo added.

"Do you know how to sail?" Miss Polly asked. "I've heard it can be very dangerous."

Farrah blinked at the plump old woman. "Why? Are there sharks or something?"

"No, sweetie," Leo assured his wife. "I think Miss Polly meant that people who aren't experienced sailors sometimes drown. But we'll wear life preservers."

"And keep an eye out for warning flags," Mary Grace told them. "My cook has arthritis, and she says we're in for bad weather."

John walked in with Mr. Tamburelli close behind him. "That guy is starting to give me the creeps," he admitted to Mary Grace as he took a bite of doughnut. "Every time I turn around, he's on my heels."

Mary Grace studied the man from Chicago for a few seconds. "Maybe Sheriff Thompson will find out something about him."

"Like he would share any information he gets with me," John muttered.

Mary Grace shrugged and sipped her orange juice. "Then you might want to check him out yourself. Your newspaper could help."

"If he's involved with organized crime, my newspaper is the last place I'd turn for help."

"So what will you do?" she asked.

"Watch my back," he said, then winked. "You got any more of these doughnuts?"

Mary Grace went into the kitchen for another tray of doughnuts, then refilled the juice pitchers. John left, followed closely by the Rayburns and Mr. Tamburelli. After they were gone, Miss Eugenia waved for Mary Grace to come over.

"I declare I'm more convinced than ever that Mr. Tamburelli is an impostor," she said. Annabelle groaned, but Miss Eugenia was insistent. "I asked him if he'd had a chance to go swimming yet, and he said he didn't even bring a bathing suit!" she announced, and all the ladies gasped.

"That is very strange," Miss Polly said with concern. "Who comes to the beach without a bathing suit?"

"Perhaps he's afraid of the water?" Miss George Ann suggested.

"Then why did he come to the beach?" Miss Eugenia demanded.

"Maybe he doesn't want to wear a bathing suit because he's got so much body hair," Miss Polly offered as an explanation, and all the ladies turned to stare.

"How do you know he has body hair?" Annabelle wanted to know.

Miss Polly blushed crimson. "Well, his arms look like they are covered with fur, and the hair on his back is so thick you can see it through his shirt."

Mary Grace suppressed a shudder and couldn't think of a thing to say in Mr. Tamburelli's behalf.

"That's it!" Annabelle cried. "Eugenia, you've found the 'missing link'!"

Miss Eugenia gave her sister a sour look. "You'll eat your words when Mr. Tamburelli is exposed."

"Well, have a nice day, ladies," Mary Grace said, then hurried to her apartment and changed for church. On the way out the front door of the Arms, she put a sign giving guests her cell number for emergencies and the time for dinner on the registration desk.

It was fifteen miles to the meetinghouse in Destin, and Mary Grace had to push the speed limit to arrive in time to set up the nursery room before sacrament meeting started. When she passed through the foyer on her way into the chapel, she was surprised to see John Wright standing by the door. He was heartbreakingly gorgeous in his dark suit, and when he smiled she almost forgot to breathe.

"I'm glad to see a familiar face," John greeted her. "I travel so much and attend other wards more often than my own, so you'd think I'd be used to sitting alone in sacrament meeting—but I'm not."

Before Mary Grace could reply, Alice Mumford rushed up. "Could you watch Devin for me?" she asked. "The chorister is sick, and they've asked me to fill in."

"Sure," Mary Grace agreed, and Alice immediately transferred her squirming toddler along with his diaper bag.

"And afterwards if you'll just take him on to nursery, maybe he won't scream for the first hour," Alice suggested.

The woman hurried toward the stand, and Mary Grace introduced John to Devin. "He is eighteen months old and a member of my nursery class," she explained as they stepped into the chapel and found seats near the back. "His father is in the bishopric, so when Alice has to lead the music, he sits with me."

"He's a cute little fellow," John said as Mary Grace began the process of spreading out the numerous items required to keep Devin happy for the duration of sacrament meeting. After putting his board books in a stack, his quiet toys in a pile, and his goldfish crackers out of sight until later, she handed him a sippy cup. Devin spotted the goldfish and lunged, upsetting the pile of toys. "Can I give you a hand with . . . something?" John asked.

"Here, take Devin." Mary Grace passed the baby to John as Brother Mumford stepped to the podium to open the meeting. The baby grabbed John's expensive-looking tie and promptly stuffed it into his mouth.

"I think he likes me," John whispered.

"Don't let it go to your head," she replied softly. "He's not very discriminating."

John smiled as the organist started playing the opening hymn. Mary Grace collected the toys, then tried to retrieve the baby, but Devin wouldn't budge from his perch in John's lap. Finally she gave up and pulled a hymnbook from the bench in front of them.

"I guess he *does* like some people better than others." John reached over and put one hand on the edge of her hymnbook. "Could you scoot a little closer?" He motioned toward the book with his head. "I'm getting eyestrain trying to see the words."

When she complied with his request, their arms touched and warmth permeated her whole body. She concentrated on the words of the song and forced herself to sing, trying to ignore the long, graceful fingers that held the other side of her hymnbook.

They made it through the sacrament without incident, but during a talk on service Devin started to fuss, so Mary Grace got out the goldfish. Devin spent the next few minutes alternately sticking crackers and his fingers into his mouth. Then the toddler reached for the lapels of John's suit coat, but John caught the gooey little hands just in time.

"Help!" John whispered.

Mary Grace located the baby wipes and removed the orange slime from Devin's hands. "It serves you right for stealing his heart from me."

"What can I say? I'm irresistible."

The little cleft in his chin deepened as he smiled, and Mary Grace felt her heart pound. Quickly she looked away and listened to the speaker. When sacrament meeting ended, Mary Grace collected Devin's things, then told John to follow her.

"Where are we going?" he asked.

"To the nursery."

He frowned. "I usually go to Gospel Doctrine."

Mary Grace looped the strap of the diaper bag over her shoulder. "Devin and I have to go to the nursery, and since he has a death grip on your tie, I don't think you have much choice." After a brief hesitation, John fell into step beside her. "Devin is having a hard time adjusting to the nursery, and the separation process is easier if his parents aren't involved."

John looked down at the baby with sympathy. "I never was all that crazy about the nursery either. They make you eat stale animal crackers, and it always smells like a wet diaper."

"You can't possibly remember anything about your nursery experience," she said as they stopped in front of a door covered with bright yellow smiley faces.

"Some things you never forget," he insisted. "And this must be the nursery." He faced the happy door. "I can smell it from here."

Mary Grace ignored this comment as she turned the knob and led the way inside. She pushed a button on her portable stereo, and instantly soft music filled the room. "You and Devin can have a seat there." She pointed to a small table covered with blocks. Then she turned to greet new arrivals.

For the next fifteen minutes, Mary Grace allowed the children to play with the toys. Devin fell asleep in John's lap, and since she needed all her wits about her to manage her class, she tried to keep from looking in their direction. After a short lesson, flannel-board story, and finger play, Mary Grace poured water into miniature cups and distributed homemade trail mix onto little paper plates.

"Would you like some?" she asked John once the children were served, but he shook his head. "It's fresh," she promised.

"I'm sure it is," he said with a smile. "But I'm afraid if I move my arms, I'll wake up Devin." She took a seat beside him, and they watched the children eat. "You must be exhausted," he remarked as she pushed a lock of dark hair from her eyes. "Are the parents going to come and get the children soon?"

Mary Grace laughed. "We have another forty minutes to go."

"Forty minutes!" John responded in a horrified whisper. "We've already been in here for eternity!"

"Nope, only an hour. We still have to take our walk, color a picture, and sing some songs."

When the kids were finished eating, Mary Grace put away the food, then lined them up for a walk. They circled the church three times, pointing out things they were grateful for as they went. John tagged a few feet behind, carrying the still-sleeping Devin. Once they were back inside the nursery room, they sang songs with a CD, then Mary Grace passed out the crayons and pieces of paper. After instructing the children to draw something they had seen while on their walk, she sat down by John.

"They're just scribbling," he pointed out discreetly.

"In the nursery we have to use our imaginations—a lot," Mary Grace explained.

When the pictures were complete, the children put away the toys, then gathered in a circle for Mary Grace to read them a book. Devin woke up during this process. Out of the corner of her eye, she watched John open Devin's diaper bag and hand the baby his sippy cup. By the time Devin's parents arrived, he was sitting quietly with the other children. He was happy to see his parents but did give John and Mary Grace a little smile as he left.

"Being nursery leader has to be the hardest calling in the Church," John exclaimed after they closed the door behind the last child. "Spending the morning here with you has really given me some perspective. The next time I'm asked to revamp home teaching routes or give a talk in stake conference, I won't have the nerve to complain."

Mary Grace smiled as John helped her stack chairs. Then she collected her equipment, and they headed out to the parking lot. On the way he pointed at the plastic bag full of trail mix that was sticking out of the top of her nursery bag. "If your offer still stands, I'll take some of that now."

"It's pretty bland," she warned as she passed him the bag. "Just Cheerios and pretzels and oyster crackers. I can't put peanuts in it because so many children are allergic, and I can't put anything sweet in because it makes the children hyper."

He opened the bag and tossed a handful of mix into his mouth. "Anything beats fasting."

"Fasting?" she repeated.

"Since going to a restaurant on Sunday would be breaking the Sabbath, starvation is my only option."

Mary Grace raised an eyebrow. "Is that a thinly disguised hint that I should invite you to eat with me?"

"Oh no," John assured her with a charming smile. "And don't worry, it would probably take more than just one day without food to *kill* me."

Mary Grace smiled at him, then slid into the driver's seat. "I guess you deserve a sandwich for assisting me in the nursery."

John put more cereal in his mouth. "I'll take you up on that, although this stuff is pretty good. If I were you I'd add M&M's, though."

Her breath caught in her throat as she watched him chew and swallow. "The children might get chocolate on their Sunday clothes," she pointed out, then started her car. "When you get to the Arms, come to my apartment and I'll feed you something a little more substantial."

John held up the plastic bag. "Can I eat all of this, or do you need me to save some for next week?"

"I would never serve my class anything *stale*," she assured him. "Eat it all." She closed the door, then waved as she backed out of her parking space. When she checked her rearview mirror a few minutes later, John and his rental car were right behind her, and during the rest of the drive home she had to resist the urge to stare at him.

When they got to the Arms, he parked right beside her and followed as she led him to her apartment. "Don't you want to go to your room and change?" she asked as they walked into her living room.

"Naw." He pulled off his tie and suit coat, then draped both items of clothing across the back of her couch.

"Make yourself at home," she remarked, and he gave her a quick smile.

"Thanks."

He sat on a stool across the counter from her as Mary Grace removed a loaf of bread, some ham left over from dinner the night before, and several condiments from the refrigerator.

John rolled up his shirtsleeves, then asked, "Is there anything I can do to help?"

Mary Grace handed him a tomato and a small knife. "You can slice this up."

He took a paper plate from the stack on the counter, then concentrated on his task. By the time he finished, she had everything else ready. "I'll let you make your own sandwiches," she told him.

"You first," he said politely. Mary Grace fixed her sandwich, then walked into the living room and sat on the couch. John joined her a few minutes later. "Delicious," he said after taking a big bite. "Even better than your trail mix."

"Since I'm providing the meal, it's only fair that you provide the entertainment," she told him.

His eyes widened. "What do I have to do?"

She laughed. "Why don't you tell me about your mission."

He sighed. "There's not much to tell. I was a dismal failure."

"You?" she asked in surprise. "All you talked about in Panama City was your mission."

"I know. But I was called to South Africa, which is a difficult mission in the first place. The social barriers combined with the political unrest make proselyting nearly impossible. But most of the guys in my mission got at least one baptism." His disappointment was obvious.

Against her better judgement, Mary Grace decided to make an admission. "You can take partial credit for my conversion to the gospel. Does that count?"

He looked up. "It might. How did I help you want to join the Church?"

"Well, for starters, by the end of that summer in Panama City I had gotten sort of . . . attached to you."

"You did?" He seemed pleased.

"At the risk of putting myself in the same category with Devin and Windy, I admit it."

"Why?" he probed.

"You're not exactly ugly," she replied with a smile. "But I think it was your righteousness that attracted me more than anything else. And the fact that you hounded me unceasingly, begging for a date."

John hung his head. "This is so humiliating. I thought you were going to make me feel better about my lack of mission baptisms, but instead you've reminded me about my inability to make you like me."

"I liked you," she insisted. "And if your mission call hadn't arrived when it did . . ." She shrugged. "Who knows?"

He smiled. "Maybe now would be a good time for you to share your conversion story."

"It might take awhile."

He glanced at his watch. "We don't have to meet the sheriff until three. We've got time."

Mary Grace told him about seeing the missionaries riding by the Arms on their bicycles. "It was raining and I chased them down, then insisted they come in and give me the first discussion."

John laughed. "Talk about a golden contact!"

"They told me to read the Book of Mormon, the New Testament, and attend church for two months. Then they baptized me."

"And when you have ten children and fifty-nine grandchildren who are all active members of the Church, I'll know my time here on earth wasn't wasted."

Mary Grace stood and held out her hand for his plate. "Something like that." She took the dishes to the kitchen and put away the sandwich fixings. John followed her and silently started helping.

Once they were finished, he said, "All kidding aside, I really am pleased that you joined the Church. Contrary to what you might believe, I do remember the nursery. My teacher was crabby and . . ." His voice trailed off as his eyes scanned her. "Well, she didn't look anything like you, that's for sure. She didn't play classical music, and the room didn't smell like flowers. I guess what I'm trying to say is that I wish you had been my nursery leader."

"Thanks," Mary Grace said as she cut him a piece of Lucy's pie left over from the night before. "I'm just grateful to serve where I can. I spent a lot of years in ignorance, and now that I know about the Savior and what He did for me, I want to show my appreciation."

He accepted the piece of pie and took a stool at the counter. Mary Grace discarded their plates, then sat across from him.

"I got a phone call from Richard Harte last night," she told him. "He said if I continued to help you, he'd put me out of business."

John put down his fork and regarded her solemnly. "Why would he say that?"

"He claims that you are trying to further your career by humiliating his family."

"I'm trying to do my job well, I'll admit that. But I'm also trying to solve his sister's murder. It seems like he'd be glad." John frowned at his pie. "Could he really destroy your business?"

Mary Grace shrugged. "I don't think so. Most of my guests are from out of town, and Mayor Harte has only been in office for a couple of years, so his influence is fairly limited."

"I don't want to cause trouble for you," John said slowly. "But I really am baffled by his reaction."

Mary Grace pointed at his plate. "Do you want another piece?"

He shook his head. "No, thanks. I'm full."

"Well, if you think about it, Mayor Harte's call was probably a good sign."

"How do you figure that?"

"Because if you're right and the Hartes really don't want you to solve the murder, you must be getting close or Mayor Harte wouldn't be threatening me."

He lifted an eyebrow. "That does make this development sound more promising. I'd almost be happy if your business wasn't in jeopardy."

"I'll be fine," she assured him. "Did you find out anything about Mr. Tamburelli?"

John was still frowning as he replied, "I've got a PI in Savannah checking him out for me. So far, nothing. If Tamburelli is not his real name, it might be hard to identify him."

"A picture might help. Maybe we could ask Windy to take a picture of him with her new digital camera," Mary Grace suggested.

John smiled. "I'll let you know if I get that desperate." He finished his pie and threw the plate into the garbage. "And speaking of Windy, I'd like to know why she came into my room while I was on the beach last night."

Mary Grace was speechless for a few seconds. "Windy couldn't have been in your room last night," she managed finally. "She asked to leave early so she could ride into Destin with some friends."

He shook his head. "That may be what she told you, but I'm absolutely positive that she was not in Destin. She was in my room, rifling through my belongings."

Mary Grace put a hand to her chest and rubbed the ache that was forming there. "You're sure?"

"Positive. The culprit left behind some red hair and the fragrance of Jell-O." He reached into his shirt pocket and removed a small plastic bag. Inside was a single strand of red hair. "Breezy is definitely the guilty party."

"Windy," Mary Grace corrected automatically, staring at the conclusive evidence.

"Whatever."

"She was supposed to put fresh towels in all the occupied rooms, but if the guest is out we just open the door and put the towels on the floor." Mary Grace looked up with a stricken expression.

"There were towels on the floor in front of the door, but Windy didn't stop there. She went through my suitcases, pulled back the covers on my bed, and even cleaned out my brush. I found her hair on the bathroom counter."

"I don't know what to say except that I'm sorry. She's really a good kid. I can't imagine what came over her."

John shrugged. "She didn't steal anything, but please ask her to stay out of my room. Even celebrities like me need a little privacy. If I want my brush cleaned, I'll handle it myself."

Mary Grace only nodded, still stunned by Windy's misbehavior.

"Well, I guess we'd better head toward Mrs. Lowery's house," John told her as he rolled down his sleeves, then put his tie and coat back on. She led him to the door, and they walked out into the warm summer afternoon. John unlocked the passenger door of his rental car. "I have directions to Mrs. Lowery's house," he said as she climbed inside.

"You won't need them," she told him. "I know the way."

CHAPTER 7

Mrs. Lowery was sitting on her front porch when they arrived, still wearing her Sunday dress. She offered them homemade lemon bars and iced tea. They explained that they had just eaten and declined both.

"I appreciate your willingness to see me," John told the old lady. "And I won't waste much of your time."

Mrs. Lowery laughed. "My time is not very valuable these days. Mostly I just sit and remember. I guess that's why I agreed to talk to you. I've been thinking about Victoria a lot lately."

"You remember her, then?"

"Oh, yes. Victoria was very memorable. Beautiful, passionate, untamed, but it's the way she died that has burned her face on my memory."

"It must have been difficult for you, especially since you knew her," Mary Grace said.

Mrs. Lowery nodded, then leaned forward. "I'm going to tell you something if you promise not to quote me." She suddenly seemed less the sweet old lady and more a savvy woman of the world.

"I promise," John accepted her terms.

"I think I might have been one of the last people to see Victoria alive."

John was instantly alert. "When?"

"That New Year's Eve, just after dark."

"Did you tell the police?" Mary Grace asked.

"No, they never questioned me, and at the time it didn't really seem important. But later I wondered if it might have been significant. I think that's why I dwell on her so much."

"Where did you see Victoria?" John prompted.

"Here." Mrs. Lowery waved toward her front yard. "It was a pleasant winter evening, too warm, really, which is why we had the severe weather later that night. I was on the porch, just like we are now, watching the clouds roll in. Then Victoria stepped out of the shadows and nearly scared me to death."

"What did you say?" John asked.

"That I was pleased to see her—and I was. She had shown some promise in composition class, especially with poetry. I asked her how she liked school up north, but she didn't answer. She was very nervous, looking around as if she thought someone might be following her. Then she said that she had written some poems and thought they might be good. I expected her to ask me to look over them for grammatical mistakes, since mechanics never was one of her strong points, but instead, she asked me to keep them for her."

"Keep them?" John repeated, and Mrs. Lowery nodded.

"As if she thought someone would take them from her. She kept clutching her coat, and I assumed she was cold, so I asked her to come inside. She refused, saying she had to go, and handed me an envelope. I believe she intended to come back and get them, but she was killed that night at the Seafoam Motel."

"Do you still have the poems?" John asked softly. "I need to get a handwriting sample for Victoria."

Mrs. Lowery extended a large manila envelope toward John, and he took it carefully.

"I looked for this after you called for an appointment. I didn't read them for the longest time, since she didn't really give me permission. But finally I decided they were mine."

John removed a small notebook and scanned the pages. After a few seconds, he passed it to Mary Grace. "Do you mind if I take this so I can make a copy?"

"I don't mind at all," Mrs. Lowery consented. "Victoria's form was immature, but her style is unique, and with a little direction . . ." The teacher's voice trailed off.

"Did Victoria tell you where she was going when she left your house?"

"No. And shortly afterwards the weather got so bad I honestly forgot all about her until I saw the article in the paper."

John leaned forward. "We interviewed one of Victoria's friends, and she said that for a time Victoria dated Randy Kirkland."

Mrs. Lowery frowned. "I'm surprised."

"That Victoria dated the preacher?" John asked.

"No, that anyone admitted to being her friend," Mrs. Lowery clarified. "By the eleventh grade, Victoria had become something of a pariah. I did know that she and Randy dated for a time. I wanted to believe that she was making an effort to change, but I'm afraid she was just trying to corrupt him."

Mary Grace frowned. "Why?"

Mrs. Lowery lifted her shoulder in a delicate shrug. "To see if she could."

"Was Victoria expelled from school?" John asked.

"It was nothing official, you understand. The school couldn't just kick out the mayor's daughter. But Mayor Harte was strongly encouraged to find Victoria another institution in which to finish high school."

"What was your opinion of Mayor Harte?" John wanted to know.

Mrs. Lowery looked surprised. "I didn't have one. I only met him once or twice."

John stood. "Thank you so much for talking to us. I might come and visit with you again if you don't mind."

Mrs. Lowery gave him a sweet smile. "I'd be delighted to have the company. You come back too, Mary Grace. I never see you anymore now that you're running Justin's hotel."

Mary Grace promised to return soon, then followed John to his rental car. As they drove to the Seafoam, Mary Grace studied Victoria's poems. One read:

Our union is more profound than touch
Our hearts are bonded in common rhythm
We live for each other
We are forever, eternal, one.

The one on the last page was very short:

A thought
A hope

A dream
A beginning
You

"So, what do you think?" John asked.

"They're sweet," she said. "But kind of melancholy."

"It sounds like she was in love for the first time." John looked over at her. "And the sadness convinces me that she and her true love were unable to be together for one reason or another."

"Or maybe the person she loved didn't love her back."

John frowned. "I guess that's possible, although from what I read, the poems sound like the feelings were mutual."

Mary Grace turned to the first page of the notebook and reread Victoria's poems until she and John reached the Seafoam Motel. Sheriff Thompson was leaning against his squad car, smoking a cigarette. As John parked beside him, he threw the unfinished cigarette to the ground and stepped on it with the heel of his shoe.

"Mary Grace," the sheriff said with a tip of his hat when she climbed out of John's rental car. Then he nodded at John and led the way up to the hotel. The surface of the parking lot was cracked and full of potholes. Once the sheriff reached the crumbling sidewalk, he continued until they reached room seventeen. He removed a key from his pants pocket and unlocked the door. Then they stepped in.

The room was very hot and musty. There was no furniture, and the carpet had been pulled up, leaving a bare concrete floor littered with paint chips. Mary Grace hugged her arms to herself as she felt a chill. John walked over and looked out the small window that faced the empty pool.

"Was this room ever used again after Victoria died?"

The sheriff shook his head. "I don't think so."

"You said the murder scene was grisly," John said, and the sheriff gave him a look of distaste.

"There was a lot of blood."

Mary Grace felt the room spin around her and put a hand on the wall to steady herself.

Several pieces of paint fell off as a result of the contact.

"Bad paint job," John remarked.

"Mr. Wilhite painted over the blood to discourage sightseers. I'm sure he didn't take time to properly prepare the walls," the sheriff remarked dryly. "Besides, that was a long time ago. Paint doesn't last forever."

As John rubbed his hand against the wall near him, hundreds of chips fell to the ground. The sheriff frowned. "Sorry," John apologized quickly. "I just wanted to test your theory." John studied the paint on the floor.

The sheriff looked like he wanted to discuss this further, but his radio went off and he stepped just outside the door to answer it. As soon as the sheriff's back was turned, John produced a plastic bag from his pocket. He pulled it open and held it against the wall, then brushed several paint chips into it.

"What? Are you like Inspector Gadget?" Mary Grace whispered. "Do you have a little of everything with you?"

John laughed. "Not everything." He returned the plastic bag to his pocket just before the sheriff walked back in.

Sheriff Thompson motioned to the door with his head. "If you're finished here, I've got a call."

John nodded. "I've got all I need. Thanks for your help."

The sheriff didn't respond, and instead just walked out and headed toward his car.

"Why did you take those paint chips?" Mary Grace asked once they were driving back toward the Arms.

"Collecting blood samples," John replied. "I'll have them DNA tested and maybe we'll get lucky."

"How? We already know that Victoria died a bloody death in that room."

"In the process of stabbing Victoria, our murderer may have cut himself as well. If we find any blood type other than hers . . ."

"It sounds like a long shot," Mary Grace said with a frown. "And your method of collecting evidence was far from scientific."

"I don't have to prove my case in a court of law, just in a newspaper article," John reminded her.

"Won't DNA testing take longer than the end of this week?"

John shrugged. "The unsolved murder articles don't have to run in sequential order. If I don't have this one solved by the time I leave,

I can keep working from a distance and then write my article when all the information is available."

Mary Grace thought of Sheriff Thompson's borderline rude attitude toward John. "You're not making any friends in Bethany Beach."

He grimaced. "That's one of the drawbacks of my job."

When they reached the Arms, they walked through the lobby and into her apartment. John retrieved his coat, then they stood awkwardly by the door. "I guess I'd better check with Lucy and make sure dinner is on schedule," Mary Grace said reluctantly.

"When you get through with that, can we look for those old registers from the Seafoam that your friend bought?"

Mary Grace thought for a second, then nodded. "Follow me. We'll check on Lucy, then I'll show you the stacks of old registers in the basement." She looked up at him. "And you'd better hope what you're looking for is there. I don't have time to search this whole place."

John smiled. "If you're instrumental in solving my case, I'll have to share my byline. You could be famous."

She rolled her eyes. "I don't have time to be famous either."

They walked to the kitchen and found Lucy asleep on the cot in the storage room.

"Looks like dinner is under control," John teased quietly.

"There are pies on the counter, and we usually keep things simple on Sunday, so I won't consider this a disaster." She looked up at him. "Yet."

Mary Grace took her keys out of her pocket and led John to the basement door. The old lock resisted momentarily, then she pushed it open, flipped on the light, and reached for a flashlight on the top step.

"Isn't there any electricity down here?" he asked as they descended.

"Yes, but it's like a tomb, and the thought of being trapped down here during a power outage gives me the creeps." Mary Grace controlled a shudder. "So I always take a flashlight, just in case."

The carpeted steps gave way to sturdy wooden ones that eventually changed to concrete.

"We're almost at sea level down here," Mary Grace explained. "Back when this house was built, supplies were delivered by ship every few months, so they had to have plenty of storage space. Mr. Bethany even included an underground dock in his house plans to make deliveries more convenient." She looked around. "There are lots of little rooms full of molded old junk."

"It's several degrees cooler down here," John observed.

"But so damp," Mary Grace pointed out. "Justin had some machines installed to control the humidity, but it still feels clammy."

They stepped out into a large room filled with crates, boxes, and old furniture. "Does this basement extend the full length of the house?" John asked, peering off into the darkness.

"I think so, but I don't know for sure. I've never liked it and spend as little time down here as possible," she admitted.

"Where does that lead?" John asked, pointing to a cavelike doorway carved out of stone.

"That goes to the old dock."

"I'd like to see it." John took a step in that direction, but Mary Grace held out a hand to stop him.

"It hasn't been used for years, and Justin told me the wooden planks are rotten. Walking on them would be too dangerous."

John looked down at her fingers on the crisp, white fabric of his shirtsleeve. Mary Grace drew her hand away and turned, hoping he couldn't see the blush that rose in her cheeks. "The registers are over here with boxes of old tax statements and other financial records."

She led him into a small room in the corner, where wooden book-shelves were built into the wall. Rows of thin, leather-bound registers filled the top shelf. Each volume had the year printed neatly on the spine. John withdrew several and flipped through them. "Here are your ladies from Georgia." He pointed to the names on a yellowed page. "From 1985."

Mary Grace smiled. "They've been coming every summer for years."

John frowned at the wall. "All these ledgers look the same."

"Justin ordered a lifetime supply of them years ago." She pointed to a corner where several boxes were stacked. "Every year I just get out a new one and send the old one to the printer to have the date stamped on it."

John walked to the boxes and examined them. Then he opened a cabinet and a cupboard. "Do you mind?" he asked as an afterthought.

Mary Grace raised an eyebrow. "Look wherever you want."

John gave her a half smile as he opened another door. When he reached the last cupboard, she turned in preparation to go back upstairs. Then John leaned down and lifted a large, green book from the cabinet. He opened the cover and flipped through several pages.

"It looks like the Seafoam didn't invest much money in their registers. The cover is vinyl, and they didn't start a new one every year."

"Is that the only one here?" Mary Grace asked.

"As far as I can tell," he replied, then looked up at her. "Apparently the only one your friend Justin saved."

Mary Grace frowned. "Why?"

John pointed at the dates scrawled on the front page. "I guess Victoria made an impression on him too."

She walked over and read along with him. "Can you tell which name she used?"

"Well, we know she was there on the night of December 31," John thought aloud as he scanned the page. "And since there is only one woman's name listed, I'm assuming Victoria signed in as Emily Dickinson."

"And Justin knew it was a false name, but allowed her to use it anyway."

John nodded. "He certainly knew she wasn't Emily Dickinson." John pulled the little book of poems from his pocket and compared the handwriting. "It's her," he confirmed. "Do you mind if I keep this for a while?"

"Keep it as long as you like. What about her true love?" Mary Grace asked as they walked toward the stairs. "Do you think he signed the register?"

"It's a possibility," John agreed. "I'll look for an Ernest Hemingway or a Walt Whitman."

Mary Grace ignored the joke. "I hope he did love her and that he visited her there," she said seriously. "Somehow it will make me feel better to know that Victoria wasn't completely alone and unloved."

John raised an eyebrow. "You're starting to take this pretty seriously."

She smiled. "You aren't the only person who likes a challenge."

As soon as they got back upstairs, John took the Seafoam's register to his room while Mary Grace woke Lucy so they could begin preparations for dinner. For the next little while, Mary Grace was too busy to worry about Victoria Harte or John Wright or any feelings she might be developing for him.

Once the food was ready, Mary Grace went back to her apartment and changed clothes. She brushed her hair and teeth, then touched up her makeup. When she rushed back into the dining room, the Haggerty ladies were already seated.

"So, did you have a nice day?" Mary Grace asked.

"The sunrise service on the battleship was very nice," Miss Polly replied.

"If you like getting windburned," Annabelle muttered.

"We ate lunch at a place called the Oyster *Bar*," Miss George Ann emphasized the last word with obvious disapproval.

"It's not really a bar," Mary Grace clarified. "That's just a trendy name."

"Well, it's a sure way to get indigestion," was Annabelle's assessment.

"Then Eugenia tricked us into following Mr. Tamburelli to Underwater World," Miss George Ann continued peevishly.

"I did not trick anyone," Miss Eugenia defended herself. "I merely suggested that it might be entertaining, and everyone agreed. And I'm more convinced than ever that he is *not* what he claims to be. He barely glanced at the singing dolphins and went out to use the pay phone while Melville the whale was being introduced."

"I wish *I'd* used the pay phone during Melville's performance," Annabelle said. "I got drenched when he did his double back flip."

Miss Eugenia leaned closer to her audience. "And I'm sure that Mr. Tamburelli's tie tack is really a camera. I got close enough to examine it a couple of times, and it was *glowing*."

Annabelle shouted with laughter as the subject of their conversation walked into the room and seated himself at the end of the table. There was a brief period of awkward silence, then Reverent Kirkland and his wife arrived and introductions were necessary. John and the Rayburns entered in at the end, and Mary Grace was required to start again.

Lucy put the food on the buffet table as Windy came in with a phone message for Mr. Tamburelli. "I'll bet it's from Silverstein," Miss Eugenia whispered to her companions after the man from Chicago stepped into the lobby and picked up the pay phone.

Mary Grace walked over to Windy and told the girl that she needed to discuss something important with her after dinner. Then Mary Grace stepped to the head of the table and encouraged everyone else to take a seat. She noticed that the reverend sat by the Rayburns, as far from John and herself as possible. Mary Grace asked Randy Kirkland to bless the food, and then the meal began.

"Did you have a nice day sailing?" Miss Polly asked the Rayburns. Farrah looked up with her signature blank stare, but Leo smiled.

"Oh yes, the water was smooth and the wind consistent. In fact, we had so much fun, we might go again tomorrow if the weather's nice."

The weather seemed like a safe subject, and Mary Grace was pleased when it was introduced. However, Miss Eugenia and Miss George Ann had a difference of opinion on the next day's forecast, and a minor argument resulted.

"Our weather is very unpredictable," Mary Grace offered as a compromise. "The weathermen are often wrong."

Miss George Ann glared at Miss Eugenia, then addressed Randy Kirkland. "So, you're a minister?"

Reverend Kirkland's fork paused in midair as he nodded. "Yes, ma'am."

"My grandfather donated the land for our Haggerty Baptist church to be built on," she told him proudly, and Miss Eugenia snorted slightly.

"That was very nice of him," Reverend Kirkland replied.

"Do you have one of those projection machines that puts the scriptures up on the wall behind you while you preach?" Miss George Ann further inquired.

Randy Kirkland shook his head. "No. We're a relatively small church and can't afford modern conveniences like that."

Miss Eugenia pointed a fork in his direction. "Don't know why you'd want a projection machine if you could afford it. Those things are a huge waste of money and downright irreverent."

"But all the big churches in Albany have them," Miss George Ann countered. "They make reading the scriptures so much easier for older people. Instead of looking down at your Bible, you can look up at the preacher." Miss George Ann turned to Randy Kirkland for support, but the reverend seemed reluctant to take a stand.

"I've never used one, so I'm not sure how well they work," he mumbled.

Miss Eugenia leaned forward. "I still maintain that it's not cost-effective or even natural. People are *supposed* to look down and read from the Bible. Why, if the Lord had wanted the scriptures on walls, He would have put them there!"

"Haven't you ever heard of hieroglyphics?" Miss George Ann demanded.

"I most certainly have, but can't see what they have to do with this discussion."

"Ancient civilizations put their religious stories on the *walls*," Miss George Ann replied with emphasis.

Mary Grace was frantically trying to think of a way to redirect the conversation when John leaned forward and spoke abruptly to Reverend Kirkland. "I understand that you were good friends with Justin Hughes."

Instead of being concerned, Mary Grace was actually relieved as she watched the reverend nod. "Yes," he affirmed. "Justin and I went to high school together."

Then John sprung his trap. "I'm investigating the death of another classmate of yours, Victoria Harte."

Reverend Kirkland glanced at Mary Grace. "That's what I hear," the preacher said, then kept eating. Mary Grace was afraid that John's insistence that she invite the Kirklands was going to be a waste of time. Then help for John's cause came from an unexpected source.

"I remember Victoria Harte very well," Cindy Kirkland announced. "She had a fixation on Randy for a while."

John raised an eyebrow as if this were news. "A fixation? You mean you and Victoria were involved romantically?" he directed the question to the reverend.

Randy Kirkland opened his mouth, but his wife spoke again. "I wouldn't say they were *involved*, and the whole relationship was pretty one-sided. Randy and I went steady throughout high school, but we had a little fight during the spring of our junior year. I thought it would be over in a few days, and it would have been if Victoria hadn't seen an opportunity and moved in."

"She was attracted to *you*?" John asked Reverend Kirkland, sounding a little doubtful.

Mary Grace studied the preacher. He was a nice-looking man, sort of reminding her of a young Ronald Reagan.

"She *stalked* him," Cindy corrected. "Victoria was one of those girls who couldn't take no for an answer. Once she got it in her mind that she wanted Randy, he never had a chance."

"So you and Victoria Harte dated," John addressed the reverend.

"Well, they went places together for a few weeks," Cindy answered for her husband. "Randy never called her, but she didn't mind calling him." Mrs. Kirkland looked shocked by this. "And sometimes she just came over to his house *without* calling first. He didn't want her around his parents, so he'd be forced to take her somewhere."

John tried Randy Kirkland again. "You didn't want to go out with Victoria Harte, but had to escort her around town to avoid problems with your parents?" John's voice had an incredulous quality.

"Victoria and I were opposites—like oil and water," Randy finally responded. "I tried to explain that to her, but she wouldn't listen."

Cindy sighed. "Even after he convinced her that they were through, she arranged to double with us to the prom."

"It sounds like she didn't hold a grudge," John suggested.

Randy laughed harshly. "She went to the prom with us to punish me."

"Why?"

Cindy picked up the conversation. "Victoria changed men more often than most girls changed nail polish. I think the thing that bothered her was that Randy was the only one to leave her and not vice versa. Our prom date was very awkward. She kept doing outrageous things to get Randy's attention. I was so glad when the evening was over."

John turned to Randy. "Did you see Victoria around town that summer?"

The preacher shrugged. "Maybe a few times. I don't remember."

"How about after she left for prep school?"

The reverend glanced at his wife, then answered. "She came to see me right before she left for Connecticut."

Cindy Kirkland's face registered surprise. "You never told me that."

Her husband looked uncomfortable. "There was never a reason to. She stopped by to tell me her father had arranged for her to go to school up north. I wished her luck and heaved a huge sigh of relief when she left."

"And you never saw her again?"

Mary Grace noticed that Randy hadn't eaten much and was twisting his fork nervously. "No." He didn't look up as he made this statement, and John caught her eyes briefly. Randy Kirkland was not a good liar.

Mr. Tamburelli returned from the lobby and took a seat at the table. Miss Eugenia turned to him at once.

"So, Mr. Tamburelli, how did you like Underwater World?"

The man seemed startled by this question. "I beg your pardon?"

"My friends and I were there, and we saw you," Miss Eugenia explained. "I even waved one time, but you didn't wave back."

Mr. Tamburelli mumbled something, then made a show of drinking his water.

Miss George Ann turned to the honeymooners. "Didn't I see you there too?"

Farrah's shrugged, but Leo nodded. "Yes, we stopped by for a little while before we picked up the sailboat."

"You left during Melville's performance too," Miss Eugenia said with sudden certainty.

"We must have been the only people stupid enough to stay through the whole thing and get soaked!" Annabelle wailed.

Farrah wrinkled her nose. "I didn't really care about seeing those smelly fish." She turned warm eyes toward her husband. "It was Leo's idea."

Miss Eugenia frowned. "Well, you missed a great show. When Kate and the babies get here tomorrow, I'll take them there."

"Make sure they wear their raincoats," Annabelle advised.

"You have friends arriving tomorrow?" Leo asked politely.

"Yes," Miss Eugenia confirmed. "Kate and Mark Iverson and their two children. They live next door to me in Haggerty, and Mark is with the FBI."

Several people around the table expressed surprise at this announcement, but Mr. Tamburelli seemed the most affected. Lucy walked in with pies for dessert, and Mr. Tamburelli took the opportunity to leave.

"I see that Pretty Boy Floyd left as soon as we mentioned the FBI," Miss Eugenia said under her breath as she ate chocolate pie without any apparent concern for the fat content.

"And *before* dessert," Miss Polly concurred quietly, then turned to Lucy. "I am a pie maker myself but often have trouble getting the chocolate custard to the right consistency. I'd love to watch you make pies one day while we're here."

Miss Eugenia snorted. "Now if that isn't the silliest thing! Spending time in the kitchen while you're on vacation."

Miss Polly drew herself up proudly. "Cooking is what I love, Eugenia—wherever I am. And I don't like to pass up an opportunity to learn."

Leo stood and pulled Farrah to her feet. "I think we'll take our pie back to our room," he said, and Farrah batted her heavy lashes at him. "Dinner was great," he added, then urged Farrah toward the lobby.

The Kirklands then said they needed to get home.

"But you haven't had any of my pie!" Lucy exclaimed.

"I'm sure they'd take one home with them if you wrap it up," Mary Grace suggested. Mollified, Lucy hurried to the kitchen to prepare one of her pies for transport.

Mary Grace walked the Kirklands to the door, and Lucy met them there with a foil-covered dish. "Here's your pie," the cook said.

"I can't thank you enough," Cindy Kirkland told her with a smile.

Mary Grace waited until Lucy had returned to the kitchen before she spoke. "I really appreciate you coming tonight, and I hope you didn't mind John asking questions."

"It was fun," Cindy said graciously. "We don't get out much." She glanced up at her husband. "Not together anyway."

The reverend smiled at his wife. "Why don't you take the pie on to the car, honey. There's something I'd like to discuss with Mary Grace."

Cindy nodded without resentment, and Mary Grace guessed that this was a request she received frequently. Once his wife was gone, Reverend Kirkland turned to Mary Grace. He wouldn't meet her eyes, so Mary Grace couldn't tell whether he was angry with her or embarrassed.

"I feel that it's my responsibility as Justin's friend to warn you to be careful with reporters. Newspaper people can be very tricky. You think they are asking one thing, but they are really asking something else. Then they twist your words and print lies."

Mary Grace was surprised by the intensity of his voice. "John's not like that," she assured him. "He's honest, and I'm sure he won't print anything that isn't true."

The reverend looked out across the parking lot toward his car, where his wife was waiting patiently. "Sometimes even printing the truth can be a disservice."

Mary Grace wasn't sure how to respond, so she waited quietly.

He smiled and shook her hand. "Well, I'd better not keep Cindy waiting any longer. Thanks for dinner."

By the time Mary Grace returned to the dining room, the Haggerty ladies had retired. John was talking to Lucy, but when he saw Mary Grace, he walked over and whispered that he'd meet her at the swing in thirty minutes.

When the kitchen was clean, Mary Grace started for her apartment. She was tired and knew that John's assumption that she would meet him was a dangerous trend, but she couldn't help herself. She walked out the back door and found him on the swing, watching the tide.

"So, did you get a lot of useful information tonight?" she asked.

"I think I have a better picture of things."

"Reverend Kirkland avoided the truth a time or two," Mary Grace reminded him. "I think he *did* see Victoria after she left for Connecticut."

"Either that or his relationship with her wasn't as one-sided as he's led his wife to believe."

Mary Grace nodded. "That is also possible."

"A straight-as-an-arrow kind of guy like Mr. Kirkland might have found a wild girl like Victoria irresistible, at least for a while."

Mary Grace studied him for a second. "You're kind of a straight-as-an-arrow guy too. Has a wild girl ever been hard for you to resist?"

He smiled. "No. Not so far anyway."

"If Randy Kirkland was attracted to Victoria, it probably didn't take him long to realize that she was trouble."

John acknowledged this with a little nod. "She was a threat to his future."

Mary Grace turned to stare at him. "Do you think Randy Kirkland killed Victoria?"

He shrugged. "I think it's a possibility."

She didn't know what to say, so she watched the waves crashing onto the shore. Finally John stood.

"I think I'll take a walk down the beach. Want to join me?" he offered, but Mary Grace shook her head.

"Monday is always my busiest day since I don't do laundry or clean on Sunday," she told him. "And I've got several phone calls to make before I go to bed, so I'd better get busy."

She rose to her feet and found herself very close to John. She looked up into his face, and her breath caught in her throat. John reached out and touched her hair. "You don't need beauty sleep, that's for sure. You're still as spectacular as you were at that Good-bye to Summer dance."

"It was a Farewell to Summer dance," she corrected. "You still remember it?"

He dropped his hand from her hair. "How could I forget? After weeks of begging, I had finally gotten you to dance with me, then Courtney got there and . . ."

"You went home to find out about your mission and forgot all about me," she finished for him.

She was teasing and expected him to laugh, but he didn't. Instead he said, "I didn't forget."

She controlled a little shiver, then turned toward the Arms. "Well, have a nice walk.," She stepped inside, resisting the urge to look back out the window. She went into the lobby and saw Windy sitting on the couch. Surprised, she sat down beside the girl.

"Why are you still here?" she asked.

"You told me you needed to talk to me about something important."

Mary Grace sighed. She had been so distracted by John and his murder story that she'd forgotten. "I'm sorry that you've had to wait, but I do need to talk to you about something. You went into Mr. Wright's room last night." It was a statement, not a question.

"Yes." Windy didn't even try to deny it.

"I don't see how you can continue working for me if I can't trust you to obey the rules," Mary Grace said firmly, and Windy began to weep.

"Oh, please don't fire me, Miss O'Malley. You know I need this job to make my car payment, and I promise I won't ever do it again."

"I'll give you one more chance," Mary Grace said with reservation. "But if you encroach on any of our guests' privacy, I won't have a choice."

Windy sniffled, then looked up at her employer. "As long as you're already mad, I might as well go ahead and tell you the rest."

"What do you mean?" Mary Grace asked, her stomach clenching with tension.

"Well, it's just that I'm so sure Mr. Wright is really John F. Kennedy, Jr. And if he gets discovered here, you'll get lots of publicity and the Arms will be famous and you'll never have to worry about getting guests again."

"Windy," Mary Grace began, "John is more than ten years younger than Mr. Kennedy would have been."

Windy continued as if Mary Grace hadn't spoken. "That's why I had to go into his room. I sent the picture to the *National Inquisitor,* but they needed a hair sample."

Mary Grace gasped. "You sent John's picture to a tabloid?"

Windy nodded. "And the hair sample too. Overnight mail."

"Windy, that is worse than just breaking one of my rules. It's probably against the law!" Mary Grace was aghast. "I can't believe you would steal his hair and look through his suitcases and . . ." She trailed off, overwhelmed by the situation.

Then she noticed that Windy was shaking her head. "I did go into his room, and I did take some hair out of his brush, but I didn't look in his suitcases." She seemed offended by the suggestion. "That would have been *wrong.*"

"You're sure all you took was hair from his brush?" Mary Grace verified.

"Yes, ma'am." Windy nodded vigorously, then looked down at the floor. "And I need to tell you one more thing. But I'm afraid you'll get mad again."

Mary Grace steeled herself for more bad news. "I won't get mad. What do you need to tell me?"

Windy chewed her lip for a second, then blurted out, "A reporter from the *National Inquisitor* is coming tomorrow. I wrote his reservation in the book, just like you said I should."

"A reporter?" Mary Grace verified. "Why?"

"For the article they're going to write about Mr. Kennedy," Windy explained.

With a weary sigh, Mary Grace stood. "Go home, Windy. We'll talk more about this later." Mary Grace waited until the girl had gone, then walked around the front of the Arms, hoping John had returned from his walk. She knocked on his door, and he opened it a few seconds later and smiled when he saw her.

"Missed me already, Gracie?" he asked.

She ignored this remark and the sudden pounding of her heart. "You're certain that someone looked through your suitcases?"

The smile disappeared from John's face as he nodded. "And my shaving kit. Why?"

"Because I just talked to Windy, and she admits to taking hair samples from your brush, which she sent overnight to the offices of the *National Inquisitor*."

"You're kidding," he said.

"No. At this very moment they may be checking to see if you really are John F. Kennedy, Jr. But the thing that concerns me is that Windy swears she did not look in your suitcases. That means someone else besides Windy was in your room."

John leaned closer. "Mr. Tamburelli?"

His breath stirred the hair by her ear, and she couldn't control a slight sigh. She clasped her hands together and stared at the parking lot. "He did leave dinner early last night. I just thought you should know." Reluctantly she took a step back. "And if you're ready for more good news, a reporter from the *National Inquisitor* will be here tomorrow to investigate *you*." If the situation hadn't been so embarrassing, Mary Grace would have laughed at the look of horror on John's face.

"Thanks for the warning," he muttered finally.

She nodded. "The way things are going, it's going to take both of us to watch your back."

CHAPTER 8

When she got back to her room, Mary Grace checked her messages. There was one from Heath Pointer asking if she'd received his flowers and promising to drop by the next day. With a sigh, she called Jennifer.

"Hello," Jennifer rasped into the phone.

"Are *you* sick now?" Mary Grace asked.

"Oh yeah. Stan too. None of us may live to see tomorrow."

"Do you need me to come over?"

"Are you kidding? Stan's mother has moved in. She dispenses home remedies, recites old wives' tales, and criticizes my house-keeping abilities with laserlike precision. If this disease doesn't kill me, she surely will."

Mary Grace laughed. "Well, call if you want me to come rescue you."

"I just pretend to be unconscious most of the time. Is John Wright still there?"

"Yes," Mary Grace told her. "But he's making progress on his story and will probably leave soon."

"Well that's good . . ." Jennifer's voice trailed off into a cough. "I'd better get back in bed before Stan's mother tries to put a garlic necklace on me. Call back tomorrow," Jennifer instructed, then disconnected.

After changing for bed, Mary Grace saw the photocopies from the old yearbooks that John had given her. She studied them for a few minutes, then found a pair of scissors and cut out all the images of Victoria Harte. She taped them to the mirror over her dresser and stared at them until she fell asleep.

* * *

"That was a close call today," the man with the cigarette said to his companion.

"Too close," the other man agreed.

"We're probably going to have to take aggressive action to protect my interests. What did you find out about the guests?"

"The Wright fellow checks out. He's a reporter from Savannah working on an unsolved murder. Tamburelli's room was clean." The men looked at each other. "A little too clean, if you know what I mean."

"Dig a little deeper on both of them."

"It's your money."

The man threw down his cigarette and stepped away. "Don't you forget it."

* * *

Mary Grace was awakened by the sound of someone knocking on her bedroom window. She blinked, trying to separate dreams and reality, then peered at the clock. It was 5:45 A.M. Then she started to cough and realized that her room was filled with smoke. Jumping from her bed, she looked around, trying to think clearly.

She had to warn her guests, had to call the fire department, had to see how bad the fire was. Reaching for the cordless phone, she dialed 911 on her way to the front desk. Once the fire was reported, she pushed the intercom button and requested that everyone vacate their rooms immediately. The smoke detector in the hall by the kitchen went off as she pushed the wooden door open.

The kitchen was so full of smoke that after she'd taken two steps, she lost her bearings. She held her breath as she tried to find the way back out, but eventually drew smoke into her lungs. Coughing, she searched desperately for the door. She felt herself falling, and her last conscious thought was that she'd let Justin down.

When Mary Grace opened her eyes, the first thing she became aware of was John's arms wrapped tightly around her. Then she moaned, "I think I'm going to be sick."

John carried her to a line of shrubbery and held her in its relative privacy as her stomach heaved. Luckily she hadn't eaten anything or the situation would have been much worse. When the spasms stopped, she sagged against John as they walked back to the parking lot. People were crowded around the Arms, and she could hear sirens approaching.

"Did everyone get out?" she asked, and John nodded as several fire trucks pulled up.

"All your guests are safe." He led her to a corner out of harm's way. Sheriff Thompson joined them there a few minutes later.

"How bad was the fire?" Mary Grace asked him.

"It was just a small blaze that started outside the kitchen door. It didn't affect the structural integrity of the building. You need a new door and a fresh paint job in the kitchen, which your insurance will likely pay for. Otherwise, I think everything's fine."

Mary Grace wanted to feel relieved, but something about the sheriff's overly cheerful tone concerned her. Frowning, she tried to concentrate. "What is outside the kitchen door that could catch on fire?" she asked and saw John and the sheriff exchange a quick glance.

"Someone set the fire on purpose, Gracie," John said finally. "Probably to punish you for helping me investigate Victoria Harte's murder."

"The mayor?" Mary Grace whispered, causing the sheriff to frown.

"You think Mayor Harte set your kitchen door on fire?" he demanded.

"I know it sounds ridiculous, but he called the other night and threatened to ruin my business if I didn't stop helping John with his article."

Before the sheriff could reply, Bobby's voice called from across the parking lot. "Mary Grace!" He pushed his way through the crowd that surrounded her, and Mary Grace stepped out of John's arms. "What in the world happened here?" The question was directed toward Sheriff Thompson.

"Looks like somebody started a fire by the back door that leads into the kitchen," the sheriff said.

Bobby considered this for a few seconds. "Why would anyone want to do that?"

"We're not sure yet," the sheriff said. "Just glad everybody's okay."

They waited in the parking lot for almost an hour before the fire department gave the all-clear signal. "It's a good thing that your smoke alarm was working," the fire chief told Mary Grace. "Otherwise, this could have been a disaster."

"Mary Grace is very safety conscious," Bobby said.

She gave Bobby a brave smile, then sighed. "I guess I'll go give my guests the good news." Mary Grace walked over to a group of people huddled near the front entrance to the Arms. "I cannot begin to apologize enough for the inconvenience you've all been forced to endure," she began. "You will not be charged for last night, and I completely understand if you all choose to change to a different hotel."

Miss Eugenia, wearing men's pajamas, stepped forward and spoke for the Haggerty ladies. "We'll all stay. Nobody was hurt, and I declare, it was kind of exciting."

Mr. Tamburelli nodded his agreement. "I'm staying," he told her briefly.

The Rayburns were more reluctant. "Farrah is just terrified of fire," Leo spoke for his wife.

"I don't like it much myself," Mary Grace replied. "If you decide you'd like to go to a different hotel, I'll help you make arrangements."

Farrah pulled her husband close and whispered into his ear. Then Leo looked at Mary Grace. "Let us talk about it; we'll let you know."

Mary Grace nodded, wondering if Farrah had found her chance to get a trip to Cancun. Turning toward the building, she said, "I want to see the damage."

"I'll come with you," Bobby offered.

Mary Grace shook her head. "You go on home and get ready for work, Bobby. Everything's fine here now."

"I can go in late," he offered.

"That won't make a good impression on your new employers. Besides, the sooner we're back to normal here, the better. You will come to dinner, though, won't you?"

Bobby nodded, then turned and walked to his car. Mary Grace took a deep breath and announced to her guests it was safe for them to return to their rooms. Once the crowd was dispersed, she followed the sheriff inside the Arms. John followed behind them. The back door leading outside from the kitchen was propped open, and most of the smoke was gone. The door itself was charred, and there was some smoke damage on the surrounding walls. Otherwise, it looked the same as always.

"See," the sheriff said. "I told you it wasn't so bad. I called Heath—"

Mary Grace barely had time to feel relief before Lucy walked into the kitchen and started screaming. "Oh, heaven help us! Somebody's trying to kill me!"

Mary Grace turned to the old woman. "That's silly, Lucy. Someone set a fire to make a point with *me*, not you."

"They set fire to the kitchen door." Lucy waved at the blackened wood. "And right here when I usually arrive!" Her voice rose again. "I think it was the KKK!"

Mary Grace frowned. "As far as I know, there's never been any Ku Klux Klan activity in Bethany Beach. Why would you say that?"

Lucy dissolved into tears. "Just because you've never heard of it doesn't mean it doesn't happen. I saw a movie on television, and it started just like this with a little fire. Next thing you know, they'll be shooting at my house and burning crosses in my yard!"

Mary Grace walked over and put her arm around the old woman. "Oh, Lucy, I think you're overreacting."

"I'm so afraid!" Lucy buried her cottony head in Mary Grace's shoulder. "I have to call my son to come and get me this minute. I'm sorry, Mary Grace, but I won't be able to work for you anymore."

This was not entirely bad news, but the timing was inconvenient. "I completely understand," Mary Grace replied. "But please stay at least through breakfast."

Lucy was already shaking her head. "My hands are shaking so bad I couldn't hold a spoon." She reached for the hotel phone mounted on the wall and started dialing. "Good land of the living, I can't get out of here soon enough!"

When Lucy's son arrived, Mary Grace assured him that there was no danger. But Lucy was crying and insisted that he take her home, so there was nothing left to be said. They left as the fire chief arrived to tell her that the crisis was over. Sheriff Thompson was with him.

"We've taken some samples of the door to run tests, but I think it's safe to say that this fire did not start on its own," the chief told her. "You need to be alert for the next several days and call us if you notice anything strange."

"I will."

"I'll have a deputy drive by here every hour or so," Sheriff Thompson promised. "And I can be here in just a few minutes if you need me."

"Thanks," Mary Grace said with a tired smile. Then the sheriff and fire chief left, and it was just Mary Grace and John in the damaged kitchen. "Well," she sighed, "I guess I'd better go to the grocery store and get some Pop Tarts for breakfast."

John smiled. "I'm not a gourmet cook, but omelettes are one of my few specialties. If you've got eggs and cheese, we could throw together a breakfast."

Mary Grace was so touched that John was trying to come to her rescue again. "You're a guest here, and . . ."

He walked over and lifted her chin with his fingers. "Hey, you've been helping me, and all this is probably my fault for involving you. Making breakfast is the least I can do."

It was impossible to think with his hand on her face, so she nodded. "Okay. Thanks." She walked to the refrigerator and started pulling out the items he had requested. "We also have bell peppers and bacon and ham."

"Ahhh," John said as he chose a frying pan from the collection hanging over the island. "Our success is ensured."

Mary Grace found a large package of frozen biscuits in the freezer and arranged two dozen on a large cookie sheet. Then she got out juice and butter and various jellies and put them on the buffet table while John created omelettes. "Do you need any help?"

He glanced up from the stove. "I think it would be best to leave it to the expert."

In spite of her anxiety and exhaustion, Mary Grace smiled. "In that case, I'm going to go put on some clothes before my guests start arriving for breakfast."

He looked at the hospital scrubs she was wearing. "You look fine to me."

Untying her apron, she moved toward the door. "Thanks, but I think my guests would appreciate it if I didn't smell like a campfire."

She hurried to her apartment and took a quick shower, then realized that the campfire smell was going to be impossible to avoid since all the clothes in her closet and drawers had been exposed to the smoke. She pulled on a cotton dress and dried her hair quickly, then sprayed herself liberally with perfume before returning to the kitchen, where John had three huge omelettes waiting for her guests.

"This one is just cheese for the unadventurous." He pointed at the next platter with a spatula. "Here we have one with peppers and onions for the ones with iron stomachs." He directed her attention to the third platter. "And finally, one for the meat lovers. I found sausage in your refrigerator and added that to the ham and bacon."

Mary Grace was touched by the effort he had put into breakfast. "I don't know how I can ever thank you."

He pursed his lips. "Hmmm, maybe you could solve the Victoria Harte murder case so I can write an award-winning article and earn my way back into my editor's good graces."

"I was thinking something more along the lines of a discount on your room for today," she replied, then picked up the plate of biscuits and took them to the dining room. John followed with the omelettes, and after arranging some fruit in a bowl, Mary Grace stepped back and surveyed their efforts. "A very well-balanced and delicious meal," she said with satisfaction.

John leaned toward her and whispered, "And waking up to a hotel fire probably gave your guests quite an appetite."

She was so distracted by his breath on her ear that she couldn't even think up a clever reply. She was saved by the arrival of the first breakfast guests. John described the choices to everyone, then offered to serve, but Mary Grace shook her head. "Nope. That's where I draw the line. Fix your plate and go sit down."

"Only if you'll sit by me," he stipulated.

With a sigh, she put some of the cheese omelette on her plate and led the way to the banquet table. Miss Eugenia chose some of the meat lover's omelette, and Annabelle made an estimate about the number of fat grams in a serving. "Not to mention cholesterol," she added.

Miss Eugenia put two biscuits on her plate and buttered both liberally. "I had bran muffins for breakfast yesterday. It all evens out."

She walked over to where John and Mary Grace were sitting. "Has anyone thought to ask Mr. Tamburelli where he was just before your fire broke out?" she whispered loudly.

Mary Grace looked around to be sure the subject of their conversation was not in the room, then shook her head. "I suppose he was in bed like all the rest of us."

Miss Eugenia raised an eyebrow as all the other ladies from Haggerty took seats nearby. "I thought it was interesting that he was the last person to arrive in the parking lot after you made the emergency announcement. Almost as if he *knew* there was no real danger."

"We've asked the sheriff to check on him," Mary Grace replied, making a mental note to determine if any progress had been made on this promise.

"Humph," Miss Eugenia showed her disdain. "I heard your cook quit because of the fire."

Mary Grace nodded. "Yes, she felt that the fire was started by the KKK, and she's terrified. I hope that she'll reconsider, but in the meantime I'm in a bind."

"I'd be glad to give you a hand in the kitchen," Miss Polly said, then blushed crimson.

"Oh no," Mary Grace said quickly. "I couldn't let you do that."

"But you need help," Miss Polly insisted.

"I'll find someone from . . . somewhere," Mary Grace said without much optimism.

Miss Polly stood up straight, a hand to her heaving bosom. "I love to cook, but I hate shopping in outlet stores and touring pirate ships and attending church on battleships." Her cheeks turned pink again as she glanced at Miss Eugenia. "And I really hate fish, especially big ones that splash you with seawater. I'm sorry, Eugenia, but that's the truth. All these years I've been coming with you and doing whatever you wanted to do. Now it's my turn." Her gaze swung over to Mary Grace. "I've always dreamed of owning my own restaurant. Cooking for your guests for a couple of days would be the next-best thing."

No one could argue. "Well, I guess all I can say is thank you," Mary Grace said finally. "After breakfast, we'll go over the menus Lucy had planned and the contents of our pantry. You're welcome to change anything, and I'll pick up whatever groceries you need."

Miss Polly nodded graciously. "That will be fine."

Just then the Rayburns walked in and stopped to speak to Mary Grace on their way to the buffet table. "We've decided to stay out the week," Leo said with a smile. "After all, lightning rarely strikes twice in the same place."

"The kitchen door was hit by lightning?" Farrah asked, her eyes wide.

Leo shook his head. "No, honey, that was just a figure of speech meaning that it's unlikely that there will be another fire here."

Farrah nodded her carefully tousled curls. "Ohhhh."

"And the sheriff promised to send a deputy by every hour or so," Mary Grace added, trying to act as though she wasn't worried about a recurrence, "which actually makes the Arms safer than the other hotels nearby."

Leo grinned. "See there, Babycakes? We'd be *crazy* to move to a different hotel."

"But you promise we'll go to Cancun next summer?" Farrah confirmed, and her husband nodded.

"I'm glad you've decided to stay," Mary Grace told them with practiced poise. "Now please get something to eat. Mr. Wright made omelettes, and they are delicious."

"Everything certainly smells good," Leo agreed, rubbing his hands together.

"I'd rather have a Hawaiian icy at that little stand on the beach," Farrah said, looking toward the door.

Leo gave them an abashed look, then led Farrah toward the food table.

John raised an eyebrow as the honeymooners moved away. "It's not hard to see who runs the show in that family," he murmured.

Before Mary Grace could respond, Mr. Tamburelli came in. He got a plate full of breakfast, then took a seat far enough away from everyone else to discourage conversation but close enough to hear what was said.

"The missing link," Annabelle mouthed as she sat down across from them. Then she raised her voice. "So, tell us what happened, Mary Grace. Did you sense danger and wake up?"

Mary Grace shook her head. "No, I probably would have died of smoke inhalation if someone hadn't knocked on my bedroom window."

John frowned. "Someone knocked on your window?"

She nodded. "That's what woke me up."

John didn't look convinced. "Maybe you just dreamed that someone knocked on your window."

"Or it could have been heavenly intervention like on *Touched by an Angel*," Miss Polly contributed.

"Why don't you think someone really knocked on my window?" Mary Grace asked John.

"The only person who *knew* about the fire is the person who *started* the fire," he explained. "And I think it's very strange that someone would go to the trouble of setting the fire, then waking you up so you could get help before any major damage was done."

Little worry lines formed between Mary Grace's eyes. "That is a little strange."

"Did the sheriff dust for fingerprints?" Miss Eugenia asked.

"I don't think so," Mary Grace replied. "But they did take some samples of the burned area and will run tests to determine how the fire was started." She gave her guests a cheerful smile. "But let's not dwell on it. The whole thing was probably just a teenage prank."

While her guests finished breakfast, Mary Grace went to the front desk. She called Windy and asked the girl to come into work immediately. Mary Grace barely had time to hang up the phone before it rang. It was Heath Pointer.

"Pete Thompson told me about the fire at the Arms!" he said with obvious alarm. "Is everyone okay?"

"We're fine, and the sheriff said all the damage should be covered by my insurance. I was hoping you could call them for me and arrange for an adjuster to come out, or whatever it is you're supposed to do when you have a claim."

"I'll handle the insurance and arrange for the repairs, but this may hurt your chances of getting a small business loan," Heath said. "I've gotten proposals from three investors, but if they get wind of an arson attack . . ."

"We're not sure it was arson. Someone might have just thrown a cigarette."

"Then how did the kitchen door get saturated with gasoline?" Heath wanted to know.

"Is that how they started the fire?"

"Yes," Heath confirmed.

Mary Grace sighed. "Okay, so it probably was arson, but it was an isolated incident and shouldn't make a difference to a lender."

"Lenders can be very skittish. Why don't you let me hire a security guard to watch the Arms during the night? It wouldn't cost much, and it would be worth the peace of mind knowing you were safe."

"Thanks, Heath. But if I feel that a security guard is necessary, I'll pay for one myself. And as far as lenders go, I want to stick with banks."

There was a brief pause, then Heath said, "That will be much harder. Private investors are willing to take more risks."

"I'll use the Arms as collateral," Mary Grace told him. "Although I had another idea that might keep me from having to take out a loan. Do you remember the Forrest Merek painting in the foyer of Justin's apartment?"

"That garish, orange-triangle thing?" Heath asked. "How could I forget it?"

Mary Grace laughed. "It may be ugly, but he told me it was valuable. The fire last night was a grim reminder that *things* can be destroyed. So I thought I might like to get it appraised and see how much it's worth. I'm not saying I'd sell it," she clarified quickly, "but I might, if the price is right."

"I've worked with an antique dealer in Destin several times, and I think he makes house calls," Heath replied. "I'll ask him to come by."

"Try to set it up this week so we can adjust the loan amount if I decide to sell the painting." *Or cancel it altogether*, she thought to herself.

"Will do. I'll stop by later and look at the fire damage. Then maybe I can talk you into going for a ride or something. You need to get away from the Arms for a while."

"I have almost a full house, Heath. I can't leave. But thanks for the offer," she told him firmly, then said good-bye and hung up the phone.

After her conversation with Heath, Mary Grace returned to the kitchen and started cleaning up the mess made by the fire and the men who had put it out. John found her there a few minutes later and began helping, even though she asked him several times not to.

"So, what are your plans for the day?" she asked in an effort to remind him that he had a job to do and couldn't spend all morning with her in the kitchen.

He considered this as he gathered dirty tablecloths for the laundry. "I've got an appointment with Sheriff Thompson at ten o'clock." He checked his watch. "And I guess I'd better start getting ready or I'll be late."

She smiled. "And you don't want to get on his bad side."

John laughed. "Oh, no, I don't want that."

He handed her the tablecloths, then she followed him to the front door. "Thanks again." The words were inadequate but had to be said.

"You're welcome. Keep your fingers crossed for me," he requested, then stepped outside.

Mary Grace couldn't keep from smiling as she walked to the linen closet. She pulled stacks of clean sheets off the shelves and realized that her laundry problems were worse than she had anticipated. The clean linens smelled like smoke and would have to be washed before she could even begin cleaning each individual room.

Mary Grace started both washers, then went into the lobby, where Windy had just arrived. Mary Grace asked her to stay at the desk and answer the phone while she dusted ash from the lobby and swept up debris that had been tracked in during the crisis. She was headed back to the laundry room when Miss Polly found her.

"We were going to go over the menus for the week," Miss Polly reminded her.

"I don't know how I could have forgotten that!" Mary Grace said with a sigh. They walked into the kitchen, and she pulled out the calendar Lucy used to schedule meals. She had chicken pot pie written in for Monday night and a chicken casserole for Tuesday.

"The main dishes are too similar on both days," Miss Polly said with a frown. "Would you mind if I changed Tuesday's menu?"

"I don't mind at all," Mary Grace assured her. She gave her a quick tour of the kitchen, pointing out appliances, utensils, pans, and the pantry. "After you have a chance to look over everything, let me know what else you need."

Miss Polly nodded. "I'll try to manage with the contents of your pantry for today, and I'll have a grocery list waiting for you in the morning."

"It would help me out a lot if I don't have to go to the store today since I have so much laundry to do," Mary Grace admitted as the desk bell rang. Windy was supposed to be in the lobby, and Mary Grace gritted her teeth as she went to see who had arrived. When she walked up to the registration desk, she found her visiting teachers standing there, *Ensign* in hand.

"Good morning!" they greeted in unison.

"We're a few minutes early. I hope that's all right," Sister Westover added.

Mary Grace let her shoulders sag. "I completely forgot about our appointment. We had a little fire last night, and all the sheets smell like smoke, so I've got mountains of laundry to do before I can clean the guest rooms," she continued. "And I've got more guests arriving soon."

The visiting teachers exchanged a glance, then Sister Mills spoke for them both. "Well, it sounds like instead of an inspirational message, you need two pairs of willing hands. We'll start stripping the beds and putting the clean sheets on them as they are ready."

Mary Grace had to blink back tears. "I couldn't ask you to do that."

"You didn't ask us," Sister Mills replied. "Now point us in the right direction."

With the help of her visiting teachers, Mary Grace had all the guest rooms cleaned before lunchtime. The sisters left with baskets of sheets, which they promised to launder at home and return the next day. Mary Grace put most of her own clothes into the washers, then walked back to the desk, composing a thank-you note to her visiting teachers in her mind. Then the front door opened and a couple walked in.

The man was tall with dark hair, and for a second Mary Grace thought it was John. Then she saw that he was holding a little girl with curling pigtails. The woman with him had light brown hair and tired eyes. A sleeping infant was curled in the crook of her arm.

Mary Grace smiled. "You must be the Iversons."

"Your lucky contest winners," Mark Iverson said, and Mary Grace wondered if he was on to Miss Eugenia's free vacation giveaway.

"Welcome to the Bethany Arms Hotel," Mary Grace greeted them. "You've been assigned to a room with a beautiful view of the ocean. It is also conveniently right next door to Miss Eugenia Atkins."

Mark raised an eyebrow. "That has its pluses and minuses."

As if drawn by internal radar, Miss Eugenia appeared at that very moment. The little girl in Mark's arms squealed with joy and lunged. Miss Eugenia caught her just in time. "I declare, Emily, I'm delighted to see you, too," the elderly lady said. "But next time wait until I'm a little closer before you jump." Miss Eugenia settled the little girl on her hip, then turned to examine the baby. "Looks like he's gained a pound since Friday."

Kate Iverson shook her head. "I doubt that, but he is eating well."

"He's not even two months old," Miss Eugenia said for Mary Grace's benefit. "And already sleeping through the night."

Mary Grace had no idea what the normal time frame was for such an accomplishment. "That's amazing," she said, hoping it was.

"Both of you look like you could use some fun," Miss Eugenia said. "Let's get your suitcases unloaded, then we'll put the babies in the stroller and go to Underwater World. They have dolphins that sing and a huge whale named Melville that does back flips."

"Your room is right this way." Mary Grace led them out the back door and around to the James J. Pettigrew Room. She helped the Iversons get their luggage inside while Miss Eugenia followed along, listing the various tourist attractions.

"There's a petting zoo that Emily will love and several baby stores in the outlet mall. There are great places to eat, and we'll have to build some sand castles."

"This vacation may be more exhausting than staying at home," Mark whispered to his wife.

Mary Grace pretended that she didn't hear and returned to the lobby. John was waiting by the front desk. "You're back already?" she asked.

"Yes. It didn't take long for Sheriff Thompson to tell me that they still can't find the report about Victoria's death. Then I tried to get him to give me his theories about what happened here last night, but he had a sudden memory lapse. I barely got two words out of him."

"Sheriff Thompson isn't a big talker, but he's a very nice man. He's helped me out many times."

John acknowledged this with a nod. "This afternoon I have an appointment with a nurse who used to work for Dr. Chandler. She's living in a retirement home, and I'm counting on her being lonely enough to be willing to talk to anyone, even me."

"Was she at the Seafoam the night Victoria died?" Mary Grace asked in surprise.

"No, but Victoria had been a patient of Dr. Chandler's for years, and after Victoria died I figure there had to have been some talk around the office."

"It was twenty-five years ago, John."

"Some things you remember." He shrugged. "I know it's another long shot, but I'm running out of time and options," he finished as a man walked through the front door.

"May I help you?" Mary Grace asked politely.

"I certainly hope so," the man responded. "My name is Roscoe Vincent, and I have a reservation."

John was eyeing the man suspiciously as Mary Grace looked down at the register. "Oh yes, Mr. Vincent, you're in the Jerome Bonaparte Robertson Room." She processed his credit card quickly, then picked up the keys and started for the front door, hoping to keep John from making the connection.

"I am supposed to meet a Miss Wendy Thigpen," Mr. Vincent added. "Would you get word to her that I'm here?" he asked, and John's eyes narrowed.

He took a step toward the new guest. "Her name is Windy, like 'cloudy,'" John corrected. "And why would you need to meet with her?"

Mr. Vincent studied John for a few seconds, then smiled. "Mr. Wright, I presume."

"Yes, John Wright, not John Kennedy. I'll be happy to let you see my driver's license."

The man shook his head. "That won't be necessary."

Mary Grace felt greatly relieved. "Because you already know that he's not JFK, Jr.?"

"Because I don't care *who* he is. We've had a report of a bona fide John-John sighting. I'll write up a story, tell the readers we're doing DNA tests on your hair samples, and print a picture taken from a distance. It will make for a nice write-up."

Mary Grace stared at the man. "You mean you're still going to print the story even though you know it's not true?"

"I'll sue," John said.

Mr. Vincent smiled. "I doubt it, since the only person you have a case against is Windy Thigpen." He turned to Mary Grace. "And everything I print will be completely true. We did receive a report that JFK, Jr. was staying here. We do have a hair sample. There is a resemblance."

"You're taking advantage of a teenager," Mary Grace accused him.

Mr. Vincent shrugged. "I'm making a living." He glanced at John. "Just like everybody else."

Mary Grace straightened her shoulders. "Well, you can make your living from another hotel. I'm afraid I can't allow you to stay at the Arms."

Mr. Vincent held up his credit card receipt. "I'm afraid you already have." He took the keys from her hand. "I'll find my own way." He walked out the front door, and John moved to follow, but Mary Grace put a hand out to stop him.

"He'll be gone in a day, and getting into a fight with him will only make his trip here more successful."

"I *hate* people like him. They are what give reporters a bad name." Before Mary Grace could respond, the front door opened again and a couple walked in.

She glanced up, then sighed in resignation. "Hello, Mother, Daddy. This is John Wright."

John turned and nodded. "Mr. and Mrs. O'Malley."

"Mr. Wright," Catherine O'Malley said, extending a hand politely.

"I'm Mike," Mary Grace's father said as the men clasped hands.

"John is a newspaper reporter in Savannah," Mary Grace explained. "He's here in Bethany Beach working on an article."

"It was nice to meet you," he told the O'Malleys. "But I'd better get busy. See you later," he added with a wave at Mary Grace. Then he walked out the door.

Once he was gone, Catherine O'Malley walked over to give her daughter a hug. "Pete Thompson called and said you'd had a fire this morning!"

Mary Grace frowned. "The sheriff shouldn't have worried you. Everything is fine."

"He's always looked out for you," Mrs. O'Malley said. "I remember that time you decided to take the sailboat out when you were seven and he stopped you."

"Probably saved your life," her husband added.

Catherine nodded. "And after Justin died, he expressed concern about you trying to run this place alone. Now it looks like his concerns were well-founded."

Mary Grace sighed. Sometimes having so many people who cared about her could be a burden. "I know that Sheriff Thompson was looking out for me, but honestly, there's nothing to worry about." She had things to do and didn't want to spend the afternoon reassuring her parents, so she decided to kill two birds with one stone. "Why don't you come back for dinner tonight? Lucy quit, and I have a new temporary chef. You can try out her cooking. Bobby will be there," she added as incentive. Both her parents were crazy about Dr. Chandler's grandson.

"I'd be glad to help out in the kitchen if you need me to," her mother offered, and Mary Grace smiled.

"That is so kind of you," Mary Grace said with a smile. "But I have enough problems already."

Mike laughed at the joke, but Catherine O'Malley gave her daughter an irritated look. "In spite of that remark, we'll be here at seven o'clock. Come on, Mike, dear. We've got errands to run."

Mary Grace winked at her father as he followed his wife out the door.

CHAPTER 9

After her parents were gone, Mary Grace sat at the desk and called Jennifer.

"Are you still alive?" she asked.

"Barely," Jennifer croaked in reply. "The doctor called in a new prescription this morning. Maybe it will help us feel better."

"If you have the flu, there's really nothing the doctors can give you," Mary Grace observed.

"Are you trying to cheer me up or send me into the depths of depression?" Jennifer demanded.

Mary Grace laughed. "Sorry. I'm sure the new medicine will work wonders. And my offer to bring chicken soup is still good."

"Thanks anyway, but Stan's mother is giving me all the help I can stand. Call me tomorrow and maybe I'll feel like talking."

After Jennifer hung up, Mary Grace went to the kitchen and told Miss Polly that they were having extra guests at dinner. "Oh, I always make plenty," Miss Polly assured her.

"Is there anything I can do?" Mary Grace asked, looking around at the ingredients spread out on the counters.

"No, dear. You know the old saying—too many cooks spoil the broth."

Satisfied that matters were well taken care of in the kitchen, Mary Grace went to the laundry room to wash more of her clothes and collect a pile of things to be sent to the dry cleaners. She was debating on whether to trust Windy with the task when another stranger walked in. Mentally reviewing the available rooms, she realized that the Arms was almost full, not counting the Edmund Kirby Smith Room, which was without hot water.

"May I help you?" she asked the man, and he smiled.

"Actually, I'm here to help you. Heath Pointer said you've got a painting you want to have appraised."

Mary Grace smiled and waved for him to follow her toward her apartment. "That was quick."

"I teach a class at the technical school on Mondays and Wednesdays, so you were on my way home."

Mary Grace opened the apartment door and pointed to the picture hanging in the entryway. "This is a Forrest Merek?" the man asked in surprise.

"I've been told that most of his famous paintings were southwest landscapes, so I figured this must be one of his early ones." *And therefore even more valuable*, she thought to herself.

"Hmmm." The man concentrated on the painting for a few seconds, then opened his bag and removed a magnifying glass. After about two minutes of examination, he closed the bag and turned to face Mary Grace. "Well, I'm finished."

"So soon?" She had expected him to take the painting with him so it could be chemical tested or x-rayed or whatever appraisers did. "When can you tell me the value?"

"Right now," the man said as he lifted his bag, "it is completely worthless."

Mary Grace was stunned. "Worthless?" She could still see Justin standing right where the appraiser was, telling her never to sell the painting. How could it be worthless?

"For one thing, it wasn't painted by Forrest Merek."

Mary Grace stared at the signature scrawled in the corner. "It has his name on it."

The appraiser smiled. "Anyone can write a name. But Forrest Merek didn't paint *or* sign this."

"How can you be sure?"

"It's not his style . . ." the appraiser began, and Mary Grace interrupted.

"He might have used a different style for one picture, especially if it was painted early in his career."

"He might have," the appraiser agreed. "But in addition to the huge discrepancy in technique, this painting was done in acrylic. Merek used only oils."

"Again, he might have been experimenting."

The man took a step toward the door. "But the most conclusive evidence is that the painting is dated almost a full year after Merek died." The appraiser pointed to the date printed under the signature in the corner. "I'm sorry, miss, but this is a forgery."

Mary Grace did her best to maintain dignity in the face of terrible disappointment. "Well, I guess there's nothing else to be said. How much do I owe you?"

The man shook his head. "Heath told me to send the bill to him."

"Thank you for coming by."

"Wish I could have given you better news," he said as they returned to the lobby.

"Me too," she agreed. The appraiser walked out, and John Wright walked in.

"Who's that?" he asked.

"The appraiser Heath sent over to look at my Merek painting."

"So, how much is it worth?"

"Nothing. He says it's a worthless fake."

John's eyebrows rose. "You're kidding."

"No, and it's very puzzling."

John followed her back to her apartment, and they stood staring at the painting.

"Why would Justin tell me to keep a worthless painting?" she asked aloud.

"Maybe he didn't know it was a fake," John suggested.

Mary Grace shook her head. "This place is full of expensive antiques. Justin knew about things like that. No one could have tricked him with a forged painting."

"So, if the painting is not valuable in monetary terms, there must be something else."

"Sentiment?" she proposed.

"Maybe somebody special gave it to him? Like his parents or an old girlfriend?"

"I think his parents died several years ago, even before this picture was supposedly painted. I guess it could have been from an old girl-friend, but why would he tell me it was valuable if it's not?"

"Maybe it's a treasure map," John proposed. "And one of those ugly little triangles points toward the chest of gold."

Mary Grace gave him an exasperated look. "Even if I thought that was a serious suggestion, all the triangles are pointing different directions. So it can't be a map, treasure or otherwise."

John smiled. "That's true. I guess we'll never know the answer. And I have to say, for a little town, Bethany Beach sure is full of mysteries."

Mary Grace acknowledged this with a shrug. "How did your conversation with Dr. Chandler's old nurse go?"

"I know all about her great-grandchildren, her fellow inmates at the retirement home, and the rash that she's developed on her back, which she thinks is a reaction to harsh laundry detergent."

Mary Grace raised her eyebrows. "Did she tell you anything about Victoria?"

John smiled. "The old nurse remembers Victoria well."

Mary Grace walked over and sat on the couch. "Because of her promiscuity or her tragic death?"

John took the chair across from her. "More because she was the mayor's daughter and one of their patients. Nurse Perkins seemed like sort of a social climber—if there is such a thing in Bethany Beach."

"Are you kidding me?" Mary Grace demanded. "Small southern towns have the tightest social circles in the world." She paused a second to think, then shook her head. "I've seen Mrs. Perkins a few times, but don't really know her."

"Well, she said that Dr. Chandler had been Victoria's physician since she was born. The mother brought her in for all her immunizations and childhood ailments, but when Victoria turned twelve her father brought her for a special appointment—to get her started on birth control pills."

"At twelve!" Mary Grace was appalled.

"Mrs. Perkins said he made a big point of how all responsible parents should follow his example and put an end to teenage pregnancy. She said it was like he was doing a campaign speech or something."

"Did she remember how Victoria reacted?"

"Very embarrassed, according to Mrs. Perkins. She blames Victoria's subsequent wild behavior on that one moment. She thinks Victoria was trying to live up to her father's low expectations and that her father was actually pleased because he could point to her and say 'Look how much worse things would be if I hadn't been responsible enough to start her on birth control.'"

Mary Grace thought of her own father, sweet and unassuming. She couldn't begin to imagine him dragging her into a doctor's office and telling everyone that since he was sure she had no morals, he wanted her started on medication to prevent pregnancy. She shook her head and felt her bond with Victoria Harte strengthen.

She looked over at John, who was still staring at the fake painting. "This was Mrs. Perkins theory," he said finally. "There's another possibility that comes to mind." She heard the dread in his voice.

"What?"

"That Victoria was being abused by her father and he wanted to make sure no baby resulted," he proposed. "Of course, I don't have any evidence to support that."

"Except that Susie Ireland said Victoria's father was the devil," Mary Grace pointed out as they returned to the lobby.

John acknowledged this with a weary sigh. "Why couldn't this be just a simple case like the others?"

Mary Grace didn't feel sorry for him. "You thrive on adversity."

He seemed surprised. "You think so?"

"You knew a twenty-five-year-old murder mystery wouldn't be easy to solve, but you came anyway."

His eyes met hers for a few seconds. "You're right. I did."

They walked back to the lobby just as Annabelle and Miss George Ann arrived. John waved to Mary Grace as she turned to speak to her guests. "So, ladies, did you have a good day?"

Annabelle sighed. "It's amazing how much more pleasant sight-seeing is without Eugenia."

Mary Grace laughed. "Where did you go?"

"We spent the day at the Sandestin Golf Resort," Miss George Ann disclosed.

"I didn't know you were interested in golf."

"We're not, really," Miss George Ann admitted. "But they have a wonderful restaurant where you can sit and look out over the golf course. It's beautiful and relaxing."

"And nobody was bugging us to run to one location after another," Annabelle added, "following suspicious-looking strangers."

"I haven't seen Miss Eugenia since the Iversons arrived," Mary Grace said.

"We saw Kate and Mark in the parking lot a few minutes ago," Annabelle told her. "They said Eugenia dragged them to a zoo this morning. Now they're headed to the store while Eugenia watches the babies take their naps." Annabelle rolled her eyes. "She thinks she's their grandmother."

Mary Grace smiled. "Well, I'd better go check on Miss Polly and see how things are coming for dinner."

"Knowing Polly, she's gone all out," Miss George Ann predicted.

When Mary Grace got to the kitchen, this proved to be true. Miss Polly had five pans of homemade chicken pot pie ready to go into the oven. "Lucy uses the frozen kind from Sam's," she told Miss Polly. "There are plenty of them in the freezer."

The older lady blushed. "I know, but I never serve anything frozen. Pot pies are easy. It only took a few minutes."

Mary Grace looked around at the flour and shortening on the counter and the potato peelings in the sink. "It only takes a few minutes to make pie crusts and peel enough potatoes for five pies?"

This time Miss Polly giggled. "I haven't had this much fun since I left Georgia." She reached for a piece of paper on the counter. "And these are the things I'll need for tomorrow."

Mary Grace reviewed the list, then offered again to help, but Miss Polly insisted she had things under control. So Mary Grace went into the dining room and prepared the tables. Since she was having a large crowd, she set up two separate tables.

At six Mary Grace went to her apartment and took a quick shower. Afterwards she put on a dress that smelled like smoke and sprayed an extra puff of perfume. Then she hurried back to the dining room.

She considered the night's seating arrangement while she helped Miss Polly put the food on the buffet table. She knew she should seat John as far away from herself as possible, and there was no way to avoid sitting by her parents. But if she put Miss Eugenia and the Iversons beside John, she could keep the conversation from becoming personal and still get to enjoy John's company. She knew Mr. Vincent would want to be near John and chose a seat for him at the other table.

As the guests arrived for dinner, Mary Grace settled them according to her mental seating chart. She put Annabelle and Miss George Ann at one table and invited Miss Polly to sit at the head of the other. "Oh, the position of honor," Miss Polly breathed. "You should sit there."

"You certainly deserve to be honored after all your hard work," Mary Grace insisted.

Bobby arrived with her parents, so she was able to sit them together at Miss Polly's right. Then the Iversons walked in without Miss Eugenia and explained that both babies were asleep, so their volunteer baby-sitter had decided to stay in the room.

"We are instructed to bring her a plate of food, though," Kate said with a smile.

Mary Grace tried not to show her disappointment as she seated the Iversons across from her parents. Without Miss Eugenia to provide distracting conversation, the night could prove to be a long one. The Rayburns came in, and Mary Grace sat them at the second table. She had almost given up on Mr. Tamburelli when he finally arrived. His face was red, and he walked with a stiff gait.

"Are you okay?" Mary Grace asked him, and he nodded.

"Sunburn," he explained shortly.

Mary Grace studied him closely. "Quite a bad one, I'd say. You should have worn sunblock."

The man shrugged. "I didn't think to bring any."

Mary Grace frowned and thought of all Miss Eugenia's suspicions about the man. She wasn't sure who Mr. Tamburelli was, but she had to agree that it was strange for a man to come to the beach without proper clothing or sunblock. She led him to the second table and sat him beside Miss George Ann, then walked back and took a seat between Kate Iverson and John Wright.

Mary Grace made introductions and told everyone that Miss Polly had prepared the meal. Then she invited Mark Iverson to say the blessing. As they filled their plates, it started to rain. "Is it supposed to storm tonight?" Mary Grace asked. She usually kept abreast of the weather so she could inform her guests, but the last few days had been so eventful that she'd forgotten.

"Just scattered thunderstorms," her father replied as they settled back around the tables. "Nothing severe."

"Not like the night you were born," her mother remarked. "You made your entrance into the world during the worst storm in Bethany Beach history."

This was exactly the type of topic that Mary Grace had hoped to avoid. "My guests don't want to hear about that," she said quickly.

"On the contrary," John contradicted. "I'd love to hear about your birth."

Kate Iverson smiled. "It sounds exciting."

Mary Grace turned to Bobby for support, but he shrugged. "I've heard bits and pieces of the story, but I'd like to hear the whole thing."

Mary Grace sighed in defeat as her mother proudly continued. "Mike and I postponed parenthood until we were both well established in our careers. That seemed like the sensible thing to do, but we found that when we were ready for a baby, my body was not. It took us several years of working with a fertility specialist to finally conceive."

"Please, Mother, not too many details," Mary Grace begged. Her parents were children of the sixties and could on occasion get carried away with their freedom of expression.

"I just wanted everyone to understand what a long-anticipated event your birth was," Catherine defended herself as Mike O'Malley reached into his back pocket and removed his wallet. He pulled out an old snapshot and passed it around.

"This is Catherine standing in front of the Christmas tree that year."

"Mike, I can't believe you still have that old thing!" Catherine cried, but her pleasure was obvious. Mary Grace suppressed a moan as she looked at the picture of her very pregnant mother smiling at the camera.

"You are their pride and joy," John whispered as he studied the snapshot.

"Which can be stifling," she returned quietly.

The Rayburns finished their meal and walked over to Mary Grace. "We've had a long day. I think we'll call it a night," Leo said.

"But you haven't had dessert," Miss Polly exclaimed.

"I've eaten so much since I've been here, I can barely get into my bikini," Farrah said with a toss of her blonde curls.

The thought of a fifty-something-year-old woman—no matter how fit—in a bikini made Mary Grace a little ill. Then she saw the look of distaste on John's face and had to put her napkin up to cover a smile. "Well, we'll see you in the morning," she told the Rayburns.

Mr. Tamburelli stood just after the Rayburns left and said that he was going to take a cold shower and see if it would help his sunburn.

"If I were you, I'd check at the drugstore and see if they have a cream that can ease the pain," Miss Polly told him, frowning at his sun-darkened skin.

"If I were you, I'd go to the emergency room," Catherine O'Malley advised. "I'll bet those are second-degree burns on your head."

Mr. Tamburelli put a hand to his tender scalp, then winced. Mumbling something under his breath, he shuffled out of the room. Mr. Vincent waved from his seat at the end of the second table. "I guess I might as well go to my room too," he said with an insincere smile. "Since I have an article to write."

Mary Grace glared in his direction, then waited until he was gone before inviting Miss George Ann and Annabelle to join them at the head table for dessert.

"We heard you telling about the night Mary Grace was born," Annabelle said to the O'Malleys as they pulled up their chairs. "And now we'll be able to hear the rest of the story without straining our ears."

"Let me get the pies first so you won't have to be interrupted," Miss Polly suggested as she stood and moved toward the kitchen.

"I'll help," Mary Grace offered, but Miss Polly waved her down.

"It's just a few pies. I can handle it."

Once the guests were served, Catherine O'Malley continued her story.

"Since I was forty by the time I finally got pregnant, my doctor kept close tabs on me," Catherine explained.

"We knew that this would be our only child, so Catherine took especially good care of herself." Mike patted his wife's hand.

"Did you have to stay in bed?" Miss Polly asked, then her cheeks turned pink.

"No." Catherine shook her head. "I had a healthy pregnancy. I was careful about what I ate, and read all kinds of books—which turned out to be a lucky thing since I went into labor while I was here alone."

"Alone!" Miss Polly gasped.

"We always have a big family get-together with my brothers and sisters during Christmas. We do it at our beach house here since it's convenient for everyone. That year Mike and I discussed having Christmas at our house in Atlanta, but it was still almost a month before my due date and I was feeling fine, so we decided to keep the tradition and spend Christmas in Bethany Beach."

"I had to be back at work the day after Christmas," Mike O'Malley picked up the story. "But Catherine didn't want to leave all the decorations out. So I went on to Atlanta and left her here, planning to come back on New Year's Eve and get her."

"The weather was unseasonably mild," Catherine told them. "I spent hours walking on the beach, looking forward to the moment when I would meet my baby."

Mary Grace met her mother's gaze, and they shared a smile.

"Mike called me on the afternoon of New Year's Eve and said he'd gotten tied up with some client."

"A tricky self-insurance policy," Mike said with a shake of his head. "Thought we'd never get it finished. By the time I left the office, the weather was getting bad, so I called Catherine. We decided that I should spend the night in Atlanta and drive down the next day to pick her up."

"The storm was bad down here too," Mrs. O'Malley told them. "Right after I talked to Mike, the power went out. I didn't want to worry him and didn't want him to be driving in the storm, so I went out to the storage shed behind the house to get the Coleman lantern. I tripped over a tree branch that had been blown down and put myself into labor."

"Actually, the doctor said it might have happened even if she hadn't fallen," Mike O'Malley amended. "Something about the position of the umbilical cord."

Mary Grace wanted to interrupt again, but she glanced around at all the rapt faces and decided to let the story run its course.

"I managed to get to Mrs. Crabtree's house next door," Catherine continued. "She was old and nearly blind, but she helped me inside my house and called Dr. Chandler. We had an awful time getting ahold of him, but finally he came."

All eyes turned to Bobby. "So your grandfather is a character in the story," Annabelle said with a smile.

"A major one," Mike agreed with a nod.

"Dr. Chandler came and delivered Mary Grace at your house?" Miss Polly prompted.

"Well, Dr. Chandler came, but Mary Grace didn't," Catherine explained. "The pains were terrible and went on for hours. In spite of the strong contractions, Dr. Chandler said I wasn't making much progress."

"Did the doctor call your husband?" Miss George Ann asked.

"Yes, at some point. I really don't remember when."

Mike O'Malley frowned in concentration. "I went out for a bite to eat, and when I got home there was a message on the answering machine. I guess it was about nine o'clock when I started for Bethany Beach, but because of the weather it took longer than usual to get here."

Catherine leaned forward. "Then Dr. Chandler told me that I needed to go to the hospital and have a cesarean section. I was scared and exhausted and begged him not to take me to the hospital until Mike got there." Catherine looked at her audience. "I know how irrational that sounds now, but at the time I just didn't think I could face it alone."

Kate nodded. "We understand."

"Finally Dr. Chandler said we couldn't wait any longer, and in spite of my protests, he picked up the phone to call an ambulance, but the lines were down. That was back before people had cellular phones and such. Poor old Mrs. Crabtree didn't drive, but she put on her slicker and walked up the street looking for a house with working phones. I had a terrible pain about then, and I think I must have lost consciousness for a time. When I woke up, Mrs. Crabtree was back. She had walked almost a mile without finding a house that had phone service."

Catherine smiled over at Mary Grace again. "The next thing I remember was Dr. Chandler standing beside the bed. He said that it was all over and I had a beautiful baby girl. I had come through the delivery just fine, but the baby was having some trouble breathing so he told me he was going to drive her to the hospital. He promised to send an ambulance for me as soon as he got there."

"Weren't you terrified?" Miss Polly asked.

Catherine considered this, then shook her head. "I was too tired to be scared. I had Mrs. Crabtree with me, and I just wanted Mary Grace to be in good hands. Dr. Chandler left with the baby, and I waited for the ambulance to come. But Mike got there first. He loaded me into the backseat of his car and drove me to the hospital. They wanted to take me to a room immediately, but I wouldn't go until I saw our baby girl. So Mike wheeled me to the intensive care nursery."

"Was Mary Grace still having breathing problems?" Annabelle wanted to know.

"No, she was breathing fine," Catherine assured everyone. "But they said it was hospital policy to put any baby born outside the hospital in the special care nursery so they could keep an eye on them."

"Mary Grace was perfect then, just like she is now," Mike said proudly. "Six pounds and two ounces. Pretty good for a month early."

"What a lovely story," Miss Polly said.

"Yes," Annabelle agreed. "Eugenia's going to be just sick that she missed it."

Miss Polly looked over at Bobby. "Your grandfather is a hero."

"He's always held a special place in my heart," Catherine said with feeling.

"I'll bet he was pleased to see you arrive at the hospital safely," John remarked.

Catherine frowned in concentration. "Actually, by the time Mike and I got there, Dr. Chandler been called away on another emergency."

John reached into his shirt pocket and pulled out a little slip of paper. "What day were you born?" he asked Mary Grace, his expression tense.

"December 31," she replied.

"A New Year's Eve baby!" Annabelle said with pleasure.

"Just in time to be a tax deduction," Mike said with a smile.

"Oh, goodness, we didn't care anything about tax deductions at the time," Catherine scolded her husband mildly. "We were just so pleased to have Mary Grace and that she was healthy."

John leaned closer to Mary Grace and whispered, "I was listening to the story. I know you were born on New Year's Eve. I wanted to know what *year*."

Mary Grace provided this information, and he made a quick note. "Why is that important?" she asked.

He looked up and shrugged. "It's not important, just interesting. You were born the same night Victoria Harte was killed, and the emergency Dr. Chandler went to handle after he got you to the hospital was almost certainly a stabbing death at the Seafoam Motel."

Mary Grace turned to her parents. "Do you remember that?"

Catherine thought for a minute, then shook her head. "I really don't. But then we were too wrapped up in you to watch television or even read the paper. And we drove straight from the hospital to our home in Atlanta when we were released."

"There wasn't much publicity," John told them. "I'm not surprised that you didn't know."

"I'm *glad* you didn't know," Miss Polly said with emotion. "It was a wonderful day in your life, and it didn't need to be spoiled by someone else's tragedy."

"Well, all this talking has made me hungry," Miss George Ann announced. "How about some more pie, Polly?"

"I won't say no to a second piece," Mike O'Malley admitted as the guests moved to the buffet table. "I think I'll try banana cream this time."

Mary Grace remained seated and noticed that John didn't rush toward the pies either. "You don't like banana cream pie?" she asked him.

He gave her a blank look, obviously still distracted.

"What's the matter?"

He shook his head. "Probably nothing. But I don't like coincidences, and this one slipped up on me."

She looked at the piece of paper in his hand. "You mean the fact that Victoria Harte died the night I was born?"

He nodded. "I wish your parents could remember something about that night that would help me." Then he smiled. "But I can see why they couldn't take their eyes off you."

Her heart skipped a beat, and she couldn't think of a sensible response. Finally he stood. "Maybe I will have some pie. How about you?"

"Whatever you're having," she managed.

The conversation changed to a debate on the candidates for president, and Mary Grace was content to listen to the others present their opinions. She watched John as much as she could without drawing attention to herself. She'd grown accustomed to his presence over the last few days, and when Friday came, it was going to be hard to say good-bye.

Her mood was a little melancholy by the time the folks from Haggerty retired for the night. As Mary Grace said good-bye to her parents, Catherine put a hand to her daughter's forehead. "Are you ill, dear?"

"I'm fine, Mother. Just tired."

"You work too hard," Catherine replied with a frown. "Heath called the other day and told me that a company wants to buy the Arms, but you won't even look at the offer."

Mary Grace was not pleased that Heath had mentioned Aztec Enterprises and their proposal to her parents. "I'm not ready to sell the Arms. Someday maybe, but not yet."

Catherine looked like she wanted to say more, but Mike stepped in. "Let's get home while the rain has stopped," he encouraged his wife. "Good night, honey." He kissed Mary Grace on the cheek, then ushered Catherine outside.

"Do you need some help cleaning up?" Bobby asked.

"No, thanks," she told him with a smile. "I'm sure Miss Polly has most everything done by now. I'd hire her in a heartbeat if I thought she'd come down here and run my kitchen."

"Well, in that case, I'll go home and leave some messages on my wife's answering machine," Bobby said, looking as dejected as Mary Grace felt.

After Bobby was gone, Mary Grace went into the dining room and started pulling tablecloths off tables. John followed along behind her, and once she had them all, he took them into his own arms.

"For a quiet girl, you had an exciting entrance into the world," John remarked as they walked toward the laundry room.

"If I had a dollar for every time I've heard that story," she told him, "I wouldn't need a loan to renovate the Arms." John distributed the tablecloths into the washers and watched as she started the wash cycle. "I guess we'd better check on Miss Polly."

John grinned. "Yeah, by now we've probably given her enough time to finish all the dishes."

Mary Grace rolled her eyes as they returned to the kitchen. Miss Polly had the dishwasher going and the whole room spotless. Mary Grace gave the old woman a hug. "You are an angel."

Miss Polly giggled. "It was so much fun! I wish I could stay here for the rest of my life."

"Me too," Mary Grace admitted, and Miss Polly giggled again. "Well, I know you must be tired, so please go on to bed."

"I will," Miss Polly agreed. "Breakfast comes early in the morning!"

They watched Miss Polly leave, then Mary Grace shook her head. "She really is an excellent cook."

"And very congenial," John added.

"And generous with her time."

John smiled. "Well, now that we're done singing her praises, how about a walk on the beach?"

Mary Grace stretched her hands over her head. "I'm too tired to walk. Why don't we just sit on the swing?"

"Fine by me."

He held the door open for her, and they walked out onto the sand. The air was still heavy with the recent rain, and a cool breeze blew up from the surf. She kicked off her shoes and luxuriated in the feel of the sand between her toes. John sat on the swing, waiting for her to sit beside him. When she did, he used his foot to begin a gentle sway.

"The thing that struck me most during dinner was how much your parents adore you," John said finally.

"Yes, they do. They are wonderful—a little overbearing and talkative sometimes, but I've never doubted their devotion." They were quiet for a few minutes, then Mary Grace turned slightly so she could look at him. "I'm going to admit something to you even though I know it opens me up for ridicule." She took a deep breath. "Which is something I never do."

He smiled. "Now this sounds interesting."

"Tonight when you realized that I was born around the time Victoria died, I had a funny feeling." He raised his eyebrows, but she forced herself to continue. "Like I'm connected to Victoria."

"Connected?"

Mary Grace was beginning to regret her attempt to explain the feeling, but she'd come too far to turn back now. "It's hard to describe, but I've had everything that Victoria didn't. Loving parents, a stable childhood, a chance to go to college and eventually find the gospel." She frowned in concentration. "Happiness."

John nodded. "But how does that connect you to Victoria?"

After a brief hesitation, Mary Grace blurted her theory out. "I wonder if your coming here wasn't by chance. Maybe Victoria wants the circumstances surrounding her death exposed, and she's counting on me to help you—almost like I owe her." Mary Grace waited for John to laugh, but he didn't.

"You've bonded with the victim," he said finally. "It happens a lot when I'm working a case, and it can be an advantage or disadvantage—depending."

"On what?"

"On whether getting too personally involved clouds my judgment."

As long as she'd told him this much, Mary Grace decided to admit the rest. "All those pictures you gave me of Victoria?"

He nodded.

"I taped them on the mirror above my dresser. I look at them every night until I fall asleep."

"Oh, Gracie," he sighed. "Now I'm jealous of Victoria."

Mary Grace laughed. "You feel strongly about her too," she pointed out. "This is more than just an article you have to write to keep your job."

"That's true," John agreed. "But as long as we're having true confessions, there's something I need to tell you."

Mary Grace nodded, her heart beating a little faster. "What?"

"Victoria Harte's case was not on the original list of unsolved murders my editor gave me."

She couldn't control a little gasp. Then he continued.

"When he assigned me to the summer murder series, I realized this was my chance to see you again. So I looked for an unsolved murder in Bethany Beach." He ran his fingers through his hair. "And this place is so peaceful that I had to go back twenty-five years!"

"Why did you want to see me again?" she asked weakly.

He looked away. "You made a big impression on me that summer in Panama City. I even considered writing you while I was on my mission."

She didn't try to hide her pleasure. "Really?"

He nodded. "But missionaries are supposed to keep their minds clear of girls and things like that, so I didn't." He glanced over and shrugged. "I even went to Emory after my mission to see you, but you weren't there."

She shook her head in wonder. "No, I was here running the Arms."

"I thought you were an archaeologist in a desert somewhere—completely out of reach—so I tried to forget about you. I dated several girls, but never got serious about any of them. The last one accused me of having commitment issues, and I wondered if she was right. Then Stan told me you were here." His eyes met hers. "I decided to come see you just to be sure that there was nothing between us."

All the air left her lungs. "And what did you find out?"

He smiled. "It's too soon to tell for sure, but it looks promising."

She looked away, uncertain how to respond.

"So, I guess you could say that Victoria called to me in the beginning, and I'm not dismissing your idea that she may be interested in our investigation, whether or not you owe her an eternal debt."

Mary Grace cleared her throat and with effort kept her voice even. "Do you think she's helping us solve it?"

"Honestly, no," he told her. "And I base that opinion mostly on the fact that we aren't doing well enough to indicate heavenly help." John stood and held out his hand. "How about just a short walk?"

She extended her hand, and he clasped it in his, then continued holding it as they walked down the beach. She savored the warm softness of his fingers wrapped around hers. Finally John interrupted her reverie. "A penny for your thoughts."

She smiled grimly in the fading light, thinking that her thoughts at the moment would cost him much more. "I was just appreciating the beautiful night."

John didn't comment on her answer, and when they returned to the swing, he dropped her hand so she could slip her shoes back on. She glanced up and saw him staring at her with such intensity that she fumbled with the clasp on her sandals. He took a step toward her and put his hand on her cheek. Then he leaned forward, and she thought he was going to kiss her, but instead he stopped, his nose just a few inches from hers. "You'd better get inside before we pass the point of no return," he said.

She closed her eyes briefly, then nodded and fled into the safety of the Arms.

* * *

The man with the cigarette stood in his regular spot behind a dune on the bluff. He inhaled deeply as another man stepped up beside him.

"What were you trying to accomplish with that lame fire?" he asked, the cigarette hanging from his lips.

"We didn't set the fire," the other man replied.

Dropping his cigarette, the first man turned in surprise. "Then who set it?"

"We don't know."

"Well, find out. We may have more trouble here than we realized."

CHAPTER 10

On Tuesday morning, Mary Grace had to drag herself from the bed when her alarm went off. She had slept fitfully, her mind tortured with dreams of John Wright and Victoria Harte. A quick shower revived her to some extent, but when she arrived in the kitchen and found Lucy making breakfast, she was disconcerted.

"You're back!" she stated the obvious.

Lucy's head bobbed. "I am back, but just for a few days until you can find someone permanent. My son says it's right that I should quit, but he said you've been good to me and I shouldn't leave without a notice."

"Well, I'm grateful to have you, even for just a little while."

As she completed this sentence, Miss Polly walked in. The two cooks faced each other, and Mary Grace tried to decide what to do. Justin had provided Lucy with a steady income for many years, but she had deserted Mary Grace in her hour of need. Miss Polly owed Mary Grace nothing but had given up part of her vacation to help. Mary Grace turned to Lucy.

"Miss Polly handled dinner for us last night. She and I made some changes in the menu, and she's given me a list of things to get from the grocery store for today. I'm sure you won't mind."

"And I'll be glad to help you prepare everything," Miss Polly said with enthusiasm. "That is, if you'll show me how you make your chocolate pies."

Lucy laughed. "I could use an extra pair of hands in here. I was always telling Mr. Justin how I needed more help, but he'd just laugh and say, 'You can handle it, Lucy. You can handle it.' And I'd be glad to show you how to make a good chocolate pie every time."

Mary Grace picked up the grocery list off the table. "Since there are two of you, I'm going to let you handle breakfast while I go to the store. I'll take care of the dining room when I get back."

"That's fine," Lucy said to Mary Grace as she pulled out a tattered recipe book. "I've been making this collection for thirty-five years, and I treasure it like my Bible," she told Miss Polly. "Once we get breakfast out of the way, we can start some serious cooking."

Miss Polly looked as pleased as a toddler on Christmas morning. "What should I do first?"

"If you'll mix up some pancake batter, I'll cook the sausage . . ."

Confident that her guests were in good hands, Mary Grace left the kitchen. She set up the buffet tables in the dining room, then walked into the lobby, where Windy was already stationed at the desk.

"You're early," Mary Grace remarked. "And we aren't even expecting any new guests today."

"The Arms is really full, and I thought you might need me," Windy replied.

Mary Grace gave the girl a smile. "I appreciate that very much, and I do need you. I've got to go to the grocery store, and with so many rooms occupied, it will take me awhile to clean when I get back. It will help me a great deal to know that you are at this desk, answering the phone and handling any customer requests."

Windy nodded. "I'll stay right here. I promise."

"And if that reporter from the *National Inquisitor* asks you any questions . . ."

"He talked to me yesterday," the girl admitted. "He said he might even quote me in his article."

Mary Grace shuddered to imagine what Windy's printed comment might be. With a sigh, she walked to her apartment, picked up her purse, then stepped out the back door into the warm sunshine. Walking slowly along the beachside walkway, she watched the tide come in. She spotted a soft drink can and a candy wrapper on the sand and leaned over to pick them up. A few feet away near a large sand dune were several half-smoked cigarettes. Shaking her head, she put her refuse collection in the nearest garbage can. Then she turned and followed the sidewalk to the front of the Arms and climbed into her car.

She stopped by the dry cleaner to drop off her campfire-scented clothes that couldn't be washed, then went to the grocery store and purchased everything on Miss Polly's list. The clerk who rang up the items for Mary Grace was one of Lucy's many cousins. "Heard you had a kitchen fire at the Arms the other night," she said. "Lucy swears it's the KKK and says she's going to call the Reverend Jesse Jackson about it."

Mary Grace controlled a smile. "I'm sure Mr. Jackson has better things to do than worry about a burned door in Bethany Beach."

"It was just a door?" the clerk verified. "Lucy said the whole room was blazing and the smoke alarms were going off."

"You can set off a smoke alarm with a match," Mary Grace pointed out as she wrote her check. "And by the time Lucy arrived, the fire was completely out."

The clerk laughed, then handed Mary Grace her receipt. "That Lucy always was one to spin a tale. I'm glad it wasn't too bad."

"Me too." With a wave, Mary Grace wheeled her cart outside and transferred her groceries into the trunk of her car. When she pulled into the parking lot in front of the Arms, John was just getting out of his car. He helped her carry the sacks of food to the kitchen, and as they walked she asked if he'd made any progress on the case.

"I talked to two more of Victoria's classmates. They were both male and both remembered her *well*, but neither one had any idea who killed her. I've sent off the paint chips, but it could be awhile before we hear on them. Last and probably least, I set up another appointment with Susie Ireland."

"Do you need me to come along?"

John smiled. "No, I think I can handle it alone this time. I brought you a little surprise." He reached into his pocket and pulled out a snapshot of Victoria Harte wearing her cheerleading outfit. "It was taken just before she got kicked off the squad," he said. "One of the guys I interviewed this morning was the editor of the school newspaper, and he gave it to me. Since you've started a shrine, I thought you should have it."

Mary Grace was pleased to have a real picture instead of a photocopy. "Thanks."

"So, what are you up to besides buying groceries?" he asked as they left the kitchen and walked toward her office.

"Well, Lucy's back, and she and Miss Polly are going to collaborate on meals, so that's a load off my mind."

"I see that Balmy is here bright and early, so that should also give you a measure of peace."

Mary Grace sat down behind her desk. "Her name is Windy."

He smiled as he leaned against the door frame. "I know. I just like to aggravate you."

"Windy's early arrival is giving me some peace of mind, but I'm sorry to say that her presence won't do the same for you."

John raised an eyebrow. "How's that?"

"Because she's already talked to the reporter from the *National Inquisitor* and given him a *quote* about you," Mary Grace replied, then smiled as he made a face. "And who knows what she might tell him today."

"You think this is funny, don't you?"

"I think it's poetic justice—a reporter being hounded by the press."

"Don't you have something better to do than torment your guests?" he asked, giving her one of his lazy grins.

"Now that I'm through with grocery shopping, I get to wash sheets and clean the guest rooms."

The smile left his face as he sat in a chair in front of her desk. "Can't you hire people to clean for you?"

She sighed. "I could, but my profit margin is nonexistent already. I'm hoping that once I get my renovation loan and the Arms stays full more, it will be like it was when Justin was alive."

"Justin didn't have to do the laundry himself?" John guessed, and Mary Grace laughed at the thought.

"Oh no. Justin had lots of employees and always made a profit."

John reached across the desk and took one of her hands in his. "Then why do you have to work so hard?" he asked earnestly.

Staring at their interwoven fingers, she tried to ignore the tingling warmth that was moving up her arm. "Because I'm a lousy hotel manager?" she managed to respond.

He shook his head. "You do a wonderful job, even though your heart's not in it." He lifted their joined hands. "Go ahead and admit it, just this one time. You'd rather be on an archeological dig in a desert somewhere, wouldn't you?"

Mary Grace struggled to keep her voice steady. "Some days I grieve for the lost opportunity," she confessed. Then she dragged her eyes up to meet his. "But right now?" She paused, frightened by the intensity of his expression. "I don't want to be anywhere else but here."

He gripped her hand a little tighter, but before he could speak, her visiting teachers knocked on the open office door. "Laundry delivery!" Sister Mills announced with a smile.

"I hope we didn't interrupt anything," Sister Westover said, her eyes focused on the desk where Mary Grace's and John's hands were clasped together.

"Oh no," Mary Grace assured them.

John gave her hand a quick squeeze, then released it and stood. "I'm John Wright. I don't believe I've met you angels of mercy."

The visiting teachers smiled. "We haven't met, but we saw you with Mary Grace on Sunday," Sister Westover said.

"And we were very curious but didn't want to pry," Sister Mills confessed, then waited expectantly.

"John and I knew each other during college," Mary Grace explained. "He's in Bethany Beach on assignment by the *Savannah Sun Times,* and he's staying here at the Arms."

"Oh," Sister Mills seemed disappointed. "We thought maybe he was an old boyfriend or something."

At this comment, John moved toward the door. "Well, it was nice to meet you ladies. I'd better go. I've got an appointment in a little while."

Mary Grace watched him escape, then focused her attention on the visiting teachers. She thanked them again for their help and listened while they gave her a quick message. After walking the sisters to the front door, Mary Grace took the clean sheets to the linen closet. She loaded her cart with the fresh sheets and towels and started cleaning on the beach side of the Arms. Being in John's company was becoming increasingly unsettling, and she hoped to give him plenty of time to leave for his appointment with Susie Ireland before she reached his room on the courtyard side.

Miss Eugenia answered the door to the James J. Pettigrew Room with a finger to her lips. "The babies are asleep, and heaven knows we don't want to wake them. Just hand me some clean towels. And give me some for Kate and Mark too. They've gone to a movie."

Mary Grace supplied the clean towels, then moved down to the rooms occupied by the other Haggerty ladies. The rooms were all cleaner than she kept them herself, and it only took a few minutes to finish the entire wing. The honeymooners had their Do Not Disturb sign on their doorknob, and Mary Grace was afraid knock, even just to offer the couple towels. So she moved down to John's door. His Do Not Disturb sign was also in place, but she knocked anyway, assuming he was already gone. A few seconds later the door was jerked open.

She put a hand to her pounding heart. "I didn't expect you to be here," she gasped. "You said you had an appointment with Susie Ireland."

"I did have one, but Susie called and canceled," he said with a frown. "I think someone might have encouraged her to avoid me, and apparently she's not as brave as you are."

"I'm sorry," Mary Grace told him sincerely, then pointed into his room. "Would you like me to make your bed?" she asked.

He smiled. "No, thanks. I'll take care of that myself. Just give me a clean towel."

She handed him one from the shrinking stack on her cart. "Well, I'd better hurry and finish the rooms."

John nodded, and she pushed on toward Mr. Tamburelli's room. There was no sign on his door, but it was locked and he didn't answer when she knocked. She stood in front of the door, clutching her master key, trying to decide whether she should open it.

"Is something wrong?" John asked from behind her. She glanced back to see that he had his briefcase in one hand and his car keys in the other.

"This is one of the awkward moments that seem to be a big part of my life," she told him with a scowl. "Mr. Tamburelli isn't answering. He doesn't have a sign on his door, so I have no reason to think that he doesn't want his room cleaned, but a couple of years ago I walked into a room under these exact circumstances and surprised a guest coming out of the shower. He hadn't heard me knock because of the running water and it was, well, terrible for us both."

John smiled. "I can imagine." He took a step toward her.

"That kind of thing never happened to Justin," she said with resignation. "Only to me."

"I haven't seen Tamburelli all morning, but then I wasn't at breakfast."

"I wasn't there either," Mary Grace told him. "I left Lucy and Miss Polly in charge and went to the store."

"If the Tamburelli guy didn't answer, he's probably out on the beach getting a worse sunburn."

Mary Grace said, "A worse sunburn than the one he had last night would be impossible."

"Or maybe he went back to Underwater World so he could take more pictures of Melville with his tie tack," John hypothesized.

Mary Grace gave him a stern look. "That is not funny."

John smiled. "Because I'm such a nice guy, I'll take all the risk out of this situation for you." He stepped forward, turned the knob, and walked inside the James Henry Lane Room.

"So, is it all clear?" Mary Grace called from the sidewalk. She started to follow him and ran squarely into his back as he made a hasty retreat. His face was pale and she was instantly concerned. "What's the matter? Was Mr. Tamburelli undressed?"

John closed the door and leaned against it. "Mr. Tamburelli is lying in the middle of the bed with a bullet hole in his forehead."

Mary Grace staggered at this news, and John put out a hand to steady her. Without conscious thought, she moved into the circle of his arms, her ear pressed against his pounding heart. She closed her eyes and listened to the steady rhythm, pretending that one of her guests wasn't dead in the room beside them. Then she heard a voice from behind her.

"Oh, excuse us," Kate Iverson said.

John released Mary Grace, and she turned to face the other couple. "Actually, I'm glad you're here," he addressed Mark. "We need your assistance. Professionally speaking."

Mark narrowed his eyes. "Professionally?"

John nodded, then pointed at the James Henry Lane Room. "Yes, there's a dead body in there."

"Mr. Joseph Tamburelli from Chicago," Mary Grace added weakly.

Kate gasped, and Mary Grace felt humiliation wash over her. What would Justin think if he knew she had brought the Arms to this disgraceful state?

Mark opened the door and looked inside briefly. "Single bullet wound to the head, not much blood. Looks like whoever killed him knew what they were doing."

Mary Grace put a hand to her temple where a headache was beginning to throb. "Miss Eugenia has insisted from the beginning that Mr. Tamburelli was not who he claimed to be," she murmured. "She thinks he might have ties to organized crime."

Mark shrugged. "Based on his execution-style death, I'd say that's quite possible. You didn't touch anything in here?" He indicated toward the door with his head.

"No," John replied.

Mark spoke to his wife. "Kate, why don't you go on back to our room and start packing."

Kate looked disappointed. "We're going to leave?"

Mark gave her a sympathetic smile. "I can't have you and the kids in a place where a man has been killed."

Mary Grace watched Kate trudge away, feeling worse than before. Then Mark turned to address her. "You need to call the police immediately."

"We don't have city police in Bethany Beach. Our law enforcement is provided by the county sheriff's department."

"Well, call them," Mark instructed. "I'll stand at the door until they get here."

"Thank you," Mary Grace responded as she moved toward the lobby. John kept pace with her. "Poor Mr. Tamburelli, or whoever he was," she said as they walked. "Not that it's important, but was the room an awful mess?"

John shook his head. "You'll have to replace the bedding, but everything else looked fine."

"Do you think the killer shot him in his sleep?"

John opened the rear door of the Arms for her. "That would be my guess."

Mary Grace wrung her hands together. "This is going to be terrible publicity for the Arms."

"One of the odd things about publicity is that it seems to help business, whether it's good or bad," John told her.

Mary Grace stopped and stared at him. "You mean people might actually choose to stay at the Arms *because* a man was killed here?"

He nodded as they reached the registration desk. "I've seen stranger things."

Mary Grace picked up the cordless phone, then walked away from Windy before dialing 911. When the operator answered, she explained the nature of her emergency, then disconnected. "The sheriff's department is sending someone," Mary Grace reported dully as she reached under the counter and took out a bottle of ibuprofen. She poured three tablets into her hand and swallowed them dry as they walked back outside. "I just can't believe that something so awful could happen here."

They reached Mr. Tamburelli's door about the same time Miss Eugenia did. She had Emily Iverson on one hip and an excited expression on her face. "I told you so!" she declared. "I knew that man was an imposter!" She turned to address Mark. "You should look into this personally since you have experience dealing with the Mafia."

Mark shook his head. "Regardless of my experience or lack thereof, this is out of my jurisdiction, and I'm supposed to be enjoying a *free* vacation." This was said with a little sarcasm.

"Well, I don't see how you can enjoy a vacation, free or otherwise, if people are dying around you," Miss Eugenia replied. "Even if you just show an interest as a citizen, it seems like you could at least *call* the FBI."

Mark took a deep breath in an obvious attempt to control his temper. "When the sheriff gets here, we'll let him decide about calling the FBI." The sound of a distant siren filtered through the humid air. "And in the meantime, maybe you could take Emily back inside out of harm's way."

Miss Eugenia shifted the baby to her other hip. "Kate says you're sending her home."

Mark nodded. "I don't see that I have much choice. As soon as the sheriff says it's okay to go, I want Kate and the kids headed back to Haggerty."

Mary Grace stepped forward. "You'll all be welcome to come again any time, free of charge," she told Mark. Based on the uncomfortable look he gave her, Mary Grace guessed that Mark Iverson had no intention of returning to the Arms at all.

The awkward silence was broken by the arrival of two sheriff's department vehicles. Sheriff Thompson climbed out of the first car with a look of dread on his face. "What's going on here, Mary Grace?" he asked.

Tears slipped onto her cheeks as she replied. "John says that Mr. Tamburelli is lying on his bed with a bullet wound in his head."

The sheriff cursed under his breath as Mark Iverson stepped forward and introduced himself. "If you want me to, I can put in a call to the FBI," Mark offered, and the sheriff nodded his consent.

"That would save me some time." Then he turned back to Mary Grace. "Nobody's been inside the room?"

"No, sir," she said, wiping her tears with the back of her hand.

The sheriff turned to one of the deputies who had accompanied him. "Call the coroner and tell him to get over here."

For the next thirty minutes, Mary Grace stood near the door to the James Henry Lane Room while the sheriff's department searched, dusted, and photographed. By the time the coroner arrived to get the body, a large group of onlookers had gathered along the edge of the parking lot. Sheriff Thompson followed the stretcher out, scratching his head.

"I've called the number listed on his driver's license but got a recording saying it was not a working number. And none of the Joseph Tamburellis in Chicago live at the address he's listed."

"It looks like Miss Eugenia was right," Mary Grace said.

"Right and wrong," Mark commented as he walked up to join them. "I just talked to the FBI office in Panama City. The dead man is not Joseph Tamburelli. He's an FBI agent named Jerry Grogan. Joseph Tamburelli is the cover that was assigned to him."

"Mr. Tamburelli was an agent for the FBI?" Mary Grace clarified, and Mark nodded.

"You're kidding," John added in astonishment.

"So he wasn't who he claimed to be, but he was *not* with the Mafia," Mark pointed out. "Just the opposite."

"Miss Eugenia was partly right, anyway," Mary Grace muttered.

John addressed Mark. "I wonder what he was doing at the Arms?"

Mark looked a little uncomfortable as he continued. "He was here as part of an ongoing investigation."

"What kind of investigation?" Mary Grace asked, praying that her headache medicine would kick in soon.

It was obvious that Mark regretted the necessity of answering. "Apparently there was reason to believe that the Arms is a drop point for a smuggling operation and has been running smoothly for some time."

Mary Grace forgot all about her headache as her mouth fell open in horror. "That's impossible. Nothing illegal or otherwise could have happened at the Arms without Justin's knowledge."

No one spoke for a few seconds. "Unfortunately, the FBI agrees with you," Mark said finally. "They believe that before his death, Justin Hughes was the smuggling ringleader. Now someone else has taken over."

"Justin was not involved in smuggling!" she denied vigorously. "He was honest, and decent, and . . . honest!" she stammered as tears returned to her eyes.

Mark held up a hand to stop her babbling. "I don't have all the details yet, but the FBI doesn't open an investigation without considerable evidence, and committing an undercover agent is even more serious."

Mary Grace felt a little nauseous but continued to shake her head. "It must be a mistake." Then an idea occurred to her. "Maybe Justin was *cooperating* with the FBI."

Mark wouldn't meet her eyes. "Not according to the special agent in charge of the Panama City office, but I'll know more soon. They're sending an agent and a four-member search team. Do you have five rooms available for them here?" he asked Mary Grace. "It would make things more convenient."

She did a quick mental assessment. "I only have four unoccupied rooms that aren't murder scenes," she told him. "Except for the Edmund Kirby Smith Room, which doesn't have hot water."

Mark looked disappointed, and John sighed. "Give one of the agents my room and I'll take the one with no hot water."

"I couldn't ask you to do that," Mary Grace said as another tear slipped onto her cheek.

John put a hand under her chin. "You're not asking, and I figure it's like Miss Eugenia said—my civic duty."

"Thanks," Mark accepted for Mary Grace. "It will just be for one night."

John shrugged. "Some of the places where I stayed in Africa didn't have running water, hot or otherwise." He winked at Mary Grace. "The Kirby Smith Room will be a step above that."

Sheriff Thompson came out of the James Henry Lane Room and asked Mary Grace to have all her guests gather in the dining room for questioning. Mary Grace walked to the lobby and sent Windy around to the rooms with this announcement. Ten minutes later everyone was assembled in the dining room, and Sheriff Thompson explained the situation.

There were gasps around the room, but Lucy took the death of a guest much more calmly than she had a small fire in the kitchen and offered to provide a light snack for everyone. The sheriff and Mark interviewed the guests individually and dismissed them afterwards. When the last guest left, they waved Mary Grace back over and John followed her.

"What can you tell us about Mr. Tamburelli?" the sheriff wanted to know.

"Miss Eugenia would be your best resource on that. She's been following him around."

The sheriff nodded. "I got plenty of information from Mrs. Atkins. I just want you to hit the highlights for me."

"He checked in on Saturday. He did not have a reservation. He did not dress like a tourist. He was very quiet and rarely spoke unless directly spoken to. Last night he came to dinner badly sunburned. According to the other guests, he did not come to breakfast this morning, and when I went to clean his room today, he was dead," Mary Grace reported succinctly.

Mark looked at his notes. "The coroner thinks he was killed about eleven o'clock last night."

"Why didn't anyone hear the gunshot?" she asked.

"The murderer used a silencer," Mark replied.

Mary Grace took a deep breath. "A *silencer?*"

Mark nodded. "A professional hit, probably related to the FBI investigation."

John cleared his throat. "I don't know if this has any bearing on what happened to Mr. Tamburelli, but I think I should mention it." Sheriff Thompson and Mark Iverson both gave John their full attention. "I did a story a few weeks ago accusing the mayor of Savannah of being a drug addict and connected to organized crime. It's possible that whoever killed Mr. Tamburelli was actually here to watch or kill me."

"Then why would they kill Agent Grogan?" Mark asked.

Mary Grace leaned forward. "Maybe they found out he was an FBI agent."

"Or maybe he stumbled across the smuggling operation," Mark suggested, and Mary Grace frowned.

"It's probably not related to this situation, but thanks for telling us," Sheriff Thompson said as he stood. Then he addressed Mark. "Once the agent from Panama City gets here, I'll turn the investigation over to him." He turned to Mary Grace. "I've asked all your guests to stay through tomorrow in case we have more questions."

"And I've given everyone my cell phone number," Mark said as he extended a card to Mary Grace and another to John.

After the sheriff left, John looked at Mary Grace. "I guess I'll need a key to the room without hot water."

Mary Grace pulled the key down from the hook on the wall. "Your new room is beachside, this way." She pointed to the left. "And I'll have to change the sheets in your room."

"I'll help," John offered, and Mary Grace was too discouraged to argue. They stopped by the linen closet and got a fresh set of sheets and some towels. Then they went to John's old room, and Mary Grace cleaned while he packed. Once he had his suitcases stacked outside the door, they worked together on the bed. As they shook out and tucked the sheets, tears came to her eyes again.

"It's okay, Mary Grace," John comforted from the other side of the bed.

She nodded but didn't respond. How could she tell him that the thought of him leaving her life forever upset her more than the fact that one of her guests had been murdered?

When the bed was made, she led him to the Edmund Kirby Smith Room and turned on the air conditioner. "No one's stayed in here for a while," she told him, surveying the room with a critical eye. "We dust it and change the sheets weekly, so I think you'll be comfortable, but if you need anything . . ."

"I know where to find you," he assured her.

Mary Grace walked over to the window and looked out at the water. "I wonder if Mr. Tamburelli had a family?"

John stepped up behind her. "He was killed in the line of duty. Being an FBI agent is dangerous work, and any family he has knows the risks."

"I doubt that's going to make them feel any better," she murmured. Then she squared her shoulders and took a deep breath. "Well, I've got to go around and personally apologize to all my guests."

John frowned. "Why? You didn't kill Mr. Tamburelli."

"No, but it happened in my hotel," she explained. "I'm sorry that you've lost valuable time from your investigation."

"For an average reporter, a delay like this could be devastating. But for one as brilliant as I am? Just a minor inconvenience."

She gave him a wan smile, then stepped out onto the sidewalk and started her rounds. Her first stop was the James J. Pettigrew Room. Kate Iverson said they were all packed up and ready to go home. Then Miss Eugenia joined Kate at the door. "The sheriff says we have to stay until tomorrow," Miss Eugenia told Mary Grace. "So we get one more day."

"I'm so sorry that your vacation is being cut short," Mary Grace told Kate.

"It certainly wasn't your fault," Kate replied. "And a couple of days on the beach is better than nothing."

Mary Grace continued on to the next room, occupied by Annabelle. "I'll ride back to Haggerty with Kate and Eugenia in the Iverson's van tomorrow," she said. "It's not that I'm afraid or anything," she assured Mary Grace, "but I miss my husband, and Kate might need help driving."

"Have a safe trip," Mary Grace said with her bravest smile.

When Mary Grace knocked on the Rayburns' door, Leo answered, looking grim, and she knew they regretted their decision to remain at the Arms after the fire. "We'll check out tomorrow as soon as the sheriff releases us," Leo said stiffly. "Enough is enough."

"I understand," Mary Grace told him, and she did understand their reluctance to stay. "You won't be charged for the nights you spent here, and I hope you enjoy the rest of your vacation . . . some-where else."

When Miss George Ann told her that she and Miss Polly planned to stay until the end of the week, Mary Grace had another struggle with tears. "Polly's having so much fun cooking for your guests that she won't leave a single day early. She told me I could go on and she'd ride the bus back, but of course I can't do that. I'll stay with her and drive Annabelle's car home."

Mary Grace blinked back the moisture that had collected in her eyes. "Well, I'm glad you're staying, and I hope that the last few days of your visit are uneventful."

She ran into John on her way back to the lobby. "Are you headed out to another big interview?" she asked.

He shook his head. "No, actually I thought I might do some jewelry shopping."

Mary Grace smiled as she realized what he meant. "You're going to force Susie Ireland to talk to you by becoming a customer?"

He nodded. "I'll have a lot of questions and need plenty of attention from the management."

Mary Grace shook her head. "You don't miss a trick."

"No, but I've dropped the ball a time or two." Their eyes met for a few seconds, then she looked away. "Has the FBI arrived in force yet?"

"Not yet." Mary Grace looked up at him. "Justin was not a criminal." It was important to her for John to believe that.

He nodded, then stepped onto the sidewalk. "There are at least two sides to every story. I've learned that from working in the newspaper business. But the important thing to remember, Gracie, is that everyone makes mistakes. If it turns out that Justin was involved with the smugglers, it doesn't mean he was a completely bad person."

She fell into step beside him. "By 'smuggling' do you think they mean drugs?"

"Probably, although not necessarily. People smuggle all kinds of things. Fake designer clothing, jewels, artwork." John looked over at her. "And a side income from smuggling would explain how he was able to run this place so effortlessly when you can't afford to hire a cook who can *see*."

"I know it looks bad, but it just doesn't feel right. Justin didn't care about money."

"Wait and see what kind of evidence the FBI has, then make your decision."

"You think Justin is guilty," she said in an aggrieved tone.

"I'm just looking at the facts, and what I've heard so far doesn't sound good. He had a house on the ocean with a dock built underneath . . ."

Mary Grace gave him a worried look. "That dock hasn't been used in decades."

"As far as you know." He stepped into the lobby and headed down the hall toward the kitchen. "We'd better check it out before the FBI does. I guess jewelry shopping can wait."

CHAPTER 11

Miss Polly and Lucy were so engrossed in a game show that they barely noticed as John and Mary Grace passed by. After unlocking the door, Mary Grace picked up her flashlight, then they started down the creepy stairway.

Once they made it to the basement, Mary Grace led the way to a heavy wooden door in a far corner, then stopped. "What's the matter?" John asked.

"I've always been a little claustrophobic," she admitted. "I hate going into closed-up places."

John raised an eyebrow. "And you wanted to be an archaeologist who spends a lot of time in tombs and crypts?"

"There are open digs," she replied, still staring at the door with dread.

"Well, we've got to find out what's down there. If you're afraid, I'll go by myself."

"You're not leaving me here alone!" she said, then straightened her shoulders as John opened the door and ducked into a small hallway. She followed with deep trepidation. The walls were close on each side of her, and the air was damp. She couldn't control a shudder, and John reached back to take her hand. She clutched his fingers desperately as they made slow progress into the unknown.

Soon the wooden walls changed to stone. "They carved this passageway right into the rock," John said with interest.

Mary Grace resisted the urge to scream and put one foot steadfastly in front of the other. They came to a set of stone stairs and descended slowly. Then they stepped onto a wooden ramp. John stopped and leaned down to whisper in her ear, "You know those wooden planks you were worried about being rotten?"

She nodded.

"Well, they are not only very new, but look like they've been treated with a water sealant. See how the moisture is beaded up?"

She looked down and saw that he was right. "But who would have replaced the planks? And when?"

John didn't answer, but pulled her forward. A few yards later they stepped into a wide, open area. "Finally, the heart of the cave," John said, taking a deep breath of fresh air. They walked down to the edge of an empty dock. "Nobody's here now, but based on the scratches along here, I'd say this dock is used often."

Mary Grace rubbed her hands up and down her arms as a cold chill shook her. "I can't believe that this is all here. I thought it was just an old ruin."

John looked toward a shaft of light, which indicated that the mouth of the cave was not far away. "Well, we'd better get back upstairs and let the FBI know about our find."

They located Mark in the lobby and told him about the cave and the modern-looking dock. "I appreciate you being up-front with that information," he told Mary Grace. "And I'd like to ask for your continued cooperation."

"What would that involve?"

"For starters, it means the search team would go over the whole place, not just the room where Mr. Tamburelli died. We can get a warrant, but if you agree voluntarily, it will save time."

Mary Grace nodded. "They can search anywhere they want to. All I ask is that they are considerate to the few guests I have left."

Mark gave her a sympathetic smile. "When they get here, I'll ask them to be polite."

Mary Grace offered to let Mark use Justin's office, and he accepted. While Mary Grace got Mark settled, John went to ambush Susie Ireland. Mary Grace left Mark making phone calls and walked to the laundry room, where she moved two loads of towels from the washers to the dryers. When she got back to the lobby, Miss Eugenia was standing by the registration desk. "Another exciting day," she said.

"I told Mark that you knew from the beginning that Mr. Tamburelli was not who he claimed to be." Mary Grace wanted to make sure Miss Eugenia knew she had received credit where credit was due.

Miss Eugenia looked pleased. "I've got a good eye for that sort of thing," she said as they paused by the kitchen door. "Kate and the babies are asleep, and I decided to come outside for a while."

Mary Grace nodded. "I'm sorry the Iversons' vacation didn't turn out like you'd planned."

Miss Eugenia shrugged. "We did the best we could."

"And at least they got one night at the Arms for free," Mary Grace agreed with a smile.

Miss Eugenia moved a little closer. "I have a question I've been wanting to ask you. It's a personal one, and I'll understand if you don't want to answer."

Mary Grace nodded, then braced herself for embarrassing questions about John or Justin or both, but Miss Eugenia surprised her. "You said you joined the Mormon Church a couple of years back, and I was wondering if you'd tell me why."

"Why I joined the Church?" Mary Grace clarified.

Miss Eugenia laced her fingers together. "I told you my question was personal, and I know I shouldn't ask. It's just that until recently, I'd barely heard of a Mormon, let alone met one. Now it seems like they are turning up everywhere."

Mary Grace laughed at this, and Miss Eugenia gave her a sheepish smile.

"I've read the Book of Mormon several times myself," the older woman added.

This was even more surprising to Mary Grace than the original question. "What do you think about it?"

"Oh, I love it!" Miss Eugenia replied, then tempered her remark with, "I mean, it's very interesting. All that history and everything."

"I have several books about South America that show evidence to support the Book of Mormon. I'd be glad to let you borrow them if you'd like."

Miss Eugenia smiled. "I would like that very much."

Mary Grace led the way to her apartment and pulled two books from a shelf in the living room. "I think you'll find these fascinating. Although nothing can 'prove' to you that the Book of Mormon is truly the word of God," she warned. "That's something you'll have to gain through prayer."

Miss Eugenia stared at the books. "How did you know for sure that it was all true?"

Mary Grace considered this. "Well, at first I didn't know that it was *all* true. I knew that I had an incredible feeling when I talked with the missionaries or read the Book of Mormon and when I prayed. Finally one of the elders had me read Ether 12."

Miss Eugenia frowned. *"For ye receive no witness until after the trial of your faith?"*

"You *have* read the Book of Mormon." Mary Grace was impressed. "Yes, Moroni gave several examples of people who experienced miracles, but pointed out that faith came first. I decided if faith was required of Moses and Nephi and Lehi and Alma, then it was required of me too. So I exercised my faith by committing to baptism."

"You just plunged ahead blindly?"

Mary Grace laughed. "I like to think my decision was a little more responsible than that. I decided that based on what I knew, I had the faith to take the next step."

"And you don't regret it?"

"Not for a second."

"Don't you miss your old church and the friends you had there?" Miss Eugenia asked.

Mary Grace shook her head. "I didn't go to church before, so there's nothing to miss."

"I've been a Methodist all my life," Miss Eugenia told her softly. "It's as much a part of me as . . ." she searched for a comparison, then held up her hands, "as my fingers. I can't imagine separating myself from the Haggerty United Methodist Church any more than I would contemplate an amputation."

Before Mary Grace could reply, a man walked through the door and introduced himself as Special Agent Wilson Hester from Panama City. "How did you get here so fast?" Mary Grace asked in amazement.

"I came by army helicopter," he replied briefly. "The search team is an hour or so behind me in a van."

Mary Grace gave Miss Eugenia a wide-eyed look, then escorted the new FBI agent to Justin's office. After the men shook hands, Mark asked Mary Grace which room Agent Hester would be assigned to.

"I can settle in my room later," Agent Hester said. "Right now I'd like to ask Miss O'Malley some questions."

Mary Grace nodded warily as they all sat down. Then John knocked on the office door and stuck his head in. "Looks like you're busy," he said when he saw the agents.

"Come on in, John," Mark invited. "This is John Wright," he told Agent Hester. "He's a reporter for the *Savannah Sun Times* and has been here since last Friday. He might have some information to contribute."

Agent Hester studied John. "I don't like dealing with the press."

John took a seat beside Mary Grace and smiled. "I'm in this office right now as Gracie's friend, not a press representative."

"Gracie?" Agent Hester asked.

"Miss O'Malley," Mark provided, and the other agent nodded.

"First I'd like to say that we appreciate your cooperation," Agent Hester began. "I was instructed to thank you on behalf of the Bureau."

Mary Grace nodded. "It seems like the least I can do since one of your agents was killed here. I'm so terribly sorry about that."

Agent Hester acknowledged her apology with a grim nod.

"And I'm convinced that a search of the Arms will help to prove Justin's innocence," Mary Grace added.

Agent Hester regarded her for a few seconds, then seemed to come to a decision. "We have pictures of Justin Hughes speaking with known criminals. We have his fingerprints on several smuggled items, and there have been regular, unexplained deposits into an account in his name for almost ten years."

Mary Grace clutched the edge of Justin's desk. She didn't know how to argue with such conclusive evidence, but the activities Agent Hester was describing were completely foreign to Justin's character.

"There have been reports of illegal activities at the Arms for over a decade, but we had no proof. Then about five years ago we got a message from someone who claimed to have a log of all the smuggling that has taken place here. He wanted immunity in exchange for the log."

"Who gave you that message?" Mary Grace asked with dread.

"Justin Hughes," Agent Hester told her. "He admitted that he had been involved but said he wanted out and was willing to turn in his partners to protect himself. Before we could work out a deal, Hughes died. We watched the Arms for a while, but there were no signs of smuggling, so we abandoned the project. But a few months ago, my office received a report that smuggling activity along the Florida coast had increased dramatically. We had a satellite take some aerial photos, and they showed some suspicious movements around the Arms again."

"Which means that someone else has revived the smuggling operation," Mark explained.

"We assume it's an old partner since the operation is running so smoothly. That's why we sent Agent Grogan in," Agent Hester told her.

"Mr. Tamburelli was looking for criminals?" Mary Grace asked.

Agent Hester nodded. "And the log Justin Hughes kept. His assignment was to look around, check the guests' room, and come up with anything he could from the inside. Then he was supposed to watch the beach at night for deliveries."

John glanced at Mary Grace. "I guess that answers the question of who looked through my things. Besides Windy, of course."

"Why didn't you send someone more experienced?" Mary Grace asked in frustration. "A better agent might still be alive."

Wilson Hester seemed surprised by this comment. "Jerry Grogan was a seasoned agent, very familiar with organized crime families."

"Well, he might have fit right in with crowds of Mafia hit men, but he stuck out like a sore thumb in a small tourist town like Bethany Beach," Mary Grace insisted. "He didn't wear the right kind of clothes, and he got a terrible sunburn because he didn't bring any sunblock." She paused for a breath, then added, "We thought *he* was a criminal."

Agent Hester nodded. "Occasionally an agent is mismatched with an assignment. It's a shame. Grogan was a good guy." The agent cleared his throat, then continued. "When the search team gets here, we'll do a thorough inspection. In the meantime, I'd like each one of you to tell me everything you know about the fire, the death of Agent Grogan, and the boat dock built into the cave under the house."

Mary Grace and John spent the next fifteen minutes telling Agent Hester what they knew. Then Mary Grace was sent to bring the guests in one at a time. No one had anything new to offer, and the honeymooners kept checking their watches throughout the interview. Finally, when Agent Hester finished, Mr. Rayburn asked if they were free to go check out.

"I'd like you to stay tonight," the agent replied, "then tomorrow you can leave as long as you give me a number where we can reach you if we think of more questions." After the Rayburns left, Agent Hester turned to Mary Grace. "Is that it?"

"There's Miss Polly and Lucy in the kitchen."

"Please ask them to come in."

Miss Polly was all smiles and blushes when she was introduced to the new agent, then sat quietly while Lucy related what she knew. Then Agent Hester turned to Miss Polly.

"You're a guest here, but you're helping in the kitchen?"

Mary Grace leaned forward. "Lucy quit temporarily after the fire, and Miss Polly stepped in to keep my guests from starving," she said in an attempt to lighten the mood, but Agent Hester didn't smile. "And even though the other Haggerty ladies are leaving tomorrow, Miss Polly is staying to help Lucy with meals." Mary Grace turned to Miss Polly. "And I can't tell you how much I appreciate that."

"I couldn't leave Lucy to handle all this cooking alone!" Miss Polly replied.

Mary Grace smiled. "Once all the Haggerty folks leave, we won't have any guests to feed," she pointed out. "The Rayburns are leaving tomorrow too."

"Cutting their second honeymoon short?" Miss Polly asked.

Mary Grace nodded. "Yes. I feel so bad that this turned out to be such an awful experience for them."

"I wouldn't feel too badly," Miss Polly consoled. "They seemed to have a good time and took full advantage of the beach. I saw them go back and forth to watch the sunsets and sunrises almost every day."

The FBI agents had been sitting in bored silence, but at this announcement they both turned to stare at Miss Polly, who explained, "I'm a light sleeper and naturally inquisitive. I spend a lot of time sitting in the chair by the window in my room, looking out at the beach."

Mary Grace frowned. "There is no chair by the window in your room."

Miss Polly blushed again. "There is now." She looked between John and Mary Grace. "I noticed that the two of you spend time together on the beach every night as well."

Mary Grace was speechless, so John responded. "We have run into each other on the beach a couple of times."

Mary Grace saw Agent Hester make a note of this, then Mark spoke. "Well, thanks for your time, Miss Polly. You'd better get back to fixing what I know will be another wonderful meal."

Miss Polly put a hand to her chest. "Oh yes! Please excuse us."

Once Miss Polly and Lucy had rushed from the room, Mark Iverson asked, "You two meet on the beach every night?"

Mary Grace shrugged. "It's become kind of a habit."

Mark frowned at John.

"We knew each other when we were in college. Our walks are completely innocent. We just talk about the story I'm helping him with," Mary Grace assured him.

Agent Hester spoke. "While you were on the beach, did you ever see any evidence of illegal activities?"

John shook his head. "No, but then we weren't looking for any."

The agent made another note, then looked up. "Well, that concludes our initial questions. We'll check in with the office in Panama City. They'll decide on our next step."

Mary Grace realized that he was dismissing them. "Okay," she said as she stood. John followed her out into the hall.

"You were great in there," he told her.

"I've had a lot of practice over the last few days dealing with the press and the police and the FBI." She shook her head. "It's been like a nightmare I can't wake up from."

They reached the registration desk as the FBI search team arrived. She gave them their keys, then showed them to their rooms. Once they were settled, she led them to Justin's office. "The search team is here," she announced unnecessarily.

Mark and Agent Hester stood, then spoke in low tones to the new agents. Mary Grace walked back to the registration desk, where John was waiting.

"So, what did Susie have to say?" she asked.

"Not much," he replied. "But she did manage to sell me a watch that I don't need." Mary Grace smiled, and John moved closer. "But the whole time I was talking to Susie, I had a hard time concentrating. I kept thinking about what you said this morning, that you wouldn't want to be anywhere but here, and wondering what you meant."

Mary Grace wouldn't meet his eyes. "Instead of making riddles out of simple statements, you should be working on your article. Otherwise you'll get in trouble with your newspaper."

"I'm already in trouble with my newspaper," he reminded her. "It made me wonder if you might be developing a crush on me."

"I'm too old for crushes," Mary Grace assured him, struggling to keep her voice from shaking.

He studied her for a few seconds, then sighed. "Well, even if I don't get any more information on Victoria, I have enough to put forth a hypothesis."

"Which is?"

Before John could respond, the FBI agents returned in the lobby and Heath Pointer walked in. "What's going on here?" the lawyer asked Agent Hester. The agent explained the situation briefly, and Heath's expression was very grim by the end. "I presume you have a search warrant?" he said.

Agent Hester shook his head. "Miss O'Malley is going to allow the search without one."

Heath turned to Mary Grace. "Can I speak with you for a minute, privately?"

She nodded, and he led her into a corner of the dining room. "I strongly object to allowing this search," he told her. "It leaves you open to all kinds of legal issues."

"Like what?" she asked.

"If they find something, they could charge *you* with smuggling!" he whispered. "We need to make sure that all your legal rights are protected before you allow them to search the Arms."

"I want this settled immediately before what's left of my business is ruined," she told him. "I'm going to let the FBI search the Arms so that they will go away and leave me alone."

"That's what I'm trying to tell you," Heath insisted. "They may not leave you alone. Especially if you allow them to search."

"Refusing to let them search makes me look guilty."

Heath sighed. "I strongly recommend that you reconsider. Contrary to what you see in the movies, justice does *not* always prevail."

"Your concern is noted and appreciated."

"There's nothing I can say to change your mind?" he asked, and she shook her head. "Would you like me to stay while they search in case they try to arrest you afterwards?"

Mary Grace smiled. "No, but I'll let you know if you need to arrange bail."

"It's not funny, Mary Grace . . ." Heath began and she could tell that a lecture was about to ensue.

"I know," she promised as she walked him to the front door. "It's a serious situation. But there is one thing you can do for me."

Heath nodded. "Anything."

"Please don't tell my parents. I don't want to upset them."

"I won't tell them for now," he agreed. "But be careful and call me on my cell phone when they leave." Then, with one last disapproving look toward the FBI agents, Heath Pointer left the Arms.

Mark moved over to Mary Grace. "Are you going to proceed with the search?"

"Yes. Against my lawyer's advice."

"The team is ready to begin," Mark told her. "You'll need to accompany them."

"I guess I'll go act like a newspaper reporter for a while," John said with a little wave.

She watched him leave, then joined the agents by the door. It took several hours to cover the entire building, and by the end she was exhausted and they had found nothing even remotely incriminating. Mary Grace couldn't help but be pleased as they regrouped in the lobby. The search team headed to their various rooms, and Mary Grace reminded them about dinner.

"It's included in the price of your room," she added.

"Thank you, ma'am," Agent Hester spoke for the group.

Once the new guests were settled, Mary Grace hurried back to her laundry. She sighed with relief when she had the linen closet restocked with clean towels and sheets, then went to the kitchen to check on dinner. Lucy and Miss Polly didn't need her assistance, so she retreated to her apartment.

She called Jennifer and spoke to Stan's mother, who said her patients were too ill to come to the phone. Mary Grace asked her to let Jennifer know she'd called, then dialed Heath's cell number.

"Are you calling me from Alcatraz?" he asked when he answered.

She laughed. "The FBI didn't find a thing," she told him.

"Well, that's good news. Have they left?"

"No, they're spending the night and will leave in the morning."

"Are they calling off their investigation?"

"That I don't know," Mary Grace admitted.

"Well, I won't make it back to Bethany Beach in time to eat a delicious dinner at the Arms, but I might stop in for dessert."

"We'd love to have you," Mary Grace assured him, then ended the call. She took a quick shower and dressed for dinner, then manned the front desk while Windy set the tables in the dining room.

All the FBI agents except for Mark Iverson sat at the end of one table during dinner and talked among themselves. They ate quickly, then returned to their rooms. The Rayburns had left a message with Windy that they were eating elsewhere, and the absence of Mr. Tamburelli/Agent Grogan was painfully obvious.

John seemed distracted during the meal, but Mary Grace was too busy trying to keep the conversation going to probe. Heath arrived just as Miss Polly and Lucy started passing out pieces of Mississippi Mud Pie. "It's really cake," Miss Polly explained to the guests.

"But it's so rich they call it a pie," Lucy added.

"And we made one without coffee for the Mormons among us," Miss Polly informed them with a giggle.

Heath accepted a piece of cake, then sat beside Mary Grace. "Bobby told me you and the newspaper guy are old friends," he said quietly. "And Sheriff Thompson said you both seemed pretty cozy after the fire."

"Cozy?" Mary Grace asked with a quick glance around the room to see if anyone else was listening.

Heath shrugged. "That's what he said."

Mary Grace saw an opportunity to put an end to Heath's futile attempts to court her and took it. "I'm not sure how John feels about me, but I'll admit that I'm attracted to him."

Heath's face paled, and she thought that he was just disappointed that she had an interest in someone else. Then she realized he was looking over her shoulder and her heart sank. "He's standing right behind me, isn't he?" she whispered, and Heath nodded. Mary Grace held her breath, waiting for the teasing to begin.

Instead John walked around to sit across from her and said, "This mud pie is great. But I wonder what they substituted for the coffee in the LDS version?"

Mary Grace couldn't gather her wits enough to reply, so finally Heath suggested, "Maybe they used real mud."

John shrugged. "As long as it tastes this good, I don't care."

Heath asked Miss Polly for another piece, then interrogated John about his job with the *Savannah Sun Times.* John admitted everything—the scandal over the mayor's arrest, his banishment to small towns writing summer filler, and his frustration with finding answers about a twenty-five-year-old murder.

"Sounds like you've had a streak of particularly bad luck," Heath remarked when John was finished.

John smiled. "Yeah, but the good thing is that I've got nowhere to go but up."

Mary Grace stood and started helping Miss Polly and Lucy clear the tables, hoping that her guests would recognize this as her signal that dinner was over. She tried to help clean the kitchen, but her cooks wouldn't hear of it.

"You look worn out," Miss Polly said as she rinsed a plate and handed it to Lucy, who then put it in the dishwasher. "Why don't you go relax for a while?"

With resignation, Mary Grace left the kitchen and walked out the back door. In the fading sunlight she could see John Wright sitting on the swing, watching the tide.

"Something was bothering you during dinner," she said as she came up behind him.

"A couple of things actually," he admitted, then moved over to make room on the swing for her.

Mary Grace sat beside him. "Like what?"

"Well, for starters, I went back to see Mrs. Lowery this evening, and she gave me a startling piece of information about Victoria Harte."

"What?" Mary Grace asked breathlessly.

"I returned Victoria's book of poems and mentioned my theory that they were written to a boyfriend. Mrs. Lowery got a puzzled look on her face and said, 'Why, I always thought she had written them to the baby.'"

"What baby?" Mary Grace asked.

John ran his fingers through his hair. "That's exactly what I said. 'What baby?' Then Mrs. Lowery sweetly informed me that Victoria was very pregnant when she came to visit her the day she died."

"Why didn't she mention that before?" Mary Grace cried.

"She said she thought we knew. Anyway, this gives my theory a whole new dimension."

"She ran away from home because she was pregnant," Mary Grace said, her mind racing. "But where did she go? And who was the father?"

"It could have been any man in town, including Anson Harte," John said grimly. "In fact, Victoria may not have known the father's identity herself."

"Then why would she come back to Bethany Beach?"

"And why did someone kill her?" John added to the unanswered questions. "And what happened to the baby? Did it die with her? Did she have it that night?"

Mary Grace gasped. "Do you think the murderer took it?"

John exhaled deeply. "I don't know. I found an important part of the puzzle, but all it gives us is more questions!"

"How will you get some answers?" Mary Grace wanted to know.

"I'm sure Dr. Chandler could shed some light on the subject."

Mary Grace shook her head. "But it's unlikely that he'll even agree to talk to you again."

"You're right. So tomorrow I think I might go see Richard Harte."

They were quiet for a few minutes, then she turned to him again. "You said for starters. What else is bothering you?"

John shook his head as if to clear it. "Why were the Rayburns out walking on the beach at all hours of the night?"

Mary Grace felt her cheeks get warm. "Reenacting their honeymoon?"

John frowned. "One moonlight rendezvous on the beach sounds romantic, but more than that is crazy," he said logically.

"You think the *Rayburns* started the fire?" Mary Grace asked incredulously.

John shrugged. "I think they're suspicious, that's all."

"Are you going to tell Mark?"

"I don't want to. Not without something to back up my theory." He stared at the ocean. "What we need is a way to check them out."

"Too bad Miss Eugenia is leaving tomorrow. We could have asked her to follow them around," Mary Grace suggested with a smile.

He laughed and drew her into his arms. She kept her hands between them, determined to maintain at least some distance. She could feel his muscles flex, and yet she knew that indulging in any fantasies would be more than merely stupid—it would be dangerous to her mental health. She was searching for the strength to pull away when he reached up and ran a finger along the line of her jaw.

Without stopping to consider the consequences, she turned her face into his palm and his fingers moved up into her hair. He paused for just a second. Their eyes met, then their lips, and for a moment Mary Grace lost all sense of time.

When he finally pulled away, tears were streaming down her cheeks. "You're the first girl who's ever cried when I kissed her!" he whispered in concern.

"I'm not sad," she said. "I just never thought a kiss could be that sweet."

He sighed, then pulled her head against his shoulder and stroked her hair gently. "So I did hear correctly at dinner. You *do* like me."

She pressed her cheek to the crisp fabric of his shirt. "I knew I couldn't be lucky enough for you to have missed that remark."

"Well, do you?" he prompted.

"I said I was attracted to you," she replied carefully. "We've established that you're not ugly."

"You think I'm handsome?"

She looked up and saw the teasing smile on his lips. "Oh, yes."

"Then we're even," he told her. "And just for the record, I'm more attracted to you than I've been to any girl since Molly Hornfeck in the third grade."

Mary Grace laughed. "Oh yeah, what did Molly have that I don't?"

"Two missing front teeth and a mean right hook." He kissed the end of her nose. "You've got to love a girl like that."

Mary Grace relaxed back against him, savoring the warmth and comfort he provided.

"But it's more than just a physical attraction," he told her. "Being with you is fun. I've laughed more in the few days I've been here than, well, in a long time—in spite of the fact that a lot of unfunny things are going on."

"Maybe you're just hysterical," she suggested.

He tilted her face up so he could look into her eyes. "See what I mean? You can find humor in every situation. This morning when I woke up, you know what my first thought was?"

She shook her head silently, not trusting herself to speak.

"I thought of you. I wondered what you'd be wearing today. I wondered whether your eyes would look tired or happy or sad or afraid. Then I wondered how long it would take me to get you to smile."

She closed her eyes briefly.

"I thought I was immune to love—unless you count Molly Hornfeck." He gave her a quick smile.

"Let's not count Molly," Mary Grace murmured.

John pulled her closer. "But really—I've been in love with you for five years. That's why none of the other girls ever appealed to me."

They were quiet for a few minutes, enjoying the surf, the salt air, and each other's company. Then an idea occurred to Mary Grace, and she jumped to her feet.

"What's the matter?" John asked, looking around in alarm.

"Nothing's wrong. But maybe there *is* a way for us to check out the Rayburns."

John raised an eyebrow. "How?"

Instead of answering, she reached for his hand and pulled him to his feet. "Come with me."

They walked into the Arms, down the hall, and through the kitchen. When they reached the door that led to the basement, Mary Grace inserted her key into the lock. Then she turned on the light while he picked up her flashlight, and they headed slowly down the stairs.

"Where are we going?" he asked as they stepped onto the concrete floor of the basement.

"We're going to look in the hotel register and see if the Rayburns are listed as guests," she told him.

Mary Grace led the way into the small office in the corner.

John nodded, obviously impressed. "And who says pretty girls aren't smart?"

Mary Grace gave him a look as she removed a volume from the shelf. "It certainly wasn't me."

He laughed, then asked, "Did they tell you what time of year they came here for their honeymoon?"

She opened the register to page one. "No. We'll have to start at the first."

"I'll read over your shoulder just to be sure you don't miss it," he said, leaning close to her as her finger began moving down the pages. After fifteen minutes and fifty pages of hotel guests, they finally found the Rayburns.

"They signed in on June 12 and left on June 18," Mary Grace pointed out.

"Yep, here they are. Just like they said." She could hear the disappointment in John's voice. "Well, it was still a good idea." He turned toward the door, but Mary Grace reached out to stop him, her finger trembling slightly as she moved it across the page.

"The Rayburns were here, but they stayed in the Nathan Bedford Forrest Room."

John raised an eyebrow. "Is that significant?"

She nodded. "They told me they stayed in the Robert Hatton Room and specifically requested it several times." She looked up at him. "The Nathan Bedford Forrest Room is courtside, but the Robert Hatton Room faces the ocean."

A big smile spread across John's face. "Bingo."

"If the people in the Robert Hatton Room aren't really the Rayburns who stayed here before, who are they?"

"That is a question for the FBI," he said as the door above them opened. He put a finger to his lips and flipped off the light switch. She turned off the flashlight as well, and he pulled her to the ground.

She huddled close beside him as they heard voices, then footsteps descending the stairs. "The Rayburns?" she whispered, and he shrugged.

"It could be Lucy, but it's better to be safe than sorry."

The echo of footsteps sounded across the open space, then they heard another door open and Mary Grace realized whoever was in her basement without permission had gone down to the docks. "So the Rayburns are involved with the smugglers?"

John nodded again.

"Coming down here is pretty bold of them considering that this whole place is crawling with FBI agents."

John frowned. "No one expected a transaction tonight *because* the Arms is full of FBI agents. It was a brilliant move, really." He looked up. "This will probably be the last time they use the Arms, and the FBI's last chance to catch them here." John thought for a minute. "I don't know how long they'll be down there, and I don't want to risk meeting them on the stairs."

Mary Grace shivered and moved a little closer to him. "Do you think they killed Mr. Grogan?"

"Definitely."

"So, what are we going to do?"

"I'm going to call Mark." He turned on his phone and pulled Mark's card from his pocket, then dialed. "Mark?" he whispered after a few seconds. "Mary Grace and I are in the basement, and we think some of the crooks just came down to the dock . . ."

John stopped speaking as the sound of returning footsteps reverberated through the hollow space. Putting a finger to his lips, John disconnected. The footsteps stopped for a few seconds, then resumed only to fade as the intruder left. Once it was quiet again, John began typing a text message with the tiny buttons of his cell phone. It was a tedious process and took several minutes. Finally John pushed Send and waited for a reply. When it came, Mary Grace squinted at the small screen but couldn't read the message.

"What did he say?"

"He's going to organize the search team into an ambush and catch these bad guys in the act."

"While we cower here?"

John put his arms around her and pulled her toward him. "I prefer to consider it cuddling."

Before Mary Grace could reply, she heard a sound in the outer room. It wasn't exactly a footstep, more like a rustling noise. She looked up at John and could tell by his tense expression that he had heard it too. He eased away from her and crouched beside the door. She moved to follow, but he shook his head. "No matter what happens," he whispered, "stay in that corner."

There was another noise, this one more distinct and much closer. Instinctively John threw his arm toward her in a protective gesture as a shadow fell across the doorway of the little office. She could hear the intruder's labored breathing, and Mary Grace put a hand over her mouth to keep from screaming. Then there was a gunshot in the distance. The figure turned abruptly and ran back toward the stairs leading down to the dock.

Mary Grace felt weak. "The FBI must have moved in," she whispered.

John turned around. "And not a moment too soon."

"Should we go down and try to help them?" she asked, but John shook his head.

"We're unarmed and would just get in the way."

They sat there, waiting for what seemed like forever before they heard Mark's voice calling to them. "John? Mary Grace?"

John stood and pulled Mary Grace to her feet, then led the way into the larger room. "We're here!"

Mark had a gun in his hand and his clothes were wet.

"Did you take time out for a quick swim?" John asked him.

Mark shook his head and pointed at the group of people who were emerging from the stairway behind him. "The *Rayburns* were unhappy about being arrested. Several of us ended up in the water trying to subdue them."

Mary Grace looked at Farrah. Her dumb blonde look was gone, and she regarded Mary Grace insolently, eye makeup streaking her face. Leo no longer seemed kind or harmless struggling against his handcuffs. Mary Grace retreated a step as Mark continued.

"We took a gun away from Leo that's the same caliber as the one that killed Agent Grogan. A few simple tests should prove whether it was the murder weapon. And we seized a load of contraband and arrested the Cuban boat crew. Agent Hester will take them back to Panama City for questioning. We hope to know more about the smuggling operation that was based here."

Mary Grace glanced at the false second honeymooners. "It's true, then? Justin was part of a smuggling ring."

"I'm afraid there's no other explanation for the dock and the merchandise that those folks just unloaded into the basement of the Arms," Mark replied. "But I believe that Justin Hughes did break his association with the criminals right before he died."

Mary Grace nodded wearily as the search team led the Rayburns and their Cuban accomplices up the stairs. "Well, now that the smugglers have been arrested, maybe you won't have to send Kate home," she told Mark.

Mark considered this. "The danger does seem to be over. I'll think about it." He turned and followed his fellow agents upstairs with John and Mary Grace close behind him. When they stepped into the kitchen they found Roscoe Vincent snapping pictures as fast as his camera would go.

"What a bonus!" he said to Mary Grace and John as he rushed to follow the smugglers and FBI agents. "If I can get this into my editor before midnight, the *Inquisitor* will have an exclusive!"

Mary Grace waited until Mr. Vincent was gone before turning to John. "What about you? Are you going to fax a report about our smuggling ring to your editor?"

John gave her a surprised look. "Why would I want to do the *Savannah Sun Times* any favors?" he asked, then leaned closer. "And why would I want to embarrass you, Gracie?"

Mary Grace felt the tense muscles in her neck relax a little. "Since the agents are checking out before they really got settled in, you can have the Robert E. Lee Room back."

He shook his head. "I don't want to change rooms again. I'm fine with Edmund Kirby Smith."

"You say that now, but you haven't had to take a cold shower yet," she warned as they started down the hall.

"Can I reserve the right to change my mind after my first shower?" he asked, and she nodded. "Fair enough." They paused by the registration desk. "Do you want to go with me to see Mayor Harte in the morning?"

Mary Grace smiled. "I've just been waiting for an invitation."

John went to his room to prepare for his interview with Mayor Harte, and Mary Grace walked around the desk to stand by Windy. "I can't believe those Rayburn people killed Mr. Tamburelli!" the girl whispered.

Mary Grace sighed. "I can't really believe it myself."

"Is everybody still checking out tomorrow?" Windy wanted to know.

"The FBI agents are leaving now," Mary Grace told her. "I don't know for sure about the others. We'll have to wait and see."

Windy frowned. "I was hoping I would get to turn on the No Vacancy sign tonight."

Mary Grace laughed. "I'm not sure it still works."

Windy looked down at her hands. "Mr. Vincent told me they got 'preliminary results' on Mr. Wright's hair samples. He's not John F. Kennedy, Jr." She looked toward the front door. "And now that he has a new story, he might not even print mine."

Mary Grace was immensely relieved by this thought, but felt sorry for Windy. "It would be pointless to run the story now that they know John is not JFK, Jr." she said gently.

"But I had a *quote*," Windy grieved.

Mary Grace patted the girl's shoulder. "You'll have other chances to get your name in print," she predicted. "Now, I'm going to bed. If you don't want to try to get to your car through all the FBI agents in the parking lot, you can sleep on my couch."

Windy giggled. "I'm *dying* to walk through all those agents. Some of them are so cute, and if I'm out there while Mr. Vincent is taking pictures, maybe I'll get in one. Then I might make it into his newspaper after all."

Mary Grace shook her head. "Windy, you are hopeless!"

The girl laughed again as she closed the register and stepped out from behind the desk. "I'll see you in the morning."

Mary Grace walked to her apartment and changed into her pajamas. Then with a sigh, she called her mother. When she broke the news about the most recent events at the Arms, her mother cried and begged her once again to sell the hotel and move back home. Mary Grace comforted Catherine as best she could, then ended the call.

Next she dialed Heath's number, and their conversation closely resembled the one with her mother except that Heath didn't cry. She couldn't bring herself to go through the story again with Jennifer, so she decided to delay that call until the next morning.

* * *

The man used his cell phone to reach his contact. "What in the world happened?" he demanded when the other man answered.

"I'm not sure yet, but the load was a total loss. They've also got both our operatives and a whole crew of Cubans."

"Do any of them know enough to cause me problems?"

"I'm too careful for that."

"You'd better hope you're right. Your survival depends on it."

CHAPTER 12

On Wednesday morning Mary Grace dragged herself from bed at six o'clock and took a long shower. As the hot water washed over her, she couldn't help but think about John in the Edmund Kirby Smith Room. Knowing that as he showered he would regret his decision not to change rooms made her smile. Once she was dressed, she went to the kitchen, where Lucy and Miss Polly had breakfast well under way.

"After Mr. Wright's success with the omelettes the other day, we decided to prepare several different varieties of quiche for the guests this morning," Miss Polly said with a wave at the beautiful pies that lined the counter. "In keeping with the French theme, we've also made croissants."

"And we'll put out fruit and yogurt," Lucy added.

"It all looks delicious," Mary Grace said as she bent to smell one of the pies. "What kind is this?"

"Mushroom. We also have sausage, ham and spinach, and onion with cheese."

"Can I help you get juice into pitchers?" Mary Grace offered, but Lucy shook her head.

"We'll handle things in here, Mary Grace," the old woman told her. "You go out there and be the hostess."

With a smile, Mary Grace went into the dining room. When the guests arrived, everyone was very complimentary about the food, and the cooks smiled proudly with each comment.

"This is way above continental," Annabelle observed.

"I'd say this breakfast rivals anything you could find on a cruise ship," Miss George Ann added her endorsement.

"Do you know how many fat grams there are in one croissant?" Miss Eugenia demanded.

"Have some yogurt," Annabelle recommended. "It's fat free. And your eye for criminals must be fading, Eugenia," her sister continued, "since the Rayburns completely escaped your suspicion."

"Actually I did think they were a little odd, but everyone got so mad when I talked about Mr. Tamburelli, I hated to mention my concerns about the Rayburns."

Miss George Ann took a seat nearby and addressed Mary Grace. "Well, I for one was completely shocked that those nice people turned out to be criminals. Please tell us what happened."

Mary Grace answered questions about the arrest of the Rayburns while keeping one eye on the door. John finally arrived about halfway through breakfast. "Have a seat." She waved at an empty space beside her at the table.

"Thanks," he sat down, then whispered into her ear. "And that cold shower this morning was *torture!*"

"My offer of a return to the Robert E. Lee Room still stands," she responded with a smile.

He shook his head as he took a bite of a croissant. "I can deal with the cold water, and I like knowing that I'm closer to your apartment in case there's more trouble."

Mary Grace bit her lip. "I can't bear the thought of you taking cold showers on my account."

He laughed and put his hand over hers. "It's my privilege, Gracie. Now, as soon as breakfast is over, I thought we'd go see Richard Harte. Will that fit into your morning schedule?"

"I'd love to have an excuse to postpone my cleanup routine," she assured him.

John gave her a smile, then stood. "I've got to run a quick errand, but I'll come by your apartment when I'm finished." He picked up a croissant. "One for the road."

Mary Grace nodded as the Iversons walked in. Once they were seated, Miss Eugenia said, "It just doesn't seem right being here without Mr. Tamburelli. Poor man."

Annabelle shouted with laughter. "Poor man! Until he died you were convinced he was with the Mafia!"

Miss Eugenia sniffed. "Be careful how you speak of the dead, Annabelle. Mother would be mortified." Then she turned to Mary Grace. "Do you have a high chair for Emily?"

"I think so," she replied. "It might take me just a minute to locate it though."

Mary Grace finally found the Arm's only high chair in a storage closet near the kitchen. When she returned to the dining room, she helped Miss Eugenia strap the baby in, then frowned at the buffet table. "None of our breakfast foods are really suitable for babies," she told Kate. "We have dry cereal if you think that would appeal to Emily more than cheese and onion quiche."

Kate gave her a grateful smile. "Emily loves cereal. Something like Cheerios or Rice Chex would be best."

"She prefers Fruit Loops," Miss Eugenia amended the order as she patted little Charles's back. "And this precious doll has already had his breakfast," she said with a smile at the baby.

Mary Grace hurried into the kitchen and returned with a variety pack of cereal. "I'll let you choose," she told Kate.

After a moment's hesitation, Kate extracted the miniature Fruit Loop box and poured a few on the tray of the high chair.

"I guess a week's worth of sugar in one meal won't hurt her," Kate said with a shrug. "After all, we are on vacation."

Mary Grace laughed, then walked over to look at little Charles. "I've never seen him with his eyes open," she said, then glanced at Mark. "He looks just like his father, and Emily looks just like her mother. It was nice that you both got a replica."

"He's named after my husband," Miss Eugenia provided. "And will you look at that!" she cried, pointing at the high chair. "Emily has divided the cereal into colors!"

Mary Grace and Kate both studied the tray. "I think it was an accident," Kate finally decreed.

"Nonsense," Miss Eugenia insisted. "Emily is a genius."

"Well, she is certainly a fortunate young lady to have a friend like you," Mary Grace told Miss Eugenia, and the old woman smiled with pride.

"Miss Eugenia took me to the hospital when I went into labor with Emily," Kate said. "They've had a special bond ever since. We had to give Charles her husband's name so he'd have a fighting chance of winning her affection."

"Humph!" Miss Eugenia scoffed. "As if anyone could help but love this darling baby."

Mary Grace offered to hold Charles while Miss Eugenia ate, and the older woman agreed reluctantly but retrieved him immediately when she was finished. Windy arrived soon thereafter and started clearing the tables in the dining room, signaling the end of the meal.

After the guests left and the dining room was clean, Mary Grace went to her room to change clothes. When she was satisfied with her appearance, she called Jennifer. "I can't believe all this action took place while I was sick!" her friend moaned. "Has John Wright solved the age-old murder case yet?"

"No, but I think he's getting close. How are the twins?"

"Fine physically, but emotionally they are probably scarred for life. Stan's mother bought them matching clothes, and the whole time I was sick she dressed them alike! That's in direct violation of the first rule of raising twins according to *101 Ways to Raise Healthy Twins*. You must allow them their individuality!"

Mary Grace laughed. "Since they're so young, maybe their individuality hasn't been completely destroyed. And I'm guessing that Stan's mother has moved out."

"And not a minute too soon. Do you know she had the nerve to reorganize my kitchen cupboards and was threatening to paint the bathroom?"

"And you let her leave?" Mary Grace demanded. "Why didn't you send her over here?"

"The woman is overbearing, Mary Grace," Jennifer replied. "I don't know how she was able to raise a son as sweet as Stan."

"Well, that's one thing in her favor, anyway. How about coming over for a root beer float tonight?"

"I'd better not press my luck so soon. We might end up with something incurable. But maybe soon."

A few minutes after Mary Grace ended her conversation with Jennifer, there was a knock on her door. She opened it to find John standing in the hallway. He gave her a quick hug, then asked, "Are you ready to go?"

"I am," she replied, then grabbed her purse.

The morning heat was oppressive and the air conditioner in John's rental car didn't work very well, so Mary Grace was uncomfortably hot by the time they reached the city hall. They rode the elevator to the second floor, then John led the way to the mayor's office and approached the receptionist aggressively.

"I'm John Wright, and this is Mary Grace O'Malley," he said. "We're here to see the mayor."

"Do you have an appointment?" the woman asked.

John shook his head. "No, but tell him that he can either talk to us or a television news crew. The choice is his."

The woman gave John a disapproving look, then stood and walked into the office behind her. When she returned a few minutes later, Mayor Richard Harte was right beside her. "Miss O'Malley, Mr. Wright," the mayor said with a nod in their direction. "I'd be glad to talk to you, but I'm scheduled to speak at the Rotary Club in fifteen minutes."

John took Mary Grace by the hand and pulled her toward the mayor's office. "I guess you're going to be late." John pointed at two chairs in front of the desk, and they sat down. The mayor came in and closed the door, his expression hostile.

"Okay, what is so important that I have to rearrange my schedule?"

"I thought maybe you'd like to tell us what happened to Victoria's baby. Otherwise I'll just have to print a supposition."

The mayor sighed heavily as he collapsed into his chair. "Victoria delivered a stillborn female infant the night she was killed. She ran away early in her pregnancy and had very little prenatal care, so I guess it's no wonder." The mayor paused for a second, then looked up. "I wasn't home during any of this. I want you to know that."

John nodded. "Who was the baby's father?"

Mayor Harte shrugged. "I didn't even know about the baby until my father told me just before he died."

"Where is the baby buried?" Mary Grace asked softly.

"In an old cemetery out on Highway 150," Richard Harte replied. "She named her Ruth."

Mary Grace blinked back tears. "Victoria loved the baby. Why wasn't it buried beside her?"

Richard Harte leaned forward onto his desk. "This is completely off the record," he told them, and John nodded. "My father thought it would look bad for him politically if it became known that Victoria was pregnant outside of marriage. So the baby was buried in a separate location, and my father took steps to make sure that the pregnancy wasn't mentioned in the papers." He turned to Mary Grace. "And even though it seems sad that the baby died, it was for the best, really. The last thing my father needed was another child at his mercy."

"We've been told that he was abusive," John said.

The mayor confirmed this. "It's true, but airing his sins in public serves no purpose now." He turned to address Mary Grace. "That's why I asked you to discourage Mr. Wright from printing this article."

"Did you start a fire at the kitchen door of the Arms?" John asked.

The mayor looked over at John with a shocked expression. "Of course not."

"But you did tell Susie Ireland not to talk to me anymore," John guessed.

"That I did," Richard Harte admitted. "Most families have secrets they don't want the world to know. Mine had more than its share. I couldn't protect my mother or my sister, although I tried. I could have turned to alcohol or promiscuity," he said in an obvious reference to his mother and Victoria, "but instead I determined to make a success of my life."

"Is there anything about Victoria's death that you'd like to tell me now?" John said.

The mayor turned his eyes toward a window. "I don't know anything about that. My father only told me about the baby."

John stood, and Mary Grace followed his example. "Well, thanks for your time. Tell the Rotary Club members that we're sorry for making you late."

As John ushered her outside, Mary Grace could feel the mayor's gaze following them.

"He was lying there at the end," she said as they stepped back out into the heat. "He knows something else about Victoria's death."

"Oh yeah," John agreed. "And now I'm just about certain that the baby's father is our murderer. Victoria must have come back to confront him, probably to expose him, and he had to silence her."

"Victoria's story just keeps getting worse," Mary Grace said as they climbed into the hot car.

John nodded grimly. "Can you tell me how to get to the cemetery on Highway 150?"

* * *

The cemetery was an old one on a shaded hill near a tiny church. "It's beautiful here," Mary Grace said as they stepped under the trees and out of the blazing sun. A gentle breeze lifted the hair from her neck, and she sighed in appreciation. They walked around carefully, studying the headstones. "Some of them are so old you can't read the names."

John frowned. "Hopefully we'll be able to read one from twenty-five years ago." They had almost given up hope when they located the small headstone in a far corner of the graveyard.

"It just says Ruth," Mary Grace said as tears threatened again. "No last name."

John scowled. "The old mayor couldn't put a last name on the marker or everyone would *know*."

They stood in silence for a few minutes, grieving for Victoria and her baby. Then they turned to leave, but John stopped suddenly. "What?" Mary Grace asked, and he pointed to a nearby headstone.

"Does that name look familiar?"

"Ruth Thompson, wife of Loren, mother of Peter," Mary Grace read aloud. "I guess that's Sheriff Thompson's mother."

John was still frowning. "Her name is Ruth, and the baby's buried right beside her."

Mary Grace compared the headstones. "That is a coincidence."

John took her hand and led her to his car. "And I've told you how I feel about coincidences."

When they got back to the Arms, Mary Grace sighed. "Well, I guess I'd better get busy."

They walked together around to the beach side of the Arms. "You need some help?" he asked.

She shook her head. "You've got your own work to do." Then she frowned and pulled him with her to a large dune near the bluff. "This is the second time I've found a pile of half-smoked cigarettes out here," she told him, pointing at the debris. "The Arms is a smoke-free facility, and all my guests know that."

"Maybe they think this sand dune is far enough away to be considered off your property," John suggested. Then his expression darkened. "Or maybe whoever is smoking here isn't a guest."

She clutched his hand a little tighter. "Why would someone who isn't a guest stand here and smoke—twice?"

John pursed his lips. "That's a good question, but I can't think of a *good* answer."

"Some of the smugglers?" Her voice was full of dread.

He surveyed the area. "They probably had a lookout posted when a delivery was expected. And this would be a great location."

Mary Grace glanced over at her apartment window just a few feet away. "If one of them stood here, they were very close to me."

"Too close." John shuddered and drew her into his arms. "You really were in danger." He pressed her face against his neck.

"But it's over now," she whispered.

John held her for a while, then murmured, "Instead of investigating Victoria's murder today, I think I might go back to Susie's stores and look at engagement rings."

She looked up at him. "Why would you do that?"

"I'm in love with you," he said softly, "and I think you love me too. At our age, marriage would be the obvious next step."

She shook her head. "We can't rush this, John. We'll need to make plans and get to know each other better, and . . ."

"Can we at least go steady?" he interrupted her.

"Do people still do that?"

He kissed the end of her nose. "If not, we can reinstitute the practice." He slipped his CTR ring off his finger and onto hers, then smiled. "Much better. Will you wear it as kind of a good faith gesture?"

She hesitated for a second before nodding. "Yes."

He gave her a sweet kiss, then they held hands as they walked to her apartment. Once inside, she threw her purse on the couch and went into the kitchen. She opened the refrigerator and offered him a drink. "I've got Sprite, orange juice, and . . ." she paused, studying their choices, "some milk that's two days past the 'best if used by' date."

"That cold shower sapped all the adventure out of me," he said. "I'll take nonexpired orange juice."

She poured them both a glass, then joined him in the foyer, where he was staring at the Forrest Merek forgery. "Thanks." He took a sip, then pointed toward the painting with his glass. "I wonder if that painting was one of the first things Justin smuggled. Sort of a memento."

She frowned as she considered this. "Why would Justin put something incriminating on his wall?"

"Especially something so ugly," John agreed. "It just doesn't make sense, and I hate loose ends almost as much as I hate coincidences." After a few seconds, he smiled and led her to the couch. "Let's sit here and visit for a while."

"I really should go out and check on Windy," Mary Grace said, although she didn't resist. "And I need to change clothes and start cleaning the rooms."

"Do you have any new guests checking in today?"

She shook her head. "No."

He put his arm around her shoulders and pulled her close. "Then that's not an emergency. And how are we ever going to get to know each other better if you're always washing tablecloths and changing sheets?"

She relaxed against him. "Okay. We can visit for a little while."

"Things must have been difficult for you during Justin's illness."

Mary Grace nodded. "I loved Justin like the older brother I never had. Watching him suffer was terrible."

"I'm sorry that he died, but I'm glad you only loved him like a brother." John kissed her temple. "So tell me—in all these years since Panama City, you never forgot me?"

She took a deep breath. "No." Their eyes held for a few seconds, then there was a knock on the apartment door. Mary Grace opened it and admitted Mark Iverson.

"Is John here?" he asked, and Mary Grace pointed to the couch.

"What? The FBI needs my help to wrap up *another* case?" John wanted to know.

Mark shook his head with a smile. "I just wanted to let you both know that Leo Rayburn is really a thug named Cornell Hill. And the gun we took from him did kill Agent Grogan."

"And I presume that Mrs. Rayburn wasn't really his wife?" John replied.

Mark shook his head. "No, her name is Estelle Harrell, and they were both employed by the smugglers."

"If they weren't married, why were they out on the beach late at night?" Mary Grace demanded, then blushed.

Mark smiled. "Watching for boats from Cuba."

"They unloaded the stuff at the dock under the Arms where no one could see what was happening," Mary Grace guessed. "Then transported it somewhere else under the cover of darkness."

Mark nodded. "Exactly. It was a great plan and has apparently been working very well for a long time. If Justin hadn't rocked the boat, the whole thing could have continued indefinitely."

"Are you trying to make me feel better about Justin's involvement?" she asked.

"Yes," Mark admitted.

"Well, it didn't work," Mary Grace responded. "I still feel awful. But what really surprises me is that they resumed their operations recently. I could have stumbled onto them at any time!"

Mark shrugged. "I guess that's a risk they were willing to take."

"And it really wasn't much of a risk, since they just kill people who get in their way," John pointed out.

"That's true," Mark agreed. "If Justin hadn't died of a very well-documented case of liver cancer, I would have been suspicious about the nature of his death. It was awfully convenient that he died before a deal could be worked out with the district attorney."

"Well, I think I can say positively that Justin died of cancer," Mary Grace confirmed. "And he actually lived longer than the doctors had predicted."

Mark nodded. "Agent Hester said he thinks the DA might have been dragging his feet a little. Apparently he doesn't like to give anyone immunity, even if it means catching bigger fish. So I guess that's where we'll lay the blame."

"And the smuggling ring is officially closed?" Mary Grace confirmed. "Mr. Grogan's murder is solved, and things can get back to normal around here?"

"Yes," Mark said with a nod. "Ms. Harrell has agreed to cooperate, so the Florida court system will be busy for years trying related cases. There could be hundreds of people involved in the scheme."

"Was she able to identify the inside man here at the Arms?" John wanted to know.

Mark shook his head. "I doubt very seriously that she knew who he was."

"If there is an 'inside man,' the obvious suspects are me, Lucy, and Windy," Mary Grace pointed out, and John laughed.

"I didn't mean *that* inside. It's someone who has access to the Arms, probably has keys, knows the layout . . ."

"And most likely worked in partnership with Justin Hughes before his death," Mark added.

Mary Grace thought for a few seconds. "I've gotten a lot of offers to buy the Arms. One company, Aztec, has been very determined. I wonder if they're involved with the smugglers?"

John raised his eyebrows. "Buying the Arms would be a smart move on the smugglers' part."

Mark jotted some notes on a piece of paper. "I'll check into it. But these guys usually hide behind fake companies and work through so many intermediaries that it's hard to pin them down."

"Heath is helping me shop for a hotel-improvement loan," Mary Grace told them. "He hasn't been able to find a bank who will finance repairs on the Arms, but said he had offers from private investors. I'll ask him who they were, and you can check them out too."

Mark nodded, then looked around the room. "This place has to be worth plenty. Even if you bulldozed the house itself, the property is in a prime location. It doesn't seem like you'd have trouble getting a bank to loan you money as long as you used this place as collateral."

Mary Grace shrugged. "With me, everything is difficult."

Mark smiled. "Let me know when you get the names from your lawyer."

Mary Grace walked them to the door, and Mark left with a wave. John lingered behind for a few minutes and, once Mark was out of sight, leaned forward and pressed a kiss on her forehead. "Well, I guess I'll go so you can start your cleanup routine." He pulled her fingers to his lips and kissed the one that bore his CTR ring. "See you later."

Mary Grace took a few deep breaths, then walked to the phone and called Heath. She asked him if he'd had any luck finding a bank willing to loan her money.

"No, but then I haven't had a chance to work on it much today. I've had a little emergency come up, but I promise I'll get to it this afternoon."

"I'd appreciate that. And could you fax me a list of the private investors who are interested in financing the loan?" she asked.

"Why? Are you considering that route?"

"I'm not sure what I'm doing yet, but I'd like to see the people who at least acted interested."

"I'll have my secretary send it right over," Heath promised. "Everything calm and quiet at the Arms today?"

"So far, but the day is young."

After ending her phone call, Mary Grace changed into work clothes, then went to Justin's office and waited by the fax machine until the list of prospective investors came through. She called Mark on his cell phone and let him know the list had arrived, then walked to the linen closet and stacked fresh towels on her cart.

When she reached the lobby, Windy was there, looking professional in a denim skirt. Mary Grace commended the girl for her appearance, then went through the front door into the courtyard, where she ran into a segment of the Haggerty delegation. They were wearing visors and smelled of sunscreen.

"I thought you were leaving today!" Mary Grace said in surprise.

"Mark decided that since the smugglers have been arrested, it's okay for us to stay," Kate Iverson reported.

Mary Grace gave them all a big smile. "Well, that is wonderful news."

"We're taking the babies to a petting zoo," Miss Eugenia said with a wave at the double stroller. "And I told Kate you'd let her fill Emily's sippy cups with apple juice left over from breakfast."

Kate's cheeks turned pink. "And I told Miss Eugenia that we could stop at a grocery store and buy our own juice."

Mary Grace smiled. "I'd be happy to provide Emily with juice. Follow me," she told Kate and headed toward the kitchen. "I guess Miss Polly and Lucy are watching TV to recuperate from their breakfast efforts," she said when they reached the empty kitchen.

"The meal was fabulous," Kate said. She looked around at the high ceilings. "It must be fun running this place. You get to meet so many interesting people."

Mary Grace laughed. "Even smugglers." She opened the refrigerator and took out a bottle of apple juice. "I do enjoy my life. I love the Arms, and I've met many fascinating people over the years. But it wasn't the life I'd planned on, and just between you and me, I'd trade it all for a husband and children."

Kate smiled. "It's funny how things turn out. I thought I would marry a guy with a normal, boring job, live my life in the Salt Lake valley, and have a house full of kids. Instead I'm married to an FBI agent, I live in a small town in Georgia, and I certainly won't be able to have a house full of kids."

"I wanted to be an archaeologist," Mary Grace admitted, "but circumstances changed my dreams, and I have to believe that the Lord had a hand in that."

Kate looked up with concern in her eyes. "Why wouldn't the Lord want me to have more children?"

Mary Grace shrugged. "We all have to have tests in this life—to see if we'll be faithful in all things, even hard things."

Tears jumped into Kate's eyes, and she looked away quickly.

"Or maybe somewhere there's a baby you're supposed to adopt," Mary Grace suggested. "It's possible that you have something else to accomplish in this life besides raising kids."

Kate frowned. "Like what?"

"Maybe you're going to invent an environmentally friendly replacement for Styrofoam or find the cure for the common cold."

Kate raised her eyebrows, and Mary Grace laughed.

"Or maybe you're going to be a room mom and den mother and do a really good job raising the two children you have."

Kate smiled as she screwed the lids on the sippy cups. "Thank you for the juice," she said quietly. "And the advice. I'll try to make good use of both of them."

Mr. Vincent was waiting in the lobby when Mary Grace and Kate walked through. Mary Grace waved as Kate went outside to join the other Haggerty folks. Then she turned to Mr. Vincent.

"I presume you're checking out?" she said coolly.

"Yeah, I've got to get back and write some spin-off articles. You might want to get a subscription to the *Inquisitor,* since your hotel will be mentioned frequently over the next few weeks."

Mary Grace ignored this remark and processed his checkout quickly. "Good-bye, Mr. Vincent." She handed him his final receipt.

He smiled as he headed for the door. "And you don't have to thank me."

"Thank you?" Mary Grace asked incredulously.

"For the free advertising," he elaborated, then stepped outside.

Mary Grace gritted her teeth to keep from telling Mr. Vincent just what she thought of him and his newspaper. After he was gone, she took the laundry cart to his room and cleaned it. Then she stopped by all the other rooms, providing fresh towels and touch-up cleaning where necessary. She had just started another load of towels when John walked in.

"Did you miss me?" he asked, clasping both her hands in his.

As he posed this question, Mark Iverson stepped into the laundry room. He glanced at their intertwined hands, then looked up at John. "I hope I haven't interrupted anything."

John smiled. "Not yet anyway."

Mark raised an eyebrow, then turned to Mary Grace. "I wanted to let you know that I got a list of the companies who have bid on the Arms and the private investors who have offered to finance your business loan. So far we haven't been able to tie any of them to known criminals yet, but I did come up with a couple of interesting facts." He paused, then continued. "Richard Harte is a majority shareholder in Aztec Enterprises, and Heath Pointer is listed as the company's lawyer."

Mary Grace stared back. "Mayor Harte is trying to buy the Arms?" she clarified. "And Heath works for him?"

"Aztec, which is a property acquisitions company, is one of Heath Pointer's clients," Mark explained. "The company has been in business for about ten years and is very profitable from what I was able to determine."

Mary Grace put a hand to her temple and tried to concentrate. "But Heath didn't tell me that the mayor was involved with Aztec. And he certainly didn't mention that he handled their legal affairs."

"The fact that he works for you *and* Aztec seems like a conflict of interest," Mark replied.

"Which might explain why you're having trouble finding someone to finance your loan," John said grimly. "Since Pointer is in charge of locating a lending institution and he also wants you to have to sell to Aztec, he might not be trying all that hard."

Mark raised his eyebrows. "That is entirely possible."

John was still frowning as he looked at Mary Grace. "Did you ever see an official appraisal on that Merek forgery?"

She shook her head. "Why?"

"Well, didn't you say Heath Pointer set the appraisal up?"

She nodded.

"Justin told you that it was valuable. If it had appraised well, you could have fixed up the Arms and turned it into a profitable business without going into debt. But the expert *Heath Pointer* hired says it's worthless."

Mary Grace felt a little knot of anxiety form in her stomach. "Are you saying that Heath told Richard Harte about the painting and they hired a fake appraiser to keep me from getting the money I need to renovate the Arms?"

"I think it's a possibility," John confirmed.

"I can't believe that the mayor would try to cheat me," she whispered. "And Heath is a *friend*. I know he has my best interests at heart." When they didn't look convinced, she continued. "He hasn't sent me a single bill for his services since Justin died."

"Maybe because he's waiting for a big payoff when you sell to Aztec," John proposed cynically.

Mary Grace moved toward the door. "There's only one way to find out. I'll have to call Heath." Both men followed her to Justin's office. John took a seat in the chair in front of the desk and Mark stood in the doorway as she picked up the phone. She pushed the speaker button, then dialed Heath's number.

"Heath?" she said when he answered. "I'm sorry to bother you again, but I never received a copy of the appraisal on that Forrest Merek painting."

"I didn't think you'd want a copy of the appraisal since the painting is worthless."

"I'd like to have a copy just to . . . keep on file," she told him with a shrug at Mark and John.

"I'll fax it right over," Heath promised, obviously anxious to end the call.

"Before we hang up, there's one other thing I wanted to talk to you about," she began. "The FBI told me today that Mayor Harte is a major stockholder in Aztec Enterprises."

There was a brief pause before Heath answered. "That's true."

"Why didn't you ever mention that to me?"

"I didn't think it made any difference."

"They also said that you provide legal services for Aztec," she told him, then waited for his response.

"That is also true. In fact, I'm the one who suggested to the board of directors that they should make an offer on the Arms. I figured that way I could get you the most beneficial terms. And I have," Heath said emphatically. "If you'd bother to read the proposal, you'd see that the contract gives you almost total control over the creation of the Bethany Arms Museum. In addition, you would receive a block of shares in Aztec, so you would share in the profits earned not only by the purchase of this property but all the others they already own. It's a good deal, Mary Grace. Not just for them, but for you too."

"You think I should sell to them?"

"I do, but I didn't want you to feel pressured. That's why I didn't mention my ties to Aztec."

Mary Grace turned and stared out the window at the beach. "If I sell to Aztec, they'll tear down the house and build a high-rise hotel."

"Probably," Heath admitted.

"You know how committed Justin was to preserving this property because of its historical value," Mary Grace reminded him.

"And the history can be preserved—by setting up a museum."

Mary Grace looked up at the intricate crown molding that circled the ceiling of Justin's office. "It wouldn't be the same."

"No, it would be better—accessible to more people. And instead of washing sheets and towels in some misguided sense of loyalty to Justin, you could move on to something meaningful."

Mary Grace was suddenly very conscious of the fact that Mark and John were listening to Heath's dismal summation of her life.

"But the final decision is up to you," Heath continued. "You can take Aztec's offer or tell them to forget it. And if you're really determined to renovate the Arms, I'll find you a bank that will loan you the money—even if I have to cosign myself."

Mary Grace felt a sense of relief. Heath *was* her friend. "Oh, Heath. I don't know what to say."

"We'll discuss it more later, and I'll have my secretary fax that appraisal over right now."

After she hung up the phone, Mary Grace stared at it for a few seconds, delaying the moment when she would have to face Mark and John and their reactions.

"I'm sorry to say this, but I'm afraid I have to agree with the guy," John said finally.

"He did make sense, and it doesn't sound like he's trying to deceive you," Mark agreed.

"I wish he'd just told me about Mayor Harte," Mary Grace told them. "I hate feeling like I'm in the dark, but I'd much rather sell the Arms to a friend than a stranger."

"So you're going to sell?" Mark asked, his expression one of surprise.

She glanced at John. "I have some important decisions to make, and it's possible that selling the Arms will be one of them."

Mark smiled. "Does your decision have anything to do with that hand holding I saw a little while ago in the laundry room?"

"Maybe," Mary Grace said demurely.

"Definitely," John amended.

The fax machine started humming, and Mary Grace walked over to pick up the pages as they came out. She glanced at each one, then passed them to John.

"Well, the appraisal looks authentic," John said reluctantly.

Mary Grace frowned, then picked up the phone book. "Assuming there really is an appraiser by the name of," she looked down at the fax, "Marvin Hunt." She looked through the business section. "There *is* a Marvin Hunt listed."

"But that doesn't necessarily mean that he came to the Arms and appraised your painting," John pointed out.

With a nod, she dialed the number and spoke to Mr. Hunt for a few minutes. He said he remembered her and the fake Merek well. He also mentioned noticing several nice antiques when he walked through the lobby, and said if she ever wanted an appraisal on them to please call him.

"Well, I guess that's it," she said after she hung up. "The Merek is worthless. Heath and Mayor Harte did not hire someone to mislead me."

John was staring at the fax. "That painting still bugs me. Something's not right about it."

"Maybe I should take a closer look," Mark suggested.

With a weary sigh, Mary Grace led the way to her apartment. The men stared at the painting for a few seconds, then John pointed at the signature and date in the corner.

"The appraiser said this date is almost a year after Forrest Merek died. A mistake like that would attract attention from anyone who knew art, not just an appraiser," he said.

"That's true," Mark agreed with a frown. "So what else could make this painting valuable?"

"I suggested to Gracie that it might be a treasure map with all the ugly little triangles pointing the way to a fortune in gold doubloons," John told Mark. "But she just made fun of me."

Mary Grace frowned at the painting. "I just said that all the triangles are pointing in different directions."

John shrugged. "So it wasn't such a great theory."

Mark walked over and lifted the painting from the wall. "The painting itself may not be a treasure map, but it still might be the key to finding Justin's log. What if there's something hidden inside the frame or glued behind the canvas?"

"Like what?" Mary Grace asked.

"A clue," Mark said, then looked at Mary Grace. "Do you mind if I take it apart?"

"I guess not," she replied, although the prospect did bother her a little.

They all followed Mark to the kitchen table, where he carefully dismantled the painting.

"If this turns out to be an important discovery, remember who thought of it first," John said with a wink at Mary Grace.

Mark worked meticulously, but once the painting and its frame lay in pieces, Mark sighed in defeat. "I guess it was a bad idea, John."

Dejectedly, they walked to the living room and sat down. "Are you sure that Justin really did keep a log?" Mary Grace asked Mark. "Or did he just say that to convince the FBI to make a deal?"

"You knew him better than anyone," John told her. "What do you think?"

She considered this for a second, then shook her head. "I don't think Justin was a liar. But then I didn't think he was a smuggler either."

"Let's hypothesize here for a minute," John suggested. "Let's pretend that I am Justin Hughes. I have been cooperating with smugglers for several years, whether out of financial necessity or boredom or coercion—it doesn't really matter. Now I'm terminally ill and I plan to leave the Arms to the one person who loves it almost as much as I do." He looked over at Mary Grace. "But I don't want Gracie mixed up with the smugglers. So I have to think of a way to get rid of them. How does that sound so far?"

Mark nodded. "Pretty good. Where's the log?"

John smiled. "I'm getting there. Okay, I've been keeping a log of all the illegal activities for years."

"Why?" Mary Grace interrupted.

"Maybe as insurance against prosecution in case he got caught," Mark suggested. "Or to keep his fellow smugglers in line?"

"Or maybe he was just a stickler for record keeping," John added. "He certainly spent a small fortune on hotel registers."

"Justin was very detail oriented," Mary Grace agreed with John. "And he was very smart," she said to Mark. "So it was probably a little of all three."

"Okay." John reclaimed their attention. "Back to my Justin impersonation. I contacted the FBI and offered to give them the log and my testimony in exchange for immunity from prosecution." He looked over at Mark, who nodded. "The FBI seemed interested, but it was taking them a long time to work out a deal with the district attorney. I needed someplace safe to put the log."

Mark looked up. "You mean somewhere besides the Arms?"

"I don't think he kept it here," John said after a moment of consideration.

"Why not?" Mary Grace wanted to know.

"Because the FBI searched every square inch of this place," John replied. "And besides, the criminals had access to the Arms. Since he was trying to keep them away from you, not attract them to you, it makes sense that he would hide it somewhere else."

"Maybe a safety deposit box or a bus station locker?" Mark followed John's train of thought.

John nodded. "Possibly. Even a house or a storage building."

"But what does any of this have to do with the painting?" Mary Grace asked.

John shrugged. "I have no idea. Maybe it doesn't have anything to do with it."

"I sure hope it isn't really valuable," Mark said, looking over at the mess on the kitchen table.

John's cell phone started ringing, and he pulled it from his pocket, then walked into the kitchen before answering. Left alone with Mark Iverson, Mary Grace searched for a topic of conversation. "So, you and Kate have decided to stay until the end of the week?"

He nodded. "And when we check out, I'll pay for our room."

Mary Grace gave him a smile. "I'm afraid that will be impossible. You won a contest and claimed the prize. It's too late to turn back now."

Mark nodded in acceptance of his fate as John returned to the living room. He looked a little pale, and Mary Grace was instantly concerned. "Is something wrong?"

"I'm not sure, but that was a tip about Victoria. I've got to check it out."

"Do you want me to go with you?" she asked, but he shook his head.

"I think I can handle this one alone."

She couldn't help feeling a little disappointed. "Don't miss me too much," he teased. Then he stood and his expression became more serious. "I'll be back as quickly as I can." With a wave he hurried out of the apartment.

Mary Grace returned her attention to Mark and saw the confused look on his face. Then he checked his watch. "Well, I'm meeting Kate and the kids for lunch, so I'd better get going too. I'll be in touch later this afternoon."

After Mark left, Mary Grace walked over to the big window and looked out at the ocean. As she rubbed her hands up and down her forearms, she wondered what Justin would say if he were there to advise her. Would he tell her to sell the Arms and put the past behind her? Would he encourage her to trust her heart to John Wright? Would he give her a hint about where he hid the log of illegal activities so the criminals could be brought to justice? Finally she gave up on an easy answer to the complicated questions of life and walked out to the front desk.

CHAPTER 13

Time crawled by as Mary Grace waited for John to return. Every time the phone rang, she jumped—and it rang often. Her mother called to see if any new disaster had befallen her, and it took Mary Grace quite awhile to assure her that things were fine. Bobby called to ask for more advice about getting his wife back. She listened with as much of her attention as she could spare and ended the conversation as quickly as possible. Then Jennifer called, and Mary Grace gave her friend a carefully edited version of recent events, all the time staring at the front door. Finally John called just as she finished dressing for dinner.

"Are you lonely?" he asked when she picked up the extension in her apartment.

The mental picture of him smiling to himself in his car made her heart race. "Just a little. When will you be back?"

"I've got one more stop to make, then I'll head that way. Could you do me a favor?"

"It depends," she replied, remembering some of his previous requests.

"Would you call Dr. Chandler and Sheriff Thompson and ask them to come over tonight right after dinner at the Arms?"

"I'll call them," Mary Grace said slowly. "But I can't guarantee that they'll come."

"I think that they'd do most anything for you, Gracie."

She sighed. "Why do you want to meet with them?"

"I think I've figured out most of what happened on the night that Victoria died, but I'm hoping if I get them all together, they'll admit the rest."

Mary Grace was skeptical. "That only happens on *Perry Mason*."

"Let's give it a try."

"Okay," she agreed. "I'll ask them to come at nine o'clock. By then, dinner will be over and the rest of the guests will be settled. But it will leave enough time for you to fill me in on your recent discoveries."

There was a brief pause, then John asked, "Promise me that no matter what happens tonight, your feelings for me won't change."

"My feelings won't ever change," she assured him.

"Remember that you promised," he said cryptically, then disconnected the call.

Mary Grace stared at the phone in her hands for a few seconds with a feeling of impending doom. Then with a sigh, she dismissed her uneasiness and tried to decide the best way to handle the invitations John had requested. She was considering and discarding several ideas when Bobby called back. When she heard his voice, she smiled.

"This is what I call perfect timing," she told him. "I need a favor."

"What?" His tone was guarded.

"I need you to bring your grandfather over here for a little while tonight. About nine o'clock."

"Why do you want my grandfather to come over?" Bobby asked.

"John wants to talk to him." Sensing that Bobby was about to object, Mary Grace pressed on quickly. "It will only take a few minutes, and I promise this is the last time. Please, Bobby. For me."

She heard him sigh. "Against my better judgment, I'll do it."

Mary Grace smiled at the phone. "Thanks, Bobby. You're the best."

"Would you call and tell that to my wife?" he muttered before hanging up.

Mary Grace spent a few minutes organizing her thoughts, then called the sheriff's department. She was connected almost instantly with Pete Thompson. "Is something wrong?" the sheriff asked, his concern obvious.

"John and I need to talk to you about something important. Could you come by about nine o'clock?"

"You're sure it can wait until then?" he asked.

"I'm sure. See you at nine." She hung up and headed for the dining room, where all the guests were assembled for dinner.

Lucy and Miss Polly had combined their efforts to make the most succulent fried chicken. "Lucy mixed the batter, and I handled the hot oil," Miss Polly explained.

"There's at least fifty years of cooking experience fried into this chicken," Lucy told everyone with a giggle. "It beats that finger-licking stuff to pieces, don't you think?"

Everyone agreed that it was the best they had ever eaten, and the cooks took turns modestly giving credit to each other. John arrived a few minutes late and filled his plate, then ate with relish. "You're not eating?" He pointed at her untouched food.

"Too nervous," she whispered.

He put another forkful of mashed potatoes into his mouth, then said softly, "Nothing to be nervous about. You've just survived a fire, discovered a murder, witnessed multiple arrests, and fallen in love. No big deal."

She rolled her eyes as Kate spoke from across the table.

"Miss Polly, you and Lucy should open a restaurant!" she encouraged enthusiastically.

"This certainly beats that stuff we had for lunch," Mark agreed. "We ate at some place called the Steel Fence."

"The Iron Gate," Kate corrected as she gave Emily a little bite of mashed potatoes.

"Anyway, I was the only man in the whole place," Mark continued with a significant look at John. "Our meal consisted of two pieces of asparagus and some carrot shavings, a little spoonful of low-fat chicken salad on a lettuce leaf, and for dessert—frozen yogurt drizzled with pureed strawberry." Mark shook his head. "I was hungrier when I left than when I got there."

Miss Eugenia gave him a stern look. "If you'd eat like that more often, you'll live longer."

Mark took another big bite of chicken. "If I have to eat like that more often, I'd rather die."

"I've never seen creamed potatoes quite this smooth," Annabelle said, redirecting the conversation.

"And the gravy doesn't have a single lump," Miss George Ann added.

"The secret is to use cornstarch instead of flour," Miss Polly explained. "And we're just so glad everyone's enjoying the food."

"Everybody better enjoy it. With all this fat and cholesterol, it will probably be our last meal," Miss Eugenia predicted ominously.

After dinner was over and the guests had gone their separate ways, John and Mary Grace moved into the lobby. "Where are we going to meet?" John asked.

"I thought we'd just go into my apartment so we won't be interrupted," she replied. "What's going on?"

"I'm going to tell them we know about the baby Victoria delivered that night," John said slowly. "But I don't want to involve Mrs. Lowery or Mayor Harte, so I'm going to suggest that the lab found amniotic fluid on the paint chips I took from the Seafoam."

"The lab didn't find amniotic fluid on the paint chips?"

"The lab hasn't found anything yet. It will probably take weeks for the analysis to be completed." He looked down at Mary Grace, concern in his eyes. "I think I know what happened to Victoria, but I hate to share my theory with you since I could be *wrong*."

"You have to tell me," Mary Grace insisted. "Nothing you could tell me would be worse than the anxiety of not knowing!"

He took a deep breath. "Remember, this is just a theory." She nodded, and he extended a piece of paper toward her. She read slowly, and soon her hands began to tremble as tears coursed down her cheeks.

"Oh, John. Your theory *is* worse than the suspense," she said, and he gathered her gently into his arms. "In fact, it's the worst thing I've ever heard." He stroked her hair and let her weep until her grief was spent. "I'm so furious and frustrated and angry," she told him. "I'd like to lash out at someone, but I don't know who!"

"Our guests will be here in a few minutes, and you can take your pick," John said grimly. "I know I can't really understand how you feel, but I'm angry too."

She took a deep, shuddering breath. "I've got to get control of myself," she whispered, massaging her throbbing temple.

He nodded. "Otherwise you'll tip them off."

She pressed her lips firmly together, then took a step toward her apartment. "I'll wash my face and take something for this sudden headache. Then I'll come right back."

John nodded again as she hurried down the hallway. Mary Grace went straight into the bathroom of her apartment and splashed warm water onto her face. Then she stared at her reflection. She saw the same large, dark eyes and the same stylishly cut, silky brown hair, but now everything had changed. Pressing a towel to her lips, she closed her eyes and prayed for strength. Then she took some ibuprofen and walked back to the lobby just as the front door opened.

Bobby walked in, followed by his grandfather and the sheriff. Randy Kirkland brought up the rear. Mary Grace was surprised to see the reverend, but John didn't seem to be. He watched as Mary Grace greeted all the invitees.

"We have pie left over from dinner if anyone would care for some," she offered, but the men shook their heads, expressions solemn.

"You didn't tell me you'd asked Dr. Chandler to come too," Pete Thompson said.

He had never addressed Mary Grace in such a terse tone, and she bit her lip as tears threatened again. "This shouldn't take long."

"It better not," the sheriff grumbled.

At this point Mary Grace abandoned all pretense that this was a friendly gathering and led the way down the hall. Once they entered her apartment, Mary Grace pointed to the couch and chairs in the living room. The guests sat down warily. John pulled a chair in from the kitchen so he could face them. Mary Grace sat on the ottoman to his left and waited for the drama to unfold.

John began the discussion by making an announcement. "I got a call today from a friend of mine at a lab in Savannah. He had the preliminary results on the paint chips we took from the Seafoam Motel."

Sheriff Thompson leaned forward aggressively. "You took *what* from the Seafoam?"

"Paint chips. I knocked some off the wall of room seventeen into a plastic bag," John admitted shamelessly.

The sheriff's face turned red with anger. "You defaced public property!"

"Why would you do that?" Bobby asked, obviously mystified.

"Because the sheriff told me the owner of the Seafoam had painted over the bloodstains to keep people from trying to get a look at the room where Victoria died. I hoped that traces of blood would still be on the back of the paint chips."

"I don't see what you expected to gain from that," the sheriff said derisively. "We already know that Victoria's blood is on the walls."

John acknowledged this comment with a little nod. "I had hoped that maybe a second blood type would show up and give us a clue to the killer's identity."

"So, was there another blood type on the paint chips?" Bobby asked, and John shook his head.

The sheriff seemed pleased by this. "Silly waste of time," he said contemptuously. "And you'd better be glad I don't feel inclined to arrest you for vandalism."

"Sit back, Sheriff, and when we get to the end of our little discussion here tonight, we can decide who needs to be arrested," John said, and Pete Thompson paled. "Can you explain why there would have been amniotic fluid on those paint chips, Dr. Chandler?" John asked, but the doctor didn't reply. He just continued to stare at John, his expression cold as stone.

"No comment?" John continued. "Well, I guess I can fill the answer in for you. There was amniotic fluid on the walls because Victoria Harte delivered a baby in room seventeen on the night she died. Her pregnancy was the reason she ran away in the first place—and why she wasn't seen around town during the Christmas holidays even though she was here."

"Victoria Harte was *pregnant?*" Bobby clarified.

John nodded. "Yes. But she didn't want anyone to know, so when she came back to Bethany Beach, she hid at the Seafoam."

"To avoid scandal?" Bobby guessed.

"Victoria didn't care about scandal," John told him. "But she had to protect the baby from her father, and the only way to do that was to keep her pregnancy a secret."

Bobby frowned. "Why did Victoria have to protect the baby from her father?"

Mary Grace found it telling that Bobby was the only one of the guests asking questions. "Because her father was abusive," she replied.

Bobby absorbed this information for a second, then asked, "If Victoria was about to have a baby, why didn't she go to a hospital?"

"I'm not sure about all of the details," John admitted. "I think that Victoria came back to Bethany Beach to confront the baby's father one last time, perhaps hoping that once he saw that the baby was about to be a reality, he would accept his responsibility."

"But he didn't?" Mary Grace asked.

John glanced at Randy Kirkland, who was staring at the floor. "No. He wouldn't help her. So she spent the night at the Seafoam, where her friend Justin Hughes was the night clerk. My guess is that she didn't know at first that she was in labor. When she realized the seriousness of the situation, she still didn't go to a hospital because she was a minor and they would have no choice but to inform her father. And as I said before, protecting the baby from Anson Harte was Victoria's most important consideration."

"When it became clear that the baby was about to be born, she told Justin and he called Dr. Chandler." John looked at Mary Grace. "But the doctor was with your mother helping her deliver." John turned to Dr. Chandler. "Which is where it gets tricky, wouldn't you say, Doctor?"

Dr. Chandler shook his head. "I don't know what you mean. I don't even know why we've been asked to come here."

John glanced down at the notes in his hand. "I want to be sure I get this right." He looked up briefly. "Feel free to correct me if I'm wrong. You left Mrs. O'Malley at eleven-thirty that New Year's Eve with a sick baby in your car. But you didn't arrive at the hospital until almost three hours later."

Dr. Chandler flushed. "The roads were very bad that night. Trees and power lines were down everywhere. It took forever to get to Destin."

John nodded as if he believed this. "The roads *were* bad that night. Mr. and Mrs. O'Malley have confirmed that," he said, and Mary Grace saw the doctor relax slightly. "But I don't think they were *that* bad." John reached out and took Mary Grace's hand in his, but his eyes never left Dr. Chandler's face. "Here's my theory. I think that when you left the O'Malleys' house, their baby was already dead."

Bobby gasped, and Mary Grace felt tears slip onto her cheeks. "Mr. O'Malley hadn't arrived from Atlanta yet, and you didn't want to give Mrs. O'Malley the bad news until he got there." He looked around the room. "That's understandable, I think."

"What in the world are you saying?" Bobby demanded.

John ignored him and continued to speak to Dr. Chandler. "You left with the lifeless baby, intending to take her to the hospital, but you stopped by your office for some reason and the phone was ringing—and had been for a long time. It was Justin at the Seafoam, where Victoria's labor wasn't going well. Justin didn't know what to do. The situation seemed dire, but Victoria kept begging him not to tell her father and refused to go to the hospital. So he called you. Over and over."

"This is pure fiction," Dr. Chandler said, but Mary Grace could see that his hands were trembling. A terrible sense of dread swept over her, and she had to control the urge to cover her ears.

"You answered the phone, and Justin explained what was happening at the Seafoam," John continued. "Victoria had lost a lot of blood, and Justin was afraid both the mother and baby were in jeopardy. So you had a choice to make. You could take a dead baby on to the hospital, or you could go to the Seafoam and try to save Victoria and her child." John paused for a second, and when he spoke again, his voice was softer. "I don't think you made the wrong choice, Dr. Chandler. Not that one anyway."

Mary Grace waited for someone to refute John's words, but no one did. Only Bobby looked more confused than she felt.

"When you arrived at the Seafoam, I figure that Victoria was already dead, but the baby was perfectly healthy. Justin was beside himself with worry, and the baby's father was there too." He looked over at Randy Kirkland. "But the father was unable or unwilling to take responsibility for a baby. And above all else, you had to keep Anson Harte out of the picture because he was the devil." John paused again, and the tension in the room was almost tangible. "And then you got an idea."

"This is ridiculous," Bobby said heatedly. "Tell him it's not true, Granddad." But instead of denying the charges, Dr. Chandler remained silent. Finally Bobby turned back to John. "So you're saying that when Granddad left the O'Malleys' house, Mary Grace was *dead?*"

"Not Mary Grace," John replied, still watching the doctor. "The O'Malleys' baby died. Mary Grace was very much alive, but her mother was dead."

"Victoria?" Bobby breathed, then swung his head around to look at Mary Grace.

"The resemblance is there if you look closely," John pointed out. "DNA tests can confirm my theory, but I don't think we'll have to wait that long. I'm sure the people in this room can clear things up if they have the courage."

Tears pooled in her eyes as Mary Grace turned to face the men she had known and trusted all her life. "Dr. Chandler?" she whispered.

Finally he sighed. "I guess I always knew this moment would come."

"Rimson," Sheriff Thompson said in a warning tone, but Dr. Chandler shook his head.

"It's over." He turned back to Mary Grace. "There are no words that can adequately describe how awful that night was. The weather was terrible; the power and phones were out. Under these conditions, I watched your mother labor to bring a stillborn baby into the world. She knew her body couldn't support another pregnancy, and she was so anxious to be a mother. That dream was now as dead as her poor infant."

Mary Grace clutched John's hand and shivered.

"Randy was just a kid and didn't have the resources or maturity to care for a child. I was a widower and knew that I wouldn't be allowed to adopt. We needed to call Victoria's father, but after the things that Justin told me about Anson Harte, I knew I could never put another child at his mercy. So we had to arrange for the baby first." The doctor paused and looked at Sheriff Thompson. The other man sighed and picked up the discourse.

"Rimson called me and asked me to come over," Pete Thompson admitted. "When I got there they were waiting in the room next door. Randy was crying, and Justin was holding the baby." He glanced at Mary Grace. "She was the prettiest little thing I'd ever seen."

Randy Kirkland spoke for the first time. "I know you're all determined to make me the villain in this, but that's unfair. I was a seventeen-year-old kid."

"So was Victoria," John pointed out, but Randy shook his head.

"Oh, no. In years she was young, but in life experience, Victoria was as old as time." Randy put his head in his hands, then continued. "I knew even then that I wanted to be a minister. My parents were supportive and helped me to plan my life so that a career in the ministry would be possible." He looked up briefly. "I did everything right. I made perfect grades, I was active in the community, I dated good girls."

"Except for your brief relationship with Victoria Harte," John said harshly, and Randy's head dropped back into his hands.

"Cindy and I had some silly fight. I can't even remember what it was about, but when word got out that Cindy had broken up with me, Victoria started hanging around. She would sit at my lunch table, meet me at my locker between classes, and even ask me out on occasion. At first I was flattered. She was exciting and beautiful." He paused. "But not the kind of girl a future preacher could *date*."

"Just the kind of girl a future preacher could compromise," John said without mercy.

"Getting involved with her was a terrible mistake," Randy Kirkland admitted. "It was like Victoria cast a spell on me, and I was powerless to resist. But after a few weeks, I knew I was going to have to break things off with her."

"Why?" John asked.

"I'm a very reserved kind of person, but Victoria was spontaneous to the point of insanity. For instance, one night I was driving her home from a party. She had been drinking and said she wanted to go swimming. She kept grabbing the steering wheel, and I was afraid she'd kill us both, so I drove down to the beach. I thought we'd wade into the water, stand there for a few minutes, and go." Randy took a shuddering breath.

"But Victoria stripped to her underwear and ran all the way out into the waves. I was afraid she was going to drown and terrified that someone was going to see us. Finally I convinced her to come out of the water, but she wouldn't put her clothes back on, so I had to deliver her to her father in her wet underclothes." Randy paused for a deep breath. "That night was a turning point for me. I knew I couldn't continue a relationship with Victoria unless I wanted to have a nervous breakdown. So the next day I told her we were through."

"But you doubled to the prom."

"Victoria didn't give up easily," Randy acknowledged. "Since I wouldn't take her as my date, she arranged to double with me and Cindy." He looked up at John. "Cindy told you it was awful, but let me assure you, she was understating it. That was the worst night of my life." He glanced over at Mary Grace. "Until New Year's Eve at the Seafoam."

"Did you see much of Victoria after the prom?"

"I made a point not to," Randy explained. "Then I worked out of town all summer, so I didn't see her again until just before school started back." He paused and everyone waited expectantly. "She came to my house and told me she was pregnant. She admitted that she'd stopped taking her birth control pills and gotten pregnant on purpose. Then she claimed that the baby was mine." He faced his audience again. "She was not known for being faithful to one person at a time, and there was no reason for me to believe her." He rubbed his temples.

"Why would she get pregnant on purpose?" Bobby asked.

"To get away from her father," Randy admitted miserably. "She had told me some of what went on in that house, and I learned more afterwards. But as bad as I felt for her, I knew that wasn't a justification for marriage."

"She wanted you to marry her?" Bobby clarified, and Randy nodded.

"But you refused?" John prompted.

Randy laughed harshly. "I had another year of *high school* and no job. I couldn't support a wife and child! And I didn't love Victoria. It would have been a disaster."

"And marriage to Victoria would have messed up all your little dreams," John said. "She was young and scared and pregnant. She needed *help*."

Randy flushed. "I did offer to help. I told her I'd pay for an abortion or even arrange an adoption. But she said the baby was hers and nobody was going to take it away. She left after she made me promise not to tell anyone about the baby."

"Which you agreed to gladly," John guessed. "Where did she go?"

Randy shrugged. "The rumor was that her father had sent her to school in New England, but Justin told me later that she ran away and went to one of those free homes for unwed mothers instead."

John didn't respond immediately, but stared at Randy until he looked away in shame. "Then Victoria came back to town right after Christmas?"

Randy nodded. "She called, and I met her out at the Seafoam." Randy's voice cracked. "She gave me one last chance to marry her."

"But you refused again."

He nodded. "There were too many strikes against us. It never would have worked."

"It would have given you some legal rights to the baby," John pointed out. "Now tell us about the night Mary Grace was born."

Randy sighed. "It was New Year's Eve. Cindy and I were at a party, and I got this hysterical phone call from Justin. He said that Victoria was in labor and had told him that I was the baby's father. He wanted me to come to the motel, but I couldn't just *leave* Cindy." Randy's tone was pleading. "As soon as I could reasonably suggest that we go, I took Cindy home and hurried out to the Seafoam."

"And by then the baby was born and Victoria was dead," John provided for him.

Randy nodded. "But don't think that the Lord hasn't punished me for my youthful sin of falling into temptation with a worldly woman," he told them. "Cindy is a fine Christian and would be a wonderful mother, but we haven't been able to have children. So my only child was given to papists and eventually joined the Mormon cult." He shook his head, as if amazed by the cruel irony.

"So much for any questions you might have had about being the baby's father," John said sarcastically, then looked away from Randy as if he couldn't stand the sight of him. Next he addressed Dr. Chandler. "You took Mary Grace to the hospital and registered her as the O'Malleys' baby?"

Dr. Chandler nodded. "And when I got back to the Seafoam, Anson Harte had arrived."

"Did he believe that the dead infant was Victoria's?"

"He never questioned it. His only concern was how Victoria's death was going to affect him politically. He said one of his major campaign promises was to reduce teenage pregnancies through education and free birth control. If it were generally known that his own daughter had died giving birth to an illegitimate child, it could keep him from being reelected. So he wanted Victoria's death to be classified as a murder instead." Dr. Chandler looked up at them. "It was the oddest thing how cold and calculating he was."

"Who put the knife in Victoria's chest?"

"He did," Dr. Chandler replied.

"Are you serious?" Bobby asked incredulously.

"I didn't know what he was doing until it was too late, or I'd have stopped him," Pete Thompson said. "But after it was done, I agreed to go along with his story."

"What happened to the O'Malleys' baby?" John wanted to know.

The sheriff shook his head. "Anson Harte said he would *dispose* of it. I was afraid he meant put it in a garbage sack and throw it in a dumpster, so I said I would arrange the burial. I named her after my mother and had her buried in a small cemetery out on Highway 150."

John glanced down at Mary Grace and gave her hand a little squeeze. "I told you I don't like coincidences."

Mary Grace couldn't muster a smile but pressed her face against his shirtsleeve.

The sheriff took a deep breath, then continued. "My wife found out about the grave and assumed the child was mine since I visited the cemetery so often." He looked up at the group. "When I agreed to the plan I thought that we were eliminating the grief, but I realize now that we just inherited it from the O'Malleys. We have grieved for that little baby. And since I couldn't explain the circumstances surrounding her birth, I alienated my wife and essentially ruined my marriage."

"Each of us paid a price for our involvement," Dr. Chandler said. "The anxiety and guilt affected my health and forced me to retire early."

"I presume that Anson Harte swore you all to secrecy," John concluded, and the doctor nodded.

"Not that it was necessary," Dr. Chandler said with a nod. "If the truth were known, the O'Malleys would be heartbroken, Mary Grace would be doomed to the same life her mother lived at the hands of Anson Harte, and we'd all go to jail."

"A week later we each got a check from Anson Harte," Sheriff Thompson said, and Mary Grace looked up in surprise. "He meant it as insurance against our having a change of heart, but I took it as an insult. I didn't plan to cash it, but when things got tense with Sadie, I used it to buy a boat and a little cabin on the backwaters. I thought it would help me gain some peace."

"Did it?" John asked.

"No."

"I used the check he sent me to finance my education," Randy volunteered. "I turned a terrible tragedy into a blessing that has brought many souls to Jesus."

John raised an eyebrow. "I guess you'll have to wait until you get a chance to talk to the Savior and see if He has that same perspective."

Randy looked away, refusing to answer, so John turned to Dr. Chandler.

"I never cashed my check," the doctor said softly. "I kept it as a constant reminder of my failure."

"What about Justin?" John asked.

"He used his money to buy the Arms," Dr. Chandler told them.

"And then you all made a point to be involved in my life," Mary Grace said. "Justin hired me to work for him every summer and taught me to love the Arms. Then he left it to me in his will."

"He wanted to tell you the truth, to explain," Dr. Chandler told her. "We discussed it many times before he died, but he finally decided that he would take his dark secret to the grave in exchange for your peace of mind."

"My parents felt so indebted to you for saving my life," she began, then had to pause to regain control of her emotions. "You were a welcome and regular guest at our house."

The doctor nodded. "I felt I had a responsibility to make sure that you were healthy and happy in the life we had given you. I mean, the O'Malleys seemed like perfect parents, but we had to be certain."

Reluctantly she turned and addressed Randy Kirkland. "Every summer you came by on the pretense of inviting me to church and Bible school and youth retreats."

"It was no pretense," Randy insisted. "I wanted desperately to share my beliefs with you."

"But not at the expense of your reputation," she pointed out.

"There was much more at stake by then," he defended his actions. "Your parents, your life, everything."

Mary Grace nodded, then looked at the sheriff. "You were more subtle. You stayed on the fringes of my life and only stepped in when I got into trouble. Like the day I got lost at the county fair or the time you pulled the jellyfish off my foot. And the ticket you fixed when I was sixteen. In your own way, you looked after me too."

The sheriff acknowledged this with a weary sigh.

"What about the kitchen fire?" John asked him.

"That was not my idea," Sheriff Thompson said.

Mary Grace looked around in horror. "*You* set the Arms on fire?"

Bobby stood. "Granddad?"

Randy held out his hands in supplication. "It was supposed to be just a small, controlled fire to distract you from helping with the investigation of Victoria's death."

"For your own good," Dr. Chandler added with a pleading glance at his grandson. "But it got out of control, and we had to call Pete."

She turned to the sheriff. "You knocked on my bedroom window and woke me up?"

He nodded. "It was either that or let you die of smoke inhalation." He gave his coconspirators a disparaging glance. "At that point I told them not to do anything else without telling me first."

Dr. Chandler leaned forward and addressed Mary Grace. "I know that you're upset right now, but I hope that after you've had a chance to think about it, you'll be able to forgive us," he said earnestly. "You have brought so much happiness to the O'Malleys."

The anguish was too fresh for Mary Grace to dispense any absolution, so she buried her face in John's sleeve.

"The O'Malleys have a right to know about the other baby," John said softly.

The sheriff nodded. "I'll tell them."

"No," Mary Grace said miserably. "I'll tell them."

The visitors stood to go, and Bobby walked over to stand beside Mary Grace. He put his hand on her shoulder, and she looked up. "I don't know what to say except that I'm so sorry."

She swiped at the tears that wouldn't stop falling. "I know. Thank you for bringing your grandfather."

"Do you want me to stay?" he offered, but she shook her head.

"No. John is here."

Bobby nodded, then followed his grandfather out into the hallway. The sheriff mumbled a hasty good night and joined them.

Reverend Kirkland lingered a little behind. Once the others were gone, he spoke. "I'd like to get to know you better, Mary Grace," he said. "Tell you a little about my family and . . ."

Mary Grace physically shrank from him, and John spoke for her. "This is not a good time."

The reverend accepted this. "You know where I am if you ever want to talk." Mary Grace couldn't bring herself to look at him, so after a few awkward seconds, he turned to John. "I guess you have all kinds of titillating details to put in your article."

John regarded him with barely concealed disgust. "I won't print anything that will hurt Gracie or her parents, and you may benefit from that fact indirectly. That's all I'll promise you."

The reverend's shoulders sagged, then he walked out the door.

As soon as they were alone, John pulled Mary Grace close and stroked her hair. She put her arms around his waist and clung to him as she cried. "I think I felt better when I was mad," she told him. "Now I just feel sad."

"Once the shock wears off, you'll get your anger back," John predicted.

"The hardest part for me in all this is the fact that *Randy Kirkland* is my father," she whispered.

John drew back and looked down into her eyes. "Mike O'Malley is your father. Randy Kirkland only provided a little DNA."

Mary Grace smiled through her tears. "I love you."

John stroked her cheek. "Oh, Gracie. Now I'm going to start crying."

* * *

"So, what do we do now?"

"There's nothing we can do except lie low and wait for this to blow over."

"Estelle is making a lot of noise."

"But you've assured me that she knows nothing that will incriminate us." There was a brief pause. "If anything should change, give me enough notice to get out of the country."

"I will on the condition that you take me with you."

"It's a deal."

CHAPTER 14

With so much on her mind, Mary Grace expected to have trouble falling asleep that night, but she drifted instantly into a peaceful slumber. During the night she dreamed that she and John were on the beach with a million stars overhead. He took her into his arms and they started dancing. Then she looked over his shoulder and saw Victoria, smiling contentedly as she watched them. With a little wave, Victoria turned and started walking down the beach. Mary Grace wanted to follow her, but then she looked into John's eyes and knew she couldn't leave him—not even for Victoria.

Mary Grace woke up suddenly, then stretched before checking the clock. It was six o'clock in the morning. Giving herself a five-minute allowance, she rolled over and stared at the pictures of Victoria Harte taped to her mirror. She thought about her dream and wondered if Victoria really had been helping them after all.

When Mary Grace got to the kitchen, she found both Lucy and Miss Polly in tears. "What's wrong?" She looked around, instantly on guard for gunmen or arsonists.

"I just can't believe that I've got to go home tomorrow," Miss Polly sobbed. "I've never had more fun in my life than I have during these past few days cooking with Lucy."

"Oh, mercy!" Lucy howled. "It's been like heaven in this kitchen since Polly came. She can read all my old recipes, even the ones with little tiny print."

Mary Grace looked from one woman to the other. "It's good that you've developed a friendship," she began carefully. "And that doesn't have to end just because you live in different cities. You can call each other on the telephone."

"It won't be the same," Lucy moaned.

"Well, there's a chance that you might be able to come back in a few months for a reunion."

"What kind of reunion?" Lucy asked, her tone more hopeful.

"I'm probably going to close the Arms, and I'm thinking about having a big farewell party. I'll invite regular guests from over the years and city officials and friends."

"It will be huge!" Lucy cried enthusiastically.

"And I'll need some excellent cooks to plan and prepare the food," Mary Grace pointed out with a smile.

"Us!" Miss Polly realized with delight. Then she frowned. "But why are you closing the Arms?"

"It's time," she replied simply.

"I believe your decision involves Mr. Wright," Miss Polly predicted shrewdly.

Mary Grace was surprised. "What makes you say that?"

Miss Polly itemized her reasons. "All those long walks on the beach, and the way you look at each other during dinner . . ."

"The newspaper man?" Lucy demanded, trying to catch up.

Mary Grace nodded, and Miss Polly leaned over to pat her hand. "He's very handsome." Then she turned to Lucy. "Maybe we could have a Hawaiian theme for our party. I attended a wedding reception last summer that was spectacular. They had a real pig roasted on a spit and fresh pineapples and leis and everything. I even have a dress my niece sent me from Hawaii. It's called a muumuu."

"I wonder how I could get me one of those Hawaiian dresses?" Lucy asked.

Miss Polly thought for a second. "I'll bet you could order one on the Internet." She turned to Mary Grace. "And with the ocean in the background, it would be perfect."

"Good morning, ladies," John said as he walked in. He stepped up beside Mary Grace and put his arm around her shoulders. "What will be perfect?" he asked Miss Polly, then turned to Lucy. "And why do you need a Hawaiian dress?"

"For the farewell party," Lucy replied.

"Mary Grace is closing the Arms," Miss Polly added.

John raised an eyebrow. "So, you've decided?"

"I just told them that it was a possibility," Mary Grace hedged.

John laughed. "Well, at least we're making progress. Excuse us, ladies." He took her arm and led her toward the door. "Come on into the dining room and eat a doughnut while you read my article."

"You're finished?"

He nodded. "It took me half the night, but it's done." He handed her a single sheet of typing paper, and she started to read.

The small town of Bethany Beach, Florida, was rocked twenty-five years ago by the stabbing death of a local teenager. Out of respect for the family, press coverage was kept at a minimum and the local sheriff's department conducted a discreet investigation. No one was ever charged in the death of Victoria Harte.

Recently I had the opportunity to visit Bethany Beach and investigate this murder as part of our Unsolved Murder Series. Based on evidence found at the scene and through the cooperation of local officials, I was able to determine that Victoria died not of a stab wound, as was erroneously reported earlier, but of complications related to premature childbirth. The stab wound was inflicted postmortem by a parent in an attempt to protect the girl's reputation. Victoria and the stillborn infant were both buried in Bethany Beach.

It is my hope that this article will clear up any questions about Victoria's death and allow her to rest in peace.

"This is very nice," Mary Grace said around the lump in her throat. "Not very sensational, and it probably won't win your way back into your editor's heart, but it also won't get anyone arrested." Mary Grace stared at the article for a few seconds, then looked up at John. "I dreamed about Victoria last night. She was waving good-bye."

"I guess her work is done," he said softly. "Have you told your parents yet?"

"No, they're coming after breakfast." Several guests came in just then, and Mary Grace gave him a quick smile before resuming her duties as hostess. When she returned, John was frowning. "What's the matter?" she asked.

"I was just wondering how soon you planned to close the Arms. I'm tired of sharing you with all the guests. I want your undivided attention."

"That might get boring," she warned.

He tugged at a lock of her hair resting on her shoulder. "I doubt that. But I'd be satisfied if you could just sit down through an entire meal so I can entertain you with fascinating conversation."

She reached out and touched his cheek. "Now that's something to look forward to."

Miss Eugenia rushed up at that moment, her face flushed with excitement. "I was just listening to the CBS Morning News, and they said that the mayor of Savannah was arrested last night for driving under the influence of an illegal substance. Then they found more drugs in his pockets and the trunk of his car. He's in jail, and they mentioned *your* name!" she told John.

"Mine?" He seemed pleased.

"They interviewed your editor, and he acted like he had known all along that the mayor was a drug addict," Miss Eugenia confirmed. "He said that you were out of town investigating another story, but that they were recalling you immediately."

John's cell phone started ringing. "I wonder who this could be?" he said as he pulled the phone from his pocket.

Mary Grace walked with Miss Eugenia to the Iversons' table, noting that most of the Haggerty group wasn't there. "Where are the other folks?"

Miss Eugenia rolled her eyes. "George Ann has a headache, and Annabelle is sleeping in. She said the only way she was getting out of bed this morning is if I tied her up and dragged her." The old woman lifted a broad shoulder. "And I didn't have any rope."

Mary Grace laughed. "So, what's on the agenda for today?" she asked the Iversons.

Kate pulled a face. "Mark has to do some paperwork regarding all the recent . . . activity here," she told Mary Grace. "So Miss Eugenia is going to take us to the outlet mall."

"They have the most precious little NASCAR jumpsuits there," Miss Eugenia explained. "And I want to get one for little Charles."

Kate gave Mary Grace a thinly veiled look of panic.

Mary Grace leaned down and whispered, "Be sure and buy it big and he can wear it for Halloween in a few years."

Miss Eugenia continued, oblivious to the exchange. "Then I thought we'd get Happy Meals for lunch and go to the afternoon show at Underwater World."

"Take an umbrella," Mary Grace cautioned.

"Annabelle already warned us about what to expect," Kate muttered, then turned to her husband, who was happily eating his breakfast. "I think you should postpone your paperwork and come with us."

Mark looked up, startled. "As much as I'd like to get drenched with fish water, I think I really need to stay here and work." He was saved from Kate's reply by John's return.

"Well?" Miss Eugenia demanded. "What did your boss say?"

John smiled. "It's amazing the difference the arrest of a mayor can make. A few weeks ago, my editor sent me out of town and told me not to show my face in Savannah until everyone had forgotten my name. Now he wants me to fly back this afternoon for interviews with the national press."

Mary Grace looked down and tried to hide her disappointment. "So, when's your flight?"

He laughed and put his arm around her shoulders. "I'm not going back to Savannah anytime soon. I'm going to finish my summer murder series whether my editor likes it or not. I'll come here on the weekends until I talk you into marrying me." He kissed her, and gasps were heard all around.

Kate recovered first. "Congratulations." She glanced at Mary Grace. "I think."

John smiled. "Thanks."

"We're not actually engaged," Mary Grace corrected. "We're still talking about dating."

"But she loves me," he told the guests, then pulled Mary Grace toward the door. "And you'd better keep the Edmund Kirby Smith Room open for me," he whispered. "If we're just *dating*, the lack of hot water will come in handy for the next several weeks."

She shook her head in mock despair. "Go talk to your editor or other reporters or watch yourself on television. I've got to tell my parents about Ruth."

"Do you want me to come with you?"

"No. They don't know you well yet, and it would make things even more awkward."

He nodded. "Well, I'll be in my room. Call me afterwards and let me know how it went."

By the time Mary Grace reached her apartment, her parents were already there waiting. She gave them both a big hug, then offered them breakfast, but they declined. "We stopped at IHOP and shared an order of Swedish waffles," Mike told his daughter. "Absolutely delicious."

Catherine was watching Mary Grace closely. "Is something the matter, dear?"

"Please have a seat." She pointed to the couch. "I have something to tell you."

Now both O'Malleys were eyeing her anxiously as they sat down.

Mary Grace took a deep breath, then began. "You remember that John Wright came here to investigate the murder of Victoria Harte?" The O'Malleys nodded in unison. "And we were surprised when we realized that she died the same night I was born?" Her parents looked at each other, then back at Mary Grace.

"What is all this about?" Mike asked.

"Remember how Mother went into labor while she was here in Bethany Beach alone?"

"Of course I remember," Mike replied.

"I wasn't exactly alone," Catherine corrected. "Mrs. Crabtree was with me most of the time."

"You had a difficult labor and were exhausted by the time I was born," Mary Grace reminded her mother. The O'Malleys didn't contradict her, but they were watching her with equally confused expressions. "Then Dr. Chandler told you that I was having trouble breathing and left to take me to the hospital."

"Yes, yes, that's all true," Catherine said with a trace of impatience. For the first time, she didn't seem anxious to rehash the details of the birth.

"John and I talked to Dr. Chandler and Sheriff Thompson last night. He admitted that when he was on his way to the hospital, he stopped by his office and got an emergency phone call from the Seafoam Motel. Victoria Harte was there, and she was also about to have a baby. The weather was bad, and there was no one else to help her, so Dr. Chandler went to the Seafoam."

"With you in the car?" Mike demanded, obviously incensed.

"And you were having trouble breathing!" Catherine added in distress. "That was completely irresponsible!"

Mary Grace shook her head. "No, Mother. I was not in Dr. Chandler's car. It was another baby, one that was stillborn. I was at the Seafoam with my birth mother."

There were a few moments of silence, then Catherine whispered, "What do you mean?"

"I'm sorry to have to tell you this. I know it will be painful, but in the end I think you'll be glad you know the truth."

"What truth?" her father asked.

"The baby Mother delivered that night was born dead."

Catherine gasped and put a hand to her chest. "Mike," she whispered.

"Just a minute," he replied. "Let's hear what she has to say."

"Dr. Chandler didn't want to tell Mother the awful news until you arrived, so he took the baby with him, and I believe that he intended to take her to the hospital. But he got the call from Justin at the Seafoam."

"Justin?" Catherine repeated with tears in her eyes. "Why would Justin call Dr. Chandler?"

"He worked there as the night clerk," Mary Grace explained.

"I remember that," Mike said with a nod.

"Justin told the doctor that Victoria Harte was in labor and having a bad time," Mary Grace continued. "By the time he got there, Victoria was dead, but her baby was alive. There was no one to care for Victoria's baby, and since you didn't know that your child was stillborn . . ."

"Are you saying that Dr. Chandler *switched* the babies?" Mike asked.

"Yes, he did," Mary Grace confirmed. "He admitted it to us last night."

Catherine began to weep in earnest, and her husband put an arm around her as Mary Grace pressed on.

"At first I was furious with him too, but after listening to the whole story, I can't say that I really blame him. Apparently Anson Harte was a terrible person, and they didn't want him to have custody of Victoria's baby. The two of you were anxious to be parents and . . . it just seemed to Dr. Chandler like the logical thing to do."

"So, what happened to our baby?" Catherine asked as she wiped her cheeks with her husband's handkerchief.

"Sheriff Thompson arranged for her to be buried in a cemetery out on Highway 150. He even named her after his mother," Mary Grace said gently.

"I think my heart is going to break," Catherine said as she clutched her husband's hand. Then she turned to Mary Grace. "It's not that we aren't glad we have you, dear. But . . ."

Mary Grace nodded. "I know. I have a lot of conflicting feelings too." She watched her mother weep and had a moment of indecision. "Maybe I was wrong to tell you," she whispered. "I could have spared you the pain."

Mike shook his head. "The truth always existed. We owe that reporter fellow a debt of gratitude."

"Nothing could make us love you less," Catherine clarified. "But now we have another daughter to love."

"And grieve for," Mike added.

"Yes," Catherine said softly, then turned to her husband. "I'd like to visit the grave."

"John and I have been there. I can take you," Mary Grace told them, but her mother shook her head.

"I think this is something we'd like to do alone. Just tell us where to find the headstone."

Mary Grace nodded that she understood. Then she took a piece of paper and wrote down the location of the baby's grave. As she handed her mother the piece of paper, Catherine tucked a lock of hair behind her daughter's ear. "I love you."

Mary Grace caught her mother's hand in hers. "I know." Then she reached up and kissed her father's cheek. "Good-bye, Daddy."

Mary Grace stood in her living room by the window that faced the beach and stared at the waves after her parents left. She hoped she'd done the right thing by telling them. They had looked so sad that she wasn't sure. She worried about it all through the morning and into the afternoon as she cleaned rooms and washed linens. She was still contemplating the wisdom of her decision and its repercussions when the phone rang at three o'clock. Thinking it was John, she reached for it and said, "Hello?"

"Mary Grace?" It was Mark Iverson instead. "I've checked, and there is nothing still rented to Justin Hughes in the state of Florida. Not even a safe-deposit box or post office box. I'm afraid that John's idea is a bust."

"Well, thanks for trying," she replied.

She hung up the phone, feeling more discouraged than before. She looked at the remnants of Justin's Forrest Merek painting on her kitchen table and felt a tear slip onto her cheek. She had let everyone down—Justin, her parents, and even her poor dead sister. Then, as her eyes settled on the name scrawled in the corner of the ruined painting, her heart skipped a beat. Before she could act on her sudden knowledge, the phone rang. This time it was John.

"Mark just called and told me the bad news about my treasure map theory," he said by way of greeting.

"John," she managed to say, "you need to come to my apartment right now. Call Mark and tell him to come too."

"What's the matter?" he demanded.

She looked back at the ruins of the Merek painting. "We've been looking for the wrong name."

John was at her door in a matter of seconds with Mark right behind him. "What do you mean we're looking for the wrong name?"

She waved toward the kitchen. "We need to find something rented or purchased in the name of Forrest Merek."

John and Mark faced each other, then smiled. "Of course," Mark said. "Why didn't we think of that?"

"Because in addition to being sneaky and secretive, women are just naturally *smarter* than men," Mary Grace told them with a shaky smile. "And I'm guessing that the 'date' under his name is really a combination or a code of some kind."

Mark pulled out his cell phone. "I'll bet you're right. We'll start a new search, and I'll let you know what we find." He walked back out into the hall while John led Mary Grace to the couch. She settled beside him, and he asked how her talk with her parents had gone.

"They took it pretty well," she told him. "They were upset, but after they have time to get used to the idea, I think they'll be fine."

She paused for a few seconds, then continued, "I don't mean to sound selfish, but it's a strange feeling to know that I'm sharing their love. For twenty-five years, I've been everything to them and now, well, there's someone else."

He studied her for a second, then said, "The existence of another baby doesn't change the way they feel about you."

"No, but this drastic shift in family dynamics will be an adjustment for all of us."

"In a way, it will be a relief," he pointed out. "They won't focus on you so totally."

"You're right."

John pulled her closer. "They'll be fine. You'll be fine. We'll all be fine."

"I know we will. But I wish my parents understood about eternal families. It would help them so much in dealing with this."

"Maybe you should talk to them about it."

"There's been kind of an unspoken agreement between us that I can be a Mormon if I want to, but they aren't interested in religion."

"If the agreement is unspoken, I don't see how you can be bound by it."

Mary Grace snuggled against him. "You're right again." Then she asked, "So, did your editor offer you a big promotion?"

"Yes, but it didn't do him any good."

She frowned. "Why not?"

"Because once I get a lot of national exposure, I won't have to work for him or the *Savannah Sun Times* anymore."

Mary Grace put her hands on his chest and pushed up so she could look into his eyes. "Then who *will* you work for?"

"I was thinking that I could freelance," he told her. "I can do that from anywhere, even Bethany Beach. That way you won't have to sell the Arms when we get married."

"You'd quit your job and move here?" she whispered.

He cupped her cheek with his hand. "Gracie, I'd move to the ends of the earth to be with you."

She closed her eyes and pressed her face into the warm hollow of his neck. Once she had regained her composure she said, "As much as I appreciate that, I think Heath is right. This was Justin's dream, not mine. I'll work with Aztec Enterprises to make sure that the history is preserved, but it's time to let the Arms go."

He kissed her soundly, then they sat quietly for a few minutes. Finally he said, "I've been thinking a lot about that summer in Panama City."

She smiled. "Me too."

"If Courtney had arrived just an hour later, or maybe the next day or the next week—we might have been married for several years by now."

Mary Grace shook her head. "No, the timing wasn't right for us then. You still had a mission to serve, and I had to join the Church."

He sighed. "I guess you're right, but I hate to think of all the wasted time."

"It hasn't really been wasted. I believe that the Lord brought us together in Panama City and meant for us to find each other again when we were ready. Looking back, I can see how the Lord has blessed our lives, and I'm grateful for everything that has happened, even the bad things."

"The bad things?"

"Like Justin needing my help and then giving me the Arms. That required me to give up my dreams of being an archaeologist." She looked up at him and smiled. "But it also put me here where you could find me. Even the trouble you had with your newspaper over the mayor of Savannah helped to reunite us."

"I guess that's true."

"We have so much to be grateful for."

"Yes, we do. And recognizing the Lord's role in our lives is an important part of showing our gratitude. *And in nothing doth man offend God, or against none is his wrath kindled, save those who confess not his hand in all things.*"

Mary Grace smiled. "I'm impressed by your knowledge of the scriptures. In fact, you're almost as good as Miss Eugenia."

John raised his eyebrows. "She can quote from the D&C?"

"I'm not sure about the Doctrine and Covenants, but she recited a passage from Ether for me. She admits to having read the Book of Mormon several times."

"So why doesn't she join the Church?"

Mary Grace considered his remark for a moment, then replied, "She's trying to decide if she can live without her fingers."

He gave her a strange look, but before she could explain further, there was a knock on the door and Mary Grace reluctantly left the warmth of John's arms to answer it. Mark Iverson was standing in the hallway. "We've run a check on the name Forrest Merek."

"And?" John prompted.

"Nothing."

John frowned. "Then you're not looking in the right places. Try somewhere less obvious."

Mark spread his hands. "Like what?"

John turned to Mary Grace. "Think about Justin and his interests. Was he a member of anything like a tennis team or a country club?"

She thought for a minute. "He was a member of the Civitan Club and the Better Business Bureau."

"That's commendable," John told her with a smile. "But I don't think that helps us. Think of someplace where he could have a locker or safe-deposit box or—"

"He went to the YMCA in Destin religiously until he got sick," Mary Grace interjected. "He had a lifetime membership because he donated a lot of money to help them build it, and he was very good friends with the manager, Marvin Shackleford. Mr. Shackleford visited Justin often toward the end of his life."

John raised an eyebrow. "Sounds promising."

"I'll check it out," Mark agreed, then left the room again.

Mary Grace stretched her arms above her head, then turned to John. "Well, now that your case is solved and you don't have to leave for Slidell until Monday, what will you do with yourself?"

"My editor from the *Times* is sending some national news guys over to interview me about Mayor Eagan. That should take up most of tomorrow. And since all your guests are checking out and your cook is quitting, I thought maybe tomorrow evening we could go out to dinner."

"We could try that place Mark recommended so highly," Mary Grace suggested.

"The metal restaurant?"

Mary Grace laughed. "The Iron Gate."

"Or maybe we can just go for a nice, long walk on the beach instead."

She laughed again. "In your dreams."

"You can count on that," he replied with a sigh. "Actually, I was thinking that I might get a tan, and I was hoping you might want to keep me company."

"I have a hotel to run."

"Yeah, but most of your guests have either been killed or arrested."

"Thanks for reminding me," she said with sarcasm, and he laughed.

"But you don't care because you're going to sell this place and move on to an exciting new life as my wife." He kissed her just as there was another knock on the door. This time John answered it. "You're getting to be something of a nuisance," John told Mark when the FBI agent walked back in.

Mark grinned. "I think you'll forgive me when you hear what I've found. There *is* a locker rented in perpetuity in the name of Forrest Merek at the Destin YMCA," he announced. "And I'd be willing to bet that the combination is," Mark looked at what was left of the ugly painting, "10-04-74."

"Justin's log is inside the locker?" Mary Grace asked.

"I think so," Mark replied.

"Well, let's go get it," she responded, but John put out a hand to stop her. He was staring at the Merek forgery, a look of wonder on his face.

"I know who it is," he whispered.

"Who?" Mary Grace asked in confusion.

"The inside guy who has been running the smuggling operation at the Arms since Justin died," John answered.

"You're sure?" Mark asked.

"It all just came together for me. Justin Hughes was a genius," he told Mary Grace, then turned to Mark. "But it's someone who will never admit guilt, so we're going to have to set up a sting."

Mark nodded warily. "Okay, what have you got in mind?"

John took a piece of paper from his pocket and scribbled a list of names. "We'll need help to prepare the trap. Mary Grace, will you call these people and ask them all to come to the Arms right after dinner tonight?"

She nodded. "Where are you going?" she asked as John moved toward the door.

"While you invite those folks to join us, Mark and I will be in your office making some more calls."

"Aren't you even going to tell me who it is?" she called after them, and John shrugged as they disappeared down the hall. Then she looked down at the list in her hand. It was a small group: Bobby Chandler, Heath Pointer, Richard Harte, and Sheriff Thompson.

After making the phone calls necessary to set up their meeting for that night, Mary Grace headed to the office to check on John and Mark, but her mother called before she could leave her apartment.

"How was the trip to the cemetery?" she asked.

"It was sad to see the tiny grave," Catherine O'Malley said. "But it's a beautiful place, and I felt at peace there."

"Are you going to change her name and move her to the family plot in the city cemetery?"

"No. She's been Ruth for twenty-five years, and it doesn't seem right to change that now. And in order to move her, we'd have to explain to the city officials what happened, and we don't want to get Dr. Chandler or Sheriff Thompson in trouble."

"It doesn't really matter where she's buried," Mary Grace said softly. "Her spirit is in heaven—which brings me to another subject. In the next few days, I need to have a serious talk with you and Daddy."

"Another one?" Catherine said with a little tremor in her voice.

"I haven't tried to push my religion on you up until now. You gave me the freedom to make my own choice, and I felt I should give you the same privilege. But I think that was a mistake."

"I'll talk to your father and let you know. Now try to get some rest tonight. I noticed earlier that you have circles under your eyes."

Mary Grace hung up the phone with a smile on her face. Things were already on their way back to normal. The phone rang again, and this time it was Jennifer.

"Have you had any more murders at the Arms?" Jennifer asked without preamble.

"Thankfully, no. But we solved the mystery of Victoria Harte's death. I'd tell you all about it, but I know you need to feed your kids."

"Stan!" Mary Grace heard Jennifer holler. "Make the boys a hot dog. Mary Grace needs someone to talk to." There was a brief pause, then Jennifer said, "I just bought myself about twenty minutes. Talk fast."

It took thirty minutes to tell Jennifer about Victoria Harte's story. Mary Grace was careful to leave out the parts about her own parentage and didn't mention the conspirators by name. Then, as soon as Mary Grace hung up the phone, it rang again.

"Your line's been busy for over an hour," John said when she answered. "I was about to get worried."

"I was talking to Jennifer," Mary Grace told him with a yawn. She checked her watch. "The time has gotten away from me. I've got to check on dinner."

"I'll see you in a little while."

After she hung up the phone, Mary Grace looked down at his CTR ring on her finger, then smiled.

Mary Grace helped Lucy and Miss Polly get dinner on the buffet table and greeted her dwindling number of guests. Once everyone was seated, she whispered to John, "Okay, the suspense is killing me. Who's the inside man?"

He leaned close and whispered a name to her. Her eyebrows shot up in surprise. "You're going to have to do some major explaining to convince me of that one," she told him.

He nodded. "Just wait until our meeting tonight."

"I think I'm going to slip out for a little while and go to the cemetery," she said.

"Do you want me to go with you?" he offered.

"No, eat your dinner. I think, this time anyway, I'd like to go alone."

He nodded his understanding, then she excused herself to her guests and drove to the cemetery on Highway 150. The summer sun was just beginning to set, making the spot even more beautiful. She had only been standing in front of the small headstone for a few minutes when she heard a noise behind her. She turned to see Dr. Chandler and Bobby approaching.

"We didn't mean to disturb you," the doctor said, looking older than she remembered.

"You're not disturbing me," she told him with a smile. "In fact, you've saved me a trip. I was planning to come by your office."

"No more questions, Mary Grace. Please," the doctor pleaded. "I've spent twenty-five years trying to *forget* what happened."

She took a step toward him and touched his frail shoulder. "I won't ask any questions, but I do want to thank you."

The old man raised his eyes to meet hers. "Thank me?"

"For my life, for saving me from Anson Harte, for all the sacrifices you made in my behalf."

Dr. Chandler's body trembled as tears coursed down his aged cheeks. "Do you forgive me then?"

She put her damp cheek against his. "There's nothing to forgive. The Lord placed me in your hands."

Dr. Chandler gave her a quick squeeze, then moved forward and stood before the little headstone. Bobby walked up beside Mary Grace. "You've given him peace at last," he said quietly.

"It was a shock to find out the truth," she admitted. "But now that I've had some time to think about it, I'm very grateful."

"I've got some good news," Bobby told her. "Annie has agreed to talk to me."

"Oh, Bobby!" Mary Grace cried. "I told you she wouldn't be able to resist you for long."

He smiled. "She hasn't agreed to let me move back home, but it's a start."

"She'll forgive you," Mary Grace assured him.

"I hope you're right."

Dr. Chandler turned and walked back to where they stood. He took a handkerchief from his pocket and dabbed at his forehead. "Too hot to stay out here long. It was good to see you, Mary Grace." With a nod in her direction, he made slow progress toward Bobby's car.

"See you in a little while," Bobby said, then followed his grandfather.

Mary Grace took one more look at the little grave, then squared her shoulders and hurried back to the Arms.

* * *

The man held the cigarette in his lips, then dialed his cell phone as he drove down the road. When a voice answered, he said, "They've found the log Justin Hughes kept. As soon as I get it, we can relax."

"They're not on to you?" the other voice wanted to know.

The man with the cigarette laughed. "They haven't got a clue."

CHAPTER 15

Once the group was assembled that evening in the dining room, John began by thanking everyone for coming.

"I hope this won't take long," Richard Harte said with a look at his watch. "I have a meeting with my campaign manager in an hour."

John pulled his cell phone from his pocket and handed it to the mayor. "You'll want to cancel that."

Richard Harte stared at John for a few seconds, then stood and walked to a corner of the room to make his call. When the mayor returned to the table, John recapped the smuggling operation and the FBI's investigation. "I know most of you were aware of those details," John said when he was finished, "but I wanted everyone to be on the same page, so to speak."

"I thought that when those guests got arrested, the smuggling ring was defunct," Heath said with a confused look on his face.

"It is definitely closed down as far as the Arms is concerned," Mark confirmed. "But the people who were arrested were hired assassins and dispensable employees. We didn't even get close to the brains behind the scheme."

"The smuggling operation ran so smoothly, even after Justin Hughes died," John told them. "There had to be an inside person assisting the criminals."

Mark leaned forward and took over the discussion. "Mr. Hughes told the FBI that he kept a log of the illegal activity that transpired at the Arms. Since two professional killers were sent to find it, we assumed it must incriminate some important people, including the inside man. But we didn't know where else to look for the log. Then Mary Grace remembered something."

All eyes turned to Mary Grace, and she blushed. "It was really just a lucky guess."

"Mary Grace told us that Justin went to the YMCA in Destin every day before he got sick," John explained. "The manager is a guy named Marvin Shackleford, and when Justin became too ill to go to the YMCA, Shackleford came to see him here at the Arms."

"Which, if you think about it, is highly suspicious," Mark inserted.

"Maybe they were just good friends," Bobby proposed.

John gave Bobby a doubtful look. "I think Justin's trips to the YMCA were really transfers of information, like when shipments were arriving, what type of cargo they would be carrying, etc. When Justin got sick, the information still needed to be passed on, so Shackleford came here."

"And after Justin died?" Bobby asked.

Mary Grace cleared her throat. "Justin told me that he had given Mr. Shackleford permission to use the beach anytime."

"Does he still come to the Arms?" Heath asked.

She nodded. "Regularly."

"Mark had the FBI do a little checking, and they found a locker at the YMCA with a lifetime rental under the name of Forrest Merek."

Bobby shook his head. "Never heard of him."

"The name from the painting," Heath said with sudden comprehension. "It *is* a fake, but it's also *valuable*."

"Exactly," John agreed.

"I hate to seem impatient," the mayor said. "But what does any of this have to do with me?"

John gave him a disappointed look. "I thought as mayor of Bethany Beach you'd want to help bring down an international crime ring that has been operating in your city for who knows how long."

The mayor frowned. "It seems like it would be better to let the law enforcement agencies handle it."

"I'm here representing the FBI, and Sheriff Thompson is actually in charge," Mark told them. "But since none of us are Forrest Merek, we will need Mr. Shackleford's cooperation in obtaining the log from Justin's locker."

"And a confession from Mr. Shackleford would be nice too," John added.

"Which the sheriff will never get," Mark pronounced with assurance. "We are hoping that if Mary Grace and Mr. Pointer approach him, Mr. Shackleford won't feel threatened."

"So Heath and I will go to the YMCA in Destin?" Mary Grace asked, and Mark nodded.

"You will tell Mr. Shackleford that Justin rented a locker in the name of Forrest Merek. Since you are Justin's heir and Mr. Pointer was his lawyer, we are hoping that Mr. Shackleford will give you the number."

"And inside that locker I'm willing to bet you will find the log that the bad guys are so anxious to get their hands on," John said with a confident smile.

"Where will the sheriff be?" Mary Grace wanted to know.

"He's got to go by and pick up a search warrant just in case Mr. Shackleford demands one," John said with a look at Pete Thompson, who nodded. "Then he'll join Mark and me outside. We'll be watching the exits in case Shackleford tries to run."

Mary Grace didn't look happy. "That sounds dangerous."

John flashed her a quick smile. "It's a perfect way to get an exclusive on the story."

"And I'll have deputies in cars all around the parking lot. Mr. Wright and Agent Iverson are really just volunteers," the sheriff clarified.

"We're a little more than that." John seemed offended by this classification. "We can stand by the exits without attracting attention. Shackleford might get suspicious if he sees a lot of sheriff's deputies."

"Which is where you come in, Mayor," Mark said to Richard Harte. "We've set up a news conference in front of the YMCA for nine o'clock tonight."

The mayor looked aghast. "What in the world will I say?"

"You can kind of rehash the recent happenings at the Arms," John suggested. "Or call for tougher gun control laws, the importance of physical exercise, more traffic lights, whatever."

"Traffic lights?" Bobby asked in confusion.

"It doesn't really matter *what* you say," Mark explained. "We just need you to get the television cameras there so that Mr. Shackleford will be distracted while Mary Grace and Mr. Pointer are looking for the log."

"What will we do when we get the notebook?" Heath asked.

"Just bring it outside, get into your car, and drive back to the Arms," the sheriff told him. "Once you're sure that the log incriminates Mr. Shackleford, my deputies will move in at the Y."

"That sounds like an okay plan," Mary Grace agreed after a few moments of consideration.

"Are you kidding?" John demanded with a smile "It's brilliant."

"It's fine with me," Heath concurred. "I never would have expected this Shackleford guy to be involved, but it does make sense."

Richard Harte sighed. "I guess I have no choice but to cooperate."

John smiled. "Sure you do. You can refuse and be one of the bad guys in my nationally syndicated article, or you can agree to help us and be one of the good guys."

"What will I be doing during all this?" Bobby wanted to know.

"You will keep an eye on things here at the Arms and help Gracie and Heath review the log when they get back."

Mark stood and pulled a gun from the holster under his arm. "Mr. Pointer, you'll need to take this—just in case," he added. "Please stand so we can figure out the best place to hide it."

Heath gave Mary Grace a smile, and he stood and lifted his arms. Mark tried several different spots, then settled on the right front pants pocket. "I'd loan you my holster, but wearing a coat in this heat would look suspicious. So the pocket is the best we can do."

They all stood and moved toward the door, and Mark gave one final instruction. "Remember, do *not* ask the YMCA manager questions or confront him in any way. There will be plenty of time for that once we have the evidence. Everyone's got cell phones?" They all nodded. "Exchange numbers, then let's go."

Before they left, John leaned down and gave Mary Grace a quick kiss. "Take care of her," he said to Heath, and the lawyer nodded.

"I was doing that long before you came along," Heath said with obvious irritation.

Mary Grace followed Heath out to his Volvo and waited for him to initiate the keyless entry. Then she climbed in and leaned forward, away from the hot leather seats.

"Well, this is exciting," Heath said as he got in and started the car. "Just like on TV."

"We've had too much excitement at the Arms lately. I'm ready to get all this over with," she replied, rubbing her temples.

Heath started the car and pulled out of the parking lot. "When will Mr. Wright be leaving?" Heath asked.

"He has to be in Slidell, Louisiana, on Monday, but he and I are sort of, well, dating, so he'll be coming back often."

Heath frowned at the road in front of him. "I can't say that's good news."

She smiled. "I'll tell you something that might fall into the good news category. I'd like to look at that offer from Aztec."

He smiled across at her. "What changed your mind?"

"If things work out with me and John, I'll have to make some changes in my life, and one of them will probably be selling the Arms."

"I think that's a wise decision," Heath replied, then he whistled the rest of the way into Destin. Mary Grace watched the side mirror for glimpses of John in the car behind them. When they arrived at the YMCA, there were two TV station vans parked near the steps.

"Looks like the plan is working so far," Heath said as he led the way past the cameramen. They waited by the front door until John and Mark were in place, then went inside and asked to see the manager.

"Hello, Mr. Shackleford," Mary Grace said when he emerged from his office. "I have a favor to ask."

"Any other time," the manager replied with a nervous look out the glass front doors. "But I've got a little situation on my hands right now."

Mary Grace planted herself firmly between Mr. Shackleford and the door. "This will only take a minute. Before he died, Justin rented a locker in the name of Forrest Merek, and I need to get something out of it. I have the combination, but not the number," she explained.

Mr. Shackleford dragged his eyes away from the crowd gathering on the front steps of his establishment. "I'm not supposed to give out that kind of information."

"I wouldn't want you to break any rules," Mary Grace said sweetly. "But I am Justin's heir, and I have been allowing you to use the beach in front of the Arms whenever you want to." She smiled up at the nervous man. "Mr. Pointer was Justin's lawyer and the executor of his estate, so you don't have to worry about our presence here being *illegal*."

A smattering of applause outside indicated that the mayor had arrived, and Mr. Shackleford looked over Mary Grace with obvious anxiety. "It's closing time. Could you come back tomorrow?"

Mary Grace frowned. "No, I'm busy tomorrow."

Mr. Shackleford surrendered with an exasperated sigh. "Okay, but we have to hurry." He looked up the locker number on the computer at the front desk, then led the way through the empty lobby into the deserted locker room. In a far corner stood locker 1254. Mr. Shackleford stopped in front of it and pointed.

"There it is," he said as he turned to leave, but Heath moved up behind him and removed the gun from his pocket, then hit Mr. Shackleford sharply on the back of the head. The man slumped to the floor.

Mary Grace couldn't control a small scream and turned angry eyes to Heath. "Why did you do that?" she demanded.

"If he saw Justin's log, he might have changed his mind about letting us leave peacefully," Heath explained.

She didn't try to hide her irritation as she knelt beside the fallen man. "We weren't supposed to do anything to Mr. Shackleford."

"We weren't supposed to question or confront him," Heath corrected her. "Agent Iverson didn't say anything about knocking him out if I sensed danger."

"I don't know how he was a threat to us," she said as she checked Mr. Shackleford for a pulse. "He was headed back out to the press conference."

"At least that's what he made you think." Heath stepped up to the locker. "I didn't hit him hard enough to really hurt him. Come on over here and enter the combination."

Mary Grace gave Heath another frown before she stood and turned the dial on the lock several times to clear it. Then she carefully put in the combination, and the locker opened smoothly under her hand. Her eyes were immediately drawn to several stacks of bills. "Is that money?" she gasped.

Heath reached in and picked up a handful. "Hundred-dollar denominations. There must be a small fortune in here."

Mary Grace picked up a leather-bound book similar to the ones used to register guests at the Arms. "And I'll bet this is the log."

Heath took it from her and flipped through the pages quickly.

"Mark also said not to read it in here but to take it back to the Arms," she reminded the lawyer.

"I'm not all that good at following rules," Heath admitted with a laugh. "And I can't believe this has fallen into my hands so easily."

Mary Grace frowned. "What?"

He held the notebook over for her inspection and pointed out his own name, which was listed repeatedly.

"I don't understand," she said in confusion.

"Oh, I think you do," he replied, and her expression changed from confused to terrified.

"*You* are the inside man? The one who has been smuggling things into the country by using the docks under the Arms?"

Heath grabbed her arm and pulled her against him. "Don't be dense, Mary Grace. Of course I am. In fact, I was the one who originally saw that the Arms had potential as a smuggling checkpoint and suggested it to some business associates of mine. The only problem was convincing Justin to cooperate. He steadfastly refused until I found out about the circumstances surrounding your birth."

Mary Grace felt the air rush from her lungs. "How?"

"Several years ago, Randy Kirkland was doing some estate planning and wanted to leave a few family heirlooms to you in his will." Heath looked over and gave her an evil grin. "Without his wife's knowledge, of course. So he told me the whole story, and I honored his confidence."

"But you used the information to blackmail Justin." Mary Grace felt furious and incredibly relieved at the same time. Justin was somewhat innocent, and Randy Kirkland did have a conscience after all.

"Yes," Heath replied impatiently. "Then when Justin died, it looked like the end of our very lucrative operation—until I realized that you were such a poor manager that we could continue without you ever getting the first clue."

Mary Grace allowed the insult to pass as she concentrated on what he was telling her. "But the FBI knew Justin had kept a log of the illegal activities before his death," she prompted.

Heath sighed. "Yes, and they sent an agent to find it, so my friends had to let their thugs—posing as guests—kill him."

An awful thought occurred to Mary Grace. "Did the smugglers have people stay at the Arms often?"

He nodded. "All the time. Like I said, you were oblivious." Heath sighed. "When this last couple ended up getting arrested, we had to shut the operation down. It's been very lucrative and I hated for it to end, but I've made enough money to last a lifetime." He shook his head. "So it's over now."

Mary Grace looked up at him incredulously. "How can it be over? I've seen the log and know about your involvement!"

"I'm sorry," he said, and he really did seem to be. "But I'm going to have to kill you."

She stared at the man she had considered her friend, then asked with a trembling voice, "What good will that do? If you walk out without me, John and Mark will stop you."

Heath shook his head, then pointed to the unconscious man on the floor. "I'll put his fingerprints on the gun and run out of the YMCA screaming that Mr. Shackleford shot you. If they thought he was the smuggler, they'll certainly buy that."

Mary Grace wrung her hands. "John figured out about Victoria. He won't give up until he knows what happened to me!"

Heath shrugged. "If that's the case, he'll have to be eliminated too." He held the gun to her head, and she closed her eyes. Then John and Sheriff Thompson stepped out from behind a row of lockers.

"Put the gun down, Pointer," John said harshly.

Heath laughed. "You have got to be kidding, Wright." He sneered the last word. "I'm the one with the gun to Mary Grace's head. You are not in charge of this situation!"

"We've got your confession on videotape." The sheriff raised a small camera into view. "That, combined with the log Justin prepared, should be enough to put you in prison for the rest of your rotten life."

"I'll admit that this does change my plans a little," Heath said with a frown. "Instead of staying in Bethany Beach, I'll have to leave the country. But I have money in accounts all around the world and friends who can arrange to have me taken anywhere." He looked between the two men. "And I know that neither one of you wants to be responsible for Mary Grace's death."

John took a step forward. "Give me the gun."

"Stay back!" Heath yelled. "I've killed people before!"

John took another step. "You won't hurt Mary Grace."

Heath laughed as John came even closer. "Of course I will. I will destroy anyone who gets in my way—including you and the bumbling sheriff over there."

John lunged for Heath just as Mark Iverson stepped out from behind him. Heath pulled the trigger on the gun, but nothing happened. Mark Iverson wrested the gun from Heath's grasp, then pulled his hands behind him with excessive force as John drew Mary Grace to his chest.

"Are you okay?" he asked, running his hands down her arms to reassure himself.

"I'm fine," Mary Grace promised, holding him tightly.

"You made a couple of crucial mistakes," Mark told the lawyer as Sheriff Thompson provided a pair of handcuffs. "Like forgetting that *I* gave you the gun and searched you for other weapons in the process."

"There were no bullets?" Heath asked in amazement.

"Worse than that," Mark said. "It wouldn't work even if it were loaded."

Heath shook his head, baffled. "So you never really suspected Shackleford?"

John answered. "We had another little meeting before you arrived at the Arms where we discussed the real plan—which was to trap *you*."

Heath looked over at Mary Grace, who was regarding him with disdain. "You helped them set me up?"

"Don't expect me to feel bad about that! You just tried to kill me!" she replied with feeling. "And you were supposed to be Justin's friend—and mine."

Heath shrugged. "So, how did I give myself away?"

"We noticed early on that you had an astounding amount of assets, but your successful law practice and good luck in the stock market seemed to explain that," Mark responded.

"And I saw you smoking once, which coincided with the cigarettes we found by a sand dune on the bluff," John added. "But I didn't seriously consider you a suspect. Then your remark about cosigning on the loan with Mary Grace made me suspicious. I mean, if you really meant it, she would have already had her loan."

"But it was Justin Hughes who gave us the final clue," Mark informed him.

"Justin?" The lawyer seemed truly shocked.

"It was that Forrest Merek painting again," John said with a grim smile. "We had joked earlier about the possibility that it was a treasure map, indicating where buried gold could be found. But Mary Grace argued that this was impossible since the ugly little triangles pointed in all different directions." John gave Mary Grace a warm look. "Suddenly it just hit me. The triangles were pointers—just like you."

Mark took over. "You had the most to gain—you had access to the Arms and the complete trust of the owner. It really had to be you."

"But without concrete evidence, we needed a confession," John added.

"Which you'll never get." Heath waved at the video camera. "Since you didn't warn me that I was being taped, that won't be admissible in court."

Sheriff Thompson gave him a cold smile. "I left it running *after* you saw the camera. So everything from that point forward is perfectly admissible."

"That tape, combined with Justin's log, should be plenty to get the district attorney's attention," John agreed.

"And you know how he feels about making deals," Mark reminded them.

Heath paled and tried to struggle against his handcuffs. "I want to call my lawyer."

Sheriff Thompson laughed. "Yeah, I'll just bet you do." He used his radio to confirm that deputies were waiting in the front parking lot to transport Heath Pointer to the county jail, then led the prisoner out of the locker room.

Mary Grace stooped down to check on the YMCA manager. "Do you think we need to call an ambulance for Mr. Shackleford?"

"It would probably be a good idea." Mark pulled his cell phone out and dialed 911 as Richard Harte walked in.

"So, how did the press conference go?" Mary Grace asked with a smile.

The mayor shook his head. "They probably think I'm crazy, but they got some good footage for the ten o'clock news when Sheriff Thompson walked out with Heath Pointer in handcuffs."

"An ambulance is on the way for the YMCA guy," John reported, then extended his hand to Mayor Harte. "Thanks for your help."

"It's the least I could do." The mayor looked over at Mary Grace, his expression almost shy. "Dr. Chandler and I had a long talk this afternoon. Maybe when things settle down a little, we could get together for dinner or something," he proposed tentatively. "So you can meet my family."

Mary Grace nodded. "I'd like that."

The sound of approaching sirens filled the air, and Mayor Harte stepped back. "Well, I guess I'll get out of the way."

"We'll be in touch," Mary Grace promised. Her uncle gave her a quick smile, then hurried from the locker room.

* * *

The cell phone rang in the gold-tone Volvo. Finally the answering machine picked up. "You've reached Heath Pointer. I'm unable to take your call right now, but if you'll leave your number, I'll call you back."

The caller disconnected without leaving a message.

* * *

When John and Mary Grace returned to the Arms, a delegation was waiting for them in the lobby. "Did it work?" Bobby wanted to know.

"Like a charm," John assured him, keeping his arm securely around Mary Grace.

Bobby shook his head. "I still can't believe that Heath Pointer is a criminal."

"I couldn't either until he held Mark's broken gun to my head," Mary Grace said. "That made a believer out of me."

Kate stepped forward. "Is Mark with you?"

"He went with the sheriff to supervise the prisoner until some more FBI agents can arrive," John told her.

Miss Eugenia pushed her way to the front of the crowd. "Okay, let's hear it. We want to know everything."

Mary Grace laughed and suggested that they go into the dining room. "There's pie left over from dinner for anyone who wants some."

"You have a seat," Miss Polly insisted. "I'll bring out the pies."

They waited for Miss Polly, then took turns describing the ambush of Heath Pointer. When they were through, Mary Grace sighed. "Even though I don't have any acting experience, I think I was pretty convincing," she told the Haggerty ladies.

"She was so good I almost believed her myself," John bragged on her behalf.

The front door slammed, and they all looked up as Mark walked through. Kate ran to him and threw her arms around his neck. "You're okay?" she asked.

He returned the embrace. "I'm fine. Where are the kids?"

"Asleep. Annabelle's with them, talking to Derrick on the phone."

"So the other FBI agents arrived?" John confirmed.

Mark nodded. "And the DEA and even a representative from the Coast Guard. Now they are all fighting over who will prosecute Heath Pointer first."

"I think everyone should get a turn," John proposed. "It's only fair."

"Poor Sheriff Thompson," Mary Grace said. "I'll bet they're driving him crazy."

Mark smiled. "He's a tough old bird. He can handle those guys." Then he looked down at his wife. "Well, since we're leaving tomorrow and Annabelle has the kids, why don't we go for a walk on the beach?"

Kate slipped her hand into his. "Sounds wonderful."

Mark looked over her head at the others. "I've got my cell phone, but don't call me unless it's life or death."

John accompanied Mary Grace to her apartment, but she wouldn't let him inside. "I'm exhausted, and I can barely resist you when I'm at my best. I think we should say good-bye here tonight."

"We've really got to plan our first date so I'll have something to look forward to," he said, then he kissed her and headed toward the Edmund Kirby Smith Room.

On Friday morning, Mary Grace woke with an unusual sense of well-being. She took a leisurely shower, then dressed in comfortable jeans and an old, sloppy T-shirt. When she walked into the kitchen, she expected to find her cooks in tears again since the day of their separation had arrived, but they were both smiling.

"I'm pleased to see the two of you happy this morning," Mary Grace said as she poured herself a glass of juice.

Lucy giggled. "I talked to my youngest son, Tyrone, last night. He lives in Macon and I told him that since the Arms was closing down, this would be a good time for me to come for a nice, long visit."

"And Macon is just an hour's bus ride from Haggerty!" Miss Polly reported with delight. "So Lucy and I can visit each other all the time."

"And exchange recipes."

"And practice pie making."

Miss Polly looked at Mary Grace and sighed. "It's a rare thing to find someone who truly appreciates a firm meringue or a smooth white sauce as much as I do."

"And I was telling Tyrone about my vision problems, and he thinks I might have cataracts. He says he'll make me an appointment with an eye doctor up in Macon and maybe I can have surgery that will improve my sight."

Mary Grace smiled. "I hope so."

The timer on the oven went off, and Miss Polly pulled on mitts as she hurried to the oven. "Biscuits are done!" she announced. "How about the grits and eggs?" she asked Lucy.

"Coming right up!" the little woman promised.

Mary Grace poured juice into pitchers and arranged them on the buffet table while the cooks brought the food in. The Iversons and Miss Eugenia arrived a few minutes later with the babies in tow. "Good morning," Mary Grace greeted.

Kate gave her a smile. "It *is* a good morning," she replied.

Mary Grace laughed. "Well, you seem much more cheerful today."

"I am," Kate agreed. "It's amazing what a leisurely walk on the beach can do for you." She winked at her husband, and Mark's cheeks turned red. "And all that intrigue last night reminded me how lucky I am to live in a nice, quiet town with a wonderful husband and two perfect children." Miss Eugenia's face fell, and Kate was quick to add, "And the best neighbor in the world!"

Miss Eugenia's expression brightened, and she gave Emily a biscuit, which the baby promptly threw to the floor. "Looks like she'd rather have cereal again," Miss Eugenia said with a tolerant smile.

"I'll get some," Mary Grace offered and started to rise.

"No, I'll get it," Kate insisted. "Just point me in the right direction."

"Inside the kitchen, second cupboard on the left."

As Kate walked into the kitchen, Miss Eugenia leaned toward Mark. "You can thank me later," she whispered.

"What for?" Mark asked.

"For the major improvement in your wife's disposition, that's what," Miss Eugenia hissed.

Mark smiled. "She attributed her new outlook on life to our walk on the beach. So I should get the credit."

"Humph!" Miss Eugenia scoffed at this suggestion. "There wouldn't have been a beach to walk on if not for me!"

He acknowledged this with a shrug. "You're right. I'll thank you now."

"For what?" Kate asked as she returned.

"Take your pick," Miss Eugenia responded. "He owes me so much."

John arrived a few minutes later. He greeted everyone and filled his plate, then bent down to kiss Mary Grace on the cheek before taking a seat beside her at the table.

"So, when's the wedding?" Miss Eugenia asked.

John swallowed a mouthful of bacon, then answered. "Mary Grace hasn't actually agreed to go on a date with me yet," he told everyone. "Let alone marry me."

"She will," Miss Eugenia predicted with a smile.

"This is so romantic," Miss Polly breathed, then dabbed her eyes with the corner of her apron.

"Congratulations on your redemption in Savannah," Annabelle remarked.

"Thanks," John said, but his tone was grim.

Annabelle laughed. "You don't sound too happy."

"I'm not. My editor sent a bunch of reporters down here to interview me today."

"They're from the national media," Mary Grace informed everyone proudly.

"Are Regis and Kelly coming?" Miss Eugenia asked.

"Not personally," John replied. "But CBS is sending a camera crew."

"Oh." Miss Eugenia's disappointment was obvious. "I just love that show. I still miss Kathie Lee, but Kelly is learning how to keep Regis in his place."

"Where are all these interviews going to take place?" Mary Grace asked anxiously, wondering if the Arms was about to be overrun by strangers.

"My editor reserved a conference room at the Marriott," John told her and smiled as she sighed with relief. Then Sheriff Thompson walked in.

"So, who won the battle over the prisoner?" John asked.

"The Coast Guard gets the first shot at him," the sheriff reported. "But Mr. Pointer is going to be spending a lot of time in court. According to a reliable source, he's singing like a canary."

"Do canaries sing?" Miss Polly asked. "I thought they talked like parrots."

"I don't know about that," Sheriff Thompson said with a smile. "But Heath Pointer would sell out his own mother if it would reduce his sentence."

This remark caused John to smile. "I'll bet spirits are high at the FBI offices today."

"They seemed pretty darn pleased," the sheriff confirmed. "Of course, all this cooperation on Mr. Pointer's part may mean that he won't do much jail time for his various crimes, in spite of our DA's reluctance to make deals."

John grimaced. "Oh well. Plea bargaining is the American way."

"Would you like some breakfast?" Mary Grace asked the sheriff.

"Thanks, but I've already eaten." He took a seat beside Mary Grace and lowered his voice. "We didn't get a chance to talk after our meeting the other night. I know that saying I'm sorry isn't close to being good enough, but I'll say it anyway."

Mary Grace smiled. "It's plenty good enough. You were faced with a choice no one should have to make, and you all put my best interest above your own."

He smiled his appreciation, then continued. "My wife and I had a long talk last night. I explained what happened, and I think things might be better between us from now on."

Mary Grace reached out and patted his weathered hand. "I hope so."

He raised his voice and included the entire table in his next comment. "Turns out there was almost $500,000 in Justin's locker at the YMCA."

"Wow." Mary Grace was impressed.

"Does that belong to Mary Grace now?" Miss Eugenia wanted to know.

The sheriff shook his head. "The money may be proceeds from the smuggling, so right now it's evidence." He looked at Mary Grace. "I heard that you were thinking about selling this place, but all of Justin's former assets will be frozen for a while."

Mary Grace shrugged. "It doesn't really matter. I'm going to close the hotel soon anyway." The sheriff looked surprised, and she explained.

"Well, congratulations," the sheriff said, then leaned forward. "And I want you to know that I think you look a lot like your mother."

Mary Grace put a hand to her dark hair. "Really?" she whispered. "I was afraid I looked a little like Ronald Reagan."

The sheriff gave her a blank look. "Ronald Reagan?"

Mary Grace nodded. "Don't you think Reverend Kirkland looks a lot like the former president?" she asked softly.

The sheriff chuckled. "I never thought about it, but you're right. He does."

John stood and held out a hand to her. "I've got to go get ready for my interviews. Will you walk me to my room?"

She took his hand, and they walked through the lobby and out onto the beach. They kicked off their shoes and let the foam bubble around their toes. "I thought you needed to get ready for your interviews."

"I've got a few minutes."

She turned her face up into the warm sunshine. "Do you really think I look like Victoria?" she asked.

John studied her. "You're a lot more beautiful, but the resemblance is there." He raised his eyebrows. "Maybe *that's* why I was so drawn to her."

"She was hoping I would be the first person to really love her back," Mary Grace whispered as a few tears slipped down her cheeks. "And I do."

John nodded solemnly. "She'd be very proud of you. And she showed an amazing amount of character and maturity for a girl so young. She ensured your safety."

"And Justin really was a good person. He did some wrong things, but in the end . . ."

John moved his right foot over until it was touching her left. "I can't really fault any of the people who have involved themselves in your life." He wiped a tear from her cheek. "Are you going to forgive them?"

"I already have." She turned and looked back at the Arms. "This place has always been a safe haven for me. I think that's part of why I held on to it after Justin died." She glanced back at him. "But I don't need it anymore. As soon as Justin's assets are released, I'm going sell it and use the money to do something in Victoria's honor."

"Maybe you could set up a scholarship for underprivileged young women, or help finance a home for unwed mothers."

She kissed his chin. "Something like that."

He grinned down at her. "If it will earn me more kisses, I'll come up with lots of good ideas! For instance, after you sell the Arms, we could move to Atlanta."

"Why? To be near my parents?"

"So you can reapply to Emory's archaeology program. Once you finish your degree, you can get an internship and I'll go with you to Egypt or ancient Mesopotamia or wherever they're digging up bones. You can look for artifacts, and I'll write newspaper articles."

She put a hand over his mouth. "I don't care where we live, and while I'd like to finish my degree, I won't apply for an archaeological internship."

"I want you to achieve your dream," he said through her fingers.

"My dreams have changed again."

He kissed her hand, then moved it so he could speak freely. "I hope I play a part in this new dream of yours."

She laughed. "You have the starring role. The only digging I see in my future will be in our yard—planting flowers and making mud pies with curly-headed, brown-eyed children who have a remarkable resemblance to John F. Kennedy, Jr."

"Oh, Gracie," he whispered. "Suddenly archaeology sounds like a lot of fun."

EPILOGUE

Six months later

Mary Grace stretched as she looked out the car window at the lights of Panama City. "So we're here?" she asked, and John nodded. "The drive went by fast. It seems like just a little while ago we were leaving the temple in Orlando."

John gave her a tender smile. "It has seemed like an *eternity* to me."

"If you had agreed to spend our honeymoon at Disney World like I suggested, you wouldn't have been driving for hours," Mary Grace pointed out.

John glanced over at her. "I know you're anxious to begin our honeymoon," he said, then wiggled his eyebrows, "but the only thing I hate worse than coincidences is unfinished business."

"What *do* you mean by that?" she asked. "And where *are* we going?" She leaned across the armrest to nuzzle his neck.

"We're going to have a wreck if you don't stay on your side of this car."

She laughed, then moved back into her seat. "Really, though, are we stopping soon?"

John checked his watch. "Pretty soon."

With a sigh Mary Grace looked down at the letter she was writing to Jennifer and reread it from the top:

Can you believe it? I'm Mrs. John Wright! If you had told me that would ever happen five and a half years ago in Panama City, well, I wouldn't have believed it. John is being very secretive about our honeymoon location. Not that I really care—as long as I'm with him.

I thought our wedding was wonderful and appreciate you and Stan making the trip. I'm sorry that we didn't get a chance to talk much. I'll call when I get back to Bethany Beach so we can catch up, but in the meantime this letter will have to do. And I also hope Stan's mother won't have broken the rest of the 101 rules about raising twins by the time you get home.

My parents seemed really impressed by the temple. The temple president and matron came into the waiting room and spoke to them personally. I thought that was very thoughtful. They've promised to start the missionary discussions when John and I get to Atlanta. Keep your fingers crossed for me.

I'm excited about going back to school, but nervous too. It's been awhile since I've taxed my brain about anything except washing sheets and keeping reservations straight. John seems eager to start his new job at the Atlanta Constitution. *If he hates it he says he'll quit and assures me that he can make enough freelancing to support us.*

My new lawyer says it may be years before the courts release Justin's frozen assets. Not that there's any rush, but I'd like to get things settled in Bethany Beach. We'll use some of the money to start the Bethany Arms Museum, and the rest will be used to fund a home for unwed mothers called Victoria's Place.

We're all still heartbroken about Dr. Chandler's death, but he died peacefully in his sleep and one good thing did come out of it. Bobby's wife felt so sorry for him that she agreed to a trial reconciliation. Hopefully things will work out for them this time. And Sheriff Thompson has retired. He said that he wants to spend more time with his wife.

Well, I guess that's all the news. I'm sure we'll visit my parents at their beach house next summer, and we can get together then. Or bring the boys to Atlanta and we'll take them to a Braves game . . .

"My goodness," John interrupted her thoughts. "That letter is turning into a book."

She smiled as she signed her new name across the bottom. "All through." She folded her letter and slipped it into an envelope as John handed her a map.

"Would you see if you can find Highway 119 for me?"

"Why are we looking for Highway 119?" Mary Grace asked as she studied the map.

He gave her a quick grin. "Can't tell you. It would ruin the surprise."

Mary Grace located the road he was looking for and gave him directions. Then she watched with growing concern as the landscape became increasingly rural. She had assumed that they would stay in one of the luxury hotels along the beach, but as the lights of Panama City faded behind them, she realized that she may have been wrong. She cleared her throat and said, "Your big surprise doesn't involve tents and sleeping bags, does it?"

He laughed. "No, we have reservations at the Beachcomber, but we have one stop to make first."

She narrowed her eyes, intending to firmly tell her new husband that she was tired of playing games, when John applied the brakes and turned off the highway onto a gravel surface. Mary Grace looked out the window and saw a squat, cinderblock building looming before them. A flashing sign proclaimed it to be the Edgewater Community Center. Mary Grace was staring, speechless, as John parked near the entrance. He opened his door, and the muted strains of a country song filled the car.

She turned wide eyes to him. "What are we doing here?"

He leaned over and gave her a short, hard kiss. "It was the only dance in town."

She struggled against the dizzying effects of his kiss and tried to understand the meaning of his words. "What?" she asked finally.

He climbed out of the car and walked around to the passenger door. She allowed him to help her out, then he pulled her against him and whispered into her ear, "Five and a half years ago you agreed to dance with me, but we were interrupted. I intend to make sure that doesn't happen this time."

Mary Grace let him lead her to the tinted glass doors, where a sign taped on the door proclaimed *Dance Every Saturday Night, No Cover Charge.* John held the door open, and she preceded him inside, where the music was fairly blaring.

The light was dim, and Mary Grace had to squint to see. To their immediate right was a makeshift bar where a little lady was dispensing soft drinks into Dixie cups. On the far wall, several card tables were set up, occupied by an assortment of elderly people. But most of the space inside the small building was dedicated to a dance floor, which was amazingly crowded. On a platform at the head of the dance area was a little folk band.

Mary Grace stared around in wonder as John pulled her toward the dance floor. He leaned down and whispered into the ear of the man playing a fiddle. The man nodded, then got the attention of the man at the microphone. A quick transition took place, and soon the strains of "You're Just Too Good to Be True" filled the room with a distinct country twang.

"Oh, John," she whispered, tears blurring her vision.

He pulled her close, and as he took her hand in his, he touched the small, silver band nestled against his CTR ring on her finger and frowned. "I still wish you would have let me get you a better engagement ring. Susie Ireland was going to give me a discount."

Mary Grace laughed through her tears. "This is the only ring I want."

"You *are* too good to be true," he said. "Today I promised before family and friends to love and cherish you always. Now I promise before a bunch of old strangers." He gestured toward the elderly people along the wall, and they waved back. "I love you, Gracie, and I have pretty much since the moment I first saw you sitting on that rock in Panama City. Today you've made me the happiest man on earth by agreeing to become my wife, and I plan to spend the eternities making sure you're never sorry that you did."

"I'll never be sorry," she told him.

He held her close until the song ended, then with a final wave to the old-timers, he picked her up and carried her toward the door.

"What's the rush?" she asked, half laughing, half crying.

"Mrs. Wright, I've been waiting long enough."

HAGGERTY HOSPITALITY

STRAWBERRY CHEESE-PIE

1 1/4 cups sugar
Juice of one lemon
1/4 tsp salt
1 9-inch pie crust (baked)
1 Tbsp milk
Fresh strawberries

3 Tbsp corn starch
1 1/2 cups water
Red food coloring
3 oz cream cheese
2 Tbsp confectioners' sugar
Cool Whip

Prepare pie filling (a jar of prepared strawberry pie filling can be substituted). Combine first six ingredients in a saucepan and cook until thick, stirring constantly. Remove from heat and allow to cool.

Mix softened cream cheese, milk, and confectioners' sugar. Spread on bottom of cooked pie crust. Arrange strawberries on top of cream cheese. Then pour pie filling over strawberries. Chill and cover with Cool Whip before serving.

CHICKEN EXTRAVAGANT

6 chicken breasts
8-oz pkg sour cream
12 slices Armour dried chipped beef

1 can cream of mushroom soup
6 slices bacon
Salt

Preheat oven to 300°F. Rinse the chipped beef and place six pieces on a lightly greased casserole dish. Rinse the chicken breasts, and salt them lightly. Then wrap each breast with one piece of bacon, and place them on the chipped beef. Put another piece of chipped beef on top of each breast. Mix mushroom soup and sour cream, then pour mixture on top of chicken. Cover with foil and bake for 45 minutes. Remove foil and bake for an additional 45 minutes. Serve with rice.

FOUR-LAYER DELIGHT

1 1/2 cups all-purpose flour
1 stick margarine
8-oz pkg cream cheese
1/2 cup confectioners' sugar

1 large Cool Whip
2 small pkgs instant Jell-O
   chocolate pudding
3 1/2 cups milk

Preheat oven to 300°F. Melt butter and pour into large casserole dish. Add flour and mix. Then press crust onto the bottom of the pan and bake for 10 minutes. While crust is cooling, mix softened cream cheese with 1 cup of Cool Whip and the confectioners' sugar. Spread mixture over cooled crust. Mix pudding according to package directions, using 3 1/2 cups milk. Pour over cream cheese layer, and let set for at least 15 minutes. Then top with a layer of remaining Cool Whip and serve.

TIGER BUTTER

1 lb white chocolate
1/2 cup creamy peanut butter
1/2 cup dark chocolate

Melt chocolates separately. Mix peanut butter with white chocolate. Turn a cookie sheet upside down and put wax paper on it. Then pour the warm white chocolate mixture onto the wax paper. Drizzle the dark chocolate onto the white and swirl together with a toothpick. Let it cool then cut or break into pieces.

EASY CHICKEN POT PIE

3 chicken breasts (boiled and chopped)
2 cans cream of chicken soup
1 pkg Veg-All frozen vegetables
Salt and pepper to taste

4 Idaho potatoes (diced and cooked until tender)
2 deep dish frozen pie shells
1 small pkg frozen corn
2 All-Ready pie crusts

Preheat oven to 375°F. Mix all ingredients, adding a little water as necessary to reach pouring consistency. Then pour mixture into frozen pie shells. Top each with an All-Ready pie crust. Press along edges with a fork, then trim with a knife. Cook for 50 minutes (or until top crust is golden brown).

SAUSAGE QUICHE

1 lb sausage (cooked and drained)　　1 dozen eggs
2 deep dish, uncooked pie shells　　3–4 cups grated cheddar cheese
1 can cream of celery soup

Preheat oven to 375°F. Mix eggs and soup together with a mixer. Put half of cooked sausage in the bottom of each uncooked pie shell. Pour half of egg mixture into each pie shell. Top with cheese—split evenly. Bake for 30–40 minutes.

MILLION-DOLLAR PIE

1 cup crushed pineapple (drained)　　10 oz. Cool Whip
1 cup chopped pecans　　1/4 cup lemon juice
1 cup condensed milk　　2 graham cracker crusts
1/2 cup chopped cherries

Mix Cool Whip, lemon juice, and condensed milk. Add nuts, pineapple, and cherries. Mix well. Pour into graham cracker crusts. Chill and serve.

ABOUT THE AUTHOR

BETSY BRANNON GREEN currently lives in Bessemer, Alabama, which is a suburb of Birmingham. She has been married to her husband, Butch, for twenty-five years, and they have eight children. She loves to read—when she can find the time—and watch sporting events—if they involve her children. She is the Young Women president in the Bessemer Ward. Although born in Salt Lake City, Betsy has spent most of her life in the South, and her writing has been strongly influenced by the Southern hospitality she has experienced there. Her first book, *Hearts in Hiding,* was published in 2001, followed by *Never Look Back* (2002), *Until Proven Guilty* (2002), *Don't Close Your Eyes* (2003), *Above Suspicion* (2003), *Foul Play* (2004), *Silenced* (2004), *Copycat* (2005), *Poison* (2005), *Double Cross* (2006).

If you would like to be updated on Betsy's newest releases or correspond with her, please send an e-mail to info@covenant-lds.com, or visit her website at http://betsybrannongreen.net. You may also write to her in care of Covenant Communications, P.O. Box 416, American Fork, UT 84003-0416.